"YOU KNOW WHAT, SANTOU?

"Until I find out there isn't a tie-in between this dead gator and your dead hooker, I'm taking it for granted that there is—and I'm going to find out what it is. Until then, don't even consider telling me how to do my job."

I shoved my way past the crowd of cops, but Santou caught up with me as I reached the door.

"Hold on, Rachel. I don't come up against much of this wildlife stuff. But you're right. It's your job, and if I was out of line, I apologize."

I didn't comment as he shifted from one foot to the other.

"What say we pool our information? You poke your nose around and learn something, you tell me, and I'll do the same by you. Maybe you're right—maybe there is a tie-in here."

"What makes you think I could possibly have access to any information you might want in my little old wildlife job?"

Santou arched an eyebrow, acknowledging the dig. "*Chere*, you strike me as a wolverine. You got something in your craw, you won't let it go till you're good and ready. I'm placing odds it's better to have you as an ally than an enemy."

I liked that.

JESSICA SPEART

To my husband, who believed in my dream.

Thanks go to Ken Goddard for his help, encouragement, and quirky sense of humor; to Jo Tyler for her insightful eye; and to all the U.S. Fish and Wildlife Service special agents who continue to fight against the odds.

AVON BOOKS
A division of
The Hearst Corporation
1350 Avenue of the Americas
New York, New York 10019

Inside cover author photo by George Brenner
Published by arrangement with the author
Visit our website at **http://AvonBooks.com**
Library of Congress Catalog Card Number: 97-93010
ISBN: 0-380-79288-5

First Avon Books Printing: September 1997

Printed in the U.S.A.

WCD 10 9 8 7 6 5 4 3 2 1

One

The marsh air hung hot and heavy, providing the perfect breeding ground for a battalion of mosquitoes that dive-bombed my body as if it were a fast-food stop. The wooden seat of the boat added further to my discomfort, biting through my pants and into my skin, while the humidity permeated my shoes and clothing to lodge solidly in my bones. Closing my eyes against the darkness of a lazy overdue dawn, I let my mind wander, bringing homespun memories of the angry honk of horns, the persistent shriek of fire engines, and the relentless racket of garbage trucks clattering down streets like heavily armored tanks. Taking a deep breath, I filled my lungs with the gas emissions and stench of New York City. But in my heart I knew better. I was stuck in a pirogue in the marshes of southern Louisiana, listening to the demented cries of nutria—fifteen-pound rodents that would have been taken for overgrown rats in New York. Shrieking like women gone mad, they led the chorus as the marsh became alive with the sounds and sights of ducks, egrets, ibis, and herons. It was the start of another steamy day.

Sitting in the small wooden boat, I tried to remember lines from off-Broadway plays, bit parts in soap operas, even the occasional commercial I'd been in that had somehow brought my life around to this, when I finally heard the sound I'd been waiting for. BOOM! The blast of a shotgun in the distance, followed by another volley reverberating in the morning air. Paddling through tall cordgrass, I tried to follow its echo, but a black Labrador saved me the trouble. Crashing through weeds and water, intent on finding its prey, the dog barely gave me a second glance as it picked up the duck in its mouth and, with a dumb smile plastered on its face, headed back to its master, anxious for a few words of praise. I was certain the dog had to be a female.

Hidden away in the intricately woven one-man blind sat Billy Paul Cochrain. We had met under similar circumstances before. Dressed in camouflage fatigues and a duck-billed cap, he was just reaching for the duck when he caught sight of my boat and looked up to see me watching his every move. He quickly pulled back his hand.

"Ain't my duck."

Once again I had blown it. Worse yet, Billy Paul knew it, too, as the same stupid grin that the Lab wore now spread across his face. He patted the dog on the head as it insistently tried to ply him with the dead bird.

"Jennifer, I keep telling you to leave them ducks alone." He chuckled as he pushed the offering away.

A female. I knew it.

I'd been based in southern Louisiana for six months now. It was my first assignment as a full-fledged special agent for the U.S. Fish and Wildlife Service. If I had known what I was getting into, I might have stayed in New York City with my defunct career as an actress. But at thirty-four years of age, you begin to panic. Not that far off from thirty-five, then forty, and finally menopause. I had thought it was time for a life change. My name is Rachel Porter, New York City born and bred.

"What we do now, Porter?"

Billy Paul grinned at me like an imbecile. I was asking myself the same question.

"You wanna take me in?"

I sighed deeply, thinking of the last time this had happened. It had been my first run-in with the senior resident agent, who also happens to be my boss, Charlie Hickok. I had hauled Billy Paul in, proudly presenting him to Charlie as my first bona fide poacher, and then waited for a few words of praise.

"You got the ducks?" Charlie asked, as he tilted his body back into a chair that creaked in protest against his 235 pounds.

One sad duck loaded with enough birdshot to resemble a piece of Swiss cheese had been my total body of evidence.

Hickok shook his head in disgust. "That's it? Then you ain't got him. Don't bring me any more of these puny, dumb-ass, nitty-picky cases wasting my time like I got nothin' else better to do."

Billy Paul's face had lit up like a jack-o'-lantern with a candle stuck inside as Charlie waved him out the door.

"You just learned your first lesson here, Bronx. One duck out of season ain't worth the trouble it takes to write it up."

I hated it when he called me Bronx. Charlie knew that. I had carefully explained that I'm from Manhattan, but he didn't much care.

Glaring at Billy Paul now as I tried to wrest the duck from the Lab's mouth, I could see that he'd just begun his morning round of hunting. There would be no other ducks inside his boat.

"This is a warning, Billy Paul. The next time I catch you, I'm hauling you in."

"Anything you say, ma'am." Still grinning, he rowed away, with Jennifer splashing in the water after him.

The only thing I hated worse than being called Bronx was being referred to as "ma'am." It made me feel older than I wanted to be. I'd learned a lot in my first six months here. I'd finally discerned that even when you catch someone red-handed, hunting an obscene number of ducks far over the legal limit, it didn't mean they were going to jail. It would have been mind-boggling if they even received a fine. Southern Louisiana meant dealing with country parishes, which meant local judges, small-town district attorneys, and rural lawyers. If they weren't related in some way to the defendant, it didn't much matter. The local lawyer won every case anyway. It was easy. They were all fixed.

Hauling the pirogue onto land, I dragged it into the weeds before jumping into my VW bug and heading off. Pink fingers of light jabbed into the blue of receding night as I bumped along a rutted road badly in need of repair. I had thought New York City streets were rough until driving down here.

Considered a demon speedster by friends and family alike, I was at home with my hand on the horn, daring taxis to pass me. While the West Side Highway is considered a motorist's nightmare, I knew most of the potholes that never got fixed. A New Yorker's badge of pride comes with being able to drive from Fourteenth Street to the George Washington Bridge while keeping their car in one piece—unlike outsiders, who hit hole after hole, knocking out tires and denting frames. City kids lie in wait for the uninitiated to pull off the road, where cars are stripped with such speed and fury that the owners are barely even aware of what's happened. This was general knowledge, and something I had been smug about all my life. No ruse could get the better of me—until I hit Louisiana and learned firsthand how it felt to be a greenhorn. Down here, road signs are considered unnecessary and directions given are as marginal as my grandmother's recipes.

My secondhand car didn't help. Taken in by appearances, I had thought it seemed too good to be true when I stumbled across it for sale. An inveterate bargain hunter, I was sure I had lucked into the steal of the century. I had. A large chunk of my hard-earned savings was legitimately stolen by the slickest car dealer south of New York City. My turquoise car was quickly turning to rust. But the major problem was the stick shift. Namely, that I'd never driven one before. Since buying the VW, which had 125,000 miles on the odometer before my foot even touched the pedal, my life had become a series of double clutches. I was a big-city rube, no two ways about it. After a night of sitting on a hard plank of wood in the middle of the water, my car, with its bad springs and thinly padded seat, offered little consolation. But I'd had a tip on some illegal duck hunting that might be taking place near Des Allemandes this morning. Besides, I needed to dry out for a while.

My life hadn't always been like this. After a twelve-year romance with an acting career that had lurched along almost as badly as my VW, I'd spent five months as a wildlife inspector at JFK Airport. It seemed I had the right qualifications for the job. None. Just two weeks of training was all that was needed. I had envisioned sifting through passengers' souvenirs while ferreting out wildlife contraband. Instead, I found myself digging through boxes of snakes and lizards on cold, dirty warehouse floors and clearing shipments of tropical fish to be rushed to the nearest pet store.

I had known there would be a problem when I decided to quit acting: what to do with my life now? Tired of worrying about frizzy hair while competing against every other actress in New York to sell GLAD Wrap, I had begun to cringe at the thought of one more audition where I was expected to be younger, shorter, prettier than I ever had been or ever could be. The relief of no longer turning myself inside out to deal with the demands of agents and casting directors was almost more than I could handle. I nose-dived into a three-month depression that found me spending my days at the Bronx Zoo, eating box after box of Crackerjacks. Twenty pounds, three months, one boyfriend, and two shrinks later, I discovered that what I related to best were animals. But I still needed a challenge, something in which my competitive nature would know no bounds. I found my calling one night watching an Audubon special on TV that focused on the illegal wildlife trade, and one man's exploits in fighting it—Charlie Hickok, Fish and Wildlife agent extraordinaire. This was what I aspired to be. I figured after all my years of dealing with the horrors of showbiz, taking on the poachers of the world would be a breeze.

Five months into the job as a wildlife inspector, I applied for special agent, and after sixteen weeks of hard training at the Academy in Glynco, Georgia, I was rewarded by making the grade. At the time, I could think of little else than my good luck. Even better, I had been immediately granted the posting I'd requested—to work under Charlie Hickok in Slidell, Louisiana.

"Good luck, kid. You're gonna need it," were the parting words of the agent who handed me my ticket. At the time, I hadn't known what he meant.

I found the field near Des Allemandes that I'd been searching for. Scattered with rice and a few inches of water, it was the perfect poacher's situation, with a levee providing near total concealment for hunters. Parking my VW out of sight, I made my way to the field, hunkering down low. The last thing I needed to do was surprise a group of angry rednecks with little tolerance for wildlife officers, who would dare tell them what they could or could not shoot. A female agent had recently been killed by a hunter who disagreed with her on the matter. I wasn't bucking to notch the number to two.

At six o'clock in the morning, the heat was already pressing down, a hot iron on the board of land below. Geese were swarming in like locusts, settling among the tall water grass to feed on grain for the coming of winter. I let my mind traipse across the water, wondering what I would be doing right now if I were anywhere but here, when six figures suddenly rose out of nowhere, their rifles trained on the unsuspecting flock. All hell broke loose as the men fired convulsively into the crowd, making it impossible to distinguish between the cries of the geese and the continuous gunfire that roared as if war had just broken out. The still-dark sky grew darker as the birds rose en masse in an attempt to fly away, but carcasses tumbled back to earth as fast and furious as the rain that tore loose from storm clouds above. The hunters reloaded quickly after each round, and the mingling of gunfire and honks of fear ripped through the air with all the fury of thunder. Flapping in the field, crippled geese frantically struggled to get away from the men, who now ran in after them, shooting until they had no more ammunition left, only to continue the carnage by wringing the necks of those birds they could reach. A battleground of dead and dying littered the field as a haze of gunpowder burned through my lungs. More than anything, I wanted to run out, flash my badge, and haul the poachers in. But I knew that would accomplish little more than to leave Louisiana one less wildlife agent to contend with. The state's unofficial motto flashed in my brain like a neon sign gone berserk: "If it flies, it dies. If it flies, it dies." Not only anything that flies, but also walks, swims, or crawls is considered fair game. Furious at being able to do nothing, I set out to at least make their escape more difficult. Drawing near the other side of the levee, I found two dented pickup trucks half-hidden in a group of cypress trees. Pulling out my Swiss Army knife, I carefully slashed each tire, taking the time to write down the license plate numbers before leaving. I had hoped the gesture would make me feel better. Instead, I felt as impotent as the geese that had tried to fly away.

This was duck patrol. It had been my assignment since the day I landed in Louisiana. It wasn't just the fact that Charlie Hickok was out to make life miserable for every waterfowl poacher around—he was also out to get rid of me. That I was not what he had expected was painfully obvious from my first day on the job.

"Goddamn! I ask for a man, and they send me a goose. What the hell am I supposed to do with some city girl?"

What he had done was to stick me out in the marshes day and night. Whenever I set foot in the office, my presence was announced by a series of duck calls that emanated from whereabouts unknown. I had been warned that women agents were few and far between, viewed only as necessary quotas to be filled. Like everything else in this world, breaking down barriers to notoriously male-dominated jobs was no Virginia Slims ad. But I had come to learn that Charlie Hickok was a name feared by both trainees and seasoned agents alike, while a posting to his station was generally reserved for those viewed as dispensable. More agents had resigned under Charlie Hickok than in all the rest of Fish and Wildlife combined. It was enough of a challenge to make me stay.

The windshield wipers on my car fought the downpour of rain, nearly blotting out the bullet-riddled signs for Nehi that dotted the countryside like giant gumdrops. Pulling into the first convenience store along the road, I placed a call to the local office of Louisiana's Department of Wildlife and Fisheries. They had the manpower available to pick up the hunters if they felt so inclined. The problem lay in the fact that, more often than not, that wasn't the case. The phone rang ten times before someone finally bothered to answer.

"Yeah?"

"If you head on over to Lac Des Allemandes, you'll find six poachers with about two hundred dead geese." Giving the officer a description of the pickup trucks and their license plate numbers, I found myself listening to dead silence on the other end.

"I don't think they'll get too far anytime soon. Their tires have all been slashed."

The silence deepened as I beat my nails against the mouthpiece before finally receiving a reply.

"Just who is this?" requested a deep Southern voice.

I had a feeling their office didn't get too many of these calls. First of all, I didn't sport the local accent. Even more suspicious, I was a woman.

"Merely a concerned citizen."

I hung up and headed back out into the rain. Times were hard in Louisiana, and, as usual, graft was rampant. Priding itself on having more poachers per capita than anywhere else in the U.S., Louisiana considers outlawing a time-honored tradition, just as much as down-home politics is a way of life. All a poacher needed was to be a registered voter, have a quarter, and pick up a pay phone, and any hunting charges would soon enough be dropped. I'd already been told it was crazy to try and fight the system. That had only intrigued me all the more.

Waterlogged, I headed back home late that afternoon. Like most other days since I'd been here, it had hardly been rewarding. Following the curve of the Mississippi River, I drove toward New Orleans. A steamy piece of bog crunched between Lake Pontchartrain and the Mississippi River, the city had originally been claimed by France in 1718, when that country swept its prisons clean of its derelicts, loading them onto boats bound for New Orleans. With a crime rate today to rival that of New York, it seemed as if some of their descendants still had a good hold on the city. When I had first arrived, I had been advised to live in or around Slidell. Rents were cheaper, it would be easier to get to work, and there was a lot less crime. But after a week of living in the local Econolodge, looking at strips of fast-food joints, creosote factories, and sawmills, I had decided to blow my budget and head where I was most comfortable. While it's not New York, at least New Orleans is crowded, claustrophobic, and noisy. I felt right at home.

Once again my salary was being eaten up supporting a small and expensive apartment, but it was worth it. Situated in the French Quarter, the tiny two-story building of pale pink plaster had black wrought-iron tiers and balconies as intricately woven as my grandmother's tatting. A miniscule courtyard and garden in back was a tropical jumble of multicolored flowers. Sweet-smelling magnolias mingled with angel's trumpets, as flaming hibiscus competed with ginger lilies for precious space. But what had clinched the deal was the artwork strewn about the place. Small concrete satyrs romped in the garden, lusting after stone angels. A devil-head fountain spouted water over its long curling tongue, splashing onto nude maidens as they slept among the water lilies, the shade from banana trees dappling their bodies with intermittent rays of sun. Plaster masks of long-dead movie stars lined the wall outside the owner's apartment, in an ode to Norma Desmond. From the owner's taste in art, I gathered I had found a kindred spirit. I knew he was the kind of man who still dressed up for Halloween.

The upstairs apartment was small, which suited me fine. Having grown up in New York, I'm uncomfortable when faced with too much space. Fronting Chartres Street, the living room led to a closet-sized Pullman kitchen, which I managed to keep clean through minimal use. The bedroom in back had French doors leading onto a balcony that overlooked the courtyard, and was vaguely reminiscent of Tennessee Williams and his cast of dysfunctional characters. Old and in bad condition, the building was loaded with atmosphere and charm.

Stripping out of wet and muddy clothes, I left what I could of the marsh lying on my bathroom floor as I turned on the water in the tub. I planned on my usual evening activity of soaking for a while with a glass of wine and a trashy magazine, when I noticed the red light blinking on the answering machine. When I pressed the playback button, a familiar, deep Southern voice reached out toward me.

"Bronx, get your ass over to 138 Ursuline Street. There's been a murder in the Quarter."

Two

The building was right around the corner from the old Ursuline Convent. Locating the apartment, I flashed my badge and pushed through the crowd already gathered outside the door, eager to catch a glimpse of the body. While the DEA, the local police, and Fish and Wildlife sometimes worked on cases together, I'd never been included on a murder before. But having viewed more than my fair share of dead bodies both on TV and in the movies, I felt prepared for whatever might await me inside. Besides, if the case was a break from working on ducks, I was grateful for it.

As I entered the apartment, my umbrella, as well as the rest of me, dripped a large puddle of water onto the floor, but I had a feeling the tenant wouldn't mind. Without being stopped, I made my way past a small circle of people, finally entering the room where the largest group huddled. What awaited me was a bloody scene. The bedroom walls were streaked with ribbons of red paint, except that the paint was still sticky and turned out to be blood. A tight knot of cops from N.O.P.D. were clustered about the body as if to keep the rest of us out. While I wasn't sure I was that anxious to look, I found I couldn't stop myself from trying to gawk over the bruisers in front, until one body got tired of my jabbing and turned around. Embarrassed at my New York aggressiveness, I flashed my ID as I backed up.

"Rachel Porter. Fish and Wildlife Service. I received a call to report here."

At five-eight, I consider myself tall, but the face that peered down at me stood a good five inches taller. A thick tangle of curly black hair held droplets of rain from outside, while a pair of deep-set, dark eyes tried to focus on the badge I held too close to his face. Taking it from me, the man examined my shield. He had a strange face when examined part by part. A long, sharp nose that could have passed for a beak led down to lips tinged around the corners with disappointment at a life that had turned out differently than planned. Deep-set eyes didn't stare so much as penetrate, with all the intensity of a laser beam focused in my direction. The lines engraved in his face looked as if they could have been etched there with acid, affirming that the wear and tear of life as a cop had more than taken its toll. Dark and brooding, he reminded me of a hawk in search of a kill. As he handed back my ID, I realized he'd been analyzing me just as closely as I had him. I felt myself fluster under his stare as I grabbed the badge out of his hand.

"Well, Rachel Porter, if you're that anxious to grab a peek, don't let me stop you, *chère*."

I'd run into a lot of that down here. Women were never referred to by their proper names, but were instead called honey, sugar, sweetheart, darling, and *chère*. At first I'd been determined to put a stop to all that. After six months, I'd pretty well given up.

"So now that you know who I am, who are you?"

He silently handed over his own ID. Jake Santou. Homicide, N.O.P.D. A cop pulled away from the inner circle, and I instinctively squeezed in to grab a glimpse of the body. I was sorry I did. Lying nude on her back was a girl of about twenty-five. But then again, it was hard to tell. Her body and face had been slashed hundreds of times, making it seem as if she had been bounced off a spider's web which had left its imprint in a myriad of fine lines. A mass of dark hair lay splayed about her head, giving her the look of a porcelain doll that had been broken and discarded. Her stark white skin, the color of fine bone china, was set in a mushrooming pool of blood as the cream-colored carpet beneath slowly turned a deep shade of crimson. An investigator busied himself dusting doorknobs, bedposts, and bureaus for any stray fingerprints, the cloud of fine dust floating through the air, descending onto the chalky whiteness of her skin and scattering a flaky cloud of dandruff throughout her hair. Glancing down at my feet to escape the surprised look of death in her eyes, I saw that the soles of my shoes were drenched in her blood. The man next to me chuckled, elbowing his companion, as I pulled back in horror and peered at the circle of faces around me. Impassive in their reactions, they had seen it all before. I backed out of the circle, grateful when somebody else moved in to take my place, hiding the bloody mess on the floor from my sight. As I walked away from the body, the soles of my shoes left a trail on the cream-colored carpet, the girl I'd just viewed following along in blood as well as spirit. Leaning against the post of her bed, I turned away from the scene, thankful that I hadn't yet eaten as my stomach took a dive. Santou appeared behind me.

"That's Valerie Vaughn. She was a topless dancer who worked a club over on Bourbon. But that's not what you were called in for. That's over here."

Santou guided me past a maze of bodies, over to the doorway of the bathroom. Chained to the leg of an iron clawfoot tub was a ten-foot alligator. Looking like a giant handbag with black and beige bands, the gator, like the girl, was dead. Grateful for the distraction, I knelt down beside the reptile. It was the closest I'd ever been to one. My only other hands-on experience was with a gator skeleton I'd seen in New York with Harry Milsus, the local forensics expert used by the FWS office there.

"Took five shots to the head."

The sight of the gator helped to ground me, momentarily taking my mind off the girl in the other room. I used to watch Harry Milsus click into his "forensics" mode and tried to copy him as best I could now. Running my fingers over the skull to probe the depth of each bullet hole, I appreciated the training I'd had at Glynco. But even more importantly, I said a silent prayer of thanks to Harry. He'd been of the belief that both agents and inspectors should know a lot more than what we were taught. He was right. He also knew what I was up against in a male-dominated Service, determined not to lay out the welcome mat for the few women trying to kick in its doors. Becoming my ally, he'd taught me all he knew.

By convincing me that, unlike wildlife inspectors, agents got all the interesting undercover work, along with job promotions and pay raises on the way, Harry was one of the main reasons I'd decided to become an agent. When he had learned I was being sent to Louisiana, he insisted that I bone up on reptiles. Harry would be happy to know that his many hours of work with me were paying off now.

All five bullets had gone in at an angle and were shallow. One of the facts Harry had made a point of was that gators' skulls are extremely thick. Whatever had killed the critter, my guess was it hadn't been five bullets that had barely nicked the skull.

"At least his death was quick. He wasn't sliced and diced like the girl in there." Santou leaned against the doorjamb, watching carefully as I tried to think of what else Harry would have told me to do.

I found myself glancing over my shoulder at the soles of my shoes. Caked with Valerie Vaughn's blood, the heels were slowly drying to a dull shade of red. Feeling woozy, I brought my focus back to the gator, though there wasn't much else to examine at this point. The rest would have to be kept for a forensics expert. The problem was that we didn't have one down here, and there wasn't a chance in hell that Charlie would send the gator out to Fish and Wildlife's National Forensics Lab in Oregon. Though the lab and its work were world famous, it didn't set well with Charlie.

"That damn thing's nothing but pork-barrel politics, soaking up money we need out in the field." That was his mantra whenever there was a budget crunch. It also saved Charlie from ever having to defer to anyone's judgment other than his own.

Though this wasn't yet a fully grown, fifteen-foot gator, I found it hard to digest the fact that someone had been crazy enough to keep it as a pet in the middle of the Quarter.

"I don't think my office received any complaints about an alligator being kept here. Do you know if N.O.P.D. ever had anything reported on this?"

"We don't get reports on this kind of stuff, *chère*. Too many other strange goings-on happening here. This gator death probably doesn't mean much of anything. There are lots of weirdos working the strip. Keeping a gator as a pet was probably a kinky turn-on for some of her johns."

My mind wandered, trying to imagine what sorts of kinky things one could possibly be involved in with a gator. I must not have been creative enough. My mind drew a blank. Glancing up, I caught Santou's stare, along with the impression that if I couldn't figure it out, he certainly could.

"I'll arrange to have the gator picked up. My boss will probably want to check this out for himself. I don't suppose you found the key to unlock this chain?"

Santou folded his arms across his body. "Nah. One thing I don't bother with is carrying a set of keys around to unhook gators. We'll get him out of there the best way we can. Don't you worry none about it." He made a motion as if to chop off the leg, sending a shiver through me.

I ran my fingers over the bullet holes once more, the rough, scaly hide pulling at my skin. No bone fragments were sticking up. No splintering had taken place. The skull hadn't even been nicked. Along with the strong odor of gator, the smell of death and decay had already begun to set in. I sensed Santou kneel down behind me and immediately tensed up, continuing to concentrate on the gator.

"What makes you so sure this gator even belonged to the woman in there? Why couldn't whoever murdered her have brought it with him in order to terrorize her?"

Santou raked his fingers through the front of his hair, snarling his nails in a disarray of curls. As he leaned in close behind me to glance over my shoulder, his breath grazed the tip of my ear.

"Look, if I'm gonna go to all the trouble of sneaking some big-ass gator into a hooker's apartment, the least I'm gonna do is to torture her with it. Maybe feed the gator a chunk or two of her. Otherwise, why bother? Besides, those slices were finely done. That's a very artistic job out there, *chère*. Took the guy hours."

Sometimes I'm slow on the uptake. The reason why I had been brought in at all was just beginning to dawn on me. I was cleanup patrol. Turning around, I found Santou watching me with the predatory gaze of a raptor as it circles its intended victim.

"So, I was called in to save you the drudgery of filling out paperwork on a dead alligator that happens to be chained to your murder victim's bathtub. Have I got that about right?" Tired and still damp from my daily dousing of rain, I would gladly have given all of this up to climb into any hot bath at the moment, with or without a gator chained to the leg.

Santou kept his voice low, forcing me to lean in toward him. "Let me give you a word of advice here, *chère*. Don't try to make this more than it is. It's just a dead gator that some whacked-out stripper kept for kicks. Nobody cares, least of all your boss. This kind of thing always means more paperwork for everyone involved. It's just the breaks that you're the one that got stuck with it this time."

My body ached as I pulled myself up off the tiles. This wasn't what I needed to hear. What I needed was dinner and a solid night's sleep, not to be arguing in a bathroom with a dead gator at my feet and a mutilated girl outside the door.

"You know what, Santou? It's just some whacked-out stripper in the other room. Who the hell is going to care about that, either? I'm getting the distinct feeling that it won't be you. For the record, as far as I'm concerned, until I find out there isn't a tie-in here, I'm taking it for granted that there is. I'm also going to find out what it is, even if I do it on my own time. Until then, don't even consider telling me how to do my job.''

Shoving my way out of the bathroom, I elbowed through the crowd, using jabs I hadn't called into play since jostling on a subway. I pushed past paramedics leaning against a wall, bored with the waiting; past the scene investigator busy capturing Valerie Vaughn's image with his camera as he focused in on every slash along the curve of her hips, each and every puncture wound outlining the roundness of her breasts. I made a determined effort not to look in her direction, not wanting to be just one more idle gawker caught up in the drama of the moment. Santou caught up with me as I reached the door.

''Hey, hey, hey. Hold on. I don't like rash judgments, and you just made one in there.''

I opened my mouth to protest but Santou cut me off before I could even start.

''I made one, too. I don't come up against much of this wildlife stuff. But you're right. It's your job, and I suppose you know what you're doing. If I was out of line, I apologize.''

I didn't comment as he shifted from one foot to the other.

''What say we pool our information? You poke your nose around and learn something, you tell me, and I'll do the same by you. Who knows? Maybe you're right. Maybe there is a tie-in here.''

His eyes darted across my face with a wound-up intensity that was ready to snap.

''Tell you what. There's someone I want to question tomorrow about this murder, who would probably be interesting for you to meet. If I set it up, I'll give you a call.'' He squinted at me, the corners of his mouth curled into a lopsided grin that clashed with the brusqueness of his stare. ''Deal?''

''What makes you think I could possibly have access to any information that you might want in my little old wildlife job?''

Santou arched an eyebrow, acknowledging the dig. The

movement of his hands caught my attention, and I glanced down to see a strand of garnet and onyx rosary beads woven between his fingers in a game of cat's cradle.

"*Chère*, you strike me as a wolverine. You got something in your craw, you won't let it go till you're good and ready. I figure you're going to shake this one around for a while. Who knows what you'll come up with? I'm placing odds it's better to have you as an ally than an enemy."

I liked that.

I had just sunk chin deep into a hot bubble bath when my doorbell rang. The buzzing stopped, only to be replaced by a persistent knocking at the door. Finally, I heard my landlord in the hallway calling out my name.

"I'm in the bathtub!" I hollered back.

Surrounded by a po'boy oyster sandwich, a glass of mediocre red wine, and *People* magazine, my evening was set. I listened as the lock on my front door clicked open and Terri Tune came in. Clad in a bright red kimono and backless slippers, he carried two large piña coladas on a tray. As the other tenant in the building, and my designated best friend, there was no keeping him out of any locked door. I had given up trying a long time ago.

"Oh, please. Are you still drinking that crap?" Picking up my glass of wine, he sniffed it and proceeded to dump it down the sink. Then he made himself at home on the toilet seat, decorated a la Terri, with a pink shag carpet. The kimono slipped open as he crossed his legs, casually dangling a slipper from his toe. Terri put me to shame, taking more time to shave his legs than I did my own. Removing the paper umbrella from the frosted glass, I took a sip.

Terri had made it his business to take me under his wing from the first day I met him. Having bought the building ten years before, he informed me that he was particular about whom he'd rent to. That I had been an actress and came from New York were all the criteria he needed. That I loved Tennessee Williams as much as he did had clinched the deal.

Working on Bourbon Street as a transvestite performer, he had saved his money to invest in real estate in the French Quarter. His best advice to me so far had been, "Don't plan on meeting Prince Charming. A girl has to learn to invest wisely for her old age." I couldn't agree with him more. I just didn't seem to be able to save money.

Picking up my po'boy sandwich, he shook his head in resignation. My mother would have been appalled at my diet as well.

"And you call this dinner?"

"Actually, I call this lunch, dinner, and a late-night snack all rolled up in one."

I'd caught Terri's act a few times. It was good. Tall and slender, he did dead-on impersonations of Barbra Streisand and Marilyn Monroe. His latest addition was Madonna. Among a few intimates, he could be persuaded to perform Tommy Tune, his idol after whom he had rechristened himself. Having danced in a roadshow of *My One and Only* for a couple of years, Terri soon decided that living out of a trunk and eating fast food was no way to live a long and healthy life, and had set his sights on something more steady—the clubs of Bourbon Street.

I had never seen Terri without his makeup. He said that if God wanted women to be natural, She would never have invented eyeliner and lipstick. Since leaving New York, I had become rather lax about my own appearance. Terri had set out to change all that, giving me a facial and a makeover the day I had moved in. I had to admit, he looked great. In fact, I might seriously have killed to look that good. Though his own hair was light brown, he preferred to be seen in a blond curly wig. With big blue eyes and dimples, he was the girl I had spent my teenage years trying to be. He was the best friend I had. I knew we would never fight over the same man. I just wished we wore the same size clothes.

I filled him in on the case over on Ursuline Street. It didn't surprise me to learn that he had known Valerie, albeit slightly. The people who worked the strip were like a small family. Most had come from other places in the country—

small towns where tolerance was a little-known word—and from families that wished they would just go away. They had. They had come to Bourbon Street and found a home. Like a carnival freak show, they performed for people who came to gawk and stare. But they were carnies in spirit only. They didn't need to travel on. New Orleans had taken them in with open arms and a yearly Mardi Gras. Terri floated the small paper parasols from our drinks on the soapy bubbles of the bathwater.

"I liked her. She was a nice girl. Though Val had her problems, there was no denying that." Terri ran his finger around the foam that had encrusted the lip of his glass.

"What kind of problems?" To me, Valerie Vaughn was still just a body resembling a picture puzzle that had been pieced back together, the tiny lines etching which part fit where.

"Oh, she bounced around a bit. She used to dance topless over at the Baby Doll, but she couldn't keep off the powder and started missing shows. Finally the Doll House took her in after she promised to go straight. She still hooked on the side, as far as I know. But I had the feeling she was into some weird shit. Word around the strip was that she had a guy involved in local politics sniffing around her. She was always looking for that Big Daddy. Val was the type of girl who either partied too hard or went into a shell. She had stopped partying lately."

"What about the alligator? They found a ten-footer chained to the leg of her bathtub."

The dye from the parasols had begun to run, staining the bubbles a drab shade of purple. I found myself thinking of Valerie and the fine slashes that had been carved into her skin. A sliver of flesh edging each pencil-thin wound had been tainted the same dingy hue. Pricking one of the bubbles, I took another sip of my drink as a shiver ran through me.

"You mean Hook. Yeah, Valerie had a thing for him. She was a local yokel from the bayous. She brought him with her, said it was the only thing she kept to remind her of home. Raised him from a baby. Used to boil chickens and feed him one a day. She said he was a notch above most men—she had gotten him to stop eating raw meat."

"Why do you think she was killed?"

I watched as the parasols slowly began to sink, having fallen through the bubbles into the lukewarm water. I looked up to see Terri watching me with eyes that had witnessed more on the strip than I would ever know.

"You got it wrong, Rach. The question isn't why—but why not?"

Three

Driving across the bridge over Lake Pontchartrain had become almost a religious experience for me. It was the demarcation line between my two different lives. In New Orleans, I was the street-wise city girl, laughing at scams others fell for. Once out in the sticks, I was a goner, a mark for wily poachers and fat, corrupt DAs.

Driving down the Boulevard in Slidell, I passed Wendy's and Taco Bell but stopped at McDonald's for a power breakfast in a white paper bag. A midsize town, Slidell is known more for its industrial attractions than its scenic charm. The main strip could be Anywhere, U.S.A., with its proliferation of fast-food joints and discount stores. Pulling into the back lot of the brick building that housed a bank, an insurance company, and the U.S. Fish and Wildlife office, I spotted the run-down, white Pontiac Bonneville. With one taillight cracked and red rust eating its way up over the fender, the car's dented license plate boasted the state's official motto: Sportsman's Paradise. No matter how I tried, I could never beat Charlie Hickok into work. He seemed to live in the place. Enid, his receptionist from the turn of the century, hadn't arrived yet. Neither had the other workers who droned on from eight in the morning until four in the afternoon, under fluorescent lights in rooms with no windows. That was the best part of being an agent: I never had to punch a clock. But I was expected to work on my own, morning through night, without having to report in. Requiring a special breed of loner, it suited me just fine.

I heard Charlie before I even entered his office. Hacking and wheezing, he was puttering about, easing into his daily routine. I poked my head in the door as he lowered his body down into his chair and started to scratch.

"Damn chiggers."

Charlie's room was a work of art. Free-form, thrown together, but a balancing act that was not to be believed. Books were piled on top of his desk at angles that defied gravity. Perched on top of that were videotapes of past busts in all their glory. Papers were strewn sky-high in piles that were known only to him and nobody dared touch. A Confederate flag hung limply on its pole in a far corner of the room.

The only personal touch to be found was a collection of framed photographs that hung on the walls and occupied most of the spare space on Charlie's desk. They were all of a woman blessed with long blond hair, a heart-shaped face, and large eyes that a doe would have envied. Rumor had it that she had been Charlie's wife. A strict Baptist, she had tried her best to keep Charlie in line, forbidding him to smoke, drink, or curse. Charlie abided by her rules as best he could, while still maintaining his normal workload of twenty-four hours, seven days a week—his schedule being the one area to which rules did not apply. Office scuttlebutt maintained that, tired of living alone, his wife packed up one day and disappeared. So did most of their furniture. Charlie simply told people that she had died. Whatever the case, the photos added a tantalizing sense of mystery, giving his office the air of a shrine.

Charlie sat behind his desk, dressed in a short-sleeve pale blue shirt and a pair of blue-and-white-striped seersucker pants. His appearance was topped off by a railroad cap that covered a head going bald. It was Charlie's way of refusing to acknowledge the fact. His neck was blotched with bright red marks where his fingers kept scratching. A nose that looked like a rose in bloom was testament to his fondness for Old Grand-Dad, and a network of small craters pitting his face proved that his attachment to candy bars had started at a tender age.

Word had it that he had been a powerhouse in his younger days. A one-man vigilante team who had taken on poachers and syndicates alike and won. The failure of his marriage, and a broken heart, had only made him all the more driven and focused where his work was concerned. The roadblock he had finally run up against had been jealousy within his own agency. That, and an abiding weakness for rubbing people's noses in his triumphs.

Charlie liked to brag that he was a direct descendant of Wild Bill Hickok. If so, he had certainly inherited Wild Bill's flair for showmanship. He had known how to publicize every sting he had ever done. The Audubon TV special was evidence of that. It led some to call him a living legend in his own mind. When higher-ups finally decided they could take no more, Charlie had been hog-tied by a promotion to a desk job. It was either that or leave the Service. He'd have sooner given up his life.

I cleared off the chair on the other side of his desk and sat down, plunking my breakfast on the only patch of open space that had so far escaped the growing fungus. Charlie joined me, pulling out his own start to the day—a Baby Ruth bar.

"Have a good time last night, Bronx?"

"Yeah. It was great. I actually got to see something that didn't have feathers on it."

That brought a smile to his face, and I felt safe in continuing. I told him about Valerie and how she had ended up looking like a demo for Etch-A-Sketch. Filling him in on the gator brought me around to mentioning that I'd heard Val was a local girl from down south in the bayou.

Charlie reached for the Hershey bar beckoning to him from his desk drawer. "Sheeet! I'll bet the tail on a horse's ass that she was Marie Vaughn Tuttle's niece. Pretty little coonass. She left the swamp to become a star. Never got any further than Bourbon Street, discovered her main talent was in twirling her titties. Last I heard, she was hooked on smack."

The first time I'd heard the expression "coonass" my Northern guilt had reared its ugly head, sure that it was a racist Southern expression for blacks. It was only later that I learned it was a term of affection for the local Cajuns. Especially coming out of Charlie Hickok's mouth. If he had been given three wishes, one of them would have been to be born Cajun.

"Who's Marie Tuttle?"

Charlie was a walking bible on the people of the bayou, and I had learned to pump him for information whenever I could. I was quickly picking up on the fact that the only way to get anything done was by befriending the folks in the swamp. Without their help, I might as well pack up my bags and start heading out once more for dog-food commercials back in New York. I was in luck this morning. Charlie was in one of his more talkative moods.

"She's a little Cajun coonass lives just outside Morgan City. Valerie was her sister's kid. When her mama died, Marie took her in. I think Valerie moved up to Bourbon Street mainly to get the hell away from Marie and gator skins. You can smell that woman from a mile away. She traffics in buying hot skins from the local outlaws and selling 'em at cut-rate prices to some of our local business scum."

Charlie scratched a raised armpit and hunkered down farther in his chair, letting the memory of former glory days wash over him.

"I busted her once, but she was out again before you could swallow your stew. A little bitty thing, but she's as mean as they come. If she were a man, someone woulda killed her by now. Lord knows, she'd as soon shoot you as look at you."

Whether or not he had put the bait out on purpose, I didn't know. But I was hooked.

"I'd like to go see her. Maybe dig around a bit and see what I can find out."

I didn't know what Charlie's reaction would be, but he'd opened the door with his call to me last night. It was a Fish and Wildlife case now, as well as N.O.P.D.'s. Still, if I were to pursue the investigation further than just writing up a report on a dead gator, I needed Charlie's permission. To my surprise, he not only gave me the bait, but pulled the hook tight so it caught in my mouth.

''Sure thing, Bronx. Have a good time.''

I decided to push my luck. ''Charlie, there's something that's bothering me about that alligator. I can't see how those bullets could have penetrated the skull. I'd like to have an autopsy done.'' Before I even finished I sensed that I had gone too far, forgetting my bounds as a rookie agent.

Leaning forward, Charlie slammed his elbows on top of a pile of papers that shifted slightly to the left. The movement was enough to set off a chain reaction reminiscent of the flicking of a domino. A delicately balanced videotape tumbled from its perch, hitting the edge of one of the photos on Hickok's desk, which tottered ominously for a moment before tipping backwards into a free fall.

Charlie moved with a speed I hadn't imagined him capable of. Jumping up from his seat, he dived across the floor and grabbed the frame right before it hit the ground. He carefully straightened the picture inside, then wiped off the glass with a tissue before reverently setting it back in its place on his desk. After a moment, he continued as if there had never been a break in the conversation.

''Well, hot damn. Not only have I got me an experienced agent, but one of those smart-ass forensic scientists as well.'' He tugged on his cap. A bad sign.

''Listen, Bronx. The goddamn gator is dead. Where I come from, five slugs to the head will do it everytime. I don't need no fancy-pants JFK-type conspiracy theories, and I gotta tell ya that I don't give a rat's ass about your woman's intuition. I'll take a quick look-see for myself, but as far as I'm concerned, it's a done deal. This case is N.O.P.D.'s problem. You wanna go see Tuttle and snoop around for a day or two, I'll write it off to some R&R. But then I want your rear end back out in that swamp. If I were you, I'd catch me some duck poachers real quick."

The drive down to Morgan City couldn't have been better. For once, the rain held off, and the sky was as endless as the Gulf of Mexico. Another scorcher of a day, even the hot breeze felt good against my face as I sped along.

Thick fields of sugar cane stood tall and green, their sweetness wafting on air usually filled with the black smoke of old, dingy factories whose stacks spewed a rank brew of toxic gumbo. Weathered shacks with corrugated tin roofs lined each side of the road, flaring rays of sunlight into my eyes with all the brightness of mini-nuclear explosions. The poverty was reminiscent of a backroad in a third-world country.

But this was southern Louisiana, where each shanty contained a family bursting at the seams. Dogs lazed in the middle of the road, rarely bothering to look up as I beeped my horn, finally swerving into the fields to go around them. Chickens pecked in the dirt, squawking their disapproval as I crept by. Children came out to stare as they heard me approach, as though it was an event not to be missed, their scantily clad bodies running alongside my car until they dropped off one by one. I beeped the horn in farewell as each figure disappeared from sight in a cloud of red dust.

Live oaks, heavy with Spanish moss, stood in front of run-down mansions that had seen better days. Bullet-riddled signs announced each small town I passed through, the holes adding a new twist of flavor to their names.

A chain gang of men worked alongside the road, spilling hot tar, their skin glistening with sweat so that their bodies blended in with the liquid they were pouring. One man gave me a smile, his body shimmering in and out of focus in the curling waves of heat, as the other men joked with each other to break up the monotony of one more muggy day in a long line of them. Looking away from the road for a moment, I came nerve-wrackingly close to driving into a ditch, providing cheap entertainment for the men, who whooped with laughter and then broke into a cheer as I quickly veered away from danger.

Stopping in the town of Houma long enough to grab a burger and a Coke, I cooled off in an air-conditioned luncheonette. Local customers unused to strangers stared at me, wondering why I would bother to stop in a town that most others were trying to leave. Laced with waterways, Houma had once been called the Venice of the Bayous. It was now a ghost town, a casualty of the oil bust which had left the area reeling and as polluted as its sister city in Italy.

Hard times could also be blamed on the declining fur trade. Trapping had always been an accepted way of life for Cajun men, and wealthy women with a hankering for skins had unknowingly helped to keep local families fed. But with furs no longer in vogue, Houma had begun a painful economic descent, its oil wealth turned to red-clay poverty.

A fifties feel hung over the place. A number of stores were closed, with their windows boarded up, the victims of recession. Even the movie theaters had felt the sting, their marquees dilapidated as if from the heartache of having been deserted for too long. I could have been passing through a time warp of plywood storefronts at an MGM back lot. But I was in the heart of Cajun country in Terrebonne Parish.

This was the pulse point of alligator country in Louisiana. It was also a hotbed for poachers, past and present, since alligator skins had boomed into fashion in the 1920s. Enterprising poachers in the bayou had been more than happy to fill the growing demand, and by the 1930s, more than half of Louisiana's alligator population had been decimated in the name of fashion. By the forties, the state's population of the reptiles had crashed, and by 1964 the hunting of gators was banned in the state. But nobody had bothered telling that to the poachers, who continued killing whatever they could drag out of the swamp.

Charlie Hickok had made a stab at putting a stop to the slaughter for a while. With his inherited showman antics, he mounted one sting operation after another, knocking out the dealers. It hadn't done much to make him popular, with either the outlaws or the power elite. Cajuns were of the belief that it was their God-given right to hunt whatever wildlife they wanted, and no damn upstart federal agent was about to tell them otherwise. Charlie had.

But he was now stuck behind a desk; a recession was in full swing; and the familiar phrase "fix the damn thing"—be it a parking ticket or an illegal hunt—was once more in vogue. Poaching was on the rise again. When you could make an easy five grand a night hunting gators, it wasn't hard to see why. Besides, nobody had ever bothered to pay much attention to the law down here. People who were smart didn't try to enforce it. The bayous of southern Louisiana followed rules all their own.

As I sped by the sign for Morgan City, the countryside took a turn for the worse, making Houma look like a shining jewel. Morgan City had a story all its own as the onetime Jumbo Shrimp Capital of the World. The discovery of offshore oil had brought good times to the town for a while, as it had in Houma. But now deserted offshore platforms dotted the landscape, and rusty shrimp trawlers rotted from disuse in murky swamps. The boom times were long gone, taking with them all the money and employment that had infused the area for a few good years.

Ply Charlie with a couple of drinks and, before you knew it, he was off and running on one of his favorites topics: how all the "goddamn" oil companies had left nothing but ten thousand miles of canals large enough for barges to plunder across, ripping through the fragile freshwater marshes of southern Louisiana, and taking with them the Cajun way of life. No longer able to make their money from the oil industry, the Cajuns had been left to keep a deathwatch as both shrimping and crabbing disappeared. All that remained of the marsh as it had been were the petrified trunks of dead cypress trees, standing like headstones in ghostly remembrance, marking the area as a watery grave.

* * *

Following Charlie's directions, I drove past Morgan City toward Bayou Vista. Marie's place wasn't hard to find. Tucked away down a dirt road, the house was nothing more than a ramshackle hut. A parcel of screaming, half-dressed kids played out front in what resembled a junkyard, with an ancient icebox and a broken-down old pickup truck falling apart piece by piece where it stood. As I parked and got out of the car, silence descended. Six kids, ranging from twelve months to fourteen years, froze in place to stare at me as if I were some foreign creature. All except the diaperless baby, who continued to crawl among rusty pieces of metal. None of the children looked like they ever bothered to bathe.

All six pairs of eyes followed me up the steps of the porch as I knocked on the screen door and looked inside. Piles of dirty laundry lay strewn about the hall floor, and a rancid odor wafted through the screen. Walking inside, I stepped over mounds of clothes and litter until I reached the kitchen, where dirty dishes were piled high in the sink, and pots encrusted with dried food sat on a table. A heap of bones with scraps of raw flesh and fur still attached lay in a corner of the floor, as large roaches moved slowly through the heat and filth, unconcerned by my presence. The house made my skin crawl.

Stepping back outside, I took a deep breath and approached the eldest boy, who watched me with a sullen stare. Golden hair stuck out in knotted clumps above a face blotched with freckles; his eyes followed my every move.

"Is your mother around?"

The silence I received for an answer was so deep, I felt sure I had hallucinated the sound of children screaming just moments before. As I took another deep breath, a pungent smell that I knew could only be gator skins drifted my way. When I turned to follow the odor that came from the backyard, the boy suddenly streaked past me, screaming at the top of his lungs as though he'd been threatened with murder.

"Ma! Watch out! Stranger coming!"

I reached the backyard in time to see all four feet and eight inches of Marie Tuttle whip around inside a wooden shed, with a shotgun in her hands pointed directly at me. Coming out, she kicked the door closed with the back of her foot. Wiry and small, she looked ferocious, and I was more than sure that, if given the slightest reason, she would happily blast me off the face of the earth.

"Who the hell are you and what the hell do you want?"

Dressed in a sleeveless pink calico smock dotted with blue cornflowers, she wore a pair of red high-top Reeboks on her feet. Strands of light brown hair fell in greasy strings about her shoulders, having pulled loose from the bun pinned to the top of her head. Her face was small and pinched, and there were gaps where there should have been teeth.

The sound of my voice was stronger and more confident than I felt at the moment. "I'm with Fish and Wildlife. I was called in on a murder in New Orleans last night. The girl was Valerie Vaughn. I was told she was your niece."

Marie stared at me, never lowering the gun.

"Yeah. She's my kin. And I already heard the news. What else you want?"

"I'm trying to find anything that might help us learn who could have killed Valerie."

Breaking into a malicious grin, Marie let loose a cackle I had only heard in Disney films, transforming herself into a short, Cajun version of Cruella De Vil—a cartoon character from my childhood who makes me cringe to this day.

"Now I remember hearin' 'bout you. You're that new duck cop whose ass has been fermentin' in duck shit and water. Ev'body knows 'bout you. You tryin' ta make some points comin' on down here stickin' your nose in where it don't belong?"

Discovering new flesh, a swarm of mosquitoes attacked me with a gung ho vengeance, but I didn't dare make a move to swat them away.

"I saw Valerie last night. I saw what was done to her. I want to catch whoever was responsible. She was your niece—don't you care about that?"

Maybe it was the fact that if she didn't care, who else would? Marie wavered.

"You gotta gun on you?"

I only wished I had. Instead, my Smith & Wesson .357 Magnum was locked away in the glove compartment of my car.

"No."

With the barrel of her gun, Marie motioned to the sullen boy covered in freckles.

"Check her out, Reginald."

Reginald? The kid had to be tough to get through life in the bayou with a name like that. What he did have were fast and efficient hands. In a quick thirty seconds, I felt as if I'd just been groped on a date back in high school. Reginald backed away, but Marie kept the gun leveled at me.

"Lucky for you you're a woman. If you'd been that asshole Hickok, I'd have blown you away by now." Marie grinned as she moved a step closer. "You know, it's mighty easy for someone to disappear back here in these swamps. It's been known to happen."

It seemed likely that Marie was responsible for more than a few people who had met with such an end.

"Were you in touch with Valerie at all recently?"

A muscle near the side of Marie's mouth twitched.

"I cut myself off from that child the day she left for N'Awlins. I knew she would come to no good in that town. I told her so. But she was flyin' high with a bunch of no-good trash."

"When Valerie was found, so was an alligator. Do you know how she got hold of it?"

Marie looked at me as though I had just come off the moon. "Don't take much brains to get hold of a gator round here. How long you been down in Louisiana now, girl?"

"Was Valerie involved with poaching gators?"

Marie's hand tightened on the stock of the shotgun.

"You know, child, you got a lot of questions for an outsider. You don't know shit about the bayou. How you think we livin' back here? How'm I 'posed to feed this gang of kids? You think only the rich folk got a right to these here gators? You wanna deal some justice, you should be taking a look at those ol' boys in your office or those state goons. I ain't gonna say what I'm doin' or ain't doin'. If that's what you want to know, you're wasting your time. Haul ass outta here now."

Complaints about the alligator tagging system were rampant. While it allowed for hunting during a thirty-day season, it benefited wealthy landowners with vast holdings of property that held plenty of gators. The bayou folks, who had always gotten by living off the land, ended up with few, if any, gators to hunt and sell. It was politics and money as usual in the land of Huey Long, and I told Marie so. Scrutinizing me a moment as if to pass judgment on whether or not I'd told her the truth, she lowered her gun.

"Reginald, go into the house and bring out two beers."

I wondered just how close I had come to being gator bait as Reginald came back out with the bottles. Marie pulled off the cap of one with her teeth and slugged down her beer, throwing me the other cold Dixie. She lowered herself onto a pile of logs with the shotgun at her feet, as a large black spider began the climb up her leg. But Marie was no Miss Muffett. Plucking off the spider as it reached the parapet of her knee, she threw it to Reginald, who lunged as if it were a reward. Tearing off one leg at a time as the spider squirmed in his grasp, he glanced over at me and grinned, aware it was something I probably hated.

I sat on the ground and leaned my back against a forlorn fender, my shirt and pants plastered to my skin as a trickle of sweat ran down my back. A baby gurgled behind me and I turned to see all of Marie's kids quietly congregated in the backyard, enjoying the free entertainment. The cold wetness of the beer seared my throat as I took a sip.

"So, you came all the way out here thinkin' I could tell you why Valerie was murdered, huh? Let me ask you. What you think it's all about?"

"Maybe she cheated on a jealous boyfriend."

Marie snorted. "Who's gonna be jealous of some drugged-out stripper? You tell me that."

"Could it have been a pimp that she worked for?"

Marie shook her head. "I didn't bring up no child to give their hard-earned money to some lazy pimp bastard. Valerie didn't have a lot of brains, but she was smart enough to work for herself."

"Was she hooked on drugs when she lived here with you?"

Finishing her beer, Marie sent her empty bottle whizzing past my head, missing me by only a matter of inches, to land on a trash pile at the back of the house.

"Reginald, bring out two more!"

Resentful of the chore, the boy glared in my direction before sauntering back to the house.

"Where you from?" Marie hoisted one leg on the woodpile, allowing me an unwanted view up her dress.

"I'm from New York."

"You got drugs up there?"

I chuckled at the thought as Reginald dropped a beer in my lap.

But Marie didn't wait for an answer. "Well, where the hell you think that stuff comes in from?"

I relied on Hollywood for my information on this subject. "The south coast of Florida has always seemed the logical place to me."

"Shit, no. The smart ones bring it in through here. Who the hell's gonna tramp across some swamp to find 'em? Of course Valerie was snortin' and doin' every other damn thing. Hell, it's easier to get that shit back here than it is to catch gators."

Reginald bent down next to Marie's foot, intent on grabbing another spider that had carelessly crossed his path. But before he could reach it, Marie grabbed the boy by the ear and pulled him toward her, slapping him hard across the face as he let out a howl. He scowled at her in silence.

"You don't know much now, do you, Miss Fish and

Wildlife? Well, I'm gonna make you just a little bit smarter.'' Finishing the second beer, she rammed the bottle down on a passing bug. ''Valerie had a boyfriend, alright. You ever hear of a fella by the name of Hillard Williams?''

Scanning my memory, I recalled seeing posters around town. His name was being touted for a hotly contested political race against the incumbent Democratic mayor, who had failed to pull the city out of its economic slump. Williams was basing his campaign on the politics of discontent, pumping up both blue-collar anger and middle-class fear by hitting on violent crime, a skyrocketing murder rate, the rocketing increase in AIDS, and an influx of illegal immigrants. Calling for antigay measures to ''take back our city,'' Williams was considered the worst thing to hit gays since the outbreak of AIDS.

''He's running for mayor of N'Awlins. That sonofabitch was also screwing my niece. But what I bet you don't know is that Hillard used to poach gators for a living. The bastard made a fortune offa it. And you wanna know how?''

Marie spit out a wad of thick yellow phlegm.

''He made it big by cheatin' everyone around here on gator deals. Had himself some rich Dago partner from up your way. They trucked those skins outta here like no tomorrow. The day I learned Valerie was letting him get his jollies off on her was the day I cut that girl off forever.''

The idea of a stripper being hooked up with the man most likely to be New Orleans' next mayor wasn't all that farfetched. America's own banana republic, the state's political history had long been fraught with corrupt politicians, from the infamous Huey Long all the way up to the present former klansman and neo-Nazi, David Duke. Louisiana loved a good rascal, and they now had another in Hillard Williams. Following in the footsteps of those before him, Williams was gaining in the polls by creating alarm bordering on hysteria among the folks of New Orleans. It was down-home politics at its most insidious.

''Hillard Williams a gator poacher?'' I was still working on digesting the fact.

"You bet your ass. Big-time."

"If he was so busy cheating all of you, why wasn't he one of those who just disappeared?"

"It ain't a smart idea to go round knocking off the head of the local Nazi party. Besides, his partner was a big-time hoodlum. We don't need that kind of trouble."

"Is he still a Nazi?"

Marie's mouth resembled a checkerboard, with black spaces and yellow teeth evenly matched, as she broke out in laughter.

"He found God, doncha know. Sweet Lord Jesus has saved him." She stopped laughing as she wiped the spittle from the corners of her mouth with the back of her hand. "Don't you believe it. You couldn't trust that bastard nohow. He'd skin the hide off anyone who wasn't looking sharp. That sack of shit tried to cheat me more times than I can remember. He's lucky he got outta here with his dick in his hand. Thinkin' back on it now, I shoulda cut it off. Maybe Valerie would still be around today."

The air was quiet but for the rattling of tins and glass settling on Marie's trash pile.

"Do you think Hillard Williams killed her?"

Marie stood up, not bothering to brush off the wood chips and bugs that clung to her dress. Picking up her shotgun, she threw the second bottle of beer onto the heap, somehow missing the tangle of children who were playing among the refuse.

"You best be going now."

Lifting her shotgun, she aimed it straight at me. There would be no more questions today. Digging in my pocket, I pulled out a card and pen, and scribbled my home address and number on the back.

"If there's anything else you think of, I can be reached here."

Marie didn't waver as I put the card down on the ground and backed away, keeping my eye on her until I felt safe enough to turn around. The children moved aside to clear a path, then fell in line, following me in silence as I walked to my car, started the motor, and pulled away. Then all hell broke loose in the yard once more, as if I had never been there. I rounded the corner and caught a glimpse of Marie as she disappeared into the wooden shed, closing the door firmly behind her.

Four

Dry lightning crackled in the late-morning heat as I headed back toward the office. With the rain coming quickly, day turned to night around noon. Along with thunderclouds, a thick white fog rolled in, and driving along the road became a more daring game of chicken than usual. Cypress trees appeared out of nowhere, gaunt skeletons beckoning me into the nearest ditch. A phantom bridge with no beginning or end floated above a field of sugarcane, held up by invisible hands. The world flickered in front of me to the tune of worn-out wipers as I thought about Marie on my slow crawl toward Slidell.

Picking up Charlie's bad habits, I grabbed a candy bar and Coke for lunch on my way back to the office. My health food days in New York seemed a lifetime ago, when I had worked out six times a week and wouldn't touch anything made with sugar. But I figured as long as I didn't start hitting the Old Grand-Dad, I was still okay.

Walking down the hall at work, I heard the usual duck calls ring out loud and clear from behind. The pile of paperwork had grown on top of my desk; it needed to be taken care of . . . someday. Clipped to my phone were pink slips with messages. One of them was from Jake Santou. Not wanting to admit it, even to myself, I was pleased he'd phoned. There was something about the man I found intriguing.

Pushing the other messages aside for the moment, I returned Santou's call. He picked up before I'd heard the first ring.

"Yeah. Santou here."

For a southern guy, he reminded me a lot of New York.

"It's Rachel Porter."

Before I had a chance to add anything else, Santou cut in.

"Yeah, Porter. I'm glad you called back. Remember the offer I made last night? Well, I've got a meeting scheduled with the political hot dog who's gonna win the next mayoral election, Hillard Williams. It's for later this afternoon. Want to come along? It'll give you a good dose of the local color. You might even pick up a pointer or two on the case."

The name set off a fireman's parade of alarm bells in my brain. If Williams was one of the first on Santou's whodunit list, it seemed obvious that what Marie had told me was true. It also appeared that Valerie and Hillard Williams had been more than just a well-kept secret. I decided to play fair and fill Santou in on my meeting with Marie, and in what context Hillard Williams's name had come up.

"Yeah, it's something I'm checking out. This is a small town, *chère*. Lots of rumors float around here. Hell, I've already heard some about you."

I skipped the bait. "What about Marie Tuttle? Why hasn't anyone been there to question her yet?"

"You just covered that for me, Porter." Santou gave a flat laugh. "Besides, she's small potatoes. I haven't got the time to waste."

I took the dig without bothering to respond. I wasn't about to make any snappy comebacks that might prompt Santou to rescind his offer. Getting off the phone, I headed into Hickok's office to inform him of my meeting with Marie, and let him know that my dance card was filled for the afternoon.

He sniggered at my report on the events of the morning.

"That gal's one little charmer, ain't she? Could make the snakes jump right out of their baskets and head back into the swamp quicker than a .45. You gotta watch that woman with both of your eyes.''

The homilies were great, but I wanted to know fact from fiction. Sometimes down here it was hard to tell one from the other.

''Is what she told me about Hillard Williams true?''

Charlie took a sip of ginger ale that had the waft of bourbon to it—a vice he'd acquired soon after the discovery that he was minus a wife.

''Well, that man never could learn to keep his pecker in his pants. In the old days, when he was raking it in poaching gators, he was one tough little dude. He's a little bitty shit, too.''

Getting information out of Hickok was like trying to pull on a strand of taffy.

''Marie said he was the head of the Nazi movement down here. Is that right?''

Hickok pulled out a nail clipper and began snapping at his fingernails, one after the other. I was beginning to understand why his wife had left home.

''That's what they say, Bronx.''

''What do you say, Charlie?''

''I say, every time you take a step, before you put your foot down, check exactly where it is you're going.''

The top of his thumbnail whizzed past me. I was getting nowhere fast.

''Listen, Bronx. Politicians down here are as crooked as a dog's hind leg, and Hillard is just about as crooked as they come. He'll do or say whatever it takes to get himself elected, and he sure as hell seems to speak for a lot of the folks around here. He says he's no Nazi. I ain't gonna argue with him on that.''

''I hear he used to have a partner from New York that Marie described as a hoodlum.''

Charlie gave a slight laugh. ''She was being charitable on that one.''

''I don't understand why the police haven't checked out

Marie Tuttle. They must know about Valerie's relation to her."

Hickok popped open a box of Raisinets, his nod to nutrition. "It's a bottom-drawer case, Bronx. Back-burner stuff for when their case load gets low, which is never. Ain't nobody in N.O.P.D. gonna lose any shoe leather over a French Quarter hooker."

The answer irritated me. "Well, maybe I'll be able to find out some more for myself. If it's alright with you, I'm going to be meeting with Hillard Williams at four o'clock this afternoon."

For once Hickok was caught by surprise.

"You want to fill me in on how you managed to pull that off?"

I didn't really, but there was no way around it. "The detective in charge of the Vaughn case invited me along. He wants us to pool information on this one."

Hickok didn't bother to look up as he emptied the box of Raisinets into his mouth. "And just who is this detective you're talking about?"

"Jake Santou."

Hickok's eyebrows shot up as he went back to clipping his nails. "I'll give you some leeway on this one, Bronx, but just make sure it's the case you're working on. I know that Cajun coonass, and I can guess what he's really interested in. And it ain't your investigating skills, neither. You just remember, you're still working for me, so I get your reports. That also means hauling your rear end back out in that bayou and working this case in between everything else."

I smiled as sweetly as possible as I walked out the door.

I met Santou outside the police precinct, where I hopped into a LeSabre so old that it made my VW look good. A red plastic crawfish and a set of black rosary beads swung from the rearview mirror, to the rhythm of late-afternoon traffic.

In the daylight, streaks of silver were finger-painted throughout his hair. Having worn a work shirt and jeans last night, he was a different person today in a brown sport jacket, chocolate slacks, and a beige shirt open at the neck to showcase the gold St. Anthony medal that lay against a chest covered with densely matted dark hair. His hooded eyes noticed me checking him out, but Santou was all business as he fought the traffic across Canal.

Originally the dividing line between the French, who considered the Quarter their own, and upstart Americans who dared to move into the area, the street now belonged to upscale department stores and the harried crowds that frequented them. A newly refurbished downtown, it could have been plunked anywhere in the U.S. and looked right at home.

We drove out toward the Garden District, passing the St. Charles streetcar on our way. Known in the past as the streetcar named Desire, which Tennessee Williams had made so famous, it slashed its way back and forth through the Garden District, its rails hot, shiny ribbons of steel under a blistering sun.

Once an exclusive section for the American nouveau riche, the Garden District is lined with one nineteenth-century gingerbread home after another. Each house had been built to surpass the next in an attempt to impress the French, who continued to view American residents as social scum. But Hillard's house took the proverbial cake. Turning on to Prytania Street, Santou parked outside the high walls of the towering mansion, stained the shade of lemon meringue pie. Walking through the wrought-iron gate, I pulled at the hem of my dress as it clung to my legs in the heat. I had tried to make myself presentable for both Williams and Santou by running home to shower and change. It had been a long time since I'd worn anything besides pants and sneakers, but it seemed the least I could do to meet a character of Hillard's notoriety.

Santou rang the doorbell, letting his finger rest on the buzzer for a minute or two. Just as I was beginning to think I'd been duped about any appointment, the door swung open, framing a hulking figure who made Santou look small. Towering at six feet five inches and weighing close to three hundred pounds, stood a man who could easily have been snatched up by any pro football team to play defense. Bearing a boxer's flattened nose and a pompadour pomaded to perfection, Hillard's butler was dressed in a red knit polo shirt complete with alligator emblem, white polyester pants, and pointy black shoes with a blinding shine. A thick gold band complete with a large, flashy diamond cut into the soft white flesh of his pinky finger. In the background, the high-pitched yap of a frenzied dog was on automatic, like a machine gun out of control.

"Yeah? Whadda youse want?"

I identified it right away as Little Italy, New York, one hundred percent.

Santou flashed his badge.

"Let me check on it." Little Italy began to close the door, but Santou quickly wedged his foot inside.

"You mind if we step in? It's awful hot out today."

I had already begun to perspire and pushed my way through the open door, urged on by a cool breeze from inside. My brashness caught Little Italy off guard.

"Yeah. I s'ppose so."

As he lumbered off, the air-conditioning took my breath away, along with the three-tiered crystal chandelier that hung in the center of the front hall. I could only guess how many gator skins had gone toward its purchase. A winding staircase stood off to the left. Made of mahogany, the steps led up to a second-floor landing that was bathed in a spectrum of colored light, the domed skylight above a mosaic of stained glass.

Little Italy suddenly loomed above me.

"Yeah. He'll see youse, but he's only gotta coupla minutes ta spare."

Following him across the floor, I caught a glimpse of myself in the French cut-glass mirror. A mass of wild red waves, my hair curled down my back, the humidity making it frizz all the more. While the summer heat had tempted me to cut it off, long hair still seemed a badge of my youth, and I wasn't ready to let it go.

Santou's newly acquired Southern drawl drew my attention back to the walking hulk in front of us.

"You working for Hillard Williams down here?"

"Whadda I look like? A guest? I'm his bodyguard." The heavy New York accent, interspersed with Santou's Cajun patter, was like being caught between a bowl of gumbo and a heaping dish of linguine with clams.

"And just why would Hillard be needing the expertise of a bodyguard in our peaceful town?"

"Hey, you're a cop. You should know this is one wacko place. I never seen so many weirdos in my life. When ya can't find a decent pizza, ya know something ain't right about a town."

"My name's Jake Santou. Who'd you be?"

I glanced at the heavy gold ID bracelet that hung from Little Italy's wrist like a chain. When he didn't respond, I answered for him. "Vincent."

Vincent's body stopped in place, a veritable Rock of Gibraltar as he turned to face me. "Nobody calls me that except my mother, and she's dead. Call me Vinnie."

The sharp rap of high heels caught my attention. I glanced over my shoulder in time to see a woman, carrying a dog the size of a Q-Tip with teeth, disappear up the stairs.

Little Italy answered my question before I had time to ask. "That's Mrs. Williams, the boss's wife. She don't take much to company."

Turning back around, Vinnie walked toward the end of the hall as Santou continued his interrogation. "You down here from New York, Vinnie?"

Little Italy didn't bother to answer as he flung open the double doors to Hillard's inner sanctum. Spread out before us was a room that rivaled the Harvard Men's Club. Paneled in mahogany, the room was drenched in a golden glow from the afternoon sun that streamed in through a large bay window. An overhead fan pirouetted silently above us, its whirling blades reflecting in the barroom mirror that hung above an immense marble fireplace. But what dominated the room was the oversize desk of cherry wood that you could have rolled a bowling ball on. Mounted directly behind it, and jutting out from the wall, was a bleached alligator skull of gargantuan proportions, beneath which sat a maroon leather chair as regal as a king's throne.

Perched in its seat was a man whose chest barely met the top of the desk, and whose balding pate was poorly disguised by a few wisps of hair combed from one side across to the other. A pair of electric blue eyes beamed at me in amusement from a face that had all the roundness of a chipmunk's, its pouches stuffed with food for the coming winter. Jumping up to greet us, Hillard Williams stood five feet tall. A butterball of a man, his barrel chest gave him the appearance of a bantam rooster. The two top buttons of his short-sleeve white shirt were undone, so that curls of wiry white hair pushed their way out in masculine defiance. A pair of red suspenders held up pants which hung below a protruding belly.

"Well, if it ain't my favorite detective. How ya doing, Jake? Good to see ya." Hillard slapped him on the back as though Santou had choked on a chicken bone. "And who's this pretty little lady here?"

I towered over Hillard Williams, and could easily have patted him on the head. Instead I held myself back, allowing him to take my hand as Jake turned on his homeboy charm.

"Why, Hillard, didn't y'all hear? Fish and Wildlife went and got themselves a female agent all the way from New York City. This is Rachel Porter. I thought this would be a good chance for her to meet the next likely mayor of our town and one of our most prominent citizens."

Hillard casually began to stroke my hand as though I were a high-strung filly in need of some calming down.

"Well, it's about time ol' Hickok did something right. Welcome to New Orleans, honey."

He gave my hand one last squeeze before I pulled free of his grasp. I tried to imagine kinky sex involving Hillard,

Valerie, and Hook, but my mind drew a blank as the man's eyes moved up and down my body, busy calculating my weight, height, and measurements.

"If there's anything I can do to make your adjustment to our city any easier, darlin', ya just holler, and I'll do my darndest to help ya out."

A movement drew my attention to the bay window overlooking the garden out back. Heavy burgundy drapes framed the view much like a stage curtain, and the bright afternoon sun flared into my eyes. Squinting against the glare, I saw a man's dark silhouette slide out from behind the bulky material and realized someone had been standing there all along. Hillard took the opportunity to grab my hand once again as he followed my gaze.

"Well, excuse my backward manners. Gunter is so damn quiet sometimes I forget he's even around. I want y'all to meet my advisor on foreign affairs. This here is Gunter Schuess."

Tall and slim, with white-blond hair cut straight across the top like coarse bristles on a brush, Gunter glided toward us with liquid grace. He was dressed elegantly in black, his skin stark white in contrast. High cheekbones jutted up like precarious cliffs. His watery blue eyes flickered over me, then dismissed me quickly as if I were of little consequence. The slightest trace of a smile touched his lips, but no glimpse of humor was to be found in his eyes. Though his grip was light as he took hold of my hand, I was left with the impression that he could easily have crushed every bone in my body. Cold and dry to the touch, his skin reminded me of Hook. I held back a shiver as I let go. Schuess then faced Santou and nodded without offering his hand.

Jake broke the tension, turning to Hillard, who watched the proceedings with amusement.

"Why, Hillard, what are you needing an advisor on foreign affairs for? You haven't even been elected mayor yet, let alone president. I thought that was another four years down the road for you."

Hillard looked pleased, as if the thought was one he'd already contemplated. Gunter quickly intervened, his voice as smooth and carefully modulated as his manner.

"In this day and age of global communications, it is to every politician's benefit to have as many contacts as possible outside his own realm. In Mr. Williams's case, when he is mayor I will take on the task of bringing European business into the New Orleans area. There is a minor problem with unemployment here at the moment, is that not so? Presenting a global platform will attract foreign business and help to alleviate the situation. It is a very farsighted solution to the problem here, and one that is sure to win Mr. Williams the election."

Gunter's strong German accent added an underlying edge to the words, giving the speech a hypnotic effect.

Turning toward me, Hillard took my hand once again.

"Did ya know I'm runnin' for mayor, sugar? Lord knows, I'm just a coonass country boy, but we got problems here, darlin', that need fixin' fast. I don't mean to scare you none, but New Orleans is like one of those big ol' oil tankers that's hit a reef and is sinking like a rock. Why, industry's leavin' here in droves, and our river port is just a lazy coon dog out in the noonday sun. All we got growin' here is people who'd rather collect welfare than work, and our murder rate's worse than where you come from. You be careful when you go out at night, you hear me, honey? I'm tellin' you the Lord's honest truth. You'll be robbed and raped and wonder what happened. And you stay away from that Bourbon Street. It's riffraff like that are turning our wonderful city of New Orleans into a city of disease and human filth."

It sounded as if Hillard were practicing for an upcoming rally. I pulled my hand out from under his, but he barely took notice.

"Most good solid workin' folks think just like me, which is why I'm puttin' myself through all this. It ain't for me, darlin'. We gotta think of our children before they're out on bread lines. Hell, you can forget about all those illegal aliens taking our jobs away. We're under siege from the legal ones, we got so damn many of 'em. I ain't no bigot, you understand. My motto is equal rights for all and special privileges for none."

As Hillard caught his breath to launch into another round, Santou cut him off.

"To tell you the truth, Hillard, we didn't come here to discuss campaign strategy and platform stands. You're the expert on that. We're here on a police matter." Santou paused a moment as he turned to glance at Gunter. "It's something you might prefer to discuss in private."

Hillard moved behind his desk as he waved us toward two plain wooden chairs in front.

"Oh, come on now, Jake. I'm sure that won't be necessary. Besides, Gunter here should be in on whatever's bothering y'all. He's my liaison with the public. Kinda like my troubleshooter, if you know what I mean."

Jake smiled. "Trouble already, Hillard? Shit, you ain't even got into office yet."

"Ain't that the truth. I just might have to call on your services some when I get there. Make you my chief of police." Turning toward me, Hillard gave a wink. "And as for you, darlin', how 'bout I set up one of them special wildlife departments here in New Orleans proper so as I can make you head of it? Put a gal like you to good use. Get you to tame some of that wild life in this town."

Hillard chortled at his own joke as he folded his hands on top of the desk. They looked tiny enough to belong to a child.

"So, what y'all here for? I got too many traffic tickets or something?" Hillard pulled out a stogie the size of one of Vinnie's fists and lit up.

"Nah. Nothing like that, Hillard. I want to talk to you about one of those topless dancers over on Bourbon Street."

"You talking about those dens of iniquity, Jake? Well, if ya got some gal you're hankering to meet, you're on your own, boy. That's outta my league these days." Hillard took a deep puff on his cigar, sending out a ring of smoke, and then winked at me as though I was being let in on a private joke. ''What y'all think? Should my administration clean up all those girlie shows, or should we keep 'em and put the taxes to good use?''

Pulling another cigar out of his pocket, he thrust it toward Santou, who declined.

''What I was wondering, Hillard, was if you might have been acquainted with one girl in particular. A dancer by the name of Valerie Vaughn. Does that ring a bell with you?''

Hillard squirmed in his seat as he smiled down at his desk. ''I was a man-'bout-town in my day. Ya know that, Jake. It's not bragging or nothing, just a fact. But I'm a married man now. Mrs. Williams wouldn't take kindly to no dancing girls coming up to the house.'' Hillard turned to look at me. ''I bet you wouldn't put up with that nonsense none yourself. Though why anybody would wanna play around on a gal like you beats me.''

Tempted to retort with a caustic remark, I held back, leaving Hillard to fill the awkward silence with quick puffs on his cigar, like an inhalator supplying him with much-needed bursts of oxygen. Gunter drifted toward the window, folding himself back in the drapes where he gazed out at the garden, as if the subject matter was of little concern.

''But this might be a girl you would have known. Her aunt is Marie Tuttle. You remember her, Hillard.'' Beads of sweat broke out on Hillard's brow, his glistening head as highly polished as a cue ball. Placing his cigar in an ashtray molded in the shape of a gator's claw, Hillard leaned as far forward in Santou's direction as he could, rising partially out of his seat.

''I'm gonna take ya up on that offer of privacy, Jake. This ain't no kinda discussion with a lady present.''

''I'm also working on the case, Mr. Williams.''

But Hillard no longer acknowledged me. ''Jake, I really would feel a whole lot easier 'bout speaking on such a delicate topic if a lady weren't present in the room.''

Not wanting to leave, I spoke up in my own defense. "Please don't be concerned, Mr. Williams. Nothing that is said is going to offend me. I'm a federal agent, and as Detective Santou can confirm, my interest in this case is totally legitimate."

Turning in my direction, Hillard rested the top half of his body on the desk and pulled himself forward until his feet were off the ground. "Sugar, this ain't New York. You're in New Orleans now, and we operate differently down here. So why don't you just relax and lighten up? You'll live longer that way."

Pushing himself back in one fluid motion, Hillard sank into his chair as he smiled at me. "First off, darlin', agent or not, ya look like a woman to me, and since I'm a Southern gentleman, there's just some things that can't be talked about in front of a lady. Secondly, you'll excuse my bluntness, but I don't see how a stripper's death's got anything to do with you protecting critters. And finally, I wish ya would stop calling me Mr. Williams. Why doncha just call me Hill."

I leaned toward him over the desk. "First off, Mr. Williams, I'm here on official business, so obviously there is a tie-in with wildlife. Secondly, my name is Agent Porter. Please refer to me that way in the future. And finally, this is as relaxed as I get." Sliding back in my chair, I held Hillard's gaze until Santou broke the tension.

"You know what, Hillard? I think I will take one of those cigars."

Pulling out a stogie from his desk, Hillard rolled it across the top. Santou caught it as it fell off the wooden edge into his hand. Carefully biting off the end, he stuck the cigar in his mouth and lit up, taking the first few puffs in silence.

"You're right, Hillard. This is a delicate topic." Turning in my direction, Santou's eyes narrowed in on mine so that I knew what was coming before he even said it. "I'm sure Agent Porter understands that as well, and won't mind giving us a moment in private to ourselves."

He couldn't have made it any clearer that this was his

interrogation, and he wasn't about to let me jeopardize it. He also couldn't have been more wrong. I minded more than he knew. Given no choice on the matter, I flashed Santou a look that left little doubt as to how I felt as I walked across the room, having been dismissed. I'd been told as a girl growing up that attitudes toward women would change, and on the surface they had. But scratch just beneath the politically correct exterior of the nineties, and all the same prejudices were alive and well, with each same wall to be knocked down as sturdy as ever. New York was bad enough. But in the past few months working in Louisiana, I'd become convinced that a change of attitude here would require nothing less than a second Civil War.

Walking out the door, I nearly smacked into the woman I had seen running up the stairs. Dolores Wlliams was dressed in black capri pants and a midriff blouse lost beneath a blizzard of sequins. She had obviously been eavesdropping on the conversation. Her hand was slapped over the muzzle of a toy poodle that, on closer inspection, could have been mistaken for a white cotton ball, but for two pink bows and ten stubby nails painted a dazzling shade of red.

As for Dolores, an overabundance of makeup worked against her effort to appear young and fresh. Heavy pancake and powder revealed a deep network of lines, while shoulder-length bleached blond hair styled in a girlish flip did little to sustain the illusion. A pair of dark sunglasses covered her eyes. What had probably been an hourglass figure at one time had come to resemble a brandy snifter. Nearly as tall as me, Dolores must have been Hillard's idea of an Aryan goddess at one time. Now she was just his bothersome wife. As she swayed precariously back and forth on a pair of red high-heeled mules, it was apparent that Dolores's lack of balance came from the Southern Comfort I could smell on her breath. I estimated that she clocked in at around fifty, though the twin ravages of age and too much liquor had taken their toll. Dolores bounced against the wall as she stuck out her hand for balance, holding on to the poodle, which I now noticed had only three legs. When she let go of the dog's snout, it bared its teeth at me, emitting a low growl of warning.

"Stop that, Fifi."

The dog looked at me with pure hatred as I started to introduce myself.

"Save your breath, honey. I heard what's going on, and let me tell you, that whore got what she deserved."

Dolores sported a lighter accent than her husband's, though her speech tended to slur.

"Did you know Valerie Vaughn?" I had the feeling Dolores knew plenty. Her remark came from a woman well aware of what her husband had been up to, and was now making him pay for it dearly.

"If you mean did I know her intimately, like we got together and had lunch, no. But I can tell you we shared more than just my husband."

I no longer cared what tap dance Hillard was doing in the next room. Santou had unknowingly done me a huge favor.

"Would you mind talking to me about it, Mrs. Williams? I'm working on the case. I'd be interested to hear whatever you have to say."

"I bet you would." She barked a loud laugh as Fifi tried to jump from her arms. Leaning heavily against the wall, Dolores studied me carefully in her inebriated state.

"You don't look like a cop to me. What are you? Undercover or something?"

"I'm with the Fish and Wildlife Service. An alligator was found in Ms. Vaughn's apartment. It had been killed as well. That's why I was called in."

"You're here about that damn gator? Jesus Christ! What a crock, though I suppose I should be grateful for small favors." Dolores pulled the dog closer until its head was buried in a sea of sequins. "Thank God that walking handbag's dead. At least there's some justice left in the world."

Considering where all the money for her house and furnishings had come from, it didn't seem a very charitable statement. Dolores swayed in my direction, nearly losing her balance. I thrust out a hand to steady her, and Fifi lunged toward me like a hungry piranha as the door to Hillard's office swung open, and the bristle-combed head of Gunter peered out. Catching sight of our powwow, he glided through the door as if he were skating on ice. Ignoring me, he caught Dolores by the arm and tried to veer her toward the stairs.

"Shouldn't you be in your room resting? None of this need concern you." Gunter's voice wove a silky web. It was obvious he was a man used to getting his way. Fifi turned toward him and growled loudly as the stump of her leg began to twitch. He pulled away for a moment, uncertain as to what the dog might do. His appearance was vaguely reptilian in the afternoon light, and I noticed, for the first time, that his eyebrows were as white as his hair, while he lacked any eyelashes whatsoever. Gunter grabbed at Dolores again, causing Fifi to launch into frenzied high-pitched barking that could have been taken for a car alarm on the fritz.

The shrill yelping jerked Dolores out of her stupor. Pulling her arm out of Gunter's grasp, she barked out her own command.

"I don't want to rest. What I want is another drink!" She glared at Gunter as he stood ramrod straight. "Now!"

Analyzing the situation through lashless eyes, Gunter humored her for the moment. "I'll see what I can do." Turning on his heel, he left the hall.

"You do that!" Dolores barked after him. With Gunter out of the way, Fifi turned her attention back to me, baring her teeth in a warning growl. Swaying toward me, Dolores considerately placed her hand over the dog's snout to keep me from being torn to bits.

"I'm a goddamn prisoner in my own home. There's always somebody spying on me." Dolores pulled back, contemplating me with glazed eyes before leaning in once again. "So, you're new in town, huh? Good. Someone Hill hasn't bought off yet. We can't talk now, but come back tomorrow for lunch. We'll talk then." Dolores hiccuped a trail of good bourbon. "I'll get Vincent to let you in."

Southern Comfort promises. My pulse raced as Gunter returned, holding a glass filled with bourbon and ice.

"I suggest you drink this upstairs." He handed Dolores the glass, his tone holding a thinly veiled threat as he grabbed her once again by the arm.

In a well-timed move, Dolores let go of the dog's muzzle so that Fifi lunged like a cobra striking at its prey, zeroing in to lock her teeth into Gunter's outstretched hand. For a moment the two froze in place, like a piece of performance art, until Gunter reached for Fifi's muzzle to try and pry her jaw loose. The dog just held on tight, digging deeper into his flesh with a determined growl. Gunter cursed under his breath as he clamped his free hand tightly around Fifi's throat. As he cut off the dog's air supply, Dolores brought the standoff to an abrupt end by rapping Fifi on the nose, and then striking a well-placed kick to Gunter's shins with the heel of her shoe. Releasing the hand with a look of triumph, Fifi came away with a chunk of flesh as blood ran from Gunter's wound.

"Someone is going to kill that damn dog someday." Ripping a handkerchief from his pocket, Gunter tightened it around the gash in an attempt to stop the spurt of blood that covered his hand and the cuff of his shirt.

"You just make sure that doesn't happen, Gunter, or believe me, you'll have a lot worse than Fifi to deal with." Dolores held her drink in a rock-steady hand, having not spilled one drop during the melee. "You'll have me on your German ass, and that's something you don't even want to think about."

There was no time to imagine how Dolores could possibly be worse than Fifi on the prowl, as the door to the inner sanctum opened and Hillard and Santou walked out.

"You're a good man, Jake. I knew I could count on ya to understand. And don't you worry none. Once I get into office, that job is yours, and that's a promise." Ignoring both Gunter's bloody hand and Fifi's reddened muzzle, Hillard bounded over to me. "You remember my offer now, honey. Don't be a stranger, ya hear? I just might have a place in my administration for a gal like yourself. It's high time we had us a head of wildlife for whatever wildlife it is we got here in this city."

Hillard once more felt comfortable enough to address me with endearments. I took this as a sign that their meeting had gone well. As for "head of wildlife," I was pretty sure he meant local dogcatcher to clean up whatever mess might be made. So far, there seemed to be plenty of them.

"So, how'd it go with Dolores Williams? I see that she was in her usual stewed state." Santou sounded awfully chipper.

"Gee, I don't know. What can you expect to get from a woman who's drunk and has her hands full with a psychotic dog? But enough about me. How was your private meeting with Hillard? He certainly seemed satisfied with the outcome." I had given Santou more than enough information for today, and had come to the decision that unless we played this straight, we might as well each work on our own. "What was all that about making me leave the room?"

Santou grinned. "It's known as Southern manners, *chère*. There are certain things Southern gentlemen don't talk about in front of a lady."

I had reached my bursting point as far as Southern charm was concerned. "Don't hand me that crap, Santou. Either we work on this together, or we're wasting each other's time."

The sun highlighted the silver streaks in his hair and deepened his sallow complexion to a rich golden brown. As we approached the car Santou took off his jacket, casually tossing it over his shoulder as he leaned against the passenger door, his eyes narrowing as they homed in on me.

"Good. I've never liked having to deal with some fragile lady. My day is now officially over, so how about having some Cajun food with me and seeing what life in Louisiana is really like? I don't imagine you've come across much of that living in the French Quarter."

His remark took me by surprise. "How did you know I live in the Quarter?"

Santou stared at me a moment, then smiled. "You told me. Last night."

"No, I didn't." Growing up in New York, the first thing you learned was never to tell anybody where you lived right away.

Santou shrugged, the smile still lingering on his lips. "Lucky guess, then."

I could feel the tension radiating off Santou's hot-wired veneer. If he was all that curious about my address, it would have been easy enough for him to find out. In spite of myself, I found I was flattered. But not enough to let him off the hook right away.

"I thought I'd been invited along on a business meeting, Santou. Not to be shunted around like some Southern belle from one room to another. You made me look like a fool back there while you and Hillard were busy playing country boys."

Whatever Santou was about to say, he consciously repressed it, wrapping his arms across his chest as though to bottle it in. Studying him in the afternoon light, I didn't see any one physical characteristic that could be called attractive all on its own, but there was something about the man that exuded sensuality.

"*Chère,* don't you know how to get along with people? Make them feel comfortable? Hillard and I are just two ol' country boys playing a bit of round-robin with each other. Nothing wrong with that." Santou's body still blocked my entrance to the passenger door. "I don't know about you, but I'm starving. Let's go for a ride."

"If all this was just to get me out on a date, you should have saved yourself the trouble. I'm not interested." I made a move for the door handle but Santou didn't budge.

"Don't flatter yourself, Porter. You're a good-looking woman, but I just got out of one mess. I don't need to get myself right back into another."

It struck a chord, echoing one of my reasons for leaving New York. In truth, I had run away. I needed to believe that if I picked up and moved, somehow my life would change—or at least my pattern of failed relationships with men. While I had always thought of myself as an independent woman, I kept making the same fatal mistake time and again. I tended to define myself by the way each man had wanted me to be.

"Listen, Porter, I'm talking dinner between two people working on the same case, that's all. But it's up to you. As far as Hillard is concerned, I knew I'd get more out of him if you weren't in the room."

"I'd expect you to tell me what you found out whether we went to dinner or not. That was the deal, wasn't it?"

Santou stepped away from the car. Opening the door, I sat down on a hot plastic cover that melted into my skin.

"Yeah, that was the deal."

Santou slid in behind the wheel and reached beneath his seat. "Jesus, Porter. What's the big deal? We're not talking date rape, just relaxing over a decent Cajun meal in a setting a whole lot nicer than this while I fill you in on the details. Is that considered torture where you come from?"

Pulling out a bottle of Mylanta, he twirled off the top and took a swig, making him seem more human. I told myself I could use a break from my daily routine of chocolate bars and po'boy sandwiches. But deep down inside, I knew it was much more than that.

We rolled past a succession of sugarcane fields as Santou regaled me with stories from his childhood on Bayou Teche. I heard about his father, who had worked the swamps collecting crawfish and frogs to be sold to pricey New Orleans restaurants, and of his grandmother, who had been a fountain of Cajun folklore for the region. As a blue heron took flight from the bayou's edge, Santou told me to quickly make a wish before the bird flew out of sight and it would come true.

"I wish you'd tell me what was so confidential that I had to leave the room for."

Santou gave wide berth to a dead cat lying in the middle of the road, all four legs stiffly raised in a salute to the setting sun. "Hillard admitted to sleeping with Vaughn a few times. Says she tempted him till he just broke down and sinned. Made it sound like that little girl couldn't keep her hands off him. But then Jesus spoke to Hillard and told him to clean up his act, what with the election coming up and all, you know."

Santou's expression remained deadpan.

"So now, while he lusts after other women in his heart, he's taken a vow to lie only in the arms of that sweet little wife of his. Hillard said he's truly sorry about what happened to Vaughn, that he doesn't know anything, and he sorely hopes she found the comfort of God before she died. Of course, the whole time he was quaking in that big leather chair of his. Seems he's worried what this kind of information could do to his campaign if it leaked out, to say nothing of his newly acquired upstanding reputation."

It was no wonder that Gunter had felt safe leaving the room. I remembered Hillard's parting promise to Santou of better things to come.

"And you swallowed that line?"

Santou pointed out an egret camouflaged in the tall grass, taking in the last rays of day. Behind the bird was a factory exuding exhaust flames as bright as the setting sun.

"I'm just throwing Hillard a little rope, is all. I thought he might have been paying her rent, but that theory went up in flames."

"Why is that?"

Santou flashed a smile. "I paid a visit to Vaughn's landlord this morning. He said he always got a check from her promptly on the first of the month. So, there's no proof there. And Hillard swears he stopped seeing her when he announced his candidacy for mayor and became a soldier for Christ."

"Do we have any reason to believe anything Hillard says?"

"I don't know, *chère*. We have here a former poacher whose previous partner still conducts his business out of a social club in Queens. Then there's Vinnie Bertucci, who's playing butler but looks like he cracks heads for a living. And all this is without even taking into account Hillard's so-called advisor on foreign affairs, Adolph or Gunter or whatever his name is. That guy strikes me as any number of things. Unfortunately, a liaison for business isn't one of them."

The sun had just set, dousing the sky a fluorescent shade of purple as we pulled up to a plain concrete building in Breaux Bridge. The pounding of music telegraphed the fact that there was more to the place than could be seen from outside. The soaring strain of fiddles and the honky-tonk notes of an accordion filled a parking lot jammed with pickup trucks, complete with hound dogs lying in the back, parked next to Grand Ams with couples necking in the front.

We made our way through the door, squeezing past countless bodies to enter a rustic room lined with long picnic tables set end to end, where the crowd sat together family-style. Overhead fans twirled as men, women, and children two-stepped around the floor in an oblong circle. A flock of business cards tacked to the ceiling fluttered in unison in the artificial breeze, their clatter mimicking an invading army of locusts. The ceiling was low enough so that, by looking up, you could take a survey of who generally occupied the place. If you lay down on your back for a few hours with pencil and paper in hand, you'd have been able to fill a couple of Rolodexes with the names and numbers of plumbers, carpenters, electricians, fishermen, hardware stores, bait and tackle shops, and traveling salesmen. Cartoon murals of the swamp decorated the walls with chartreuse alligators, jaws looming wide open in readiness to swallow up the giddy crowd.

The band onstage, playing loud and nonstop, consisted of three generations of women costumed in red-and-white polka-dot dresses that flared out like bells, while the men wore blue-and-white striped shirts, with white pants held up by flame red suspenders. A lanky reed of a man with a drooping mustache and dark, soulful eyes sang in French, the melancholy lyrics soaring up to the rafters in a blend both piercing and nasal.

Santou grabbed my hand and pushed his way through the crowd until he found a spot big enough for one, squeezing us both in at a long wooden table. A giant bowl of steaming red crawfish and a pitcher of beer appeared just as a Cajun square dance began.

Feeling a tap on my shoulder, I swung around to face a sprightly old man decked out in a string tie and green suspenders who asked me to dance. I tried to bow out as gracefully as I could, but the old man refused to take no for an answer.

"If ya gonna eat Cajun, ya gotta dance Cajun."

"He's right, Porter. It's the rule in this place."

Taking a quick drink of beer, I headed out onto the floor. I grew up in a time where dancing meant rarely touching your partner, but Cajun dancing was exactly the opposite. Holding me in a tight embrace, with enough complicated twirls thrown in to keep me off-balance, the old man had a charitable amount of patience. But by the time the dance was over, I was panting from exertion while my senior citizen partner was still raring to go. Finally taking pity on me, he allowed me to return to my table, where bowls of jambalaya and another pitcher of beer had miraculously appeared. But more food brought more music, and the challenge seemed to be to get me up on the dance floor as much as possible. It wasn't until a waltz began that Santou stood up, locking his eyes on mine as he held out his hand.

"Come on, *chère*. This one is mine. We're going to *fais do-do*."

"*Fais do*, what?"

"Dance, *chère*. You know how to do that. You just relax and give yourself over to me."

Out on the dance floor, his hand burned into the small of my back as I told myself it was too soon to get involved again. The stubble of his chin bit into my cheek, and a surge of heat rushed through me. Pushing slightly away, I caught my breath. I'd been hurt far more in my last relationship than I had ever wanted to admit. It had been enough to make me leave my home. Santou pulled me close again, his hand tightening around my waist as our bodies moved together in slow, quiet rhythm. Closing my eyes, I let myself sway up against him, enjoying the sensation until his hand began to work its way down my back. Pushing away harder this time, I still felt the heat from his body against mine, even though we were inches away. In an effort to rein in my pulse, I turned back to business.

"So, where do we take it next on trying to nail Hillard?"

Santou stopped abruptly in place, looking at me with a dark brooding that I hadn't expected.

"Hillard's right. You need to lighten up. You don't know when to relax and have a good time."

"Listen, I just want us both to keep in mind that this is still business. Let's not forget that."

"I don't think there's any problem there."

Releasing me, Santou walked off the dance floor over to the other side of the room, where a game of darts was in progress. Taken aback by his abrupt change of mood, I stood alone for a moment before moving over to join him. Santou kept his eyes on the game as he spoke.

"Darlin', I get the feeling you like challenges, so I'll tell you what we'll do. I'll make you a deal. We'll play a game of darts. If you win, I'll tell you everything you want to know about Hillard this evening."

"And if I lose?"

Santou turned to me and stared for a moment, once again leaving me with the impression of a hawk in search of its prey. It was enough to dampen whatever heat I'd had left, as I warned myself that this was a man not to be trusted.

"If you lose, no more business tonight. We just have fun. That too threatening for you, *chère?*"

"Not at all."

I waited for the game in progress to end as I drank another beer. I had discovered that, as a rule, men tend to take it for granted that women are automatically bad at darts. It was a notion I always enjoyed dispelling. Darts was a game I'd excelled at ever since I was a kid, and people at the bar I'd frequented in New York had learned not to waste their money betting against me. If I didn't get one bull's-eye after another, I considered it an off game. Beer tended to focus my aim, and I'd had more than my fair share tonight. I knew, taking the darts in hand, my aim was as good as ever.

"Your turn, Santou."

By the time our first game was over, the few spectators had turned into a crowd. Having lost hands down, Santou looked over at me as if silently revising a premature judgment.

"You must have beginner's luck, Porter. Let's try again."

There was nothing I preferred to do. With the second game as much a wipeout as the first, Santou insisted on a third, but by now my aim was deadly. I scored one bull's-eye after another, until he threw down his darts in defeat.

"You win, Porter. It's business as usual for the rest of the night."

His voice held a hard edge that led me to believe he wasn't used to losing. Back at the table I bought a pitcher of beer, and Santou polished off a glass before leaning in toward me.

"You conned me, Porter. I won't let that happen again." Pushing himself back in his chair, he stared out at the crowd.

"It's your own fault, Santou."

Glaring at me, he poured himself another beer. "How do you figure that?"

"You set yourself up by taking it for granted I was a rank amateur who wouldn't know how to play the game."

Santou downed the second glass and drew close, causing my pulse to soar as he placed his hands just above my knees. "But that's exactly what you are, Rachel. You're a stubborn novice who's burning with something to prove. That's what makes you so dangerous."

His palms seared my skin, and I felt his breath on my face as I tried to collect my thoughts. On the one hand, I wanted to slug him. On the other, Santou was the most fascinating man I'd met in a long time. Pulling my eyes away from his stare, I shifted my chair so that his hands slid off my knees, breaking the heat of the moment.

Santou leaned back and studied his glass. "So, what do you want to know?"

With my pulse once more in check, I quickly assessed the situation. If he chose to think of me as a novice, so be it. I wasn't about to back out of this case.

"What is Vinnie Bertucci doing down here?"

Santou poured himself another beer before answering. "I'm not sure. But if I were to take a guess, it probably ties in with Frank Sabino, Hillard's former business partner. They were in the gator business together, big-time. Had a racket trucking illegal skins up to a warehouse in Newark, where they were stockpiled and then shipped over to Japan. Sabino was busted on it years ago. Hillard managed to slip out of any charges. Supposedly there was bad blood between them after that, but I wouldn't bet on it. It's a good ruse that's used to cover up a multitude of sins."

Santou poured the last of the beer into my glass.

"Next question."

"What's the story on Dolores Williams?" I hadn't told him of my appointment with her for tomorrow, and I didn't intend to.

"She used to perform synchronized water skiing at Cypress Gardens in Florida a lifetime ago. Had a body not to be believed and a vocabulary to match. Stories differ as to how she hitched up with Hillard, but she's been in an alcoholic haze ever since."

Santou slowly held up a finger. "One last question *chère*, just like Aladdin and his magic lamp."

I asked him the question Hickok had skirted. "Was Hillard the head of the Nazi movement down here at one time?"

"Hillard was, is, and always will be involved in the movement, and anyone who tells you different is outright lying. It's the man's religion."

The band started up again, playing a slow tune. Looking over at Santou with his burning eyes and unruly mop of hair, as crazy as it was, I knew what I wanted to do.

"Let's dance."

We moved across the floor and this time I relaxed, dismissing any thoughts as to how unprofessional I was being, only too glad that Charlie Hickok was nowhere in sight.

As we drove home along the twists and turns of the bayou, stars illuminated the night, looking like handfuls of iridescent confetti that had been tossed up into the sky. A breeze fluttered through dead cypress trees along the road, and their shawls of Spanish moss glistened like finely spun spiderwebs caught in the glow of the moonlight. The country was quiet except for the sound of Santou's car, his muffler a jarring and discordant note out of tune with our surroundings.

"You're more dangerous than I first thought."

The sound of his voice startled me. "What do you mean?"

"You're deadly with darts."

A truck roared by the other way and for a moment I thought of home. "In all fairness, I probably should have warned you."

"You're dangerous in other ways, too." Santou kept his gaze straight ahead.

"How's that?"

"You ask too many questions. If you're not careful, you're going to find yourself in a lot of trouble."

"Are you telling me not to ask questions, Santou?"

I heard a light clicking sound against the steering wheel, and turned to see Santou's rosary beads moving between the fingers of one hand.

"People play their games differently down here, *chère*, and you don't understand the rules yet."

"What are the rules?"

"Pay attention to warnings and take them seriously. They're only given once, and then it's out of Southern courtesy."

So far I'd received my fair share of warnings from everyone involved in this case—Marie, Hickok, Hillard Williams, and now even from Santou himself. The beads continued to hit against his steering wheel like a tongue clucking a steady stream of disapproval.

"Why the rosary beads, Santou?"

He held them up to the moonlight. "My grandmama gave them to me, saying they would keep me safe. I find they help me to think straight." Clenching the strand tightly in his fist, he held them for a moment before slipping them back into his pocket.

It was late by the time we reached my car at the police station. Santou reached over to unbuckle my seat belt, his hand grazing the bare skin of my legs.

"I'll drive along with you just to make sure you get home safe."

It was an offer I felt best to decline. "Thanks, but I'll be okay."

As he walked me to my car, I fought off the overwhelming desire not to spend the night alone. "You'll give me a call if you find anything else on Hillard?"

Santou draped his lanky frame against the car door. "Until we find something solid linking him to Vaughn, there's not much more we can do at the moment. Besides, keep in mind that just because Hillard fits nice and easy, it doesn't necessarily make him our killer."

"Then where do we go from here?"

Reaching out, Santou wrapped an arm around my waist and pulled me tightly against him. Kissing the lobe of my ear, his lips brushed against my cheek in a slow move toward my mouth. I intended to stop him. But I didn't. Not until I felt myself balancing on that delicate ledge along with my good intentions. Pulling away from temptation, I slid in behind the wheel, turning on the car's engine as he leaned in the window. Dropping his rosary beads into my lap, Santou turned and headed back toward the station.

Five

I was at Prytania Street by twelve o'clock sharp the next day. Though my car looked out of place in the neighborhood, with its badly dented front fender and a taillight that had given up and died months ago, I had dressed carefully for the occasion, wearing one of the two skirts I owned. My intention was to look presentable yet conservative. After Hillard's fawning attention toward me yesterday, I didn't want Dolores getting the wrong impression. With my finger on the buzzer, I waited in the heat for Vinnie to answer the door.

Just as yesterday, his manners were impeccable.

"You again?"

His uniform today consisted of baby blue polyester pants and a maroon-and-navy sports shirt. His hair looked as if it hadn't been slept on, with every pomaded strand arranged perfectly in place.

"Mrs. Williams is expecting me. Mind if I come in?"

"Couldn't stop ya yesterday. Why should today be any different?"

I stepped inside.

"Wait here."

A familiar rat-a-tat-tat bark announced Dolores's presence as she tottered in, with Fifi growling under one arm and an amber-colored drink held in her other hand. Her sunglasses were lodged on top of a puffy swirl of blond hair, allowing me full view of hazel eyes swimming in a sea of red. A soft nest of pouches formed downy pillows beneath, highlighted by white concealer that had been applied with a heavy hand. She had come a long way since her days as a performer with a body to kill for. Neither time nor Hillard had treated her particularly well. She was dressed in hot pink capri pants, and a long sequined top, gathered into a large knot in front, fell past her hips.

"This way, sugar. We'll talk out back in the garden." She leaned toward me, carefully covering Fifi's snout. "Less chance for prying ears to hear anything that way. What's your poison?" She gave her glass a swirl, but after all the beer I had consumed last night, the thought of anything alcoholic sent my stomach plunging.

"I'll just have an iced tea, if you don't mind."

"Mind? Why should I mind? Vincent!"

Little Italy stuck his head out from around the corner.

"Waddaya want?"

Dolores rolled her eyes as if her life consisted of one trial and tribulation after another. "Bring an iced tea outside and another bourbon while you're at it." Turning around, Dolores came close to losing her balance as Fifi yipped out a warning. But with a remnant of grace from her past, she caught herself at the last moment, managing not to spill her drink as she continued to walk outside. "You'll love the patio. It's great." She pulled a lounge chair into the sun. Settling into it, she leaned back, angling her face to the left.

"I need another fifteen minutes on this side to even out my tan."

Her skin already looked like an expensive Coach leather bag. Lying across her lap, Fifi pulled back her lips in a jagged-tooth grin that dared me to come close to her mistress. Ignoring the suggestion, I dug inside my purse in search of sunglasses as I turned my chair away from the sun.

"Do you know how I knew that Hillard was screwing around on me?"

I twisted my chair back around to catch her expression.

"How?"

"Because the old fool kept sneaking off with my jewelry, giving that bitch one piece at a time. Do you have any idea what it's like to find something missing every week and wonder if you're losing your mind?" Dolores barked out a loud laugh that sent Fifi flying into the air. Grabbing the pooch, she held Fifi tightly against her chest as the dog panted rapidly. "That's what he used to tell me, you know. It was all in my mind—that I was drinking too much and should check myself into some rehab center. The old goat."

"How did you find out it was Valerie?"

"In this town? Are you kidding? I had people banging down my door to tell me Hillard was involved with some cheap coonass stripper. After that, finding her was easy. I just had Hillard followed."

"You hired a private detective?"

"Damn straight! You think I'm going to have my jewelry disappearing on me only to end up on some little whore? I did hard labor for those stones."

I needed to tie Hillard in with Valerie for more than just a few passing nights. The P.I.'s report could corroborate that and probably pass along some extra dirt as well.

"I'd like to speak with the detective you hired. Where can I find him?"

Dolores sucked down the rest of her drink. "Oh, he's long gone. Left town right after he gave me the info. Who knows where the hell he went. He didn't even bother to collect his last check—not that he needed to, after the minor fortune I paid him. Hell, he probably retired on it."

No P.I. that I knew of would ever voluntarily miss a payment, no matter how much money he had already made on a case.

"But you're sure it was Valerie that Hillard was giving your jewelry to? There couldn't have been anyone else?"

"Listen, sugar, I'm not stupid. I know he's fucked around on me plenty. But Hillard has his own code of honor. No more than one whore at a time. He's loyal that way. Besides, when I finally confronted the bitch, she was wearing a locket that I used to keep Fifi's picture in. Can you believe it? I go to threaten the tramp, and she answers the door wearing my own goddamn necklace! Used to call herself a coonass. Cheap piece of ass is what she was. I never did get the necklace back. She called me crazy and slammed the door in my face. But Hillard finally admitted it. He admitted everything, after what happened to poor little Fifi."

Vinnie came out with our drinks, and Dolores become conspicuously quiet. Grabbing the fresh glass with one hand, her arm stayed tightly wound around Fifi, whose compact body was beginning to fry in the sun like a well-done pork sausage. Drops of saliva fell from the dog's tongue onto Dolores's capri pants, in a pattern that resembled a Rorschach test. Squinting into the sun, Dolores let go of Fifi just long enough to grab on to the front of Vinnie's shirt.

"Where the hell are my sunglasses, Vincent? Where did you goddamn put them?"

Vinnie towered above her, almost blocking out the sun, his right hand bunching up in a fist. But Fifi wasn't dead from the heat yet, and she let loose a warning growl. Slowly bringing her arm back around Fifi's neck, Dolores put her glass of bourbon to the dog's snout and watched her gratefully lap up the liquid.

Satisfied that his point had been made, Vinnie smoothed out his shirt, tucking it in tightly around his thick waist. "They're on top of your head like they always are."

"Well, for Christsakes. Can't you see my hands are full? Put them on for me. Make yourself useful around here." I expected Little Italy to break her in two. Instead, he acted as though he were dealing with an overbearing child.

"Muzzle the pooch."

Dolores obediently did as she was told, covering Fifi's mouth with her hand as Vinnie struggled with the sunglasses.

"Alright, alright. Enough already. They're on."

"I'll let youse know when lunch is ready." Vinnie stood looking at us for a moment before lumbering away. I waited until he had disappeared inside.

"Is it safe to be talking with him around?"

Lifting her glass away from Fifi, Dolores took a sip of her drink. "Who? You mean Vincent? He's a big dumb lug, but he's harmless."

"But doesn't he work for your husband?"

Dolores choked on her drink, spraying the liquid onto Fifi's head. "Who the hell doesn't? You stay in New Orleans long enough, you probably will, too. So, where was I before?"

"Something happened to Fifi?" I volunteered.

"Oh, yeah. One night Hillard says he's going for a walk. Get a little night air. I know damn well where he plans to go, so I tell him, oh no. You want to go for a walk? You take little Fifi with you. Well, the bastard up and takes Fifi to that whore's. I know this not only because he was gone for three fucking hours, but Fifi came back without a leg. Like I wouldn't notice." Sticking a finger into her drink, Dolores fished out a piece of ice and rolled it along Fifi's back. The stump of the lost leg twitched in an imaginary scratch. "That damn gator of hers took Fifi's leg like it was some kind of hors d'oeuvre. Hillard almost died that night—I just about killed him. That's when he stopped seeing the bitch. I made sure of that. I warned him if he ever saw her again, there wouldn't be one voter in New Orleans who didn't know about it. I told him it came down to a choice between that whore or winning the election. I don't believe in that Tammy Wynette 'stand by your man' crap."

Dolores held out a hand for me to inspect. Weighing down her ring finger was a large sapphire encircled with diamonds.

"That piece of fooling around cost Hill big time. I made him go out and buy me a whole new batch of jewelry. But I still want the rest of my jewelry back, and I want it back now!" Dolores's voice rose in volume and Fifi jumped up nervously, scanning the area for any sign of danger.

"Would you be willing to make a statement about this to the police?"

Dolores gave me a boozy stare of astonishment. "Of course not. That was part of the deal I made with Hillard.

He's protected up the wazoo. In fact, you're probably the only one not on his payroll yet. That's the only reason why I'm even telling you this. You see, there's not a damn thing you can do with this information. But you can be sure Hill will find out that I told you, and I just love yanking that man's chain. As long as he behaves, I stay quiet. One false move, and his family-man cover is blown to high hell, along with his run for mayor. I just like to give him a reminder every now and then.''

She was shrewd, but I had my doubts that Hillard was living up to his end of the bargain, no matter how sure Dolores seemed to be.

''Do you think Mr. Williams had anything to do with the death of that girl?''

Dolores burst into a raspy barking laugh. ''You gotta be kidding me. That man barely has the strength to get it up, let alone kill anyone. That's a good one.''

As though on cue, Vinnie lumbered outside and clapped his hands.

''Chow time, ladies.''

Vinnie started back toward the house, but Dolores's shriek brought him to a halt.

''Vincent, where the hell do you think you're going? Help me up out of this thing.''

Vinnie handed me her drink as Dolores covered Fifi's muzzle. The dog was as good as her own private bodyguard. Kind of like a gun with its safety latch removed. Vinnie rousted Dolores out of the chair in one swift move that sent her tottering toward the house. I followed, staying a few paces behind in case she fell.

We entered the dining room, where two places were set in front of the seat Dolores plunked herself down at: one for herself and the other for Fifi. Vinnie lumbered in from the kitchen with a steaming bowl of pasta. Its aroma brought back the memory of Little Italy on a warm summer night—of cafés serving up steaming espresso and homemade canolis from dawn to dusk, while local groceries burst at the seams with 101 different kinds of olive oils and exotic vinegars. The pungent aroma of salamis and hams beckoned to passersby, while big wooden barrels filled with olives stood tantalizingly close to rows of freshly baked bread.

But Dolores apparently wasn't hungry. "What the hell is this?"

"Linguine with clam sauce. What's it look like?" Vinnie set down the bowl with a thud.

"How many times do I have to tell you that I don't eat this crap? I'm on a diet!"

"And how many times I gotta tell ya this stuff ain't fattening? And where'd ya get a mouth like that on ya anyhow? All youse women down here are supposed ta be ladies."

Dolores grabbed her drink. "All I have to do is take one look at you to see how low-cal this crap is. Get this stuff out of my face and get me another drink. I'm going upstairs."

Dolores pushed herself away from the table, knocking her chair backwards. Spinning around, she swooped Fifi up in one deft motion and reeled toward the stairs.

"What that broad wants ya could transfuse her with. She don't need no food ta get fat." Vinnie shook his head in disgust as he lifted the bowl from the table.

My stomach growled loudly at the thought of another candy bar in place of real food for lunch. "Too bad. It smells great."

The bowl froze in midair. "Ya like Italian?"

I remembered Vinnie's words from the other day. "I love it. The trouble is, you can't find any good Italian food around this town."

Vinnie put the bowl back down and began to heap pasta onto my plate. "This ya could die for. It's my mama's own recipe. Takes me three hours just ta make the sauce. I shuck my own clams. That's the secret. I also got garlic bread in the oven. Hold on a minute."

The meal was the best Italian I'd had since coming south. Even better, Vinnie sat down and joined me.

"This is a good Chianti. Ya gonna like it."

Vinnie wound a huge ball of spaghetti onto his fork and popped it into his mouth. "You a cop?"

I suspected it was a question that Vinnie would be particularly interested in. "No. I'm an agent with the Fish and Wildlife Service. I was called in on the Vaughn case because of the dead gator found in her apartment."

Vinnie grunted as he kept on eating.

"By the way, I thought nobody was allowed to call you Vincent except your mother."

Vinnie stuffed a piece of garlic bread in his mouth. "The old broad reminds me of her. She was a pain in the butt, too." Vinnie pushed the garlic bread toward me. "You ain't on no diet. Here, have a hunk ta wipe up the sauce with. So, all that really concerns ya is dead animals. I got that right?"

"More or less."

"Well, if ya looking for dead animals, it's too bad there ain't one around here. Maybe we could fix that for ya." Vinnie burst into a high-pitched silly giggle that could have belonged to a young high-school girl. "I'm only kidding ya. I love animals. In fact, I like 'em better than most people. Here, look."

Vinnie pulled out a medal dangling from a heavy gold chain inside his shirt. "See, this here's my patron saint. St. Francis of Assisi. He helped all them little animals." Vinnie poured me some more wine. "So where ya from?"

"New York. In fact, I used to live on Mott Street."

Vinnie stopped eating. "No shit. What number?"

"Seventy-eight. Apartment 2B."

"Hey, my cousin owns half that block. Ya probably seen him. Fat guy with a cigar always stuck in his mouth."

Looking at Vinnie's girth, I could only imagine. Still, it was possible to detect that at one time he had been a good-looking man. But that had long ago been buried beneath a mound of heavy pasta, thick steaks, and too many rich desserts.

"So, what are you doing down here, Vinnie?"

Vinnie didn't look up as he demolished the mound of linguine in front of him.

"I wanted a change of pace, if ya know what I mean, and New Orleans is better these days than Miami. Too many spics down there. Here ya just got coonasses." Vinnie broke into a giggle again. "I love that word. Coonasses."

"So you're sort of a 'Man Friday' around here for the Williamses?"

Vinnie giggled some more until tears formed in his eyes. "Man Friday. Yeah, that's what I am. I gotta remember that. That's a good one."

"You wouldn't know Frank Sabino by any chance, would you?"

The giggling stopped as Vinnie put down his fork and stared at me.

"Yeah, I know Frank. Why? Do you know Frank?"

"I used to hear his name around New York. It seemed a strange coincidence to come down here and find that he used to be in business with Hillard. I was just wondering if you might have worked with him also."

Vinnie mopped up the sauce on his plate with the last piece of garlic bread, wolfing it down in one fell swoop.

"Ya know, youse should really stick ta dead animals. And since there ain't none of 'em around here, if you're finished eating, I'd say lunch is over."

I decided to head back to the office to report my findings to Charlie, and see if I could begin to piece together any of the ragtag ends. He was ready for me the moment I walked in the door.

"Bronx, get in here!"

Charlie was busy scratching furiously away at his neck, which by now was the color of rare roast beef. "Goddamn these chiggers."

Pushing his cap back on his head, his fingers strayed to his scalp, smoothing an unruly lock of hair that was no longer there. He stared at a photo of his former wife, mulling over what he was about to say.

''What are you doing tonight, Bronx?''

I froze, thinking the worst.

''Jesus Christ, you're damn antsy. Calm down. You ain't nothing like my type. I just thought we'd go do some fishing.''

''What kind of fishing do you do at night?'' I didn't think my company was something Charlie particularly hankered for all that much.

Hickok guffawed as though the joke were on me.

''Fishing for outlaws, of course. Something you ain't been too successful at during your stay down here so far. You game, or you got your evening chock-full of other nocturnal activities?''

By eight o'clock that night we were on the road in Charlie's old pickup, headed toward the west bank of the Mississippi, with a small trailer hauling his mud boat behind. Charlie's driving consisted of a series of near misses as he continually came close to hitting anything in his path, be it cars or animals, as his truck straddled both sides of the road. Deciding it would be best if I closed my eyes, I'd just begun to doze off when he hit a rut in the road, making my head bounce off the roof with a resounding thud. I looked over to see Charlie grinning in delight.

''Who are we looking for anyway? Anyone in particular?''

''Not we, Bronx. Me. You're just along for the ride. Maybe learn a thing or two on the way. See if I'm wasting my time, or if there's any hope of making a real agent out of you.'' Charlie pulled out a Baby Ruth and proceeded to have his dinner. He threw me a Nestlé's Crunch, and I joined him in the evening meal.

''I'm out after the most notorious outlaw in the country. One Trenton B. Treddell. He's a wild man, Bronx. That s.o.b. has been getting away with murder for years. But I'm gonna catch his ass. I can feel it.'' Charlie was on a roll. ''Trenton's been killing the shit out of wildlife for years. The man's a downright game hog. But when I get hold of him, and you'll notice I say *when*, I'm gonna eat his lunch for him.''

I'd heard about this from others who had worked with Charlie. Trenton Treddell was his Moby Dick. He'd been after the man for years. In fact, he'd been out chasing Treddell the night his wife finally left. The running joke in the Service was that someday Trenton would end up catching him. More than a few in Fish and Wildlife felt that was the only way they'd ever get rid of Charlie. A few had even suggested paying Trenton to do the deed.

"How long have you been after this guy, Charlie?" It seemed a reasonable enough question. But then, I was dealing with Charlie Hickok. Reasonable wasn't a word in his vocabulary.

"Listen, Bronx, when you learn to do your job and become a real agent, then you can think about criticizing me. But until that day comes—and it seems like one hell of a long way off, if ever—you just set your fanny back and watch a pro at work."

I never knew how Charlie was going to react until it was too late. The most volatile man I'd ever met, he was also a walking encyclopedia on the bayou and Cajun life. It all depended on whether or not he felt like sharing his knowledge with you. So far, he'd rather have worked with a trained baboon than with me. I closed my eyes again as he continued to mutter away. But a few minutes later, he was back into a loud harangue.

"I'm feeling good tonight. I'm going to show that sucker how the cow ate the cabbage. One of my missiles is coming, and it's gonna hit ol' Trenton right between the eyes."

I made the mistake of yawning.

"Listen up, Bronx. This is a war zone out here." He slapped at a mosquito that had left me for greener pastures. "Hell. I gave up my goddamn life for this job, and this is how the Service pays me back. If I had a good team of agents, I could clean up this swamp in no time. But it ain't never gonna happen with the amateur material they keep sending me."

"Right, coach. Possibly with a SWAT team you could get rid of all the poachers around. But since I'm the only team you've got, maybe it's time you started making better use of me."

I hadn't come along to be insulted. Besides, the worst he could do was to relegate me once again to full-time duck patrol, and that was already a foregone conclusion.

"And since we seem to be clearing the air, Charlie, there's something that's still bothering me about that gator the other night. I just don't think those bullets penetrated deep enough to kill it."

"Something keeps bothering me too, Bronx. And that's having some smart-ass Yankee female as a rookie agent. But it seems like there's nothing I can do about it. You just gotta learn to live with the cards you've been dealt. And in these here parts, I'm king of the hill as far as catching outlaws goes. And the cards you've been dealt is to deal with me. As far as that gator is concerned, I don't need no goddamn fancy-pants forensics lab to tell me what I already know. The gator was shot to death. That's that. Period. *Comprende?*"

I kept my mouth shut for the rest of the ride. We were headed into Jean Lafitte Reserve near Barataria, famous for its pirates of past and drug smugglers of present. It consisted of nine thousand soggy acres of marsh, swamp, bayous, and wetland. A fortune in drugs had been smuggled in through here. Also a refuge for otter, mink, and nutria, it was teeming with gators. Lafitte was a national park considered taboo territory by poachers. Most wouldn't dare to go near the place. For Trenton, it was a favorite hunting location.

Finding Charlie's "lucky spot," we parked and unloaded the mud boat. Not a sound was to be heard except for the slapping of water against wood. A sheet of black velvet covered the sky and dozens of stars peeked out through tiny moth-eaten holes. Pushing off, we entered the swamp, and soon even the pinpricks of light disappeared.

Age-old cypress trees slid by as we made our way through a watery maze. A bullfrog croaked in angry protest at our presence. Sounds are always different at night. The tiniest noise in the swamp becomes magnified a hundred times, until every bit of space hums with its own peculiar song. But soon even the noise died down, making it all the more frightening. Charlie loved the swamp, which was something I'd never yet understood. Even during the day there was always an eeriness to it. At night it was terrifying. Every tree became sinister, every animal was threatening. It was here that bodies were dumped and left to rot. People swore that spirits wandered among the cypress trees at night, with curtains of Spanish moss their only camouflage.

This was one of those suffocatingly hot Louisiana nights when not even a breeze dared invade the area. A swarm of mosquitoes danced about my head in a frenzy of midsummer madness, buzzing inside my ears like a radio that hadn't been tuned. Charlie began to scratch and slap, muttering an occasional curse under his breath. He finally broke the silence.

"It's so quiet you could hear a damn gnat scratch its ass."

Except for him, he was right. Charlie directed the boat down different fingers of the swamp that shot off without any rhyme or reason. When I finally spoke, it was in a whisper.

"How do you know where to find him?"

"What the hell you whisperin' for, Bronx? Afraid a ghost'll hear you comin'?" Hickok could smell fear and immediately zeroed in on mine. I silently hated him for it. "I can find him 'cause we been doin' this for years. The man knows where I am, and I know where he is. It's sorta like a game of hide-and-seek."

The idea was so ludicrous that it broke the tension for me. "And you haven't caught him yet?"

"Listen up, Bronx. This man is the best there is at what he does. I'm gonna get him. There's no two ways about it. But he's dangerous in that he has no fear. It's a test of skills that's takin' place here."

I had the sneaking suspicion that if Charlie ever caught Trenton, there wouldn't be much in life for him to look forward to. From where I sat, I could sense his adrenaline flowing. In turn, my own began to pump a mile a minute.

"There's the sucker now!"

I looked around madly but saw nothing in the darkness of the swamp.

"Nice and slow, we're gonna sneak right up behind him."

As if he were doing the opening step in a mating dance, Charlie eased along until I could just make out the marsh ahead. Another boat sat with a lone figure in it. Even in the darkness, I could tell the rig was twice as big as our own. A huge engine attached to the back purred in anticipation of our arrival. It wouldn't be much of a race. We were in a stock Chevy thumbing our nose at Mario Andretti in one of his Formula cars.

Charlie glided our boat slowly forward, feeling his way as tentatively as a debutante at her first ball. But there was no sneaking up on Treddell, who turned to watch our approach. He stood up, and his looming figure cut a shadow across the moonlight, causing my heart to clench.

Charlie goosed the throttle, and we flew toward Treddell's boat with a lurch. As we picked up speed, so did Treddell. When Charlie unexpectedly slowed, so did he. A cat-and-mouse game ensued, a pure and simple tease. Trenton would allow us to get tantalizingly close, then quickly pull away, conducting a series of figure eights, twists, and turns that would have made an ice-skater proud. Charlie tried to follow suit, nearly causing our boat to capsize and landing my heart in my throat.

What must have been less than fifteen minutes seemed like a good hour as Charlie and Trenton played their game. Looking over at Charlie, I saw him in his element—a man determined to win or to kill me trying. I gripped the sides of the boat until my knuckles ached.

Suddenly Treddell threw his boat in reverse, nearly causing us to crash. Throwing back his head, he let loose a devilish roar as he took off again, abruptly veering off to the side. He hightailed it into a tall patch of cordgrass and cut the engine. His boat bobbed seductively, the grass around his craft swaying as if it were a skirt buffeted by a breeze. I held my breath, waiting for the next move, when I heard the faint whisper of a laugh glide across the water toward us.

Having held out as long as he could, Charlie finally blasted the engine, 150 horsepower sending us cutting through tall grass toward Trenton. The hull barely skimmed the surface as we flew atop the marsh, and the motor screamed with glee. Water whipped up and razor-sharp grass slashed against the side of our boat like miniature daggers as we approached him. My pulse sped along with the engine, caught up in the excitement of the chase.

Trenton waited until the last moment before letting loose, his boat rising out of the water as if it were about to unfold a pair of water wings. An expert in building airboats, he had mounted 220 horsepower to the rear of a light pontoon craft which hit close to seventy miles an hour, leaving us far behind.

Charlie followed Trenton's zigs and zags as best he could, as Tredell's airboat churned up water and weeds that blew back in our faces. Up ahead, the marsh became impenetrable but for a narrow channel that cut through in the shape of a horseshoe. With only one entrance in and one exit out at the opposite end, it led onto a lake of open water.

Entering the canal, Trenton barreled ahead in a race to the other end as we followed behind. The wind picked up, and I found myself squinting into a thin mist of water that hung like a sheet of fine rain. But the breeze also carried a pungent aroma that had precipitously crept into the night air. An odor which was unsettlingly familiar, and blasted an alarm siren inside my brain.

Shielding my eyes against the oncoming spray, I peered at what seemed to be a group of swaying orange figures in the near distance. Dancing on top of the water, they stretched their long, lithe limbs up toward the sky, high-kicking like a chorus line of leggy Rockettes. It wasn't until we drew closer that the figures converged into a fiery wall of flames, and the biting sting of smoke hit our eyes.

Charlie stared for a moment in disbelief before the impact of what we faced hit him.

"Holy shit! That bastard's set a blaze that's coming right at us!"

Trenton had reached the other side of the horseshoe, dumping his spare gasoline along the way. After that, all it had taken was one simple match to turn the canal into a roaring death trap. Charlie threw the throttle into reverse, not bothering to try to turn the boat around. The motor choked up, and for a brief instant I felt sure we were about to go up in flames as the fire came roaring toward us, an angry critter out of control. The heat of the flames greedily licked the night air, the hot breeze a furnace eager to engulf us. The crackling of fire on water sizzled in my ears, and my skin prickled from the heat, as our engine caught hold and we sped backward through the waterway. In a game of touch-and-go, Charlie's mud boat and the roaring fire kept a steady pace. My fear froze as the flames picked up speed, but Charlie miraculously swung the boat out of the canal with only a few yards to spare.

Charlie had gone in search of a race, and Trenton had more than obliged. Smoke ripped through my lungs, and tears stung my eyes as I looked back to see Trenton's craft parked at the end of the horseshoe, a sentinel standing guard. His motionless figure peered out from thick, black billows of smoke. Looking like Lucifer personified behind a screen of sinuously dancing flames, he began to laugh, a deep, menacing laugh that rang out through the night, echoing off the edge of the swamp to encircle us before slowly fading away as the fire continued to crackle. We sat in silence, watching the night burn, the roar of Trenton's motor now no more than a ghostly whisper.

Charlie cursed a nonstop blue streak out of the marsh, into the swamp, past dead cypress trees, and beyond ghosts that knew well enough to stay out of his way. He cursed until we reached shore and loaded the boat back onto its hitch. A crimson hue rose up from the swamp and burned the velvet sky, eclipsing the stars. I held my silence until we were almost home.

"I want to thank you for that lesson on how to catch outlaws, Charlie. It's been a night I'll never forget."

"Not one word, Bronx! You hear me? Not one word of this to anyone, or you'll be out on duck patrol so long you'll forget what another human being looks like." Charlie was in the blackest mood I'd seen yet. "We got our asses whupped tonight. We got 'em whupped good. That ain't nothing to be proud of."

I wondered if something inside him had finally snapped. "Does this mean you're giving up?"

"Hell, no! I'm only just starting. The important thing is to be a poor loser, and that's exactly what I am. That's the only way to win, Bronx. Don't you ever forget that."

It was a lesson I'd spent my entire life learning. It was what had me sitting in a pickup truck weaving through the bayou night. It also gave me a window into Charlie Hickok's soul. Neither of us could walk away from a challenge. Sometimes, it was the only way I felt I really existed at all.

"We did get close, Charlie."

Charlie pulled his cap down with a tug.

"Coming close don't count in nothin' but horseshoes, Bronx."

He had a point. I just wasn't sure what it was.

Six

Charlie's mood didn't lighten up over the next few days, and, as a result, I found myself once more back out on full-time duck patrol. He sent me off with a few words of wisdom.

"Listen up, Bronx. You signed your life over to this outfit. That means you hit the road, you stay on the road, you catch the bad guys, and you stop 'em dead in their tracks."

This was easier said than done. A new scam in vogue was to make an anonymous call reporting a poaching in progress. I'd rush to the area only to discover that I'd been kept busy on a sham. Meanwhile, a group of poachers would be leisurely blasting six hundred grosbeaks out of their nests just twenty-five miles away. This time of year was a free-for-all on grosbeak babies. Not only did they have the bad luck of being a favorite food for Cajuns, but they were also dumb enough to sit on branches awaiting their fate.

In another ruse, one good ol' boy would be set up to take a fall on a minor poaching charge, spiriting me away from where the real dirty deeds were going on. One or two ducks over the limit ate up a day of my time, filing papers and heading to court. Twenty-five dollars later, Bubba or Billy or Tommy Lee would be set free to join the others. It was the perfect flimflam.

In order to placate Charlie's black mood, I spent five

nights in a row at Bayou Lafourche, scouring the area for poachers. Hitting a different spot each night after dark, I'd stake out a likely location for poaching and wait for the evening deluge of rain to begin. Dawn found me soaking wet, sore, and waterlogged down to my bones as I trudged through miles of marsh in search of suspects. Steam-cleaned from the heat rising with the sun, I'd rush home each afternoon to catch a few hours' sleep before heading back out on another late-night marathon.

But my luck appeared to have changed this evening. There was no sign of rain as I headed down Highway 55, my headlights illuminating battered road signs flashing exotic names—Chauvin, Boudreaux, Dulac, and Cocodrie—all in the heart of Cajun country. Pointe Au Chien was on my card for tonight. Twenty miles outside of Houma, the Pointe is flat and nearly devoid of trees. I'd at least be able to watch the geese take flight in the morning.

I'd begun to choose my spots by instinct. The obvious thing to do was head west of the Pointe, where a ricefield lay close by. I was after the poacher who was smart enough to lie low in the cordgrass of the east. Parking my car, I grabbed my flashlight along with my .357 and headed for the water.

The air was filled with the scent of gunpowder. Holding my flashlight to the ground, I searched for any telltale signs of a hunt. But this was my fifth night out with little sleep, and I was tired of kicking around in the dirt. About to give up, I caught the light's gleam off a mound of spent cartridges that glittered like a pile of fool's gold. Whoever had been here just a short while ago had had a field day—not that it did me any good now. But at least I knew I was right. This was an area worth staking out.

Feeling absolved by my find, I looked for a spot to rest and wait for more luck at first light. A large muskrat nest sat close by. Long and wide, with tightly woven twigs, it was the closest thing I'd had to a bed in five nights. I curled up on it and played with the idea of asking for a transfer.

Life without Charlie. The phrase had a nice ring. Dealing with the man was becoming more difficult by the day. On top of that, Louisiana had come to seem like a hopeless skirmish with no end in sight. I didn't mind the fight. But if I was willing to sacrifice my sleep, existing on little but Cokes and candy, I needed to see at least a modicum of progress.

Tracing the routes of dozens of stars above, I was still on a fruitless search for Orion's belt as the sky grew light and a new moon slowly grew old. A circle of geese hovered overhead, trying to decide whether or not to land. Either way, there was more than a good chance they would end up being blown to smithereens. I tried to shake my morose mood, when something else grabbed my attention.

The muskrat nest beneath me had begun to shake. I knew it wasn't from muskrats, unless they'd taken to snoring, too. Jumping off as I pulled my gun, I kicked hard at one side of the nest and then the other.

"Quit kicking!"

Curious as to whom I'd been lying on top of all night, I planted myself in the shooter's position I'd learned at the Academy, my gun held steady in both hands.

"Come out or I'll shoot."

"Jesus Christ. Hold your fire!"

A pair of yellow rubber boots appeared, followed by jean-clad legs the size of hamhocks. Next came hips wriggling their way free from a tight squeeze, as a wide waist and round belly clad in red-and-black checks jiggled out. The effect was that of a fully grown adult emerging from a cocoon.

The insect turned out to be none other than Hunky Delroix, a poacher I'd already caught three times for illegally shooting ducks. This was getting to be a bad habit. A big man, Hunky weighed in close to 260 pounds. But even more distinctive was his near-fluorescent, carrot red hair with full beard to match. I was unsure how he had managed to squeeze himself inside the nest in the first place; he was swathed in sweat from the exertion of working his way back out. His shirt clung tightly to him, outlining each roll and bulge of fat on his frame so that he resembled the Michelin man. Panting hard, Hunky sat down on the muskrat nest.

"Jesus Christ, don't shoot me, Porter."

"Don't tempt me, Hunky. This isn't a very good morning for me. Ever hear of PMS? I think I have it."

Twigs and reeds stuck out from his hair and clothes, and a stench hung about him that made me wonder if the man ever took a bath, or just soaked in marsh water.

"What were you doing in there?"

"What the hell do you think I was doing? I was hiding from you."

At least I now knew where all the spent cartridges had come from.

"Why don't you pull out the rest of your gear. The gun first. Slowly."

A new twenty-gauge 1148 Remington appeared, attesting to the fact that Hunky had been pulling in money from somewhere lately.

"Leave it on the ground and kick it over to me." I picked the gun up, not wanting to leave anything to chance. "Let's see the rest of the goodies."

I must have arrived at the Pointe just as Hunky had been about to leave. The ducks were all neatly packed in a burlap sack.

"All right, Hunky. Let's go. I'm taking you in." Another day, another twenty-five-dollar fine.

Hunky wrapped his arms around his massive frame and stamped his feet in protest, an overgrown child in the midst of a temper tantrum.

"You're taking the food right out of my babies' mouths, that's what you're doing, Porter. You're causing my babies to go hungry."

I knew his babies. Two hulking boys of fifteen and nineteen, who'd already been brought up on numerous poaching charges of their own.

"I have the feeling it's more like I'm putting a kink in an upcoming party."

Hunky had plans for his daddy's seventieth birthday. Custom required not only that all his kin be invited, but that he feed them as well. In this case, that amounted to sixty-four people. They'd just have to eat something other than duck.

"Oh, for Christ's sake Porter, you know my cousin's only gonna get me off anyway, so why don't you give yourself a break and just let me go? I promise I'll never do it again."

He grinned as he crossed his heart and spit in the dirt. His cousin was Delbart Lumstock, famous throughout the area for his defense of poachers. While his courtroom skills were mediocre at best, he excelled in backroom politics. In the old boy network, Delbart was on top of the heap keeping the wheels of justice sufficiently greased. Busy poachers had made him a wealthy man. And for those cases too slimy even for Delbart to weasel out of, only the minimum fine was applied. I'd been here long enough to know how the game was played. In fact, I was beginning to learn how to play it myself.

"For me to let you go, I'd need something in return, Hunky."

A look of relief passed over his face.

"Sure. Whatever you want. How about a couple of ducks?"

"No. A couple of ducks isn't going to do it. I want you to tell me where I can find Trenton Treddell."

The color drained from Hunky's florid complexion. "What you want him for?"

"What do you care, as long as it's not you I'm after?"

It was easy to guess why Hunky was panicked. Notorious for his explosive temper, Trenton had once caught a man who had tried to turn him in. After Trenton finished with him, the man had never looked the same. It was an example that had not been forgotten.

"Are you going to tell me where to find him, or do you

want to spend your morning having me haul you in? It doesn't matter to me, Hunky. In fact, it'll get me out of the swamp for the rest of the day."

Carefully weighing the situation, it was evident Hunky had a lot of hunting left to do.

"If I tell, you can't say where it came from."

"He'll never know, Hunky. I promise."

Five minutes later, I not only had explicit directions to Trenton's house, but the time he usually arrived home after a morning of hunting. Picking up the sack of ducks along with Hunky's shotgun, I headed back to my car.

Hunky watched in stunned silence and then waddled after me. "Hey, wait a minute! Where you going with my stuff?"

"I never said you'd be getting these back, Hunky. Only that I wouldn't bring you in on charges. The ducks were illegally shot and are being confiscated. As for the gun, I'm sure Delbart will be glad to retrieve it for you. And try not to poach anymore, because the next time I catch you, I'm taking you in just to screw up your day."

I'd at least be able to keep him from killing anything else for a few hours. As for the ducks, I'd leave them at the first shack filled with kids on my way. While Charlie would have fried my rear end for that, my job was to keep ducks from being shot in the first place. At this point, they might as well feed some hungry kids.

As for my deal with Hunky, I'd never be able to tell Charlie, though I knew he would have done the same thing himself. As with the rest of life, he lived by a double standard: what was fine for him was not okay for me. I intended to change all that.

I was headed for the outskirts of Gibson, a small town just before Morgan City. With a natural swamp close by, it was Trenton's kind of place. I was hoping this would be my ticket out of hell. I needed something to get me into Charlie's good graces and out of permanent duck patrol if I was ever going to make it in my new career. I wasn't asking for much. Just a break. Where Charlie Hickok was concerned, that was crossing the line. But I was willing to take the risk, even if it meant having to deal with the looming specter of Trenton Treddell. He had unknowingly gotten me into this mess. The least he could do was help get me out.

A slight breeze brought the distinct smell of swamp water on the air as the rising humidity cooked the odor of muskrat into my clothes. It was early yet. Too early for Trenton to return. I stopped at a local restaurant as my stomach began to growl. I had forgotten what it was like to have three well-balanced meals a day, subsisting on Hickok's eye-opener of a candy bar and a quart Mason jar filled with iced Coca-Cola. I sat down for a leisurely breakfast.

Two overly greasy eggs, underdone fatty bacon, and a side of grits later, I was back on the road, vowing to follow Charlie's example from now on. At least I had a full thermos of coffee. With an erratic schedule that dictated catching a few hours of sleep on the run, I was relying more and more on caffeine these days. Long gone was my devotion to juicers, vitamins, and health food. Even Terri had thrown up his hands in defeat, calling my haphazard lifestyle the "kamikaze beauty technique."

Following Hunky's directions, I pulled off the main blacktop and headed down a narrow dirt road, hitting every hole and bump along the way. A lumbering movement off to the right caught my eye, and I slammed on my brakes to see a nutria scurry by. A small alligator basking in the sun slithered into the canal as my VW spewed up dry, dusty plumes of dirt in its wake. Another five minutes of bone-jarring bounces passed and there was still no sign of human life. I felt sure Hunky had swindled me, even now having a good laugh over the con he had pulled.

My faith was restored as I rounded a bend and saw the outline of a dilapidated house looming ahead. In bad need of new paint, the one-level ranch had rows of wooden shingles missing. Tape had been stuck on most of the windows, and a Confederate flag was draped across the front door. Parked out front was a vintage pink Cadillac, with tail fins that easily ran the length of my car. Off to the side stood a small wooden shack, home to chickens pecking for bits of grain, and a pot-bellied pig which buried its face in the earth, its nose blowing up tiny dirt devils of dust. A large wading pool was fenced off to the left, holding a multitude of baby gators. It looked like Trenton was an efficient one-man hit team, exploiting the reptile from both ends of its existence. Busy collecting eggs to hatch on his own, he had a steady pool of skins coming in once the gators were grown. All was quiet, with a heavy air of neglect about the house and grounds.

I knocked at the front door, not expecting an answer. If Trenton were here, he would have made his presence known by now. I tried to peer through the front window, but drapes obscured my view, their dirty cream lining shredded in long, thin strips. Turning around, I followed a trail of parched brown grass back to my car, a thin trickle of sweat running down between my shoulder blades. I resolved to sit there and wait till Trenton returned home.

Then I caught sight of a woman coming around from the back of the house, moving with the force of a bulldozer picking up speed, her sights set on knocking me down. Her piled-up mound of flaming red hair resembled the muskrat nest on which I'd spent my night. Her body was beyond Rubenesque, with a royal blue top stretched tightly over her chest, the deep V-neck accentuating heaving breasts that pushed forward like twin torpedoes. Black stretch pants seemed grafted onto her skin, outlining every muscle, clump of cellulite, and grainy ounce of fat in excruciating detail. Chanel perfume permeated the air, mixing with the noxious odor of stagnant water and rotting waste. Color-coordinated, her coral lipstick matched her manicured nails, long and sharpened to fine deadly points. From Hunky's description I knew this to be Dolly Treddell, Trenton's wife.

"What do you want here?" Dolly didn't carry a gun like Marie. She didn't need to.

"I'm looking for Trenton Treddell."

Dolly planted her legs firmly apart, her hands clenched in fists on her hips.

"And just what do you want with Trenton?"

"I'm with Fish and Wildlife. I'd like to talk with him for a few minutes. Is he at home?"

"Is he at home?" Dolly mocked, her imitation of a Northern accent a strident bray. "No, he ain't home, and unless you got a legal and dated warrant, I suggest that you trounce yourself right on outta here. We don't take kindly to no Fish and Game agents in these parts."

As tough as Trenton, the woman knew her law. She didn't flinch as my hand made a calculated move toward my .357.

"I just want to speak with Mr. Treddell, that's all. I'm not here to cause any trouble."

Pulling at her bra strap to realign a breast, Dolly didn't see it that way. "If you're with the government, you ain't nothing but trouble. I want you off my land right now."

She began to roll forward as a Ford Explorer came tearing down the dirt road from behind, its chassis heading straight at us. Determined not to go alone, if that was Trenton's intention, I threw an arm around Dolly's neck, pulling her close. The Explorer churned up a geyser of gravel as it slammed on the brakes just before impact. The car door flew open and I found myself face-to-face with Hickok's Moby Dick. At five feet eleven inches and weighing a solid 180 pounds, Trenton was as tightly built as his airboat. Impeccable in pressed jeans and a blue oxford shirt, he had the relaxed look and deep cocoa tan of a tycoon just back from vacation. His sleeves were rolled up to reveal rock-hard biceps that Popeye would have envied. Broad shoulders and a bodybuilder's neck led up to a head sporting a mane of shiny silver hair. Steel blue eyes looked out from a face that maintained a neutral expression. The only odd feature on his face was an overly long nose that could have passed for a gator's snout. He wasn't at all what I had expected.

Glancing down, I saw in his hand an illegal shocking machine used to catch fish. Strings of perch and sockalee dangled at his side. Restraining a dangerous desire to laugh, I realized that I had him. The man Charlie Hickok had been after all these years. It was this simple, if I was crazy enough to try and pull it off.

"Are you Trenton Treddell?"

Treddell looked as though he hadn't a care in the world. "That's me. And may I inquire as to who you are?"

His voice was as deep, soft, and smooth as an old forties' matinee idol, throwing me for a loop.

"I'm Rachel Porter with Fish and Wildlife, and you're under arrest for illegally shocking fish."

Once in jail, all it would take would be a phone call to Delbart Lumstock to make him a free man. But until then, I had him. It was something even Hickok hadn't done before.

Treddell stood waiting for the punch line, until the charge began to sink in. His steel blue eyes turned to two lethal darts that were an icy shade of grey. His hands rounded into fists, the knuckles a bony ridge of threatening projectiles beneath the skin. The nerve under one eye twitched, and the muscles in his neck bunched tautly, thick as cords of rope.

It was Dolly who broke the silence, pulling back to get a better view of the suicidal woman beside her.

"You fucking bitch! Who the hell do you think you are? Do you have any idea who you're dealing with?"

She moved toward me with ten coral claws unfurled as I reached for my gun. But Trenton intervened, holding her back before she hurled herself at me.

"There's nothing to get upset about, Dolly. She's just doing her job and wasting her time."

I was left with an unsettled feeling as a second passenger stepped out of the van. Gaunt and gnarled as a windblown cypress, he had long, stringy hair straggled in different lengths. It fell below his shoulders to form three distinct girdles of color in a garish rainbow around his head. His ribs protruded through a black tee shirt, while his jeans rested on the bones of his hips. One gaunt arm had an elaborate tattoo of a gator crunching down on a human skull. A tiny gold alligator dangled from one pierced ear. His blackened nails clung to strings of perch and sockalee in both hands, exactly matching Trenton's catch. As he moved slowly to stand beside Treddell, the three made for the strangest trio I had ever seen.

Trenton reverted to his former smooth self. "Let me introduce you to Gonzales, my swamp creature."

For a fleeting second, I wished I had never sought out Trenton Treddell.

Gonzales's eyes flickered toward the road, and I half expected him to bolt, but a stern look from Treddell held him in place.

Looking askance at my wreck of a car, Trenton motioned toward his own Explorer. "Are we supposed to travel in your vehicle, or would you prefer to take mine?"

I struggled to hear the question above Dolly's shriek.

"You aren't actually going to let this bitch take you in!"

Trenton maintained a cool demeanor. "We'll be back before supper, Dolly. No need to worry." He held up the strings of fish. "Can these be left for tonight's meal, or do we need to bring them along?"

Stunned by his decision to let me bring him in, I wrapped my uncertainty inside a brisk demeanor.

"We'll take my car. The fish are evidence."

Trenton didn't blink an eye. "Then I suggest you fold them in a tarp and place them inside the trunk. Slidell's a long way off, and they'll have begun to rot by then."

There was no menace in his tone, but I felt myself shiver.

With calm deliberateness, Trenton walked to my car as Gonzales followed, both dropping their fish on the ground as they climbed inside as best they could. Twisting his gaunt body into a fetal position, Gonzales took what there was of a backseat. Trenton folded himself into the front as Dolly watched in disbelief. Rolling up the fish, I tossed them into the trunk and joined the two men inside. We pulled out to a stream of curses as Dolly stood in the middle of the road, shaking her fists in rage.

"You're a fool, Trenton Treddell!"

Her words echoed after us as the house disappeared from

view. Trenton gazed out the window in silence. His long silver hair hid his face from my view, camouflaging whatever he was thinking. We were halfway down the dirt road by the time my own stupidity struck me. As I slammed on the brakes, the men turned toward me and stared.

"Under the circumstances, I think it would be best if I handcuffed you both."

In no position to wrestle each man to the ground, I didn't want to pull my gun after getting this far without it.

Trenton studied me for a moment in silence. "Agent Porter, if I wanted to escape, don't you think I would have done so before we stuffed ourselves into this tin can you call a car? I'm coming along with you willingly. Otherwise, you wouldn't be alive to tell about this day."

Trenton had made his point. Starting the car up again, I continued down the road.

"Why don't you tell me what the angle is?" I asked. "Just why are you letting me arrest you?"

Trenton slowly smiled. "Charlie Hickok and I go back a long ways. He's been working hard to catch me for the last twenty years. He can taste it, he wants it so bad. I don't mind the game. Sometimes I even enjoy it. But the older that man gets, the more ornery he's become. He needs to be taught a lesson. Letting you bring me in is the most humiliating thing I could do to Charlie Hickok. It'll add a notch to your belt, and you'll owe me one. Besides, Delbart will have us out in time for dinner. Isn't that right, Gonzales?"

Gonzales guffawed in the backseat as he slapped a thin thigh. "Dis'll get ol' Charlie Hickok good. 'Wil' Bill' I call him. Dat man, he gonna go crazy."

Treddell was right. Whether Charlie admitted it or not, this would be a notch in my belt. It was something that Hickok would have to recognize sooner or later and deal with. The arresting officer on Treddell's file would bear my name, written proof in black and white that would never go away. It would be an event that everyone in the Service would eventually learn of. For better or worse.

Treddell turned to face me. ''Now it's time for you to answer a question, Agent Porter. What made you decide to come after me?''

I thought of the flames that had nearly engulfed me. And of Charlie's black mood ever since.

''I was in the boat with Hickok a few nights ago.''

Treddell continued to gaze at me blankly.

''The night you drove us out of the marsh by setting that fire.''

Gonzales howled, slapping his thighs in rapid succession as a low chuckle escaped Treddell's lips.

''Oh, my. Oh my. This is gonna be good. It's just a game we play, Agent Porter. I knew Hickok had plenty of time to back out. But I had no idea there was a woman with him.''

''Would it have made any difference?''

Trenton caught sight of a baby gator and, holding his two fingers together in the shape of a pistol, pretended to take a potshot.

''Probably not. So, you came after me for revenge?''

''No. I came after you to get Charlie Hickok off my back.''

Treddell pulled a packet of Red Man from his shirt pocket. He delicately lifted a small wad of the chewing tobacco between his thumb and forefinger as if it were a piece of priceless china, examining it for a moment before slipping it behind his bottom lip. A few brown strands fell onto his pants and he picked up one sliver at a time, placing each back in the pouch before throwing it over the seat to Gonzales.

''How did this game between you and Charlie get started in the first place?'' I was counting on Treddell to fill me in the details that Hickok never would.

Trenton spit a stream of tobacco out the window, taking care not to hit my car.

''I think it had to do with the forty gators I was skinning a night. But that was years ago when I was a young man. Charlie was new around these parts and he came gunning for me. Thought I'd be as easy as all those other turkeys he'd managed to catch up till then. He didn't know at the time that he was dealing with the King of the Outlaws.'' Trenton attempted to stretch, but there was nowhere for him to move in the tiny front seat. ''Then there was the night of our boat race. Since then, it's been a blood feud between Charlie and me.'' Trenton looked over and smiled. ''He ever tell you about that one?''

''Charlie only tells me stories about the ones he caught. Up until recently, I didn't know there were any that got away.''

Gonzales fidgeted in the backseat in a futile search to find a comfortable position. ''Dat Charlie! He don't tell de good stories den! Trentone, he got plenty of dose.''

Trenton leaned his head out the window. This time a breeze blew the brown wad of tobacco juice back against the side of my car. ''It was another one of those nights when Hickok was set on bringing me in. He'd been hearing about my exploits from all the small fry he was catching, and I think his ego was itching. I'd already been pretty busy that night snagging gators, but I still had plenty of hours to go and a lot more killing to do. I heard his boat before I spotted him. But I knew who it was.''

Gonzales tossed the Red Man back and Trenton took out another wad before folding the pack up and putting it away.

''He thought he had me this time. We were both in our putt-putt boats and pretty evenly matched. But what Charlie failed to realize is that no one knows this marsh better than me. I grew up here. I know every twist, every turn, and every tree stump there is. I'm like the Vietcong, and Charlie ain't nothing but another upstart invader. So, I decided to teach him a lesson. I took him for a ride that he'd never forget, showing him the ins and outs of my hometown. He was good. Kept on my tail and never let up. But he started getting a little too smug and stopped looking where he was going. So I let him get real close, almost have a taste of me. Meanwhile, I'm leading him to his doom.'' Trenton gave me a sly glance. "Just like the other night. I'm that elephant with the big tusk that Hickok is hankering after, and he wants me real bad. So there I am, heading for a big stump barely sticking out of the water, when I swerve. And Charlie's wondering why the hell I just veered out of the way. Well, let me tell you, that boat of his went flying up in the air like he'd just been shot out of a cannon. It was better than *Smokey and the Bandit*. He had a lot of explaining to do, to get himself a new boat after that. I missed him there for a while."

Gonzales guffawed, spraying a mist of tobacco juice on the backseat as I tried to picture Hickok flying off into the wild blue yonder.

"Then you don't hate Charlie Hickok?"

"Oh my, no. I consider him one of my best friends. He just doesn't know it. Without Charlie, I'd never have earned the reputation I have today."

Passing the turnoff for Morgan City, I wondered if such a legend had ever have heard of Marie Tuttle. Or a onetime gator poacher by the name of Hillard Williams. With a long drive ahead, I told Treddell bits and pieces about the Vaughn case. After I finished, Trenton was quiet for a long time.

"I knew that little girl many years ago. At one time, Marie Tuttle was a close friend of mine."

His tone of voice led me to believe that friendship had only been part of it. While the image of Marie in her high-top sneakers didn't jell with the near-prissy neatness of Trenton Treddell, there had been no sign of any husband at her place. Thinking back on it, one or two of her kids even bore a slight resemblance to the man sitting next to me. Trenton asked for the details on Valerie's death, and I filled him in, going so far as to tell him about Hook.

"I gave her that gator."

The remark took me by surprise. "But that gator was only a few years old. I thought you hadn't seen Valerie since she was a child."

Trenton stared dead ahead, and, for a minute, I was afraid that was all the information I was going to get.

"The last time I saw Valerie was when I gave her that

gator. It was a going-away gift. She said she wanted to take a part of the bayou along with her. She needed to leave for a while. Dry out, I suppose. I never thought it would be to New Orleans. That wasn't where I'd arranged for her to go."

The fact that he'd been in touch with her up until that point was something I wanted to know more about. I drove on in silence, hoping that, given the time, he'd continue his story.

"She'd been living with my son at one time. Dale was quite a boy. Best poacher in the bayou. I always planned for him to work with me when he grew up. Even as a boy, he could catch and skin gators as well as any man. But Dale decided to strike out on his own. At least that's what he said." Trenton reached into his pants pocket and pulled out a tissue, spitting what was left of the tobacco in it.

"Then his plans changed. He started working for a local prick dealing gator skins big-time. The guy was shipping the skins to his partner up North. They had organized a racket that was making them a fortune, hauling gators out of the swamp by the ton. Dale was working nights killing the gators and spending his days skinning them. He was a gold mine, doing the work of three men for the price of one. Damn fool kid was letting them take advantage of him, and for what? Nose candy. When he got tired, they'd dole it out and he'd keep going. Took no time at all to get the kid hooked. Roped him in and made a damn coolie out of him. That's what they did. Soon enough, Valerie was on the stuff, too.

"Problem was, those two kids began wanting more than they were getting, and in no time at all, Dale was in deep debt to those scum and working it off for free. That's when he and Val started on crack. It was cheaper and easier to get hold of. Hell, that shit's all over the bayou." Treddell stared out the window. A gator came into view but he barely seemed to take notice.

"Next thing I know, Dale's stealing from his own home. Taking Dolly's jewelry, the TV, stereo, VCR. Anything he could get his hands on to sell. Dolly was ready to kill him.

Val tried hooking to raise some money, but didn't have much luck at that. Never could get her prices down right."

The only image I had of Valerie flashed in my mind, lying in a pool of her own blood. She hadn't had much luck in New Orleans, either.

"I finally kicked both of them out. Told them not to come back till they were clean. I hadn't raised a son of mine to become a damn junkie. Problem was, they never could seem to get straight."

Trenton took an idle potshot at an egret as the bird unfurled its wings, disappearing against the glaring rays of the sun. "Next thing I know, Dale's stealing from the scum he'd been working for. Then one day, he just up and disappeared. Valerie came around looking for him. I did some snooping myself, even threatened to kill anyone who had done him in. But I never knew for sure. I beat up his boss real bad—nearly killed the son of a bitch. But I didn't find out a thing.

"Meanwhile, Marie was beating Val black-and-blue. Seems Val had been selling information to Dale's boss in exchange for drugs. Telling him where to find the caches of gators caught for Marie. Val was whittling it out of the few local peckerwoods that slept with her. Got them to bragging about how many gators they'd killed for Marie, and where they'd hidden their stashes. Then Val would run right over and sell the information for a few hits of snow. When Marie found out, Val ended up with two black eyes and a broken rib before she got away.

"The girl came crying to Dolly and me. Dolly still held a soft spot for her, so I gave her some money and arranged for her to go away. Try and make a fresh start. I felt it was the least I could do for Dale, so I set it up for her to stay with friends of mine in Bogalusa. But she never got that far. She stopped in New Orleans and never left."

"How did Valerie end up calling the gator you gave her Hook?"

Pulling a pack of sugarless gum from his shirt pocket, he

handed me a piece. "I asked her that once. I thought it had to do with Captain Hook, at first. I told her she'd have to get herself a nice loud clock so she'd always know where the damn thing was."

Trenton stuck four sticks of gum in his mouth, taking a moment to chew.

"She said *Peter Pan* had nothing to do with it. That was just fantasy, her gator was real. She had named the thing Hooked, but then shortened it. Said she named it after her own bad habits of being hooked on dope and hooking for a living, and that no amount of time would ever change that. So she'd just as soon skip getting the clock."

Something struck me as all too familiar about Dale's boss. "The man that your son worked for. Whatever happened to him?"

Trenton gave a low, mirthless laugh. "He moved away from the marshes. Got out of business right before the feds came down on him. Interesting timing, don't you think? He suddenly decided to go straight, right before the cops beat down his door. Hell, he'd made enough money to go on to bigger and better things. I hear he's running for mayor of New Orleans these days, and he'll probably end up getting the damn job, too. He's got the money and contacts to buy all the votes he needs. The bastard is Hillard Williams."

I pulled over to the side of the road and stopped the car. "Did you ever hear from Valerie after she settled in New Orleans?"

Trenton gave me a strange look that led me to believe he knew more than he was telling. "I heard from her once. Seems she had hooked up with a flunky of Hillard's for a while. A guy by the name of Buddy, who helped him run his gator business. After Buddy got tired of paying for her bills and dope, she panicked and called me. But I know a lost cause when I see one. She'd already burned me once. That was the last I heard from her."

"You'll be interested to know she found someone else to bail her out."

"Anyone I know?"

I had a feeling that Trenton didn't even have to ask.

"Hillard Williams."

Seven

Trenton sank into a reflective silence as I played with fitting more pieces of the puzzle together. I hadn't heard from Santou since our evening out last week, and wondered if he was having any more luck than I was. I tried to come up with a dozen reasons why he hadn't called since then, but they all left me feeling like a fool. It was at times like this I wished there was no such thing as a biological urge.

The day was steaming up. Hot tar bubbled beneath my tires, and gators and snakes sought out scraps of shade for a few minutes of relief. Perspiration stained Trenton's neatly pressed shirt, while Gonzales's stringy hair clung tightly to his head. I was used to the shabby conditions I traveled under, and generally thought little of it until others were forced to suffer with me. Stopping at the first convenience store along the way, I let the two men stretch while I sprang for three bottles of Nehi and a box of Moon Pies. The *Times-Picayune* caught my eye with its headline about the race for New Orleans mayor. I bought a copy and handed it to Treddell as we piled back into the car. With three more weeks to go, Hillard was leaping ahead in the polls. An editorial credited this to his plan for bringing foreign investment into the economically depressed city.

Lifting a pair of wire-rim glasses out of his pocket, Trenton carefully adjusted them on his nose as he studied the article.

"Listen, darlin', this sonofabitch isn't doing anything that politicians haven't done here for years. New Orleans is a witches' brew of drugs and crime. Hillard's coming in promising to change all that. Hell, people know the man has made a lot of money in some shady ways. But they figure maybe he has the gift. Maybe he can help them make money, too. What they don't understand is that Hillard is part of the damn problem. He's smart enough to hit people where they hurt." Trenton punched at an ink-smeared blurb with his finger. "He's saying here that all New Orleans is gonna be wiped out from this AIDS epidemic, and that it'll cost us millions unless we do something about it right now. And you know what? People are scared enough, they'll elect the old bastard thinking he's gonna solve the problem for them. That he'll ship all the gays up to New York or Miami or anywhere else but here."

It was true. Hillard was smart enough to tie every issue into money and what it would cost, giving it all the lethal power of a barrel of fertilizer and diesel fuel mixed together just waiting to blow. A volatile mix of rednecks and liberals, skinheads and gays, New Orleans was reminiscent of Berlin in the thirties.

"But New Orleans doesn't have a lock on hard times and bad luck, Trenton. Take a look at New York—just walking in Central Park has become a crapshoot. And when was the last time New Orleans dealt with international terrorism? Most cities are melting pots overflowing with homelessness, drugs, and rampant unemployment."

As Trenton turned the front page with a flick of his wrist, the paper snapped in the air like a gator latching onto its prey. Gonzales fanned himself with the second section as Trenton swallowed the remainder of his Moon Pie before bothering to respond.

"Times may be hard everywhere, *chère*. But they're harder here. We've always depended on what God set down in the ground to make our living, whether it be gators or sugarcane or oil. When oil went belly-up on us, so did the whole damn state economy. You think Washington, D.C., has got it bad? Sugar, we got a billion-dollar deficit in this state and no way of paying it off. That's why I've always relied on gators. They haven't dried up yet, and I don't expect they ever will. No matter what Charlie Hickok says."

McDonald's, Burger King, and Wendy's flashed by as I turned into the Fish and Wildlife lot, pulling in next to Hickok's dilapidated Pontiac. My fingers sizzled against the hot metal of the trunk as it opened, and the stench of rancid fish flew out. Holding my breath, I hauled out our cache. Decomposing rapidly in the heat, the flaccid skins glistened with a heavy coating of oil. Four stray cats appeared out of nowhere, leaping high in the air and purring seductively in hopes of a handout. Before I could get the trunk closed, two of the felines jumped inside. Grabbing the shocking machine, I left the trunk open and let them have their way. Gonzales and Treddell held the strings of fish at arm's length as we struggled to make our way to the building past a rapidly growing number of furry bodies. Erupting into loud howls, their gentle rubs against our legs became more frantic, and the frenzied pack began to eye us much in the same way as three large bags of cat chow.

Slipping inside, I slammed the door behind us to face a different kind of crowd. A few disembodied heads poked out of doorways as the smell of rotten fish hit with all the force of a bombshell. The heads disappeared just as quickly, catching sight of our group. None of the usual duck calls sounded to announce my arrival. Instead, the hall was as quiet as the swamp in the middle of a sweltering July day.

I was left with mixed feelings. On one hand, I was reveling in my success. On the other, I knew that Treddell was out to embarrass Charlie, making him the laughingstock of the bayou. Word would travel fast that Hickok had been done in by a greenhorn girl and a Northerner to boot. It was the ultimate low blow. Trenton and Gonzales traipsed through enemy territory with little concern, secure in the knowledge that they'd be free to walk out in just a few hours. But I was here for the long haul.

By now the situation was out of my control. In reality, it

had been ever since I'd set out this morning in search of Trenton Treddell. Nothing could stop this from taking place now. Not even Enid Moore.

A reed-thin woman with steel grey hair and deep blue veins like road maps on the back of her hands, Charlie's secretary spent her time stationed directly in front of the air conditioner knitting thick wool sweaters, which were piled high like dead sheep behind Hickok's desk. Having been in Charlie's employ for longer than anyone could remember, Enid was as much a piece of the office furniture as Charlie's well-worn desk. Predatory when it came to what she considered her private domain, Enid ruled with an iron fist. She even controlled Charlie on occasion, when no one else could. She'd been around long enough to watch numerous rookie agents come and go. I had the sneaking suspicion that, in most cases, she had even contributed to their demise. Having already informed me that being an agent was an inappropriate job for a woman, she pumped this opinion into Hickok daily. Not that he needed much reinforcement. Her usual greeting to me was a withering gaze that seemed automatically to mark off the number of days I had left in Charlie's employ.

Enid skipped the usual formalities today. Grabbing her handkerchief, which reeked of English Lavender, she pressed it tightly to her nose and mouth, attempting to block out the stench that was headed her way. Putting a hand up to stop me, she quivered as she caught sight of Trenton Treddell. The look of sheer terror in Enid's eyes hammered home the realization that I might be about to blow my career to smithereens all on my own, without her help.

I stuck my head inside Charlie's office, where he sat twirling the lead tip of a pencil in his ear, gloomily contemplating the pile of paperwork rising before him.

"You got a minute?"

Charlie appeared not to notice the offending smell of rotting fish. I cleared my throat, but he didn't even bother to look up. In a bad way since our run-in with Trenton, nothing had taken place to improve his mood. I didn't expect this would make him feel any better.

"What the hell are you doing here, Bronx? You're supposed to be out catchin' me some damn poachers."

Trenton's voice boomed out from the hall behind me. "That's exactly what she did, Hickok. If I were you, I'd congratulate the girl."

Charlie's head snapped up as he sniffed the air, a bloodhound who'd just received a whiff of its prey. Slowly removing the tip of the pencil from his ear, he sat stock-still, staring over my head.

"Who the hell is that?"

Trenton grinned broadly as he pushed past me and strolled into Hickok's office to plunk himself down in a chair. He casually threw his shocking machine and the strings of rotting fish on top of Charlie's desk.

"Your agent here caught me red-handed shocking fish and brought me in. Wasn't much I could do about it. She caught me fair and square. Got Gonzales, too."

Gonzales shuffled past me with a smirk. "Sure did, Wild Bill. No doubt 'bout dat." He added his string of fish to Trenton's pile as a circle of rancid oil worked its way through Charlie's papers.

Charlie sat in silence, finally letting loose a whistle as he leaned back in his chair.

"Well, I'll be damned."

Trenton grinned, putting his feet on top of the desk. "I presumed you already were. You must have thought the devil had finally caught up with you when that fire came hard on your ass the other night. You were halfway to hell, boy."

I stood glued in the doorway, certain the volcano I had unleashed was ready to blow. I expected it to take my career along with it in an explosion that would resonate for years.

Charlie chuckled soft and low. "I knew it had to be the devil or Trenton Treddell."

Interlocking his fingers behind his head, Trenton appeared to be just passing the time on a slow day of poaching.

''Hickok, we have different views of the devil. I've been sure you were Lucifer dressed up in that costume of yours for years.''

The two men grinned, each giving the other his due.

''That was a good stunt, Trenton. It surely was. One to add to the list.''

Hickok waved in my direction with the back of his hand. ''Get another chair for Gonzales here, and how about some coffee? You boys want a cup of coffee?''

If Trenton had formerly been his idea of the devil, I was about to become his new one.

''That's your secretary's job, Charlie. I just bring in the outlaws you've been trying to snag for years.''

Pigheaded and egotistical, Charlie seemed determined to ignore the fact that I was the one who had managed to arrest Treddell. He glared at me as I glowered back. It took Trenton Treddell to break the deadlock.

''You got one gutsy agent there, Hickok. Not many would have had the nerve to come calling at my house, facing up to Dolly to try and find me.''

''That's because no one else would have been that stupid.''

Charlie motioned me to come close, and I did. Old Grand-Dad mixed with Hershey bars lingered on his breath as he pushed himself up, his face a few inches from mine.

''What did I tell you, Bronx? Didn't I tell you that Treddell was mine? You're in deep trouble now, girl. I mean deep, deep trouble. You sure know how to screw up a man's wet dream. I oughta get you transferred to Texas and teach you what hell is really like.''

Charlie was taking it better than I had thought he would. ''Well, it can't possibly be any worse than working for you, Charlie. I'm damned if I do my job, and damned if I don't. But either way, I'm not the person in this office who gets the damn coffee.''

Without taking his eyes off me, Charlie spit out an order to his secretary, who had inched her way over to the door.

"Enid! Get me some coffee, four cups, and two more chairs on the double!"

I had just won a skirmish in the war.

Charlie and Trenton drank coffee and Old Grand-Dad as they reminisced about old times. After more than two hours of socializing, it was hard to guess they'd been enemies for years. With the day dragging on, I wondered if Charlie was ever going to move things along. I was curious to see how he planned to bring charges against a man who had now begun to seem like a long-lost brother. But Charlie droned on, dredging up one showdown after another over the past twenty years. Trenton finally brought it to an end.

"I'll make that phone call now, if you don't mind Charlie. I'll just give Delbart a ring and tell him to get on over here and bail us out."

Charlie slammed his feet off the desk onto the floor.

"I goddamn do mind! Why, hell! You don't need to call that damn shyster lawyer. Ain't no way I'm putting your ass in jail."

Charlie poured another round of Old Grand-Dad into each cup.

Treddell eyed him suspiciously. "What are you talking about, Hickok? You've been after me all these years just to knock back a few drinks?"

Charlie scratched along his ribs, the chiggers having begun their trek south. "Listen here, Treddell. First of all, the rules are that I gotta catch you myself. This thing here don't count."

That rule must have gone into effect the moment I walked in the door with Charlie's number one quarry.

"Second, when I catch you it's gonna be on something good that'll stick. Not on any piddling charge."

Charlie was tap-dancing as fast as he could. Shocking fish was right up there. It was something he'd have been glad to stick Treddell with if he had been the one to catch him.

"Third, there's something much better I've got in mind for you. I want you to help me nail that horse's ass of all asses, Hillard Williams. We gotta bring him down before he gets to be the goddamn mayor of New Orleans, for Christ-sake. How does that interest you?''

Trenton leaned over the desk, his chest touching the fish that had begun to turn to soft mush.

''Agent Hickok, you got yourself a deal.''

I trailed Hickok out the door and down the hall all the way to the men's room, following him inside.

''What are you doing Charlie? You don't even know what's going on with the Vaughn case! I'm the one who's been doing all the leg work on this, and there's no way Trenton Treddell fits in here.''

Charlie unzipped his fly as I turned my back.

''Listen up, Bronx. That man's had a burr in his rear end for years about Hillard. He holds him responsible for his son's death, and he's got a score to settle. 'Course there ain't no way that's ever been proven, but Trenton's like a man on fire with a need for revenge where that asshole's concerned.''

''But he's a poacher! What are you going to do? Dress Hillard up as a gator and let him loose in the swamp for Trenton to shoot and skin?''

Charlie chuckled as he zipped his fly back up. ''That's a good one, Bronx. Might even work.'' Moving over to the sink, he ran a few drops of water over his fingers before shaking them off. ''Listen, I've seen Treddell in action and when that man's after something, believe you me, it don't ever get away. What's more, he knows these swamps better than any man alive. Whatever Hillard's been up to, he opened the door for us when Valerie was murdered.''

''Jesus, Charlie. We don't even know Hillard's the one who did it. Even Santou said that. Besides, what does the swamp have to do with any of this? We're talking about a murder that took place in the French Quarter.''

Charlie pulled a Baby Ruth from his shirt pocket and began to munch away. ''I ain't saying nothing's going on or ain't going on. I just plan on keeping all my options open, and Trenton is one of 'em. Sheeet, I been after that man so long, I might as well get some good use outta him, seeing how you've taken away what little fun I had. Hell, we'll just start us a new game with bigger stakes."

That's when I knew Charlie was holding back. I also knew that whatever information he had, I'd never get it out of him unless he chose to tell me.

"We're going back in there, Bronx. I expect you to keep your mouth closed and let me do the talking. You gotta use psychology on a man like Trenton. Get him to see things your way. So keep your trap shut, and don't cause me no problems."

Whatever game Charlie was up to, I'd play along for now. But if he had any intention of leaving me out of the loop, he was in for a major surprise.

"It ain't just the murder of that girl, Trenton. Hell, I'm not even sure Hillard's the one who did that. Could have been any pissed-off john she dragged in like some stray cat. But he's stirring the pot something funny. I can feel it in my bones. The man's as crooked as a dog's hind leg."

Charlie's toothpick broke in half. It remained lodged between his teeth, where he'd been busy digging at a shred of chicken. The fish had been removed. All that remained was an oil slick, and a bucket of Colonel Sanders's fried chicken covered up most of that spot now.

"Hillard's been stirring the pot for years, and all you law-enforcement boys have just been letting him get away with it. And Valerie wasn't just any girl, Hickok. If Williams had anything to do with it, that man's going to pay in the worst way."

"Well, that man's about to meet his match. He ain't come up against you and me yet, Trenton. We're the dynamic duo who are gonna zap that sucker's ass."

All this talk of the "dynamic duo" was beginning to get on my nerves. No mention of my involvement had yet been made at all. With his feet propped up on the desk and fingers laced behind his head, Charlie conveniently appeared to have forgotten just how Treddell had come to be sitting in his office in the first place. I decided to speak up on my own behalf, no longer giving a damn as to the consequences.

"There's something you're forgetting here, Charlie. I'm the one who's been working on this case from the start. I've been the one to meet with Marie Tuttle and Hillard Williams and his wife. And just to jog your memory, I was also the one that arrested Trenton. At this point, I'm more tied in to the players than you are."

Scratching one underarm, Charlie glared at me in a silent warning.

"Exactly what is it you want, Bronx? A gold star?"

"What I want is to be kept in on this case. Everyone knows who you and Trenton are. No one's going to tell you much of anything. But I'm an unknown factor in these parts. I'm a woman most people refuse to even take seriously. I'm the best weapon you've got for digging into what's going on."

Treddell nodded in agreement. "She's got a point there, Charlie. No reason we can't all work on this thing together."

Hickok gave me a long, hard stare, but I was in no mood to be sloughed off.

"Alright, Bronx. You're in. But let me warn you, this ain't no child's game we're playing. Things could get rough. Hillard's got as far as he has by being a damn person who'd rape his own mother and laugh about it. So you just better be ready for some straight-out hardball playing. I'm aiming to find out what Hillard's been into and put the kibosh on it. And I mean to do it before this damn election takes place."

"Do you think it might somehow tie in with that dead alligator?" Remembering the baby gators in Trenton's backyard, I looked down at the alligator boots that were on his feet now. Gator poachers, past or present, never seemed able to stray too far, for too long, from the critters.

"Will you let up with that damn thing? There's something going on here a hell of a lot bigger than that. I just haven't figured out what it is yet."

By the time the meeting finally broke up, the sun was beginning to set. I had hoped Charlie might offer to drive Trenton and Gonzales home. But with a pile of paperwork in front of him and a half-finished bottle of Old Grand-Dad by his side, there was little hope of that. I volunteered my services, and we once more piled into my tiny VW.

Trenton was quiet at first. Staring out the window, he pulled apart a Moon Pie and threw the chunks out to dogs that we passed.

I made a stab at conversation. "It must feel strange, suddenly joining forces with the man who spent the last twenty years chasing you through one swamp after another."

Trenton idly put a piece of Moon Pie in his mouth.

"It takes an outlaw to catch an outlaw, *chère*. Because an honest man has no idea how we do things. Old Charlie's got outlaw blood in him. I'd bet twenty gator skins that he didn't tell you about that. You be sure and ask him about his early days the next time he's on your back."

If Charlie had been an outlaw at one time, it was something I hadn't heard whispered before. But it did help to explain his obsession with trying to convert poachers once he had caught them. It was a policy that hadn't sat well with the Service. They weren't in the business of reforming outlaws. Even worse was the fact that Charlie spent both the agency's money and time on the attempt.

Trenton took a bite out of the last Moon Pie before throwing the remainder out the window. "As far as Hillard goes, you can wager a month's salary on the fact that he's up to his neck in no good. That man can't do right for doing wrong."

I felt sure Trenton knew more than he had told either Charlie or me.

"Just what is it you think Hillard is up to?"

Trenton laughed softly. "I think he's doing what he's always done. He's just doing it on a bigger and better scale now."

"You think he's still dealing in illegal gator skins?"

"Darling, that was always just a sideline for him and his

partner. That's never where the real money came from. I'd say he's still dealing in drugs big-time. Gator skins was just the perfect cover."

"Does Charlie know about this?"

Pulling out a soft leather pouch, Trenton's callused fingers deftly laid a perfect line of tobacco onto a thin skin of paper. Flicking a few wayward brown strands into place with his thumb, he quickly rolled the cigarette into a tight cylinder, wetting down the glued seam with his tongue. A fleck of tobacco clung to his lower lip.

"To tell you the truth, I don't know whether Charlie knows about it or not. But he'll find out soon enough. Going after Williams is like declaring war. He's got some big guns on his side. We both have our own reasons for wanting to bring Hillard down. Just as long as we do, that's all that matters to me. This is payback time."

Striking a match against the dashboard, Trenton lit the cigarette, inhaling deeply. Burning with the intensity of a flare framed against the blackness of night, the cigarette moved rhythmically as Trenton took steady puffs, staring out the window at his own private demons. The smoke curled lazily in a slow-twisting dance, its aroma bringing back the apparition that had appeared through a curtain of fire the other night. That same man sat next to me now.

Gathering up my nerve, I questioned Treddell about the stockpile of baby gators in his backyard. I was answered by a volley of high-pitched, delirious laughter from the backseat—the same hysterical scream as nutria out in the swamp. I'd forgotten that Gonzales was even there. Trenton calmly continued to smoke.

"The gators are my own personal collection. Some I let go, some I keep as pets, some I skin, and some I eat. Some I use for dealing out a little bit of my own bayou justice."

I was only surprised that Trenton hadn't already brought Hillard to justice in his own way, sure that he blamed Williams for both the death of his son and now for Valerie's. The night music of the swamp rose in crescendo along with a croaking choir of wood frogs and the long, lonely hoot of a distant owl, as Trenton's house came into view at the end of the lonely dirt road.

Eight

The next day I decided it was time to pay Jake Santou a visit. He'd finally left a message on my machine. Two little sentences. "See you're out. I'll call back." I wasn't holding my breath. Or as Terri was fond of saying, "By that time, you'll be old and grey and your boobs will have fallen down to your knees." My vanity had assumed he'd have called before now. And though I hated to admit it, I'd been thinking about him in those moments before I fell asleep and immediately after waking up. During my days in the bayou, and my nights alone in the marsh.

I'd expected him to keep me posted on any new information he'd dug up on the case. The fact that I'd heard nothing from him until now had me puzzled. While I wasn't expecting Hickok to throw any clues my way, I'd hoped for more from Santou. But I had another reason for stopping by. I wanted to snoop around Valerie Vaughn's apartment. I'd had no opportunity to do much of anything besides examine Hook the other night, and while I'd picked up bits of information about Valerie from Trenton and Marie, I wanted to get a feel for who she was on my own. In order to do that, I needed a key.

Fighting my way through downtown traffic, I circled the precinct three times with no luck. The streets were packed as usual, without a parking space in sight, forcing me to cram my VW into the first illegal spot I could find that wasn't already taken. I walked inside, the squad room buzzing with activity. Men in blue hurried past as I headed toward the detective division. Hookers on their way to and from jail glanced at the clock in annoyance as their working hours ticked away. A battered transvestite screamed at his pimp, swaggering in a black cowboy hat and snakeskin boots, while a druggy sat trembling in a corner, drenched in cold sweat as he moaned aloud. I entered the detective division, where garbage cans overflowed with torn pizza boxes. Phones rang incessantly with no one in sight. Spotting Santou's name on a door, I peeked into a cubbyhole with walls the color of week-old oatmeal. The stench of fried food and hot sauce clung to a sparsely furnished room, the wooden desk and chairs looking like rejects from Goodwill. Stepping inside, I walked over to the desk, where a sack of McDonald's french fries lay next to a cup of coffee, the creamer floating on top in tiny white curds. A blue plastic bottle of Mylanta sat nearby. A poster of skeletons dancing down Bourbon Street decorated one wall, while on the other side of the room hung a corkboard covered with papers. Wandering over for a closer look, I saw it was the schedule of a man who never went home but spent twenty-four hours a day on duty. Tacked next to it was a list of Santou's cases. Arranged in numerical order, Valerie Vaughn rated a ten. Rock bottom, along with the notation L.P., standing for low priority. I was about to shuffle through a pile of papers on his desk when Santou walked in the door, his head hanging down, absorbed in his thoughts. Halfway across the room he sensed he wasn't alone. His body jerked, and his hand automatically reached for the gun at his waist.

"A bit jumpy today, Santou?"

An ancient window fan creaked irregularly, like an old man drawing his last breath. Stale air circulated around the small room, making it seem even hotter than it was outside.

"Jesus Christ, Porter! You scared the hell out of me. Don't you know better than to do something like that?" Pushing a thick lock of damp hair off his brow, he stared at me for a moment before attempting to smile.

"Sorry I haven't been in touch, *chère*. But I've been bogged down pulling all-nighters on duty. I'm juggling so many cases these days that I'm having a hard time keeping them all straight."

Although I had hoped for a warmer greeting, he at least was letting me know up front what I had already gathered from the papers on his board. He'd done nothing on the Vaughn case so far.

He rubbed his eyes as he sat behind his desk and took a sip of cold coffee. "Man, I could use a break. What's say we put all this behind us and run away for a while? Maybe spend a week south of the border."

"I've got an even better idea. Let's go someplace where the temperature falls below ninety degrees."

"You're on, *chère*." Santou crossed his hands behind his head and leaned back in his chair. "Now all we have to do is find the time. I'll show you my calendar if you show me yours."

"It's a deal."

There was no doubt in my mind that this was not a man to get involved with. The problem was, the process had already begun. What made him attractive was exactly what I knew would be nothing but trouble. Dark and brooding, Santou had a melancholy that I found irresistible. It was the last thing I needed to drown myself in.

"At the moment, I'm here about something else."

Santou's eyes burned through me, burrowing past all my good intentions of not getting sucked in further. "Denial's bad for the soul and other parts of the body, *chère*."

"What I want is a key and permission to enter Valerie Vaughn's apartment."

Santou's scowl came back with a vengeance. "You aren't going to find anything there. We've been through that place top to bottom. Besides, I could get in big trouble by giving you that key."

"If you've already scoured the place, what's the problem? It shouldn't matter if I have a go at it. It's not as if I'll be messing up any crucial evidence—unless there's something you're not telling me. But then, we have an agreement, don't we, Santou?''

I conveniently ignored the fact that I hadn't yet mentioned my own visit with Dolores Williams, or what I had gathered from Trenton Treddell. I was learning that everyone had secrets to be kept until the proper time. If Santou had any information I needed, I wanted to have something of value to trade.

Jake sauntered over to the office door and closed it before sitting down again. Leaning forward, he kept his voice low.

''Word has come down from the top that Vaughn's place is strictly off-limits.''

''That's rather vague. What 'top' are we talking about? The mayor? The chief of police? Or does Hillard Williams have a say in all this?''

Santou ignored my questions. ''All I can tell you is what I've been told. This has been deemed a sensitive case. Even I've been taken out of the loop on this one.''

Considering that the investigation was officially listed as low priority, none of this made any sense. It also led me to believe that Santou wasn't even coming close to telling me what he knew.

''Why should a stripper's apartment be considered so sensitive? Does Hillard already have his hooks into the Department, even before election day?''

Santou rubbed his eyes with the heel of his hands, as if wishing this would all go away. I wondered if that included me. ''You ever hear of scandal, *chère?* It doesn't necessarily have anything to do with why the girl was killed. But just maybe there's some embarrassing material lying around. She was a hooker with a long list of interesting clientele. It seems she entertained a good number of our city's high and mighty. I can't see why reputations should be destroyed if these people weren't involved in her murder. That includes Hillard Williams.''

His eyes were bloodshot as he put his hands down. Maybe he was being paid to keep off Hillard's back, but I wasn't.

''Since when did it become part of your job to play go-between for Hillard and the police? Did I miss something last week when we were at his house?''

A muscle twitched under Santou's left eye as he reached for his coffee and finished it off, sour curds and all. I almost felt sorry for the man.

''Look, Jake. I don't mean to accuse you of anything, but Hickok hasn't given me any official word to get off the case yet. Besides, if the place was already gone over with a fine-tooth comb, what am I going to find? Someone's toothbrush with a name tag on it?''

I felt sure that whatever incriminating evidence had already been found was long buried.

''Who's handling this investigation now, anyway?''

Santou reached inside his desk and pulled out a roll of Tums. ''All I can tell you is that nerves are on edge about this one. The captain is handling the case himself.''

Popping two of the antacids in his mouth, he followed it with a swig of Mylanta. Whatever pressure had been applied to Santou was beginning to show. Heavy lines under his eyes verified the fact that he hadn't had a decent night's sleep in the past week.

''Believe me *chère,* I don't like this any more than you do.''

The fact that someone was working so hard to keep the lid on this case was all the more reason to get inside Vaughn's apartment as soon as I could.

''I'd be coming at this from a wildlife end only, Jake. I don't care who Valerie was sleeping with or who she wasn't. But there's something about that gator that's been bothering me, and that's what I'll be searching for. I'll be careful. I'll be in and out without anyone knowing I was ever there. I'm good at this, Jake. I swear I won't get caught.'' I'd never done anything like this before in my life.

Against his better judgment, a smile began to pull up the corners of Jake's downturned mouth. ''I was right about you the first time, *chère*. You are a wolverine.''

Rummaging in his drawer, he brought out a key and slid it along the top of the desk. As I reached for it, his other hand came down hard on top of mine, his eyes locking in on me as he turned the intensity up.

"Whatever you find, I get. I'm as curious as you are to know what's going down. I'm putting myself on the line for you. Just remember that when you're in there, and don't do anything stupid. If you get caught, so do I."

I tried to slide my hand away, the key lodged securely beneath it. But Santou held me firmly in place.

"I'm trusting you, *chère*. I mean it; don't disappoint me. I want anything you find reported to me. You got that? No secrets here."

"No secrets."

The jagged teeth of the key cut into my skin, and my heart beat rapidly at what I was about to do. The fact that Vaughn's place had been gone over didn't bother me in the least. Finding things that no one else ever could was a talent I'd developed as a kid, beginning with where the Christmas presents had been hidden.

Santou's door flew open without warning, as if a sudden gust of wind had ripped through the precinct. Sliding my hand along the top of the desk, my fingers folded into a tight fist that I brought to rest in my lap. Following Santou's gaze, I turned around to see Captain Conrad "Connie" Kroll standing directly behind me.

"Social hour is over, Santou. Unless this is police business, I want to see you in my office right now."

A man who didn't waste words, he glanced at me briefly. His eyes were weighed down with heavy folds of flesh that fell over the tops of his lids. The soggy nub of a burned-out stogie bobbed up and down from where it was held clenched between his teeth, and a buzz cut had left the top of his head looking like land only recently razed. At five feet six inches tall, his body was irregularly proportioned, with short arms, a longish torso, and a neck the size of a tree stump.

"Wrap it up on the double and save the broads for your time off."

Kroll left the room having barely bothered to acknowledge me.

Santou popped another Tums into his mouth. "He doesn't know who you are. Let's keep it that way. It's safer for both of us. Just get in and out of that place as soon and as fast as you can."

An electrifying rush sped through me as I gripped the key to Valerie Vaughn's apartment tightly in the palm of my hand.

I hadn't been back to Vaughn's street since the night of the crime, and for all my bravado, I wasn't so sure how I felt about returning. Stopping at a small café directly opposite her building, I grabbed a cup of coffee and watched for a while in case anyone else might be making a visit. I tried to eat a Danish, but slides of Valerie lying in a pool of blood flashed through my mind in rapid succession. A full body shot detailed the mass of red lines that ran across her breasts, her stomach, down her thighs, and up her arms, flashing on to her hair as it lay in clumps of blood about her head. Replacing this with a close-up of her face, I panned in tight to focus on eyes wide-open in fear, hoping for an image that would tell me who her killer had been. But all I saw was pain and death. Part of the cherry glaze had fallen off the Danish onto my fingers. Looking at it, I began to feel sick and stopped eating.

After about twenty minutes, I gathered my courage and walked over to her building. My footsteps echoed dully on the cobblestone street. Ducking inside, I headed up the stairs to the second-floor landing. I felt as if lead weights had been tied to my legs, my steps growing heavier the closer I drew. Already in a knot, my stomach tightened even more as I was hit with a case of nerves. Moisture coated the palms of my hands, and my heart beat as fast as my legs shook, until I could barely stand. This was the way I had always felt before stepping onstage for a role. But in comparison, that seemed easy. This was for real.

Yellow police tape stretched tautly across the door, declaring the property out of bounds. Kneeling, I stared at the lock and inserted the key, holding my breath as I pushed the door open. Shimmying under the flimsy barricade, I crawled inside as the door closed shut behind me. The apartment looked the same as it had the other night. Except this time I was alone. I've always held the belief that dwellings retain the energy of the person who lived there, along with whatever events have taken place. Standing still for a moment, I felt the unsettling sense of a violent death hanging over the room like a heavy pall. Breaking into a cold sweat, I could almost hear the pounding of silence. The quiet was that foreboding.

"All right, Rachel. You're playing a role. That's all this is. The part of a detective who's brave and smart and strong."

I waited, but no image came to mind.

"It's a role. It's a role. It's a role."

Taking a deep breath, I decided I would be Valerie, simply going through my things as if in search of something missing. The problem was, I didn't have any clue as to what that might be. I headed for the first thing I saw—an old writing desk with drawers. When I sat down in her chair, the wooden back lodged sharply between my shoulder blades, and I found myself wondering if Valerie had experienced the same sensation whenever she sat here. I opened the large middle drawer and rummaged through its contents: unpaid bills for body lotion, perfume, and lingerie from Victoria's Secret. A smaller drawer contained stamps, envelopes, and a magnifying glass. Pushing my hand all the way to the back, I pulled out a photo of Marie Tuttle standing next to a dead gator three times her size. She smiled and rubbed its belly as if gently sending it off to sleep.

A side drawer contained Polaroids of a woman who was nude but for black spike heels and a Mardi Gras mask festooned with feathers and sequins. A whip slithered down her leg like a long, black snake. Chained to the table behind lay Hook. With her long, curly black hair and hazel eyes, the shots were of Valerie in a variety of erotic poses.

Lodged behind the snapshots was a small black address book, its pebbly texture rough in my hands. It seemed inconceivable that someone would have bypassed such evidence. It was. Page after page was torn out so that the book resembled my high-school diary. Planning for the day my mother might find it, I'd torn out all the juicy bits, hiding them someplace else. I held little hope that Valerie's missing pages would be found.

Gathering my courage, I moved toward the bedroom. Streaks still decorated the walls, but they were no longer bright red. A dark crimson stain on the carpet took the form of Valerie's body as a wave of nausea came over me, and the room swayed from side to side. I started to head into the bathroom but stopped dead in my tracks. Hook's chain was still attached to the bathtub. So was part of his leg. Swallowing hard, I leaned against the doorway, closing my eyes and bending over so that I wouldn't fall.

"It's a role. It's a role. It's a role."

As soon as the queasiness passed, I stood up and turned to face Valerie's room.

Get busy. Start looking somewhere, anywhere. Don't think. Just move.

Opening the closet door, I examined her clothes. Trash and flash dominated her choice of wardrobe. It's what I would have chosen if I had been given the role of a stripper. Thrown haphazardly on the floor in a heap were dozens of spike heels in a rainbow of colors, the kind we'd referred to in college as "fuck me" shoes. A variety of low-cut blouses in leopard spots and tiger stripes hung bunched together, while a black jumpsuit with a fishnet midriff and sheer panels dangled close by. I could smell her body's aroma, faintly pungent, with the scent of musk oil sprinkled on a few of her items. At the end of the rack hung a garment bag. Pushing everything else to one side, I unzipped it to reveal a full-length mink coat. Running my hands over it, I shivered, feeling the skins that were as dead as Valerie was. It was lined in satin, and the label near the collar read "Louis Furs, Key Biscayne, Florida." Monogrammed on the inside pocket were the initials D.W. I wondered if Dolores had ever sobered up enough to realize that, besides her jewelry, she was missing a coat. I wondered if Valerie had minded the fact that Hillard couldn't be bothered buying her one of her own.

Going over to her dresser, I opened the drawers, careful not to look at the spot where Valerie had died, just behind me. One drawer held a collection of crotchless panties and G-strings, along with her Mardi Gras mask, carefully wrapped in thin tissue paper. An assortment of spandex pants and satin short shorts filled a second drawer. Rooting through her things, I felt like one more voyeur peeking inside Valerie's disjointed life. With no idea of what I hoped to find, I had little choice but to keep going just as others had before me, ready to rip through whatever secrets I could find.

It's only research. There's no other way to learn who she was without searching through everything. It's homework. Nothing more. My thoughts felt hollow inside me.

The third drawer revealed a vibrator and batteries, along with a blue velvet box which contained silver Chinese balls and a cock ring. Behind her erotic toys lay a black leather whip curled on top of a Bible. Taking the book out, I opened it to where an inscription on the inside cover read, "To my darling daughter. Always follow His way." It was signed, "Love, Mother." Returning the Bible to its spot, my fingers touched a pile of condoms and French ticklers that had been shoved all the way to the back. The last drawer held an assortment of scarves in different lengths and colors, covering hundreds of strands of bright, gaudy Mardi Gras beads. Pushing them aside, I caught a glimpse of two boxes, each nestled in a far corner. I picked up the smaller one, made of smooth oak. Its lid slid easily off. I hoped to find love letters or a diary, but instead it was filled with a dime-store variety of tiny plastic reptiles and fish handed out as lagniappe, or favors, during festival time. Bright red crawfish with claws outstretched were mixed in with translucent squid and tiny green gators, jaws open wide to reveal rubber teeth and red tongues. Replacing the lid, I pulled out the second box. Larger in size, it was covered in a pretty blue satin. As I lifted the lid, a tiny ballerina in her tutu of pink mesh sprang to life, circling round and round in a silent pirouette. I had owned a jewelry box exactly like it as a child. On a bed of blue lay a tiny charm bracelet, from which dangled an alligator, a heart, and a miniature replica of a Mardi Gras mask. I thought of my own jewelry box, and of how much I had taken for granted as a child. I had believed every dream I had would come true. When I came to Louisiana, it was as a disillusioned adult trying to run away from unrealistic expectations and heartbreaking failures. But I hadn't been able to lose my demons on the way. Only temporarily in hiding, they were biding their time, ready to spring out again on some dark night. Then where would I run? I wondered if Valerie had felt the same way.

As I was about to close the lid, I remembered what I had loved best about my jewelry box. Reaching beneath the ballerina's wooden pedestal, I felt the same smooth button that had always assured me my treasures were safe. Pressing it, I lifted the figurine to reveal the hidden compartment beneath. Just as I had, Valerie used this hideaway for her own prized possessions. Neatly folded up inside were a few newspaper clippings. They weren't the treasures I had hoped to find, but they must have been important to Valerie. Straightening one of the clips, I saw that it was an article on the neo-Nazi movement in Germany. The report could have been written during Hitler's reign. Instead, it was of riots and fire bombings today. Just as in the U.S., Germany was struggling to deal with a liberal asylum program as its own economy continued to decline, with unemployment the only figure steadily on the rise. So far, there had been two thousand right-wing attacks in the past year, leaving twenty-five people dead. Gypsies and Turks had been the main targets, but Jews were once again leaving the country. A government report had conservatively placed the number of right-wing extremists in Germany at forty thousand, with four thousand of those considered violent skinheads. A country of passionate extremes, Germany had swung 180 degrees since the left-wing terrorism of the seventies. In the hard-pressed nineties, the Red Guard had been replaced by a different fanatical face.

The second clipping concerned a right-wing terrorist group, the Nationalistic Front. Led by Meinolf Schoenborn, the group had come under intense scrutiny by the German police. This had led to a raid, in which forty of its 130 members were arrested. The photo that accompanied the article was of a neo-Nazi rally in Bayreuth. The motley mob could have been any rowdy gang after a rock concert, except for the placards spewing hate and the sneers on their faces. On closer look, one face in the crowd stood out, catching my attention. Peering over Schoenborn's shoulder was a face startling in its elegance. But it was the eyes, nearly translucent and coldly detached as they calmly gazed through time, space, and newsprint, that held me. The face belonged to none other than Hillard's liaison, Gunter Schuess.

The last article Valerie had kept was about a fledging terrorist group that replaced the now-defunct Nationalistic Front. Like a cancer out of control, National Unity had erupted in small pockets throughout Germany, ritualistically torturing immigrants, Jews, and gays. The group was best described as a tightly organized death squad. Financed by the international drug trade, they had been supplied with Uzis, AK-47s, and other high-powered weaponry. But four months ago, the German police had accidentally stumbled upon their headquarters. In the ensuing shootout, thirteen members of the group had been killed. Their leader, Heinrich Breslau, had managed to escape, along with seven others, vowing that their fight wasn't over.

I gathered that Gunter had been involved with the Nationalistic Front and possibly even the splinter group that followed. The question was, what was he doing in Louisiana now, working for Hillard Williams? I had considered Hillard a small-time Nazi, goose-stepping out in a bayou. But this brought events into an entirely different league—one that had been important enough for Valerie to have hidden articles on. Folding the clippings, I placed them in my pocket. Two other items remained buried away at the bottom of the box. The first was a matchbook from a restaurant. I searched inside the cover for a hidden message, but none was there. Simply a book of matches; perhaps it had been a memento from a romantic evening or a meeting place for business. Except that the restaurant was along distance from New Orleans. Located along Bayou Teche on the other side of Morgan City, it was close to Marie, not far from Trenton, and a long way from the Doll House. Sliding my fingers along the bottom of the box, I pulled out one last secret that Valerie had hidden away—a strand of rosary beads. Curious as to what she might have asked for in her prayers, I tucked it into my pocket along with the matchbook and news clippings.

Replacing the boxes, scarves, and Mardi Gras beads, I closed the drawers, wondering what items people would scavenge through one day in an attempt to decipher who I had been. Turning to face the room, I flashed on Valerie and the sounds of a struggle. I walked out of the bedroom, closing the door hard behind me. But the cries passed through the walls, refusing to let me escape. Reining in my vivid imagination, I didn't have a clue where to look next.

If I were Valerie, what would I do? Where would I hide what I didn't want found?

I had managed to discover one of her hiding places. It was more than likely that Kroll had already uncovered the others. I wandered into her kitchen, a shiver going through me as I poked around. I no longer had to do character work. The kitchen could have been my own. Opening the cupboards, I saw mismatched plates from a variety of secondhand collections. No two glasses were the same. A casserole dish was chipped and discolored with burn marks. In the drawers, her knives, forks, and spoons were pot luck, just like mine. Maybe I knew Valerie better than I had thought.

Her refrigerator verified it. It's strange how you can tell if a refrigerator is kept full and has just been cleaned. It has a different feel to it than one that is generally empty. Valerie and I both kept the latter kind. Inside were a few cans of beer and diet soda. A half-empty bottle of cheap white wine, minus the cork, sat lodged on the inner shelf of the door. A container of cottage cheese held large green curds instead of white. Checking the freezer, I guessed it hadn't been defrosted in years. I usually solved that problem with a hammer and chisel. Valerie had never gotten around to it. A box of fried chicken and a quart of chocolate ice cream lay wedged between two thick layers of ice. The only things that could fit, they depressed me. It reminded me too much of my own life.

"What would Valerie do? What would Valerie do?"

Wandering back out, I glanced at my body in the full-length mirror in her hall, imagining myself in her clothes. At one time, I might have looked great. But along with acting, I had given up my daily routine of working out. In no time at all, an almost-perfect figure had changed into a body I could get by with if I didn't wear anything tight, and made it a practice to take off as few clothes as possible in any given situation. And then I knew what I had been looking for.

As a stripper, Valerie had made her living with her body. That meant she had been conscious of her weight. She also kept a large container of ice cream in her freezer. I had, too, when I lived in New York. I'd been told by someone in the know that it was the best place to hide anything small and of value. Going back into her kitchen, I removed the container from her freezer, pulled off the lid, and checked inside. Sure enough, its contents had been removed, then carefully repacked and patted back down into place. Having worked cash jobs off the books to support an acting career, I'd been taught how to hide a wad of carefully wrapped bills. Valerie must have learned the same trick.

I began to dig, dumping the ice cream into her sink, until the spoon hit the plastic bag buried near the bottom. I grabbed it by the knot at its top and ran it under hot water, the chocolate running off in muddy streams. Finally, it became clear enough to see a white cloth carefully folded inside. Ripping the bag open, I pulled back one corner of the cloth at a time, revealing perfectly shaped stones the color of ice that reflected the light from the bare bulb above—a necklace formed from dozens of diamonds. Creating an intricate choker of swirls, the stones led down to one enormous pear-shaped diamond. Along with the necklace was a business card for Global Corporation, located on Mulberry Street in New York, in the heart of Little Italy. I had the feeling it was no jewelry store.

I stashed the card in my pocket along with Valerie's clippings, and placed the necklace back into its shroud. While Hillard might have covered Valerie in Dolores's old fur and a few of her baubles, I doubted that this had been one of them. Carrying such a fortune outside was more than I wanted to deal with—New Orleans easily matched New York when it came to muggers working the streets. But I couldn't leave the diamonds here. I had little choice, other than to move quickly and pray. I buried the necklace at the bottom of my bag, one more thief stealing pieces of Valerie's life. Having gotten what I came for, I closed her door behind me.

The streets of New Orleans are never quiet. This is the land of jazz and zydeco. There's always the fanfare of tourists and the hullabaloo of Bourbon Street, with its never-ending party. That's part of its charm. It's why I chose to live in the city. I like its street hustlers, its tap-dancing kids, the carnival characters, the barkers for girlie shows. I'm a sucker for the French Market with its beignets and café au lait, for lining up for abuse and oysters at the Acme Restaurant, and paying through the nose for a hurricane at Pat O'Brien's. I love the music that pours out into the street in a spicy gumbo of Dixieland-meets-the-blues. It's the pulse that runs through this town twenty-four hours a day that in bad times lets me know I'm alive. I've always found the idea of being surrounded by people I don't know appealing. Some might call it passive participation, requiring no active form of commitment. I call it reassuring.

But the undercurrent I caught that afternoon as I stepped outside Vaughn's building was something I hadn't heard in years. I felt it before the pitch actually reached my ears.

Electricity filled the air like a high-tension wire that's been cut, lying in wait for the first stooge who'll walk by and pick it up. Coming up through the pavement, the vibration worked its way through my legs and into my chest, the dull thud of pounding feet beating like a drum with an urgent message. Every nerve in my body hummed to a station whose reception was getting stronger by the minute. The torrid air crackled with a high-pitched frequency that would have had dogs baying at a clear blue sky. Standing perfectly still, I recognized the sound for what it was too late. The hum built to a howl as a throng of bodies burst onto the street.

Dressed for a combination of Halloween mixed with Mardi Gras, the crowd was a breathtaking array of colors and styles, sequins and feathers. Men garbed in everything from miniskirts to evening gowns had costumed themselves as WACS, airlines stewardesses, and Hillary Rodham Clinton. A contingent of women rounded the corner, some dressed in priests' robes, others attired in black leather and studs. The one thing they all had in common was the expression of stark panic plastered on their faces.

Men ran past, holding on to tattered signs and wigs, with their clothing in shreds. Blood ran down faces and arms and legs, from heads that had been cracked open and flesh that was gashed. A rock flew by, striking a woman in the back of the neck. Tripping, she fell to her hands and knees, to be trampled on by strangers in their headlong rush from something unseen. The scream of senseless words was swallowed up in the terror that gripped the street, their meaning lost before they could reach me.

Sensing the swell that was swiftly building into a melee, the café where I had sat just an hour before pulled its shades closed, locking the door to those who tried to push their way in. I held my bag tightly against my body as I found myself propelled along by the crowd, an unwilling participant caught up in the frenzy. I tried to get back inside Valerie's building, her apartment suddenly a safe haven. But I couldn't turn around, let alone make my way through the throng that was now a stampede. I tried to ask the woman melded against me what had happened. Busy maneuvering her own escape, she ignored my question as she scrambled over a body that had fallen down in front of her. Looking at placards that read "Silence Equals Death," I remembered talking to Terri about the gay rights march that had been scheduled to take place today. I'd been too busy to think about it until now. But the march was supposed to have been held on the opposite end of the city, and should have been over hours ago.

I didn't have time to sort any of this out. A deadly combination of rednecks and skinheads exploded around the corner behind us and onto the block, in pursuit of the retreating crowd. My own panic began to rise as I found myself pinned against a wall, helplessly watching the ensuing uproar. Thrusting my hand in my pocket, I grabbed onto the news clippings I'd found inside Valerie's jewelry box. The dry paper rustled against my skin, its crackling whispers insinuating I'd opened Pandora's box, unleashing the event now taking place. I froze at the thought as someone bumped up against me and screamed into my ear, telling me to run. Turning my head, I caught a blur of studs and swastikas. Hunting caps, black boots, shaven heads, and angry faces began gaining on the frightened crowd.

I spun around to join the others in running for my life, as bats and bricks knocked into bodies around me. Cries of *Heil Hitler!* echoed in the air. A bottle whizzed dangerously close, crashing into the back of the man to my right. Broken glass splintered in a swirling kaleidoscope beneath frantic feet as shards became pulverized into flying lethal slivers. No longer able to distinguish the drumming of feet from the pulsing of blood resounding in my ears, I looked around to see signs with large black letters that screeched, "Kill Aids Before It Kills You" and "Clean Up The Quarter." Twisted mouths shrieked obscenities, while eyes filled with murderous rage picked out their victims, one by one.

Looping the strap of my bag around my neck, I wrapped it in my arms as if it were a child in need of protection. My heart pounded to the rhythm of heavy feet now in stride with my own. A face moved in dangerously close. Its lips, branded with canker sores, puckered into a tight circle as if in search of a kiss. Instead, a thick wad of saliva hit my cheek. I felt it running down my face and desperately wanted to wipe it away, but didn't dare let go of the treasure I kept gripped close to my body.

Too late, I felt the heavily booted foot coil itself around my ankle. I tripped and fell, trying to pull myself up, but was knocked back down. Another angry stranger grabbed the woman next to me. His hand jerked her head back and I heard her vertebrae pop one by one like a row of champagne bottles exploding on New Year's Eve. Glancing up at my own assailant, my body now locked in place between his feet, I watched in stunned fascination as thick hands rose above his clean-shaven head, clasping a sign that proclaimed "Support Hillard Williams." It whirled above me like a sword, ripping down through the air as I raised my hands to try and brace myself against the blow. Its message erupted in a loud explosion inside my head as I crumpled, floating into a warm, liquid darkness.

Nine

I woke to a painful throbbing in my head and a mouth filled with the taste of dry, sour blood. Carefully running my tongue over my teeth, I could feel that my lower lip was split open and distended as though I'd received a double dose of Novocain. The gritty texture of gravel and dirt bit into my skin, and a heavy pain in my chest made me wonder just how badly I'd been hurt. Cautiously moving one hand, I felt beneath my ribs, grateful to find that my bag was still there. When I lifted my head the street whirled around me, a battlefield littered with moaning and broken bodies. Laying my cheek back on the ground, I knew I should try to get up, but my aching head wanted nothing more than to stay put.

A hand came down in front of my face, and I braced myself for the worst.

"Are you okay?"

I let out a painful breath and turned the question slowly over in my mind. I was carefully rolled onto my back, and looked up to see the double image of a man. A lump the size of a grapefruit decorated his forehead. I concentrated on focusing the twin images into one.

"I think I'm all right."

"Let's check."

He slowly helped me sit up and I heard myself groan. Then I doubled over in pain. My stomach felt as if it had been scooped out with a dull plastic spoon. My pants were torn straight down my legs, with fine shards of glass embedded like shrapnel in my skin. Blood mixed with dirt to form a gooey paste. As I slowly moved one leg, my knee cramped up, and I cried out in pain. The sob caught under my ribs, crawling into the space where my purse had been lodged. But all that was secondary to the fireworks going off in my head. I found myself thinking of Santou, and wondering why there were no police in sight.

"We were lucky."

I looked at the man in front of me, whose bruise had begun to turn the color of purple, and wondered what he was talking about.

"It's a lot worse over on Bourbon Street."

"What happened?"

"You weren't part of the march?"

"No. I just happen to have lousy timing."

A sharp spasm of pain went through me as his fingers probed for any broken bones.

"Didn't you know there was a gay rights march going on?"

"I'm afraid I forgot." I felt like a fool with no ethics.

"I'll bet you never do that again."

I tried to laugh and found that I couldn't.

His fingers continued their search. "The march started later than planned. We even changed our itinerary because of rumors that something like this might happen. We were hoping they'd get discouraged and just go away. But our local neo-Nazis are a dedicated bunch of boys, with not a lot to do and plenty of time to kill. Somehow they discovered our new parade route and planted themselves in teams to attack, splintering us up in different directions. From there it was easy pickings."

"Did you change it with the police?"

"Of course. It always has to be cleared with them first. In fact, the police were milling around when we first started out."

His fingers touched my head, and I let out an involuntary yelp.

"Nice lump you've got there. You better get yourself to the emergency room and have that checked out."

As he took his fingers away, I saw they were stained with blood. I had the squeamish feeling it was mine.

"Do you think you can walk? I'm getting transportation to ferry people over to the hospital. If you wait over there with the group on the corner, I'll see that you're taken care of."

I didn't want to move. "I'm okay. Really. Thanks, but I can get home by myself."

He took hold of my elbow and lifted me up. "I didn't say home. I said emergency room. You're going to need to be checked out. Get yourself over there now."

He pointed to where a number of people were huddled together, as I tried to figure out the fastest route home.

"Thanks. I'll do that."

Every inch of my body throbbed in pain. Leaning against a door, I tried not to think about the cut on my head as I watched the man move off. I had told him I was all right. What I felt like was hell.

Sticking close to walls, I made my way home, clutching my bag in one hand as I held myself up with the other. I had no intention of going to the hospital. I'd been to too many in recent years, visiting friends who rarely left. Just as with a Roach Motel, once you checked in, you never checked out.

Ursuline Street isn't far from where I live, but it seemed to take forever. Hobbling along, I maneuvered around the bodies that littered each block, all in different states of injury. I had yet to see a cop. It was as if a holiday had been declared for the N.O.P.D. Word just hadn't filtered back to a public who had the audacity to clutter up the streets. The French Quarter was strangely silent.

Placing my ear against the coolness of a brick wall, I heard the sound of water splashing from a fountain hidden from view. I closed my eyes and conjured up a herringbone courtyard awash with flaming hibiscus, letting the sweet scent of magnolia take my mind off the steady throb of pain. Cautiously applying two fingers to the gash on the back of my skull, I was relieved to find a sticky paste instead of gushing blood. I felt sure that with a hot bath and a few hours' sleep, everything would be all right.

Finally making it home, I fumbled with my keys as I prepared to confront one last obstacle—the long rickety flight of stairs that led up to my landing. Slowly climbing one step at a time, I sat down when I reached the top, resting on the doormat Terri had given me the day I moved in. Woven in golden straw, two skeletons were locked arm in arm in a dance of death. Home had never looked so good.

I had just begun to appreciate my mother's wisdom on having a heating pad and ice bag on hand, when the pounding began. Closing my eyes, I hoped it would just go away. But the pounding continued until I realized the sound wasn't coming from inside my head, but outside my door. It was followed by a deep, heart-wrenching moan that had me up on my feet before the rest of my body was ready to follow. I hobbled like an old crone, reaching from chair to table to wall for support. Having been in a perpetual hurry all my life, I silently asked forgiveness from every senior citizen I'd come close to knocking over in my frenzy to get somewhere fast.

The stench of urine hit hard as I opened the door. Curled on the doormat at my feet lay a bloody beaten mess. A few thin strips of cloth were embedded in a back which had been brutally beaten. The flesh quivered like a trembling heart. For a moment I was tempted to slam the door and lock myself in, as a cold, sickly sweat drenched my body. I didn't want to faint. Not outside. Not with whatever this was at my feet.

"Rach. Help me."

Staring down at the grisly form, I realized it was Terri. Having lost his blond wig, his hair had been chopped in rough patches. Deep red gashes were slashed in his skull. His blue eyes peered out from behind two narrow slits, the skin swollen and puffy from repeated punches, while blood ran from a broken nose into his mouth, making it appear as if he'd just crawled out of a boxing ring. The remains of his

Bo Peep outfit were torn and slashed, but a small woollen lamb was still clenched to his chest, its belly slit open. The bloodstained stuffing led a trail up the stairs. I dragged him into my room as carefully as I could. What he needed was to get to a hospital fast, but calling an ambulance proved to be as impossible as finding a cop on Ursuline Street. I finally broke through the constant busy signal, only to be informed there was no telling how long it would be before one could arrive.

"Is this an emergency?"

I hung up without bothering to answer. Trying to drag Terri down to my car was out of the question. Not only would it injure him more, but I could barely lift my own weight at the moment, and I didn't trust my car under the best of circumstances.

I picked up the phone and called Santou. If the police couldn't be bothered controlling a riot, at least they could drop off the injured at the nearest emergency room. Like every other cop must have been that day, Santou was at his desk.

"I need some help, Jake."

I tried to keep any emotion out of my voice, not wanting to appear either helpless or hysterical. But Santou jumped to his own conclusions.

"What's the matter, Porter? Did you get inside the apartment? Damn it! There was some kind of trouble, wasn't there?"

Valerie's apartment. It seemed a world away. I had almost forgotten I'd been there at all, except for the soreness lodged beneath my ribs where I had kept hold of her hidden treasure. Yet Santou thought that was why I was calling—that I had somehow let him down. I found it hard to believe he was unaware of the riot that had just taken place. By now, everyone in New Orleans must have heard the news. But thinking back, there had also been no television crew in sight. It was as if the city had conspired to keep the entire event a secret.

I filled him in on the bare essentials, then listened to the silence. I could almost hear him mentally listing the pros and cons of getting involved. I hadn't yet told him what I'd found in Valerie's apartment. I'd decided that if he couldn't bother to help, I would tell him I'd found nothing at all.

"Hang on. I'll be there."

I hung up before my emotions got the better of me. It was just possible he really hadn't known about the riot. Or maybe he just wanted to learn what I had found out. Either way, it would get Terri to a hospital, and for the moment, that was all that mattered. I brought out a basin of cold water and a pile of wet towels from the bathroom, laying one across Terri's eyes. The palms of my hands looked as if they'd been washed in ground glass, and my left knee had already blown up to twice its normal size.

"Rach?"

I held Terri's head in my lap as I rinsed out a wet cloth. "Don't try to talk. Someone will be here soon to help."

But he reached up and held on to my hand. "I might be needing that plastic surgery sooner than I planned. What do you think?"

His voice came out as a deep rasp, and I told him he sounded like Harvey Fierstein.

"Good God. As long as I don't look like him."

I started to laugh, but it hurt my ribs.

"There were some real fuckers out there today, Rach. These Southern boys are into some nasty S&M. It was enough to make The Whipping Post look like amateur hour."

It hurt for him to talk. But I also knew he was afraid not to. If you stop talking, you might pass out. If you pass out, you might die. I let him continue.

"You know that kimono you love, Rach?"

"You mean the purple one with the little geisha girls performing obscene acts?"

"Yeah, that one. It's yours. I want you to have it."

"Jesus, Terri. Will you stop it? You're not going to die. Besides, if you were, I'd want the fuchsia one with the naked boys running around."

"Bitch. You know I plan to be buried in that."

Terri shivered. I grabbed a blanket from the chair behind me and began to wrap him up.

"What the hell are you doing, Rachel? Putting me in my shroud? It's one hundred fucking degrees in here!"

"You shivered. I thought you were cold."

"Jesus. If I were cold in this weather, I'd really be dying. No, I was just thinking about being buried, and it gave me the creeps. All those disgusting little maggots nibbling away. It would be a crime to lose such a great body."

"Are you talking about me?"

Terri's head rolled in my lap as his laugh turned into a moan. "That's another thing I've been meaning to talk to you about, sweetie. You've been putting on a little weight lately. Guess it's that healthy diet you're on."

I tried to move my leg as a piece of glass buried itself deeper, but a groan from Terri froze me in place. He let out a low sob and his chest quivered, as though the flesh were no longer attached to bone. I found myself holding my breath until he spoke again.

"You have to admit. This does give me the perfect excuse for a trip to see that gorgeous plastic surgeon in Rio. Not that I planned on resorting to this. But it does make the pain more worthwhile."

The blood from Terri's head had soaked through my pants, and I started to worry that maybe he really was dying. Slowly counting to one hundred, I told myself Santou would magically appear by then. "It's nice to know you still have your values in the right place, Terr."

Footsteps echoed on the stairs, and for a brief moment I had a flash of skinheads rushing from house to house to finish what they'd begun. My heart picked up speed, pounding against bruised ribs, until I caught sight of tousled curls and Santou's beak of a nose poking their way in through the door. He took a long look at us sprawled on the floor, before moving in.

"Jesus Christ."

"Yeah, I know. We look great."

"Sorry I took so long, but the streets are a mess."

I silently swore that next time I'd let Santou beat me at darts. "I understand. It's a real problem when you've got to watch out for bodies beneath your tires." Taking the cloth off Terri's eyes, I gave Santou a better view of the damage. I felt petty for ever having mistrusted him. "You'll never know how grateful I am that you made it here."

"Yes I will, Porter. Hey, buddy. Ever been in the backseat of a broken-down old LeSabre? You're gonna love it."

"No. But I can vouch for the backseat of an Acura Legend. Maybe you should think about a trade-in if we're going to get serious." Terri gazed through puffy lids as best he could as Santou knelt down beside him. "My hero. If Rach didn't already have dibs on you, I would."

"I'll keep that in mind. Anything broken I should know about?"

Terri placed an arm around Jake's neck. "Nothing that a little plastic surgery can't fix."

Picking him up, Santou started out the door. "You're not going to make me come back and carry you down, too, are you, Porter?"

I would have let him win a second game of darts if he had. "Not a chance."

I followed as best I could to the street, where Santou's car was parked in front of a tow away zone. Having placed Terri on the backseat, he gently propped a blanket under his head. It was a side of Santou I hadn't seen before. The man was full of surprises.

The going was slow as we made our way to Charity Hospital. While most everyone was out of the street by now, pieces of torn clothing lay scattered about, giving the scene more the air of a rowdy party than the riot it had been. Remnants of red ribbons and black armbands lay like discarded party favors. An ostrich boa blew up against the curb. Wigs sat on sidewalks looking like small abandoned pets, while sequins and rhinestones paved a fictional road to Oz.

But there was also darker memorabilia to be seen. Broken bottles and wooden bats streaked with blood decorated the streets. A few people limped past while others sat motionless along the curb, vacant stares their only expression. We drove past the café on Ursuline Street, where the front window lay shattered on the ground in thousands of fragments. The owner knelt picking up pieces of glass, a pool of crystal at his feet. The only thing missing were the skinheads who had run rampant just a few hours ago. Nowhere in sight now, it was as if they had all collectively crawled back into the woodwork.

Santou pulled up to the emergency entrance, flashed his badge, and, as if by magic, two orderlies appeared. I assured Terri I'd wait to see what the doctor said, as the orderlies took him out of the car and slid him onto a gurney.

"Just don't touch my plants, Rach. Promise me that. You'll kill them. This may be the wrong time to tell you, but you don't have a way with anything green."

He was right. My own plants looked as dead as the cypress in the marsh. I had just begun to limp behind the gurney, when I felt the pressure of Santou's hand on my shoulder.

"Where do you think you're going, Porter?"

Annoyed at the question, I tried to move on, but Santou's hand held me in place. "I'm going in with Terri to make sure he's all right."

Santou popped a Tums in his mouth as he motioned toward the wheelchair. "You're going in, all right, but you're sitting in this."

"No way. I'm not a patient."

Stopping an orderly, Santou pointed in my direction. "Sorry to bother you, but could you tell me if this woman looks like a patient to you?"

The orderly checked me up and down and then grinned, the sunlight glinting off a gold-capped front tooth. "To be honest with you, she looks like hell. But don't you worry none. We'll patch her up almost good as new.''

Santou pressed me down into the wheelchair. ''I think that says it all.''

''Yeah. It was a real professional opinion.'' I allowed myself to be wheeled inside, where I was handed countless forms to fill out for both Terri and myself. Engrossed in the bureaucracy of hospital procedure, it took a full second before I realized that Santou was no longer standing beside me. I twisted around to see him heading for the exit door.

''Hey! Wait a minute. Where are you going?'' I hadn't planned on being left here. I figured a quick look-see by some guy in white, and I'd be out the door myself.

Santou made an impatient wave toward the waiting room filled with walking wounded. In torn and bloodied costumes, most looked like victims from the parade. ''You're going to be here a while, so I figured I'd do some poking around and see what I can find. I'll be back to pick you up in a few hours. Just don't limp off anywhere.''

Turning around, he walked out, leaving me stranded.

I've never been a good patient. I can't stand needles, and the sight of blood, especially my own, will usually make me faint. Even worse is the smell that lingers in hospital corridors. I feel certain that the stuff, markedly generic in odor, is bottled and sprayed up and down the halls at least twice a day. This place was no different. The sea-green walls closed in around me while the number of battered bodies multiplied by the minute. Most of the stories were the same. The gangs that attacked had seemingly come out of nowhere, disrupting and destroying the march. It was nearly inconceivable that a bunch of rednecks had been so highly organized. With their hunting caps, tattoos, and loud bluster, I knew the kind of guys these were. Hand them some Dixie beers and a gun, and they're your average poacher out to best the game warden. I wouldn't have thought they were capable of much tactical strategy. It made me wonder what else I'd been wrong about. I watched as one victim after another sped by faceup on a gurney, attended to by doctors and nurses barking out orders on their way to fast-food operating rooms. The anticipation of waiting was more than I wanted to deal with alone. I got up and placed a call to Charlie Hickok. I figured if I was going to take a day or two off from the marsh, I should at least tell him why. I informed Charlie where I was calling from, only to be met with a moment's silence on the other end of the phone. Then all hell broke loose.

"What in the goddamn tarnation were you doing in the Quarter in the first place, Bronx? Seems to me that's a long ways off from any scum out there taking potshots at my ducks."

The dull thud in my head kicked into high gear. I worked hard to compose myself before answering. "I was doing some work on the Vaughn case, Charlie. Remember? You, me, and Trenton are all in this thing together. I managed to get a key to Vaughn's apartment and had just finished snooping around the place, when I walked out and got caught in the riot."

Charlie cleared his throat and took a slug of what I could tell, even over the phone, was bourbon. "So? What did ya find?"

I found myself hesitating, unsure of just how much I wanted to divulge. I'd paid dearly for the information, and unless Charlie was going to treat me as an equal on the case, I wasn't ready to hand over all my hard work with no return. I decided to tell him only what I'd found on Schuess.

"Hell, taking a wild guess, I'd say that Schuess is one Nazi el kooko kooko. Seems to me like Hillard's got himself into a shitload more trouble than he can handle this time." Charlie chuckled at the thought. "No problem, Bronx. Take some time off and dry your boots out. Trenton and me have got this thing covered."

"What have you found out so far, Charlie?" I knew he'd been digging just as hard and fast as I'd been. He had to have come up with some information of his own. If he filled me in, I'd share the rest of the goodies on Global and the diamonds with him. Otherwise, it was information I'd keep to myself for now. It was all up to Charlie.

"Don't you worry none. Me and Trenton will take it from here. If I need you for anything else, I'll call. Otherwise, you just head on back to the marsh once you've rested up. Its about time you got back to what you were hired for."

Charlie couldn't have made my heave-ho off the case any clearer if he'd rented a billboard to advertise the fact.

"And just what is it exactly that I was hired for?"

"Goddamn it, Bronx. How many different ways do you need to hear me say it? You're a dirt-level rookie, who keeps trying to horn in on things you aren't ready for yet. When I think you're capable of handling something like this, you'll be the first to know. Until then, you'll stick to what I tell you."

He hung up before I could answer. I should have known that Charlie would edge me out of the way once he got involved. I'd done all the footwork, and now he was riding the tail wind in search of the glory. Having been put in my place, I was now expected to behave the way any rookie would who had been reprimanded. Instead, I intended to respond in what I considered to be Charlie Hickok fashion. If Charlie didn't want to work with me, I'd just work the case on my own.

Feeling as bad from Hickok's brush-off as I did from my injuries, I heard my name called out and was soon following a nurse through the swinging double doors into a hotbed of activity. I didn't belong here. In New York, I was someone who had dosed up on multivitamins and herbal concoctions, and went to nutritionists just to avoid all this.

I was placed in a small examining room, where I was told to strip and slip into a hospital gown. Hanging open down the back, the gown did little to offset my sense of vulnerability. Recent years had been plagued with keeping track of friends on their way in and out of hospitals: people who should have been hunting for apartments, planning vacations, rehearsing their next show. Hospitals were places to die. I wasn't supposed to be here. By the time a doctor finally came in, I was ready to bolt.

With dark hair cut short for no muss or fuss, Dr. Sandra Kushner moved at the same breakneck speed I did—ninety miles an hour set on cruise controls. In her mid-thirties, she wore just a light dab of lipstick for makeup. Dark eyebrows slashed across her brow and a long, sharp nose gave her a strangely patrician air. Hazel eyes analyzed me in a quick, impatient glance. At five feet five, the woman was a powerhouse. From her no-nonsense air, I knew she had to be from New York. Picking up my chart, she began a succession of rapid-fire questions.

"Rachel Porter. Are you from around here?"

"No. New York." Being a Northerner in Louisiana is like being a stranger in a strange land. You tend to seek out others of your own kind.

"City?"

I nodded as she began her examination, homing in on every unseen injury. "You're from the boroughs?"

She smiled, aware that I'd caught the difference in our accents. "Long Island. How long have you been down here?"

"Six months. You?"

"Three years." She noticed me flinch as she touched a sore rib. "Fish and Wildlife, huh? What do you do?"

"I spend the majority of my time trudging through marshes and swamps."

Taking out a large Ace bandage, Kushner wrapped it firmly around my rib cage. "Jewish girls from New York don't do that sort of thing."

I didn't even ask how she could tell. Almost no one ever could. "No. They don't work in hospitals in Louisiana, either."

We smiled, both acknowledging the fact that we were either running from or in search of something neither of us could really define. I jumped as she touched the back of my head.

"Somebody did a nice job back here."

"I'm glad you like the handiwork. I hate to think what he would have done if he'd really had the chance."

"I think we can get away without shaving the area and putting in stitches. I'll just clean around it and trust that you'll rest, if that's all right with you."

I opted against the skinhead look as she moved on to my other wounds.

"You banged up your knee pretty well. Have a nice time at the parade?"

"Wrong place, wrong time. I wish I could say I'd been there by choice, but it was sheer accident."

Brandishing tweezers, she swiftly pulled out the debris embedded in my palms and knees. As a reward for good behavior, I received a tetanus shot and one of cortisone to help bring down the swelling, along with an elastic knee brace to wear. My parting gift was a container of painkillers.

"Well, Porter, for someone who had no intention of being there, you ended up with assorted contusions, a bum knee, and quite a lump on your head. If I were you, I'd stay out of the way of neo-Nazis. You'll live longer."

My knee and head throbbed as I waited for the Percocet to kick in. "I came with a friend who was in pretty bad shape. Is there any way I can find out about him?"

Kushner glanced down at my chart. "Sure. Give me his name and I'll check on him for you."

With Kushner out of the room, I shed the hospital gown and slipped back into my tattered street clothes as I waited for word on Terri. The fact that I was no longer officially a patient helped to take my mind off my aches and pains, and focus it where it belonged—on the necklace of diamonds I'd left lying inside my purse at home.

It didn't take long for Kushner to return with news on Terri.

"Your friend didn't fare as well as you. We're doing a battery of tests on him now, and it looks like he'll be here at least another couple of days. Give me a call tomorrow, and I'll find out what I can for you then."

"I appreciate it."

She made a note on her chart. "Just think of it as a favor for a fellow New Yorker."

Halfway out the door, another thought struck me. "Do you ever perform autopsies in your spare time?"

Kushner gave me an odd look, unsure of whether or not to smile. "Any particular reason you want to know? Perhaps with a loved one in mind?"

I chuckled as I thought of Hickok. "No. Nothing like that. In fact, we're not even talking human. Sorry. Stupid question."

Putting the chart down, Kushner pulled herself up on the examining table. "No, not at all. Besides, now you've got my curiosity aroused. All I want to know is if it's legal."

I limped back into the room, the brace a vise around my knee. "That's a hard one. I'd say it's perfectly legal. My problem is a boss who's hedging on having an autopsy done, out of sheer stubbornness and obstinate male ego."

Kushner laughed as she drew small concentric circles in the air with her feet. "I've dealt with the same problem around here. Believe me, it's not that unusual. But it sounds like the patient is. What kind of animal are you talking about?"

"Reptile. A large one."

She rubbed a finger along the bridge of her nose as another patient was rushed down the hall on a gurney. "I wish I could help you, but . . ." Gesturing toward the commotion out in the hall, she smiled and then shrugged.

But I wasn't ready to give up so easily. Not after Hickok's abrupt dismissal of my work.

"Would you know someone else who might be willing to do it without legal authorization? I swear on the Empire State Building, it's for a good cause."

Kushner gazed off in the distance for a moment, then turned back with a look of sheer inspiration. "I just might have the guy for you. He's a veterinarian and fellow New Yorker who's heavy into animal rights, which means we're constantly battling over medical experimentation. Sam's one of these old sixties idealists who's probably crazy enough to do just about anything, if you can provide him with a politically correct reason.''

''How would helping to solve a murder case involving a big-time wildlife poacher strike him?''

''I'd say you've got your man.''

Ten

The waiting room had pretty much cleared out by the time Santou returned to get me. I'd spent the last half hour watching frightened people being shunted in and out, with injuries ranging from broken bones to bodies that looked as though they'd been put through a meat grinder—mostly victims of the riot. I was caught between two conflicting emotions. Though I wanted to thank Santou for his help, I also had the overwhelming urge to punch him out for being on a police force that didn't seem to care.

I slid into Santou's LeSabre, wanting nothing more than to sleep for a solid eight hours without any dreams of Valerie, Hickok, or the maniac who'd plowed a sign into my head.

"So, Porter, you want to tell me all about your day before, during, or after dinner?"

It hurt for me even to think. Having to deal with carrying on a conversation over dinner was another dimension altogether. "Listen, Santou, I appreciate the trouble you've gone to, taxiing me back and forth. But look at me. I feel like shit, and all I want to do is go home." What I really wanted more than anything was another Percocet.

"Home is exactly where I'm taking you, Porter."

This time we drove down Bourbon Street. Santou flashed his badge, and we were waved on through an area that had been blocked off to all other traffic. I had expected to find a scene out of war-torn Beirut. While torn clothing and splintered signs abounded here as well, what surprised me was the fact that most of the buildings and porno theatres remained relatively untouched, except for those that were explicitly gay. Terri's club, Boy Toy, was one that had incurred skinhead wrath. The front window was shattered, and part of the building had been torched, but Terri's publicity shot as Madonna in a lacy white bustierre, bikini panties, garter belt, stockings, and high heels still hung outside. "Kill All Fags" had been spray painted over it in large black letters.

As we drove down block after block, it became obvious that the riot on Bourbon had been carefully planned. It was as if someone had laid out which businesses were to be hit. Considering the amount of money generated on the strip, it wasn't hard to imagine why. But it did make me curious. A few of the clubs had even had the foresight to board up their windows. I made a mental note as to which buildings they were, and decided to try and find out who the investors might be.

Santou parked in front of my apartment, placing his N.O.P.D. sign clearly on display. Opening the passenger door, he helped me out.

"You'll have to make it upstairs on your own steam, *chère*. I've got packages to carry."

I concentrated on the long flight of steps ahead, not bothering to ask Santou exactly what he was bringing in. All my energy was directed on keeping as much weight off my left leg as possible. The second-floor landing still reeked with the odor of urine, and my straw doormat was stained with Terri's blood. Unlocking my door, I stepped inside and scanned the room for my purse. Spotting it on the floor where I'd left it, I limped over to my secondhand chair, removing the ice bag I'd carelessly left on its seat. A dark, wet puddle covered the pale green fabric. Too hot and tired to care, I plunked myself down as I watched Santou come through the door with an armload of groceries. The man rarely seemed carefree. Tonight he looked even less so.

''You picked a good day to get beat-up, Porter. We got us some fresh catfish, and I'm in the mood to cook.''

The mention of food set my stomach rumbling, and I realized I was starved. The last time I'd eaten was the cherry Danish before my expedition to Valerie's. I was in no shape to get up and cook for myself, something I rarely did even under the best of circumstances. Instead, I watched Santou put the groceries away and generally check out my living conditions. I hadn't cleaned the place in weeks, and, at the moment, my freezer was in worse shape than Valerie's.

''I figured you wouldn't have much here to cook with. Looks like I was right.''

Santou looked perfectly natural puttering about as he hummed to himself, but I didn't appreciate the crack. I'd been made to feel that I wasn't domestic by everyone from my mother to my former fiancé. They were right, of course. But it was still a sore spot. I believed in the philosophy of takeout: if you live by yourself, why bother cooking food that's just going to go to waste? I considered myself a responsible adult by bringing my meals home in little aluminum containers.

The catfish sizzled and the collard greens smelled better than I had imagined they would. It was the most cooking that had been done in my kitchen since I'd moved here.

I was more aware of my mismatched plates and utensils than ever as we sat down to eat. I hated the thought of someone coming in and making assumptions about me as I'd done with Valerie, but it wasn't hard to do. Santou poured himself a glass of red wine, quickly downing it in one gulp.

''What? No Mylanta chaser?''

His eyes narrowed as they focused in on me, and he was silent for a moment.

''Want to tell me what you found at Vaughn's place this afternoon?''

I picked at the catfish, trying to figure out what it was about his question that bothered me. ''Why don't you tell me first why there were no cops around for today's festivities? Or weren't the police aware that a potentially explosive march would be taking place today?''

I reached for the wine bottle, having come to the decision that one glass along with a Percocet probably wouldn't kill me.

''They were out there, Porter. There was no trouble on Canal where the march started, and that's where everyone had been ordered to report.''

I pictured a long line of cops hanging out on Canal watching the march disappear off in the distance. ''Why didn't they move in when all hell broke loose?''

''That's the million-dollar question. They were ordered back to the precinct to change into riot gear as soon as they got wind of trouble. Seems it took a long time to order them back out on the street again.''

''And who was the one giving the orders?''

Santou took a drink of his wine. ''Captain Connie Kroll.''

''The same charmer I had the pleasure of not meeting early this morning.''

''The one and only.''

''Interesting guy. First he ropes off a murder investigation, and then sits back as all hell breaks loose in the Quarter. He wouldn't happen to be tied in with Hillard Williams by any chance, would he?''

Santou frowned. The creases in his face cut deep through his flesh. ''Everyone knows Hillard. You can't hang a man for that.''

The words reverberated in a hollow cavity behind my eyes where a migraine was beginning to form. My daily quotient for civility was close to running out.

''Well, just what can you hang a man for down here? I know poaching doesn't seem to matter. How about committing murder? Does that pose a problem? Or is it only the slashing of hookers that doesn't count? I mean, what the hell is it that you guys are paid to do, anyway?''

Santou sat back and stared through me as though deciding

my fate. When he spoke again, it was with an icy distance that let me know in no uncertain terms that I had overstepped my bounds.

"Listen, Porter. I work damn hard to do my job right, and that ain't always easy around here. I've paid my dues and been put through the fire more than you'll ever know. I've learned that sometimes you got to straddle both sides of the fence to get what you need. That's why I'm good at what I do. It's a trick you could do well to acquire. I put my ass on the line today by giving you that key to Vaughn's apartment. Now you owe me some information. As for the march, I'll dig around and find out what I can. Other than that, you want to press charges against the guy who bashed in your head? Sure, no problem. Describe him for me. Can Bo Peep identify who beat him up? I'll be glad to do the paperwork. Otherwise, if you've got a problem just say so, and we'll call whatever this is that we've started here quits."

A combination of Percocet and wine had me dead tired and close to bursting into tears. Everything seemed hopeless at the moment—from taking the time to try and slap a poacher in jail, to attempting something as simple as having a conversation. In the past when I'd reached this point, I generally handled the problem by walking away and burning my bridges behind me—especially when it came to my relationships with men. This time I couldn't figure out whether Santou was a bridge I couldn't afford to burn, or just one I didn't want to yet.

"I apologize. I've never been very good at getting beaten up in riots. It's something I'm trying to work on. Mind if I start over?"

Santou drank another glass of wine, never taking his eyes off me. Exuding both a red-hot anger and white-hot lust that caused my pulse to race, his seductive mix of danger and sex was as irresistible as it was frightening. My face flushed as he continued to stare. Noticing it, the barest trace of a smile flitted across his lips. I took a deep breath and tried again.

"What happens to Connie Kroll if Hillard gets into office?"

"Same thing that happens to him no matter who gets in. The man stays. He's rock solid. Kroll's a lot like old J. Edgar Hoover was. He's got dirt on everybody in town. Starts a file as soon as each new baby is born." Santou leaned back in his chair, examining me more casually now. "It would take a bomb to dislodge that man. Problem is, nobody's got one big enough to do it."

"Does he have a file on you, Santou?"

Leaning back to grab a box of toothpicks on the kitchen counter, he pulled one out and began to chew it to bits. "I suppose he does, at that."

"Does he have one on Charlie Hickok?"

"Porter, he's probably already started one on you."

The thought put a stop to the rush I'd been feeling.

"So, if you wanted to find out about someone, all you'd have to do is take a peek inside his files, is that right?"

Santou finished off the wine. "Don't even think it. They're kept under lock and key I don't know where, and I'm not sure I want to. I've just about used up my nine lives already. I'm trying to hold on hard to this last one."

By now, the roar in my head had died down to a mild throb. "The last thing I remember during the march was being slammed on the head by a sign encouraging me to vote for Hillard. Do you think he could have been behind what happened today?"

"No way, *chère*. Don't waste your time on that end. He's not stupid enough to chance it, not this close to the election. Too many votes would be lost if he openly sided with the rednecks. Besides, he's found Jesus, remember?

"Hell, Porter. Today's ass kicking could have been from any number of groups. We've got Confederate Hammer Skins, the Aryan National Front, White Aryan Resistance, and Church of the Creator. Take your pick. We've even got splinter groups of the Nationalist Skinhead Knights and the Fourth Reich Skinheads. Any one of them could have been responsible. They're so damn disorganized most of the time, its hard to keep a finger on them. They form; they break up; new ones start.

"That's not to say that someone close to Hillard couldn't have organized the butt kicking, though. This was a solid-gold opportunity for a little right-wing political consciousness raising, and if that were the case, I'd have to put my money on Buddy Budwell."

The name sounded vaguely familiar. "Who's that?"

"One mean ol' fat boy who's come a hell of a long way from his roots. He used to be poor white trash from back in the swamp. He worked his way right on up through the ranks in Hillard's gator scam. There ain't nothing too down and dirty for ol' Buddy to stick his hands into. Whatever's going to get him his pot of gold is his religion. That and being a Nazi. He was Hillard's second-in-command when Hill headed up the delta contingent. Buddy's like a son to him. Hell, he could *be* his son. I hear Hillard used to pop his mama regularly; could be Buddy was a product of that loving union."

I remembered now where I'd heard his name before. It had been through Trenton.

"So Buddy's still at Hillard's beck and call?"

"Who's to say? Buddy's a respectable businessman these days. Deals legally in gator skins, selling them around the world. Shit, he even sells to rock stars. He's made a fortune at it. If Buddy's dipping his fat little fingers into something illegal, he has a hell of a cover. Up till now, we've never had any reason to look into it. Fact of the matter is, we still don't."

That was something I disagreed with him on. Buddy was a man I wanted to meet soon. Reaching into my bag, I pulled out Valerie's necklace and plunked down a fortune in diamonds next to Santou's plate.

"Jesus, Porter! Where in the hell did you find this?"

"Yeah, I've grown kind of fond of it myself. The question is, how come you guys didn't discover it?"

Picking up the necklace, Santou ran his fingers over each stone. I tried to envision it around the neck of either Dolores or Valerie, but neither fit the bill.

"Hell, as far as I know, that place was torn upside down and right side up."

"Obviously not inside out. Someone forgot to check her freezer."

Santou's fist tightened around the necklace. "She kept a fortune in diamonds next to some frozen chopped meat?"

"She had it buried inside ice cream."

His eyes drilled into me until I felt like a bug about to be pinned and dissected. "You dug through ice cream in a dead woman's freezer? You want to tell me how you happened to come up with that idea?"

I decided to skip over the details and just give him a broad outline. "I used to work off the books in New York. I ended up with lots of cash, and needed some place to stash it. I figured a container of ice cream would be the last place anyone would ever look."

Santou shook his head as the corners of his mouth twitched into a grin. "And they wonder if the sexes think differently. How did you know what you were looking for?"

"I didn't. I just knew that Dolores Williams's jewelry was being siphoned off by Hillard and ending up around Valerie Vaughn's neck."

"And how did you know that?"

"Dolores told me." I pulled out the card for Global Corporation, placing it next to the diamonds. "This was under the necklace when I found it. It might be worth looking into."

Santou picked up the card and turned it over. "How many jewelry stores do you know of on Mulberry Street, Porter?"

"That's exactly what I thought."

Leaning over, he kissed me lightly on the lips. "Good work. I'll clean up."

Santou washed the dishes as I sipped some more wine. If this was what togetherness could be like, it wasn't half-bad. So far, I'd made it my business never to stop long enough to wonder if I might be missing out on something. Biological clock was still a distant phrase, even though mine was running out fast. Even my mother was beginning to give up hope I'd ever settle down. After my last relationship ended, I'd sworn to myself "never again." Now I was beginning to wonder if perhaps I'd been too hasty. The riot had shaken me more than I liked to admit. Getting smacked in the head made me realize I was vulnerable. Being with Santou made me aware of just how lonely I sometimes felt.

"You going to be okay here by yourself tonight, Porter? I could camp out on your couch if you like."

For the briefest moment I was tempted not only to tell him to stay, but to forget about the couch.

"It's a nice offer, but the couch has more springs than fabric on it. I don't want you impaled in your sleep." Hesitating, I decided against it, still not ready to take the plunge. "Thanks, I'll be fine."

I handed him the key to Vaughn's apartment as he headed toward the door. Pulling it halfway open, he turned back around to face me. Looking at his unruly mop of hair and those eyes that penetrated me, my pulse began to race, and I was prepared to change my mind. All he had to do was ask.

"Listen, I wasn't going to bother telling you before, but you're bound to find out. I got a call from Dolores Williams. Somebody poisoned her dog."

It was late that night as I was drifting off to sleep, courtesy of another Percocet, that I realized what had irked me about Santou during dinner. He never bothered to ask if I had made it as far as Vaughn's apartment before getting caught in the riot. It was as if he already knew. But something troubled me even more, something I was only able to tap into as I began to fall asleep.

Dragging myself out of bed, I searched through the pockets of my torn pants until I found what I'd been looking for. I closed my hand tightly around it and sat back down on my bed, hesitating for a moment before opening the drawer of my nightstand. Santou's garnet-and-onyx rosary beads lay nestled inside, the ones he had given me that first night. Then I opened my fist. The beads were an exact match to the rosary I now held in my hand. The one that had been secreted away inside Valerie Vaughn's jewelry box.

My body ached as I crawled out of bed the next morning, cramped muscles protesting my decision to work that day. Three cups of coffee and a Percocet made me feel only slightly better. The makeup I applied did little to hide the damage that colored my skin various shades of purple. This was a job that required Terri's expertise. His fine hand would have worked magic, camouflaging the profusion of bruises that had mysteriously appeared overnight. But Terri was occupied with his own injuries at the moment, leaving me to realize just how much I'd come to depend on him for everything from friendship to beauty tips. Weary from a dream-filled night of running feet and the rat-a-tat barking of one very dead dog, I headed over to the Garden District, past the esplanade on St. Charles, and on to Hillard's lemon meringue pie of a mansion. There had been no love lost between Fifi and me, but I felt bad for Dolores. The dog had been her lifeline. I was worried what would happen to her now.

Vinnie answered the door at his usual lackadaisical pace, eyeing my bruises up and down before saying a word.

"Youse been playing football on ya time off, New Yawk?"

Seeing him in his lime green shirt and white polyester pants, I knew Vinnie couldn't have been the one who had done the dirty deed of killing Dolores's dog.

"Hey, if some punk boyfriend did that ta ya, say the word and he's dog meat."

I appreciated the sentiment, but all it did was remind me of Fifi. "Speaking of dogs, that's why I'm here. What happened?"

Vinnie motioned me inside. "I know how ya hates ta sweat. Seems like something the mutt ate in the backyard didn't agree with her."

"Do you know what it was?"

"I got a good idea. I seen a guy looking the same way

once at a restaurant in the Bronx. Big swollen tongue you couldn't of rolled back in his mouth. The wise guy with him blamed it on the shellfish. I say it pays ta know who's doing the cooking. Personally, I like ta cook for myself."

"So, what was Fifi eating?"

"The mutt kicked off on a nice chunk of lean ground sirloin. Her favorite. Course, I'd been wondering what happened ta the makings for my meatballs. I always buy the best for my sauce, ya know. So I was pretty p.o.'d about the whole thing."

"Where was Mrs. Williams at the time?"

Vinnie scratched absently at his crotch. "Now, that's the funny thing. She was sleeping it off upstairs in her room like she does every afternoon, ya know. But she always kept Fifi in bed with her. Damn mutt even has its own pillow. Youse oughta see the thing. We're talking lace, with its name, whadda ya call it, hand sewn, in the center. Anyways, I'm at the stove cooking some sauce when the old bat starts screaming at the top of her lungs, 'Where's Fifi? Where's my little Fifi?' How the hell am I supposed ta know where her damn dog is, if she don't?

"So's, we start looking for the damn thing. I'm down on my hands and knees checking under beds, inside closets. She even had me move the damn furniture, like that little porker could squeeze into a tight space. Finally, she's screamin' and cryin' that her dog's been murdered. Listen, that was one nasty mop of hair with sharp teeth. But what kinda person is gonna kill a little dog, am I right?

"So we hit the backyard, and there's Fifi, a chunk of meat still in her mouth, lying on her side like she's taking a nap. I wouldn'ta put it past the mutt to play dead just so's it could nab me. But I let Mrs. W. go and check it out. Sure enough, Fifi's stone-cold dead. Not even a twitch from the stump. Now she's screamin' that one of us murdered her dog, and says we're gonna all have to take some kinda lie detector test. Wants me ta go down ta the police. I mean, I hated that mutt, but I ain't no dog killer."

I believed him, but I also felt sure the dog had been intentionally poisoned.

"Was anyone else besides you and Mrs. Williams here at the time?"

Vinnie finished manicuring a fingernail with his teeth, spitting the loose clipping onto the floor.

"Mr. W., he was out somewhere's, I don't know where. I don't keep tabs on the old man. And the Kraut? That sneaky sonofabitch could be behind me right now, and I probably wouldn't know it."

"Do you think I could speak to Mrs. Williams?"

"She's locked herself in her bedroom and said she ain't coming out. I'm just supposed ta keep putting a glass of bourbon and ice outside the door every half hour. She's slugged down about a pint so far this morning. Good thing I keep it well stocked."

"I think it would be a good idea for me to take Fifi's body and have it autopsied. That way we could begin to figure out what kind of poison was used, and possibly trace where it came from."

Vinnie sniffed the air as the scent of lasagna wafted out from the kitchen.

"Whadda ya, kiddin' me? She's got the damn dog locked up in there with her. Ya could always try gettin' it away from her, but youse are on your own with that one."

The last thing I needed to do was get in a tussle with Dolores over the body of her dead dog. Anxious to get back to the kitchen, Vinnie cut me some slack.

"Listen, kiddo. I don't like no animal killers any more than you do. I mean, if you're gonna snuff someone, you should pick on a guy your own size, you know what I mean? I got something that might help ya out. I picked up what meat was left on the ground where Fifi keeled over. I don't want nothing else dying, ya understand? I still got it. Ya wants it, it's yours. Wait here and I'll dig it outta the freezer."

The meat would be almost as good as Fifi herself. I waited

beneath the crystal chandelier, the sun scattering miniature rainbows on the polished floor around my feet. The morning light felt like sharp lasers drilling into the back of my eyes, and I found myself concentrating on the kaleidoscopes of color in order to take my mind off the steel pincers of pain beginning to form in the back of my head. I was taken by surprise when the door to Hillard's private chamber opened. Gunter walked out, looking as cold and distant as the newspaper photo I now had of him. He wasn't alone. His companion was a scrawny weasel of a man with a long, thin nose reminicent of the hose attachment on a vacuum cleaner. His eyes squinted, darting back and forth as they took me in. Wearing a sneer, along with a toupee that resembled roadkill, the man was dressed in the uniform of a state agent for the Louisiana Department of Fish and Game.

A hint of a smile flitted across Gunter's lips. "Agent Porter. What an unexpected surprise. Are introductions necessary here, or do you two already know each other since you are both in the same line of work?"

The state agent wiped the palms of his hands up and down his legs, leaving track marks of sweat on his pants. "She don't know me none. Not a hotshot fed like herself. They don't have nothin' to do with us state boys who work hard for a livin'. But I sure as hell know who she is."

A homegrown enmity between federal and state agents in Louisiana had developed into an "us against them" mentality. Just as with the folks in the bayou, I was considered the outsider coming in, trying to shove a law down their throats which they had no intention of following. State agents played by bayou rules. Sometimes they even made up their own.

"Then you have an advantage over me. Do I get to know your name, or is this part of the game where I'm supposed to guess?"

The man continued to sneer, shoving his hands deep in his pockets, his fingers wriggling about like a family of tiny moles trying to escape through the fabric.

"That's a good idea. Why don't you spend some of that free time of yours doing that."

Nodding to Gunter, the man strode past me out the door. Gunter's lips twitched, though his eyes remained as dead as ever.

"That was state agent Clyde Bolles, and I don't believe he likes you, Agent Porter."

"I'll learn to live with it."

Gunter wasted no time on small talk. "May I ask what you're doing here, please."

"I want to speak with Mrs. Williams. It won't take up much time."

Gunter looked toward the staircase before bringing his attention back to me.

"Who let you in, Agent Porter?"

"The butler, of course."

"Of course." Gunter sighed and motioned toward the stairs with a sweeping theatrical gesture, turning his body around as if to block any sudden moves on my part.

"I am so sorry, but Mrs. Williams is indisposed today. Perhaps you heard. Her dog took ill yesterday and died." He gestured with the same hand that Fifi had taken a chunk out of, the white gauze still bearing telltale stains of dried blood.

"I heard the dog was poisoned."

"Interesting. And I thought it was just a piece of bad meat."

I was left with little doubt as to who the supplier had been.

Gunter moved in toward me until I found myself backed up against the front door.

"I'll let Mrs. Williams know that you stopped by to convey your condolences. It will mean so much to her."

Leaning in close, he turned the knob and opened the door behind me. Worried that Vinnie might pick this moment to come lumbering back in with the meat in his hand, I allowed the door to close in my face and then headed to the back of the house. Having refused this morning to put on the brace I'd been given to wear, a jolt of pain shot through my knee as I slowed to a hobble. But I didn't have to go very far before I spotted Vinnie hidden behind a profusion of overgrown shrubs. The lime green of his shirt blended in with the plants, while his face peeked out from between the deep pink flowers of an azalea bush.

"This is the best I can do for youse."

Thrusting a small foil-wrapped package into my hands, he turned and was gone before I looked up to thank him.

Eleven

As I drove back toward Canal, I wondered what kind of business a state game agent could have with Gunter Schuess. Clyde Bolles appeared to be a beneficiary of small-town political patronage—a favor that had been owed and paid off by supplying Bolles with a job.

Wanting to get a progress report on Terri, I stopped by a pay phone along Decatur Street. The news Dr. Kushner gave me was good. Aside from needing lots of rest, Terri was on the mend.

"Just keep an eye on him, Porter. He has this obsession with staring at himself in the mirror while chanting the names of top plastic surgeons like it was some sort of mantra. Why don't you swing by the day after tomorrow and take him off my hands."

That sounded like the Terri I knew and loved. Kushner added some more information that I'd hoped to hear.

"I also spoke to Sam Leonard, the vet I told you about. Seems he's bored with his same old routine, so I filled him in on you. That was last night. He's called me three times since, wanting to know why you haven't phoned him yet. So do me a favor and give him a call before he pesters me to death."

"Thanks. I'll return the favor sometime."

"You can buy me a drink when this is all over and we'll call it even."

With some free time on my hands, a pay phone in front of me, and a ball of raw meat thawing out fast, I decided to call Dr. Sam right away. A male voice answered on the third ring with the same impatient tone I occasionally found myself using.

"Yeah, hi. Animal Health Clinic here."

"I'd like to speak to Dr. Leonard, please."

"Well, I'd say that depends on who you are."

Sam Leonard was in bad need of a new receptionist—one who didn't abuse clients before the first appointment had been made.

"This is Rachel Porter. Dr. Leonard's expecting my call."

"You aren't kidding. I've been waiting around hoping to hear from you all morning. How the hell are you?"

"Dr. Leonard?"

"Yeah, yeah, I know. You'd think I wouldn't have to answer my own phone, but my receptionist is out to lunch so I'm doing double duty. So are you free or what?"

"You mean do I have some time available?"

"Yeah, like right now. Lucy's due back in ten minutes. Let's grab some lunch, and you can fill me in on what you have in mind, lay out the plans, hit me with the dirt."

I hadn't imagined working with a kamikaze vet champing at the bit to disobey the law. But I also didn't have a wide range of candidates to choose from. I'd have to check him out and decide from there. We agreed to meet at Mother's, a local spot on Poydras Street. It seemed a safe enough place since it was always jammed.

"How will I recognize you?"

"I'll be the good-looking guy with the long grey ponytail, grizzled beard, and jeans. How about you?"

"I'm the tall strawberry blonde who looks like she just walked into a wall."

Dr. Sam chuckled. "Yeah, Sandy told me about that. So, I'll look for a Yankee decked out in red, black, and blue. See you in half an hour."

I gave myself a quick once-over in the rearview mirror.

Yellow bruises shone through my makeup, as if I'd contracted a bad case of hepatitis. Giving up on vanity, I turned my aggression on a Jaguar instead, beating it out for a parking space that was up for grabs. By the time I got to Mother's, the line for a table was halfway out the door. I pushed my way up front, but no one fit Sam's description. I started heading to the back of the line when a hand gripped me by the shoulder and swung me around.

"Hey, Rachel. Follow me."

Grabbing my hand was a man already beginning to jostle his way through the crowd, looping himself in and out of bodies like only a true New Yorker can do. A long grey ponytail swung past his shoulders, hitting the back of a lavender tee shirt. Jeans were slung low on his hips. Air Nike sneakers gave a bounce to his walk, so that his head bobbed up and down like a duck at a shooting gallery. Dr. Sam had a table ready and waiting with a pitcher of cold sangria half polished off. I was impressed.

"How did you manage this?"

"The guy who owns the place, his dog's a patient of mine. Hey, it's that old New York adage of who you know."

Taking a sip of sangria, I studied the man across from me. A coarse mass of salt-and-pepper hair was pulled back tightly. A beard and mustache covered the bottom half of a pockmarked face. Unruly eyebrows reached straight out toward me, hovering above hazel eyes which smiled from behind a pair of round tortoiseshell glasses. He was the classic sixties-liberal case study. A Dead Head graduates from school, decides to experience life on the road, travels around the country living in communes until landing in New Orleans, where he tunes into the ongoing party and then proceeds to tune out, never bothering to leave.

"So, you got it figured out yet, Rachel?"

"Sorry. You're just not what I had expected."

"Good. Okay. So you want to know what's in this for me. Let's run through it before we eat. I've got a bad stomach. I'm beginning to think it's ulcers."

Dr. Sam listed a political history that involved lab animal

break-ins, spraying red paint on seals up in Canada alongside Brigitte Bardot, and harassing Soviet trawlers during whale hunts. But that had been years ago. Since then, his life had settled into the routine medical duties required for his practice. Restless and itching to do something he shouldn't, he was looking for some trouble. I gave him the rough details of what I wanted him to do, which was basically to autopsy a gator found at the scene of a highly suspicious murder. I also told him I was looking to tie it into a scam involving heavy hitters whose names I couldn't yet divulge.

Agreeing to help me out, Sam gobbled down a plate of shrimp étouffée in record time, ordering a piece of sweet potato pie before I had barely begun to dig into my seafood gumbo. His paunch attested to the fact that he'd been enjoying the good life more than climbing over the walls of any research labs, lately.

"So did I pass the test, chief?"

"Like an Eagle Scout with flying colors."

"Great." His hands massaged his stomach. "Man, this is just what the doctor ordered. I feel like I've been born again."

I took out another Percocet and poured some more sangria. "Kind of like Hillard Williams, huh?"

"That scumbag running for mayor? His dog is a patient of mine. Now there's your deep-fried couple. The wife's a lush, which is understandable. It's probably the only way she can get through each day with the man."

I reached for my sangria as the Percocet caught in my throat. "You used to treat Fifi?"

"Still do. Nasty little bugger. But hell, I'd be, too, if I'd had a gator chomping down on me like some hors d'oeuvre." Reaching into the bottom of the sangria pitcher, he forked out a maraschino cherry and popped it in his mouth, the red juice staining a few hairs on his beard.

"Sorry to have to tell you this Sam, but you just lost a patient. Fifi met with some foul play yesterday. I have reason to believe she was fed poisoned meat. In fact, I have a sample in my car. I was hoping you'd analyze it for me."

Sam dipped his fingers into his water glass and wiped the cherry juice from his beard. "Yeah, sure. No sweat. Man, I wasn't crazy about that dog, but she didn't deserve a death like that."

The remark conjured up visions of Valerie and Hook. "Will you be able to do an autopsy on the gator anytime soon?"

Sam picked at the fruit on the bottom of the pitcher, demolishing one piece after the other. "Sure. You got a way to get it over to me?"

It was the one piece of logistics I hadn't stopped to consider. There was no way to transport a ten-foot alligator in my Crackerjack box of a car. Fortunately, Dr. Sam picked up on my panicked state of hesitation.

"Don't worry about it. I've got a van. Tell you what, I'll even help you carry the body. Feel better now, Rachel?"

"You're a lifesaver, Dr. Sam."

"Yeah. That's what most of my patients tell me. So, what say we put this gig in motion and take the van out for a spin this evening? Is that copacetic with you?"

It was the best news I'd had all day.

I arrived at Sam's at eight o'clock that evening, anxious to be on my way, get the deed over with, and hightail it back with the least amount of trouble possible. Getting out of my car, I was met outside his office door by a rottweiler as ferocious as any I'd seen. Pitch-black, with a head the size of a serving platter and a mouthful of razor-sharp teeth, the dog emitted a series of gruff barks, sending my adrenaline soaring. I froze in place, and felt the rough surface of a tongue lick the back of my hand.

"That's Shep. A real killer, isn't he? I'm trying to teach him to attack at the first sign of trouble."

Sam stood behind his screen door, grinning broadly.

"How's he doing?"

"Miserably. The dog loves everyone. He hasn't yet realized exactly where it is that he lives. I mean, we've got the projects on one side, all the looney tunes from the strip on the other, and rednecks running the rest of the show. But I figure based on looks alone, he's got to have some value as a deterrent.''

Dr. Sam wheeled out an ancient Chevy van painted in a wild array of colors, a piece of art history from the days of *Sgt. Pepper's Lonely Hearts Club Band.* I didn't have the heart to tell him that riding through Slidell in such a kool pop was the equivalent of flashing a neon sign for the local cops to pull us over. Sam climbed into the driver's seat and opened the passenger door from the inside, the outside handle having fallen off long ago. It creaked open with a high-pitched shriek.

''Don't say it. I know what you're thinking, but I can't let it go. It would be like admitting I've grown old.''

I kept my mouth shut, understanding only too well. We barreled over the bridge across Lake Pontchartrain, a breeze passing through the windows as the wind picked up. Beaming off the black water, the light of a near-full moon was topped by whitecaps which danced across the lake, frothing like freshly whipped cream. We were heading directly into a squall.

As the rain began to pour down, Dr. Sam handed me a small piece of rope. I followed its length along the dashboard outside the window, to where it was knotted onto the windshield wiper on the right hand side of the van. Sam held an identical piece of rope in his left hand.

''Start pulling.''

''You've got to be kidding. Your wipers don't work?''

''I never actually drive this thing. It's a relic. But you needed something large enough to stick a gator in—am I right, or what?''

The only thing good about the storm was the fact that not many police would be out looking to roust ''undesirables'' passing through town. The rain transformed the honky-tonk main drag of Slidell into a Fauvist painting. Fractured by the jerky movement of the wipers, brightly lit signs competed in a riot of color, blurring to soft edges so that McDonald's-BurgerKingWendy's all became one. The rain battered the roof of the van, tiny snare drums in fevered competition. Pouring in through the open window, the rain soaked my pants until the fabric was almost sheer against my skin.

I changed the string from one hand to the other as my arm began to ache, continuing to tug at the wipers to a silent beat as I counted time in my head. Pulling out a bag of red licorice twizzlers, Dr. Sam handed me a long rubbery stick as I pointed out the building between drops of rain.

"Pull off over there, where the bank is."

Turning off his lights, Dr. Sam made a sharp right turn into the lot. The only other car there was a powder blue Dodge Shadow belonging to Deke, the night watchman for the building. Between nine-thirty and ten was when Deke took his dinner break for Kentucky Fried Chicken, just down the block. He had told me it was a ritual he'd rather die than miss. I was counting on that tonight. With any luck, we'd be in and out before he returned. Checking my watch, I saw that it was 9:35. Nabbing one dead gator in twenty minutes shouldn't prove to be much of a problem.

I unlocked the door of the building and led the way down the hall toward the FWS office. Our footsteps rang out on the linoleum floor, echoing down the empty corridor. Dr. Sam held my flashlight as I punched in the code to shut off the alarm, and held my breath. I stared at the plaque, with its warning that we were about to break into a government agency, as I pushed the office door open, my body tensed and ready for flight if a siren went off. I didn't put it past Charlie to change the code without telling me just for the hell of it. I stood perfectly still waiting for him to jump out of a darkened corner, materialize behind a door, appear from under a desk, confront us from any one of a dozen possible places, and pounce in righteous indignation. But the room remained completely silent. All except for Dr. Sam, who paced around in search of a garbage can. Having stuck the last piece of licorice in his mouth, he chose this moment to throw away the empty twizzler wrapper. The sound of crinkling cellophane crackled in the quiet of the room, setting my nerves on edge. Retrieving the wrapper from where Sam had thrown it at the bottom of Edna's perfectly clean and empty garbage can, I handed it back to him.

"Hold on to this, please."

Dr. Sam took it from me. "Yeah. You're right. It's not like they're going to notice an alligator is missing from here. We don't want to leave any clues behind."

He didn't know yet that I also planned on his help with returning the gator once the autopsy had been performed. I glanced inside Charlie's office to make sure he wasn't there drinking in the dark, then led the way to a room large enough to hold a chest freezer the size of a gigantic trunk and little else. I had made a copy of its key a few nights earlier, stopping by close to midnight with a bag of donuts for Deke along with an excuse about a missing folder. The key had been replaced early the next morning, before either Charlie or Edna had a chance to notice it had ever been gone. But what confronted me now made me question just how clever I had really been. My flashlight illuminated the silver glow of a brand-new lock, bolting the freezer's lid solidly in place. I dashed out of the room to rummage through both Charlie and Edna's desks in a desperate search for the key, as I glanced at the clock on the wall. Already 9:45. I didn't expect much sympathy from Dr. Sam as I walked back empty-handed and explained the situation.

"Oh ye of little faith. Buck up, Rachel. It's not a major problem."

Bending over to examine the lock, he pulled close to a dozen keys from his front pocket. Different sizes and shapes, they clanged together.

Dr. Sam caught my look of surprise and chuckled. "And here you thought I was just really hung. Disillusioning, isn't it?" Checking the lock once more, he fingered through his collection. "It's a Schlage, so this shouldn't be too difficult."

Dr. Sam was beginning to seem more and more like a pro, and I wondered if I should be concerned. "I'm grateful you're on my side, but is there a reason why you should have a match for this lock?"

He didn't bother to look up as he tried out a few keys. "I was able to get a bunch of masters from a locksmith."

"Don't tell me. His dog is a patient of yours."

Sam grinned as the lock snapped open. "Successful heart surgery on his bulldog made him a happy man. When he heard about my nasty habit of losing keys to the cages at the clinic, he gave me a set of masters to make life easier. And it has, don't you think?"

Together we lifted the lid of the shiny silver coffin. Hook lay inside, frostbitten, but still in one piece except for the leg that had been lopped off in Valerie Vaughn's apartment. I grabbed the tail while Dr. Sam locked an arm around Hook's neck. Hoisting him out on the count of three, we lowered him to the floor as the lid slammed shut, snapping the lock back in place. It was then that I heard the office door open. No clock struck ten, turning me into a pumpkin. Instead, the white glare of Deke's flashlight glimmered in the outer room. Silently crouching with Hook between us, we watched the light slash back and forth, reaching up to filter in through the small glass window of the door we hid behind. Satisfied there were no intruders, Deke moved down the hall. While we were safe for the moment, I had no idea how we would escape with our cargo. I turned to face Sam where he knelt, Hook's head still under his arm.

"You wouldn't happen to treat any pets belonging to a night watchman by the name of Deke Domange, would you?"

"Not even close."

Several thoughts flashed through my mind as I tried to conjure up what to do next. My answer came as Hook slowly began to defrost. Sneaking back into Charlie's office, I dug through a pile of paperwork in the bottom drawer of his desk until I came to a freshly opened bottle of Old Grand-Dad. There was no one Charlie could think he was hiding it from, except possibly Deke. Besides a weakness for Kentucky Fried Chicken, Deke had a confessed love for good bourbon.

Taking a moment to explain my plan to Sam, I sneaked out of the office and back down the hall, opening and closing the door to the building loudly. Within thirty seconds, Deke's flashlight had me in its view, blinding me as though I were a jacklighted deer.

"Hey, you—Miss Porter. What you doin' here this time of night?"

Deke had the rawboned look that comes from having spent a lifetime working outside. With a face like a hound dog, and an emaciated body that was the result of his wife's death and cooking for himself for too many years, he had the glazed-over expression that people sometimes get when they're just passing the time waiting to die. Deke had spent most of his early years working on an oil rig. He was laid off, along with the rest of the workers in southern Louisiana, around the same time that his wife had died. It was then that he'd begun to hit the bottle hard. He claimed it was his only relief from a lifetime of memories that he'd just as soon forget. But he always waited until arriving home at six in the morning before drinking himself to sleep. I felt like dirt for what I was about to do.

"Hey, Deke. I was just about to celebrate catching a big poacher. Ever hear of Trenton Treddell?"

Deke whistled as he gave me a nod. "He's a big fish, that one. Famous all over the bayou. You catch him all by yourself?"

"I sure did. So, I've decided to celebrate. Only I had to stop by first to pick something up from my desk. How about sharing a drink to toast my success?" I held the Old Grand-Dad out in front of me. "I hate drinking alone. Would you join me for just one?"

Deke looked at the bait, trying to control the urge. I wanted to drop the bottle on the floor or smash it against a wall. Instead, I held it closer, tempting him.

"I don't know, now, Miss Porter. If anyone ever found out, they'd be mighty unhappy to know I'd been drinking on the job."

"I'll never tell, Deke. So, how is anyone ever going to know?"

A light went on in his eyes, that wasn't from thoughts of

women or money. Only the smell of bourbon could bring Deke to life anymore.

"Alright. Seeing that you're celebrating and all, Miss Porter, I'll join you in one. But only one, and then I gotta stop."

"There wouldn't happen to be any plastic cups in the bank employees' room, would there?"

Having thrown a retirement party for one of their employees earlier in the week, they'd left not only cups, but also a bag of ice stashed in the minirefrigerator. Opening the door to the bank, we let ourselves in and I poured the first round. He sipped at his bourbon as though he was stepping onto a patch of thin ice. I quickly replenished his drink and then took a sip of my own. It didn't take long for Deke to drain his cup. I excused myself with the ruse that I needed to get something from my desk and headed out the door, glancing back in time to see Deke pour himself another good-sized drink. He was set for the rest of the night. Grabbing paper towels from the bathroom, I mopped up the puddle of water that had formed around Hook and stuffed the towels inside my pockets. Ten feet of gator was carried out the door, through the hall, and into the rain, where we placed him carefully on the floor of the van.

The rain came down hard as we made our way past the fast-food stops, late-night video stores, and onto the highway heading back toward Lake Pontchartrain. New Orleans glittered in the distance, its carnival-colored lights reflecting off the lake. Raindrops refracted the glow, so that the city appeared to be on fire. I tried not to think about the stench of dead gator that had begun to fill the back of the van. After the evening's events, I wanted a drink as badly as Deke had wanted one just a short while ago.

One of the best things about New Orleans is that you never have to worry about where to go. The town never sleeps. People always say that about New York, but the truth is that New Orleans is the place to be if you want to drown yourself in a party that doesn't end. New York is a place to keep bumping into yourself alone. I didn't want to be alone right now, and I didn't want to just be with strangers. Not for a while.

It was quiet at Dr. Sam's clinic as we pulled in, except for Shep, who growled loudly, his barks mixing in with the rumble of thunder. Unloading Hook, we took him inside. Shep sniffed at the dead gator and then backed away to a far corner of the room, as if not trusting Hook even in death.

"Let me buy you a drink. It's the least I can do after what you've been through tonight." I wanted to go someplace loud where I couldn't hear myself think.

"We both look like hell."

"We'll go somewhere dark."

I let the rain run through my hair, down the back of my neck, and inside my shirt as we walked quickly, making our way to the Old Absinthe Bar. A speakeasy from the twenties, it was just what I was looking for: dark, crowded, and with a nearly intolerable noise level.

The waitress stared, but we paid little heed as we headed toward one of the small tables in back. I ordered a cognac, and the heat from the tightly packed room slowly steamed my clothes dry. A band played the sweet/sour notes of the blues that always made me feel good to feel sad, the guitarist wringing a tear from every string as the group of five jostled for space on the small raised stage.

Someone brushed against me, and I looked up to see a blind man searching for clear passage with his cane. Making his way through the throng of tables, he was pulled up onto the stage. He was dressed all in black, and his hair fell below his shoulders in soft, loose waves the color of drifting snow. His skin was as starkly white as Valerie's. The singer for the group, he wore dark glasses to cover dead eyes, reminding me of Deke.

I ordered another cognac. By two in the morning, finally sated, I glanced over at Sam, who looked equally beat. He held his head up with the palm of his hand, his eyes fluttering closed until the next loud chord jerked him awake.

We walked back through streets filled with other sleepless people who couldn't face going home alone. By the time we reached Sam's clinic, my head ached from bruises and booze. Crawling into my car, I promised to drive safely and go straight home.

Instead, I headed back toward Lake Pontchartrain. Stopping at the first all-night liquor store I found, I bought a bottle of Old Grand-Dad. The squall had died down to a light mist, but the world still held its fine, blurry edge. I wasn't sure if the effect was from the rain or the cognac, and I didn't much care. Trying to find a distraction from the thought of a warm bed and soft pillow, I turned on the radio that mostly played static, filling my head with the same erratic sound.

Back in Slidell I stopped at a McDonald'sBurgerKing-Wendy's and picked up four cups of black coffee and two Egg McMuffins to go. Pulling in next to Deke's Dodge Shadow, I unlocked the door to the building and headed to Charlie's office, not worrying about the alarm that I had never bothered to reset. I put the new bottle of Old Grand-Dad back where his other had been, carefully replacing the pile of papers on top. Everything was once more in order. Activating the alarm, I closed the door to the office and locked it behind me. The dead silence of the hall echoed the hollow sound of my feet as I went over to the entrance of the bank and let myself in. Deke was sprawled out on the couch in the employees' room fast asleep, the empty bottle on the floor beside him. Propping him up, I slapped some cold water on his face until he began to stir, and then held the hot coffee to his lips, forcing him to take constant, steady sips. A few laps around the building, three cups of coffee, and two Egg McMuffins later, Deke was apologizing to me for his behavior, and I felt like the villain I was.

It was five o'clock in the morning, that witching hour when the first fingers of dawn haven't quite overcome the darkness of night, when I climbed the stairs to my apartment to try and catch a few hours of sleep. I pulled off clothes that smelled of smoke, cognac, and dead gator, and crawled into bed where I lay on my back. The blades of the overhead fan fluttered the sheet against my body, which still ached from a riot that had only taken place the day before. For as long as I could remember, my life had been on fast forward.

I was tired, dead tired, but my mind wouldn't stop. The red light on my answering machine flashed on and off. I ignored it, not wanting to deal with anything other than trying to sleep.

As usual, I left the standing lamp on in the corner of my bedroom. My demons weren't stilled by a couple of drinks. They came out in the dark, not going away until the first light of day. That was why I always left a light on—except for those occasions when I didn't sleep alone. But those had become more and more rare in the last few years, and my demons had felt more at home, sneaking in when I least expected them. If I'd thought I could drown them in a bottle, I would have been tempted.

Twelve

I woke up at eight later that morning, my head an overripe melon ready to burst. My second-to-last Percocet and a cup of black coffee temporarily mended the damage until the phone rang, jangling my nerves and splitting the pain wide open again. When I answered the phone, my voice had all the texture of a gravel pit that had been trounced on by a two-ton Mack truck.

"What the hell is the matter with you, Rach? You sound like a bad imitation of Lauren Bacall. And by the way, you're the one who should be calling me. After all, I'm the one who's in the hospital."

I added guilt onto a pounding headache, having meant to call Terri yesterday and forgotten completely about it.

"Don't you return your phone calls anymore? I must have left ten messages for you last night. You had me worried half to death."

I counted the flashes on my answering machine. There were eleven. "I had a rough day and went out for a few drinks last night."

"I hope it wasn't that cheap crap that you seem to have such a fondness for."

Terri made me smile in spite of myself. "Only good cognac. I promise."

"Cognac, huh? You must have had a rough day. Tell me you weren't drinking alone."

Terri was the closest thing I had to a Jewish mother down here.

"No. I had company."

"A certain detective we both know and lust after?"

"No. Just a friend. How are you feeling?"

"I'm fine, and don't try to get me off a topic I enjoy. God knows how long it's going to be before I get to do anything other than live vicariously, and you're not providing me with very good material. Listen, Rach, you're missing the boat here. I know my men, and beneath that brooding exterior, the detective is hot. So, what's your problem?"

Thinking of Santou put my nerves on edge. I had just enough doubts to make me question the man. He also tempted me enough to make him that much more interesting.

"I don't know, Ter. There's just something that strikes me as odd."

"Is that necessarily bad?"

I knew Terri wouldn't let me off the hook until I had explained. "The day of the riot?"

"Go ahead; it's one I'm not likely to forget."

"I was in Valerie Vaughn's apartment digging around."

"Want to tell me how you managed to get inside Val's place?"

I smiled in spite of myself. "I was given a key, compliments of one hot detective."

"That's it, Rach. We're talking salt of the earth. The man rescues me from off your floor, and lets you play peekaboo at a murder scene. What more do you want? I don't ever want to hear another word against him."

"Then you're not going to like what's coming. While I was rummaging through one of Valerie's drawers, I found a set of rosary beads. They're an exact match to the ones Santou gave me, that he said had belonged to his grandmother. Doesn't that strike you as odd?"

"What—that they're the same? So what? You thought he gave you one-of-a-kind designer rosary beads? Maybe it was a popular pattern a few years back. Like they've got an extensive choice of design in the bayou? Get a grip, Rach. You're making excuses. I know when you're scared."

Terri's humor grounded me better than anything else could. "When can I bring you home?"

"I thought you'd never ask. How about early this evening? That way I'll get in another backrub. Besides, what would life be like without three more bad meals? It'll help me appreciate my freedom. By the way, you haven't forgotten to feed Rocky, have you?"

Terri's cat hadn't been named for Stallone's movie, but after the boxer Rocky Graziano. Or at least for Paul Newman, who had portrayed the boxer on film. "No, I've been feeding Rocky and ignoring your plants. But when I spoke to Dr. Kushner yesterday, she said you were grounded until tomorrow."

Terri grunted petulantly. "What can I tell you? She changed her mind. I think she's got her nose out of joint. Speaking of noses, she could use a bit of hers lopped off. I've been suggesting the three of us get a group rate for some plastic surgery. I must have pissed her off somehow."

I had no doubt about that. I assured Terri that I'd check on his release orders and swing by after dinner.

I pressed the playback button on my answering machine and listened to Terri's ten messages, which ranged from wondering what swamp I was stuck in, to prayers that I was doing something hot, hot, hot. The eleventh call was from Dolores Williams.

"D'ja hear how they killed my little Fifi?" She broke into a long, wrenching sob before continuing on. "Those bastards murdered her. But I'm gonna make 'em pay for it. An' that goes for that dead whore of a coonass, too. I'm goin' to the newspaper. Hell, I'll make sure it gets on TV—one of those *Hard Copy* shows. By the time I'm through, that old goat'll be runnin' for cover. Let 'im just try 'n stop me."

I heard a hiccup, another sob, a long pause, and then a click, as she hung up. I thought briefly about stopping by to check on Dolores, but decided to put that on hold. From the sound of it, she had consumed enough bourbon last night to knock her out cold until noon. Besides, my plans for the morning were already booked. After feeding and watering Rocky, I intended to pay an unannounced call on Buddy Budwell.

The sky was calm and clear as a pristine lake after last night's storm. I checked in on Rocky, then wheeled out toward Thibodaux. The town was best known by a handful of tourists for a dilapidated plantation called Rienzi. Originally built as a place for the queen of Spain to sack out after escaping Napoleon, it had never been used. What had settled in town instead was Buddy Budwell and his booming business in alligator heads and skins. I guessed that this was the place where Hillard had originally run his gator scam. The fact that Budwell hadn't moved from the spot made sense. Now that alligators were off the endangered species list and limited hunting was legal, Buddy was sitting pretty, with all his contacts and hunters already in place. Former outlaws with an entrepreneurial flair had made out like the bandits they were, simply switching the signs on their doors from "illegal" to "legal," with business running right along as usual.

While I didn't have the exact directions to his shop, I had every reason to believe Buddy was well-known around these parts. I stopped at a 7-Eleven along the way to pump some gas, and then sat down for a bowl of hot boudin. I was hoping some food would settle the volatile mix of Percocet and coffee, which was playing havoc with my system. The girl behind the counter who served up my rice and pork sausage was as thin and spindly as a heron. Her small head perched precariously on top of a long, slender neck, and she wore a tube top and short shorts. Brown hair hung listlessly past shoulders that hunched over as if she were cold.

"Do you know where I can find Buddy Budwell's shop?"

She looked at me blankly, her fingers lacing together and pulling apart in a slow, jerking motion.

"He sells souvenirs to tourists. You know, alligator heads and skins. Ever hear of him?"

She shook her head, drawing her shoulders tightly around her. As she turned her palms faceup in the air, I had a clear view of the track marks on her arms.

I paid for the gas and the meal and continued on, following Route 1 along the sinuous path of a lazy bayou. Lily pads burst with a profusion of flowers that made me want to forget about track marks and riots and poachers. A young boy appeared up ahead, a mirage holding a walking stick twice his size, as he emerged from a dense wave of heat. Covered in freckles and denim, he kicked at the bloated body of a frog that was ready to burst. I stopped the car next to him.

"I'm looking for Buddy Budwell. Do you know where his shop is?"

The boy planted the toe of his sneaker on one of the frog's legs. He poked at the taut white stomach with the end of his stick, and a thin stream of fluid appeared.

"You go down a ways to a sign where an arrow points left," he said. "You have to turn there."

Thrusting the stick into the frog's stomach, the boy watched it burst like an overinflated balloon, spewing its contents onto his dirty white sneakers. He mixed the guts into a pasty stew as the intestines baked on the top of his shoes.

Driving on, I glanced back. The boy had bent over his conquest and now lifted the remains of the flattened frog in his hand. Bringing his nose down, he took a good whiff.

I came to the roughly cut wooden sign and turned off the blacktop onto a gravel road, following the trickle of a stream as it meandered along before abruptly ending. In the distance, gunshots ripped through the air, cleaving the silence of an otherwise languid morning. Opening the glove compartment, I pulled out my .357 and tucked it under my shirt. I had no idea what to expect from my meeting with Buddy Budwell.

I drove about a mile before I came upon two vehicles sitting in front of a nondescript cement building. Planted in the middle of nowhere, its only sign was a metal RC Cola plaque, shot full of holes embedded in the building's front door. The Ford Escort parked directly in front had seen better days. Chunks of paint had peeled off in large rusted patches, and its sole decoration was a cardboard air-freshener hanging from the rearview mirror. On each of its sides was the photo of a different naked girl. The Toyota Land Cruiser next to it was in better condition, its logo announcing Gators to Go painted in neat black letters against its cream-colored body.

Against the wall of the building, two long wooden benches held a macabre display of alligator skulls. A smaller bench displayed fully fleshed and preserved heads. Their eyes gleamed wickedly, and long snouts led to sharp teeth glistening as pearly white as bleached bone.

I parked my car next to the Escort and followed the reverberation of gunshot blasts around to the back of the building, where a man resembling a large side of beef stood taking careful aim at a target.

Standing six feet tall with a shock of blond hair, he had skin a bloody shade of red. One pudgy cheek was pressed tightly against the barrel of a twelve-gauge Remington pump. A finger the size of a sausage pulled back on the trigger, and the rifle recoiled hard against his shoulder. Half-moons of sweat stained each underarm. He pumped another round into the chamber, a spent shell falling onto a mound of other empties at his feet.

Standing next to the man was State Agent Clyde Bolles. He ran to set up a fresh can for Budwell, nervously jumping back before another round could be shot. Spotting me as he turned around, Bolles flapped his arms wildly but Buddy ignored him, knocking the target neatly off its mark and onto the ground before bothering to see what all the fuss was about.

Still retaining a baby face with all of its fat, Buddy wiped the back of his hand across a scraggly mustache that could have passed for a smudge of dirt. Clyde ran up to his side, his mouth drawn into a sneer as his eyes darted back and forth between us.

"This here's what the feds are hiring these days, Buddy. Pretty funny, ain't it?" Clyde laughed in a series of hiccups, his fingers twitching nervously in the air.

Buddy pulled a navy handkerchief from his back pocket and wiped the sweat from his face. "Ain't it time for you to be heading out, Clyde?"

Watching him grind the heel of his shoe into an anthill, I half expected Bolles to refuse to go. Instead he hacked up a thick wad of phlegm, spitting it out on the ground before heading to his car. He revved up the engine and tore away in his Escort, a trail of gravel spewing behind him.

Buddy bunched up his soiled handkerchief and shoved it back in his pocket as he gave me a grin.

"Don't mind that peckerwood none. He ain't all bad. But everybody knows these state agents. They spend most of the time with their thumbs up their ass, bitching about their bad luck and hating everyone for it."

Buddy's bicep flexed as he lifted his rifle and a tattoo of Porky Pig sprang to life, complete with horns, a pitchfork and a shit-eating grin.

"You're the new agent, right? Rachel Porter, isn't it?" I nodded my head. "Hell, maybe you'll be an improvement over that last bozo they had. Poachers had him chasing his own tail. He wasn't much good except for a laugh. So, what can I do for ya, sugar?"

"I just wanted to come by and introduce myself. I was hoping you might show me around your operation."

"Sure enough, darlin'. Come on inside and we'll grab us a couple a beers."

The inside of Budwell's bunker was kept cool by a large fan whirling above. Gator skulls held down the piles of papers scattered on top of a wooden desk and along the Formica countertop that divided the room in two. A cot with its sheets askew sat in the corner of the room. Next to it was a small black-and-white TV, the volume just high enough to hear a woman on *Love Connection* describe her latest romantic disaster. From somewhere in the room, a clock ticked loudly, passing the time.

"I hear tell you're ticketing the hell outta those ol' boys in the marsh. Lord knows Delbart's keeping busy, what with hauling ass back and forth to court and all." Buddy screwed the caps off two bottles of beer and handed me one. "Don't you worry none, sugar. I won't go telling your boss on you for drinking on the job." He winked slyly as his lips engulfed the neck of the bottle.

"How's business these days?"

"Shit! Ol' Charlie must have already told you how I was an outlaw, so I ain't gonna bullshit you none. Poaching was mighty good to me in the ol' days, but the legal business, it's even better if you can believe that."

Looking at his surroundings, it would have been hard to tell. Buddy caught my glance. "I like to keep a low profile around here, but I'm pulling in about a million and a half a year. Hey, I even got movie stars and rockers calling me to send 'em some gator heads. Why, Clint Eastwood's got one of mine hanging in that restaurant of his."

Buddy ambled over to a heavy vault door, grunting as he tugged it open to reveal a huge freezer room. Large wooden barrels stood stacked from floor to ceiling, filled with piles of salted gator skins, the excess lying in a heap on the floor. Buddy surveyed the scene with pride.

"Yeah, I get calls from rock stars, movie stars. Even that Madonna. They all want gator heads and skulls to put in their houses. It's hot stuff out in Hollywood these days. Makin' me a rich man."

Buddy sorted through a mound of skins piled like a bunch of old clothes for Goodwill. "You see this here? It's all going over to the Japs. I take yen, I take lire, I take deutsche marks. If it's any kinda money, I take it. It's all the same to me."

Buddy slapped his stomach in satisfaction, jiggling a layer of fat as we walked back out. Throwing some wrinkled tee shirts off a crate and onto the floor, he motioned for me to sit while he plunked himself down in an old easy chair.

"Between you and me, outlawing was the best thing I ever did. Hell, most of us dealing legal these days got our start through poaching."

"It looks like you've got quite a business going for yourself." I decided to play a hunch. "I hear you're also keeping pretty busy working on Hillard's campaign these days."

Buddy grinned and gave me a wink. "That's right, I sure am. And mark my words—we're gonna make him mayor, too. N'Awlins is in bad need of someone like Hillard. Straighten that hellhole right out."

Slugging back the rest of his beer, Buddy's cheeks puffed out in large fleshy pouches.

"It must be hard finding the time to run a big business along with a campaign."

Buddy hefted his bulk out of the chair with a forward swinging motion. "When something's important, you find the time for it, know what I mean?" Opening an icebox that could have sold as an antique, he grabbed two more beers. "What's your interest in all this anyway? You wanna stuff some envelopes for us? Ain't ol' Charlie keeping you busy enough, running ragged after all those boys out shooting his ducks? 'Cause the way you look, I'd say they're winning."

Buddy handed me another beer and lowered himself back into the chair, landing with a heavy thud.

"If you're referring to my bruises, I was caught in that march in town the other day. Got whacked on the head for it, too."

Buddy let out a belly laugh. "That'll teach you to look both ways before you step out on the street next time. Better yet, don't hang around with fags."

I put the second bottle of beer down on the floor next to the first, which I hadn't touched. "Is Hillard still heading up the movement down here these days?"

Buddy's tongue flicked across his bottom lip. "Naw.

Hillard's outta that now. I suppose you also heard I used to be his second-in-command.''

Smiling, I shook my head. ''Yeah, at one time. But I heard you're running the whole show now.''

''Sugar, who'd go and tell you a thing like that?'' He winked as the neck of the bottle slid partway down his throat. ''You ain't Jewish, are ya?''

''What do you think? Do I look like I am?''

Buddy laughed as *Love Connection* turned into *Concentration*.

''Naw. I'd been able to sniff you out if you were.'' Emptying his second bottle of beer, Buddy picked up one of mine. ''Who knows, what with the two Germanys back together, maybe they'll learn to do it right this time. Except those damn Jews are just like cockroaches. Seems you can't kill 'em off, no matter how hard you try. Getting to be the same way with fags. That AIDS thing is gonna kill the rest of us, but the damn fags will still be out there marching for their damn rights. Now that's one problem we're gonna try to do something about.''

Buddy smiled as he stretched out and propped his feet on top of his desk, knocking a gator skull to the floor. ''So, tell me. Didya meet Hillard yet?''

Picking up the skull, I held it in my lap. ''I was at his house not long ago.''

''On a social visit like this one?''

''No, it had to do with an investigation into the murder of a dancer, Valerie Vaughn.''

Buddy twirled one of the empty beer bottles on his finger. ''So what were you doing there?''

''I was called in because of a gator found in her apartment.''

Buddy put his feet down and leaned in close. ''Bunch of wackos in that town. Listen here, sugar. Ain't nobody don't fool around if they get the chance, know what I mean? But Hillard had nothing to do with that two-bit piece of ass. She wouldn't have been worth his getting in trouble over.''

"You knew Valerie?"

"Yeah, I knew Valerie. Who didn't know Valerie? But you don't go and shit in your backyard, and N'Awlins is Hillard's backyard. Besides, that wife of his woulda killed him."

If Buddy could lie for Hillard, maybe he could fill in some blanks as well.

"Tell me about Gunter Schuess. Is he involved with the movement down here?"

Buddy snorted in disgust. "That arrogant asswipe? Naw. He's just pulling the wool over Hillard's eyes with that liaison bullshit. He's getting himself a free ride for a while. But let me fill you in on something, since you seem to be so interested. American Nazis don't need the damn Germans. The Krauts, they think they're better than us, you know what I mean? Shit, we could teach those bastards a thing or two would make their heads spin." Buddy leaned back as he let out a burp. "But I don't bother myself with none of that, cause I'm just a good-natured ol' swamp boy. I love everyone."

He grinned in a way that made my skin crawl. Taking a quick glance around the room once more, I spotted a sawed-off shotgun. It poked out from a pile of clothes where it stood against a wall. Buddy followed my gaze.

"You got a hankering for guns, sugar? That there ain't nothing. I got me a real beauty at home. A goddamn Remington with a silencer that I used to hunt gators with in the old days. I figured it would come in mighty handy in case I ever bumped into a game warden I hadn't bought off. It could shoot his ass to kingdom come and never make a sound."

Buddy watched me closely, then broke a smirk. Logic told me to get up and leave, but there were a few things I still needed answered.

"Clyde Bolles is a strange kind of guy. Since he seems to have taken such a dislike to me, is there anything I should know?"

Buddy reached down between the buttons of his shirt and slowly scratched his belly.

"Doncha know? Ol' Clyde used to be a poacher himself before he got a job with the state. Now I'm giving him tips on who's poaching gators these days. I don't need no scum cutting into my business. Now that I'm legitimate, that is." Buddy laughed as his hand heaved up and down on his stomach. "But Clyde, he's kind of a loner. Don't like no one messing around in what he considers his territory. At the moment, you're sitting in part of it."

I stood up to leave, placing the gator skull on top of the jumble of correspondence and bills. Catching a glimpse of a black matchbook that looked vaguely familiar, I leaned in closer as I bent down to pick up my beer bottles. On the way back up, I managed to get a better look. The matchbook was from Pasta Nostra.

Driving back along Route 1, I swerved around a walking stick that had been thrown in the middle of the road. The boy standing there earlier had disappeared from sight. The empty stretch of road ahead glistened under a hot white sun like a long string of black licorice. Passing by the 7-Eleven, I saw the girl in her tube top and short shorts sitting on a wooden step, lazily fanning herself with a wilted newspaper. I was more confused than ever after my visit with Buddy. With no clear-cut lines dividing the poachers from the politicians from the gay bashers, it was all one big roux being stirred in the hotpot of southern Louisiana.

The raucous cry of a great blue heron rose up from the bayou. I pulled my attention back to the road just in time to slam on my brakes as a pickup veered toward me. Swerving at the last second, it barreled down a narrow dirt road, coughing up hairballs of dust. The whirlwind it had thrown up settled back down to earth in time for me to catch sight of the license plate, with its letters HONK. It was Hunky Delroix, getting even with me for our tiff the other morning. On another day I might have let him go, not wanting to bother with a Bayou car chase, but this morning I needed to vent my frustration.

Peeling out after him, I dodged one pothole after another in a road leading to nowhere as Hunky churned up a layer of dirt that fell like fine volcanic ash. Squinting at the road ahead, I rounded a bend in time to see his vehicle fly up in the air and then crash back to earth with a heavy thud, the frame settling onto a tire as flat as a pancake. Pulling up a few yards behind, I watched as Hunky waddled around, trying to assess just how bad the damage was. The axle of his pickup rested on top of a sharp rock that was lodged in the middle of the road.

"That's what you get for cutting me off, Hunky. It wasn't a nice thing to do."

Glaring at me, he returned his attention to the tire that was beyond any hope of repair. "Dammit, Porter. I ain't having no luck these days."

I sympathized with him on that, feeling pretty much out of luck myself.

"There's a 7-Eleven not too far back. I'll make a call and have the nearest service tow you out."

Hunky kicked at a spider as it scurried out of his way. "I ain't got no money for that. I'll change the damn thing myself. I got another tire in the back was mended not too long ago."

Evidently, Hunky was used to flat tires. If he wanted to kill himself in the heat, it wasn't my place to argue with him. Getting out of my car, I joined him to examine the damage.

"Where were you heading off to so fast anyway, Hunky? You got something in the back here I should know about? Maybe another bag of ducks?"

Hunky's face flushed bright red as though he had just stepped out of a sauna. "I ain't got nothing back there, Porter. You got me the other day. Even took my gun, remember? Why don't you just leave me alone now? I got everything here under control."

Tiny beads of sweat rolled down his face and onto his

beard, where they clung like miniature Christmas balls. Sauntering over to the back of his pickup, I peered in. Hunky trailed after me.

"I've changed my mind. Maybe you oughta go call that tow truck for me, Porter. Okay? Will you do that?"

"Sure, Hunky. Just as soon as I see what's going on back here."

Stepping up on the rear fender, I swung myself over the tailgate and into the bed of the truck. I landed on a burlap sack stuffed with millet seed, used for baiting a lake and shooting geese. Pushing aside a fishing pole and a container of worms spoiling in the heat, I rummaged through a pile of old clothes grungy to the touch, stiff from dirt and sweat. Beneath those were some cardboard boxes flattened to cover the floor of the truck. Seeing nothing there, I realized Hunky's reaction to me had become like that of one of Pavlov's dogs—except instead of him getting hungry, I just made him sweat. Ready to give up and head back out, I took a final look around.

"Porter, I want you outta my pickup right now. Don't you need some kinda warrant or something to go searching back there?"

That did it. There had to be something, and I was going to find it, even if it meant tearing the truck apart piece by piece.

"I don't need any search warrant, Hunky. But if you've got a problem with this, feel free to have a chat with Hickok after you fix your tire."

Pulling up the cardboard, I discovered a long wooden pole with a sign nailed to it. I turned it over and read, "Kill All Fags. Get Rid of AIDS. Vote Hillard Williams." Looking at Hunky, I now knew one other person who had been at the march that day.

"Nice sign you got here, Hunky. I was hit over the head with something that looked an awful lot like this. In fact, I had to go to the hospital because of it."

Hunky cleared his throat, shifting his weight from one foot to the other. "I got a constitutional right to express myself, same as everybody else."

"You're absolutely right, Hunky—you do. But it stops at bashing people over the head to make your point. Assault and battery of a federal agent is an offense punishable with jail."

"I don't know what you're talking about, Porter."

"I think you do. In fact, I think you're the one who gave me those contusions. Yep, it's all coming back to me now. I think I'm going to have to press charges against you."

"You're a crazy woman, Porter! You know that? I didn't even see you at that march! You can't throw me in jail for something I didn't do!"

"It's your word against mine, Hunky and I think the police just might believe me before they do you."

He stood with his head hanging down, his hands stuffed deep in his pockets, muttering to himself.

"What was that, Hunky?"

"What do you want this time, Porter?"

Hunky was the only key I had.

"I want to know who was responsible for planning the riot, and where you hold your meetings."

Hunky stamped his feet, pawing at the ground. "Are you outta your mind? I can't tell you that stuff!" Letting loose, he kicked the flat tire. "Besides, I don't know."

"Let me make this easier for you, Hunky. You're aware that I caught Trenton, aren't you? Well, he wants to know awfully bad who it was that gave him up. Since he's willing to work with me, I feel kind of obliged to tell him."

Hunky's complexion went from red to ash grey in a matter of seconds. When he finally spoke, his voice came out in a rasp.

"You can't tell him. You promised me! I'll be a dead man!"

"You're right. And I'd feel really bad about that Hunky, so I'll tell you what. I'm going to make you a deal. You tell me what I want to know, and I won't bring charges against you. I also won't tell Trenton who it was that turned him in. Is it a deal?"

Hunky's brow furrowed in a mass of deep wrinkles as he worked out every angle.

"If I tell you what you want, you can't use this Trenton stuff on me again the next time."

"Agreed."

Hunky doubled over as if he were fighting off gas pains. "Shit. I can't believe I gotta tell you this stuff."

Leaning against the sign, I showed no pity.

"Alright. It was Buddy organized the thing. He's just trying to help Hillard win the election, was all."

"Who else was involved besides Buddy? Was Hillard in on it?"

"He mighta known about it. I don't know. It wasn't like he was at the meeting or nothing."

"Who else was there?"

"Nobody you'd know, Porter."

I'd been a fool to think this was going to be easy. "Was a German there by the name of Gunter Schuess?"

"Yeah. He was there."

"What's his involvement? Is he one of the leaders?"

Hunky glared at me.

"No. He ain't no leader. Buddy's the leader. Schuess wants to be the leader. But he ain't our leader."

This was obviously a sore point. I decided to poke around and open it up. "I don't think he should be the leader either. After all, this is America, so why should a German think he has the right to come in and take over an American group?"

Hunky warmed to the topic. "That's what I say. You know, this Kraut comes here telling us all about how powerful his group is over in Germany, and how they're getting the upper hand. Well then, how come he suddenly has to leave and come over here? Huh? We don't need the kinda trouble that he got in over there."

The best thing about Hunky was that once he got worked up and rolling, he generally had a hard time stopping himself. "What kind of trouble did he get into back there? Did the members of his group kick him out?"

"Shit, Porter. The police bombed their headquarters. So Schuess is laying low over here for a while. But all the Kraut cares about is our money. Says it's all one big brotherhood, and how we should be helping them out. I say bullshit. I don't see no one helping us out any over here."

The information matched what I'd read in Valerie's clipping. "And how are you supposed to get all this money for him and his group?"

Hunky's eyes glazed over, aware that he'd given away more than he should have. "I don't know, Porter. I don't go to them meetings much anymore. I'm too busy trying to keep food on my table, thanks to you."

"Where's your meeting place, Hunky?"

His eyes headed up the road, and for a moment I had the uneasy feeling we weren't totally alone. "I can't tell you that. It changes all the time. We don't stick to one spot."

"We have a deal. You don't give me this information, and the deal is off. It's your decision, but I know for a fact that Trenton is home today."

"Jesus Christ, Porter! No wonder you're still single. You don't know when to stop twisting a man's balls."

"I guess it's just one of those things my mother forgot to teach me. Make up your mind now, Hunky. I haven't got all day."

"Alright. I can tell you one place. As I said, I don't go much to the meetings no more." Pulling at his pants, Hunky leaned against the truck as he looked around. "Buddy's got a place, a hunting camp they use for meetings. It's right outside Morgan City on Bayou Maringouin. And don't ask me how to get there, 'cause I don't know. You gotta have a boat, and you gotta know the swamp. That's all I can tell you."

"Thanks, Hunky." I climbed down from the pickup and walked toward my own wreck of a car. I already knew the man who could take me to Bayou Maringouin when the time was right.

"And I'm not the one who hit you neither, Porter!"

"I know that, Hunky."

As I turned my car around, I saw Hunky kick his flat tire hard, as though he was wishing it were me.

Thirteen

Stopping by the Central Grocery long enough to dash in and grab a muffuletta sandwich for lunch, I made it home just after noon. The mail had already arrived and my mailbox slot was jammed wide open, a thick manila envelope having been rammed tightly inside. Cursing the U.S. Postal Service under my breath, I struggled to get the envelope out. The one time I'd managed to get hold of the mailman, I'd asked if he could deliver my mail so that it didn't look as if it had been shipped in from Beirut. I'd paid dearly for that. Since then, everything I received appeared to have been put through a wringer.

Eating my sandwich straight out of its wrapper, I tore open the envelope to find a videotape. It had been packed without any note as to what it was. For a moment, I wondered if the mailman had been playing musical mailboxes again, purposely stuffing Terri's mail in my slot. Not owning a VCR myself, I knew no one who would have sent it to me. Postmarked from New Orleans and marked to my attention, no return address had been given, leaving me without any kind of a clue. I grabbed the keys to Terri's apartment and headed downstairs.

Rocky mewed and launched into commando mode as I let myself in, attacking me from behind to land squarely on my back. Clinging tightly as I tried to push him off, he raked into my skin with his claws. It was only when I finally gave up that he loosened his grip and climbed onto my shoulder. Rubbing his head against my cheek, he purred loudly into my ear—like most men once they've gotten their own way.

Walking into Terri's apartment was always like entering a museum of the exotic and strange. The hallway was cluttered with charcoal portraits of dead movie stars, and a hand-painted border ran across the top of each wall. Displaying a slight variation on the Kama Sutra, all the figures were male in a variety of acrobatic positions. In the living room was a photographic history of Terri, from the obligatory pose as a baby lying naked on a lambskin rug, to his earliest days as a hoofer. Autographed photos featured him in wacky poses with Liza Minelli, Bernadette Peters, Cher, and his idol, Tommy Tune. Reviews of his one-man show on Bourbon Street were framed on the wall, as was a poster of himself dressed as Marlene Dietrich from her movie, *The Blue Angel*. Small sculptures of male nudes, always well endowed and minus the head, were artfully placed about the room.

I turned on the VCR, pushed the tape in, and settled back into the black leather couch. Rocky made himself at home, rolling up into a tight ball of fur on my lap. The first image appeared, looking like an old black-and-white B-movie. What I took to be a barren landscape slowly evolved into the back of a man's head, as bald and smooth as a ball bearing. Turning around to face the camera, Hillard Williams was caught in a most casual pose. Picking his nose, he appeared oblivious to his surroundings, which clearly weren't part of his home. Even more interesting, Hillard was totally nude and seemed unaware that he was being filmed as he sat down on a couch. The focus grew sharper and a table appeared in the background. Chained to one of the metal legs was Hook. After a moment, another figure wandered into frame, the stout torso of a man covered with dark, shaggy hair. Looking like some creature who had lagged behind in the evolutionary process, the figure walked around and sat down to join Hillard. Though the profile of the man's face was slightly blurred, the silhouette was oddly familiar. Pushing Rocky off my lap, I leaned forward hoping to get a better view. With the nub of a cigar clenched tightly between his teeth, a neck the thickness of a freshly cut sequoia, and a crew cut that would have done a marine proud, Captain Connie Kroll turned toward the camera and froze as though he were posing for a mug shot.

I pressed freeze frame and stared at the two upstanding pillars of the New Orleans community, already able to guess what was about to take place. As I turned the tape back on, a mass of dark, wavy hair filled the lens. A jolt of recognition ran through me as the body of Valerie Vaughn sashayed into view. It was startling to see her alive, having first viewed her as a mutilated and bloodless corpse. Dressed in high-heeled boots and black leather gloves with a thin gold chain at her waist, she planted herself in front of the two men with a whip curled loosely in her hand. She unfurled it with a snap of her wrist, and Hillard ejected off the couch like a spent bullet and onto his knees at her feet. Valerie excelled in the role of dominatrix, debasing the city's two most powerful men.

Like a bad porno film, Hillard and Kroll took turns performing one "lewd and lascivious act" after another. Illustrating the very thing Hillard was preaching against and that Kroll had taken an oath to obstruct, the tape was pure dynamite, capable of blowing both men's careers to smithereens. At one point, Valerie turned her back on her two companions to wink at the camera and, for a moment, I felt sure that wink had been meant for me. A chill ran through me as if Valerie had lunged out of her grave and reached in to twist at my soul.

Rewinding the tape to her entrance, I watched the performance again, slowing the action as she turned to the camera so that we stared at each other once more, conspirators in her secret. The perfect tool for blackmail, the tape could have been how she ended up owning the diamond necklace. It might also have been the cause of her death. It was obviously one of the reasons why Connie Kroll had closed off a murder investigation to all but a select few.

The tape ended, but Valerie's image remained seared in my mind. Whoever sent it must have been Valerie's cohort, the person who worked the camera. I thought back on everyone I had met so far, trying to figure out who it could be. I ended up drawing a blank. The tape raised more questions than it answered. If Valerie had used it as blackmail, it left me wondering if Hillard and Kroll had been her only two victims.

I also questioned why it had been sent to me at all. While it could very well be pointing in the direction of Valerie's killer, it might also have been meant to derail Hillard's election. Or perhaps Valerie's accomplice was now worried for his own life. Whoever mailed the tape knew more about me than I did about them.

As a child of the sixties, I'd cut my teeth on news reports of Vietnam, the secret war in Cambodia, and the Watergate tapes. I had grown up with the likes of Nixon, Haldeman, and Ehrlichman, so I expected people in power to be dishonest more often than not. I felt like a fool for being surprised by any kind of corruption, whether it took place in the ranks of the New Orleans Police Department or involved a girl from the bayou.

Going back upstairs, I walked into my apartment, where the red light on the answering machine beeped with steady precision. A message had been left by Santou. While I was pleased at hearing from him so soon after last night, I couldn't shake the feeling that something wasn't quite right. It was a feeling I'd had ever since discovering the rosary beads inside Vaughn's apartment. Terri put it down to my fear of yet another failed relationship, but it was more than that. The rosary was an exact match of the one Santou had given me the night I'd gone out with him. And while my heart didn't want to believe there was any connection, my gut instinct told me the coincidence was just too great. I wanted to trust Jake. But for the moment, I couldn't. Besides, for all I knew, Santou was also aware of the tape's existence and anxious to get his hands on it for his own reasons.

For the time being, I would confide in no one, and that

included Charlie Hickok. He'd frozen me out of the case; I saw no reason to run to him with every bit of information I found. I wanted to work on my own for now. If and when I needed his help, I'd be sure and let him know. It was the same arrangement he had laid down to me.

Playing the tape back, I listened to Santou's message a second time. The good news was that he had managed to track down Global Corporation. With its base in New York and a subsidiary company in Germany, the owner was listed as one Frank Sabino, with Hillard as chief executive officer. Buddy Budwell headed up the board of directors. The list of goods they dealt in ran the gamut from alligator skins to rip-offs of designer jeans to the buying and selling of diamonds.

The bad news was that Dolores Williams was in temporary residence at his precinct. Having been caught breaking into Valerie Vaughn's apartment early this morning, she had been slapped with a charge of first-degree murder.

Chaos reigned as usual as I made my way down the halls of the precinct. Detectives dressed up as pimps headed out to work, while pimps that had just been arrested tried to pass themselves off as detectives in an attempt to sneak out the door. Santou had left word to steer clear of him if I made the trip over. Up until now, Dolores's arrest had been kept quiet, with few outside the department—or even within—aware of the fact. If the press got whiff of the news, it would blow up into a front-page scandal.

While I wasn't concerned about the effect on Hillard's campaign, I didn't need to be spotted by Kroll. By now, I had an inkling of just how dangerous the man could be. Getting on his bad side was something I'd try my best to avoid. Santou had suggested we have as little contact inside the police department walls as possible, and that suited me fine.

I stopped to ask a clerk directions to the holding cells, and a shock of white hair in the distance caught my eye. Gunter Schuess quickly slipped into a room as the door was shut behind him. The office belonged to none other than Captain Connie Kroll. It seemed Gunter had become Hillard's liaison in more areas than just foreign affairs. He was probably here to clean up the mess—I felt relatively sure that Kroll would be more than happy to oblige. The fact that Dolores had been arrested in the first place threw me for a loop. Besides Hillard's apparent connection with Kroll, it was obvious that Dolores was no killer. The entire incident had the smell of a scam about it.

Getting back into Valerie Vaughn's apartment had been easier than trying to work my way in to see Dolores. I found myself up against a sergeant who was hot and bored, and liked making me squirm. Thirty pounds overweight, he was the Southern version of Arnold Schwartzenegger gone to seed. In a fight against reality, he had pushed himself into clothes that were far too small. The buttons on his shirt pulled one way, while the buttonholes fought to go the other. The waistband on his pants was undone and folded over a belt that was barely holding on at the last notch. The sergeant sat at a desk facing the doorway and stared blankly at an empty crossword puzzle, his jaw chomping slowly up and down on a wad of bubble gum.

"I'm here to see Dolores Williams."

"No can do, sugar."

I pulled out my shield, hoping it might carry some weight. "I'm a federal agent with the Fish and Wildlife Service. This involves a case I'm investigating."

"Don't matter none to me, darlin'."

"Would it be possible to at least tell Mrs. Williams I'm here?"

"Can't do that for ya, honey." Chewing on his pencil, the sergeant turned his attention back to the puzzle.

But I wasn't willing to be that easily dismissed. I moved to the side of his desk and glanced down at the paper in front of him. The puzzle in the Sunday *New York Times* had been one of the things that had kept my mind functioning during my three-month stint of depression, where I had subsisted on eating Crackerjacks and sobbing at the zoo. Compared to that, this one was a breeze. Without thinking, I jumped in to help.

"If you get the answer for six down, you'll be able to solve four and eight across. It'll also give you a big clue for twelve down."

It was enough to get the sergeant's attention. It also came close to getting me blown out of the room as his macho pride shifted into overdrive.

"No shit, darlin'. What are you—the puzzle queen?"

Backtracking, I made the usual female genuflections, hoping to work my way into his good graces. "No. It's just that I've seen this puzzle before. Not that I was able to figure it out myself. But I did see the answers for it."

His teeth chewed up along the body of the pencil until he reached the blackened stub of the eraser. Biting it off, he rolled the eraser around on his tongue before spitting it out.

"So, you got a good memory, huh?"

I moved behind him to get a better view. White horizontal lines marked the back of his neck like a road map where folds of fat overlapped, untouched by the sun.

"Only because I worked so long on this puzzle, and just couldn't get any of it right."

"But you remember some of the answers?"

"I remember six down."

"Give it to me."

I gave him the word, and then another and another, until he finally came up with one of his own. He grinned and stretched as twelve down was filled in. Kicking out the chair across from him, he motioned for me to sit down.

"So, what's your interest in the lady back there?"

"I'm working on the case involving the alligator found at Vaughn's apartment. I haven't had a break on it yet, and my boss is on my back. If I could at least speak to Mrs. Williams, I'd be able to report back to him on it. It might help to get me off the hook for a while."

The sergeant picked at a pimple on his forehead. "That wouldn't be Charlie Hickok you have to report to now, would it?"

"The one and only. He's been making my life a living hell."

The sergeant's stomach rumbled, and I pulled out a Milky Way bar from my bag, laying it on the desk. He stared at it for a moment before picking it up. "That's some lousy bribe."

"I know. But it's all I've got. Unless you'd like a few more clues on that crossword puzzle."

Ripping open the wrapper, he took a bite as he tipped back his chair and glanced around. "Hickok, huh? There was a time I thought being a wildlife agent would be a pretty sweet deal. Then I met that man. Decided to become a cop, instead. I feel for ya on that one, darlin'."

Finishing off the candy bar, the sergeant got up from his chair and walked across the room, filling the doorway as he stretched, glancing up and down the hall. Sauntering back to the table, he put his full concentration on the crossword puzzle in front of him. He spoke without looking up. "It's lunch hour, so you're safe. But five minutes. That's all I can give ya."

I was willing to take anything I could get. Thanking him, I made my way down the corridor to where Dolores sat in a cell all alone. She looked like hell. I couldn't be sure whether it was from drying out or mourning for Fifi, but she looked as if she had aged ten years overnight. The fine network of wrinkles around her eyes formed heavy pouches like so much extra baggage. Her mascara ran in black muddy rivulets, settling in polluted reservoirs on either side of her nose. Her girlish flip was gone, replaced by coarse, peroxided hair that had been pulled back sharply from her face. Looking old and haggard, she quietly sobbed as she twisted the shreds of what had been a tissue in her hands. No more the former glamour girl working hard to retain her youth, she was a shriveled old woman behind bars. She cried out upon seeing me, her mouth working back and forth like a mute trying to speak. Grabbing the bars in front of her, she shoved Fifi's collar toward me.

"They murdered my Fifi!"

I held on to her hand. "What happened this morning, Dolores?"

"They poisoned her and left her to die a horrible death." More tears filled her eyes as her nose began to run. Wadding shreds of the tissue together, she blew her nose hard, using up all the slivers she had pieced into a round ball. I searched through my purse and handed her a pile of blue tissues that must have been stashed at the bottom of my bag for years. Her hands shook as she ripped the tissues one by one into thin strips.

"You wouldn't have anything to drink in there, would you? I'd feel a lot better if I had a drink."

It was impossible not to feel sorry for her, and angry at whoever had brought this about. "We'll find who did this to Fifi. I promise. But you have to tell me why you went to Valerie Vaughn's apartment this morning and broke in."

Dolores's bark of a laugh burst out, and for a moment she was her old self again. "Is that what they're saying? I wonder which of the bastards cooked that one up."

"You didn't break in?"

"Hell, no. I had a call from someone telling me to show up right away if I wanted to get my jewelry back. So I went. When I got there, the door was already open. There was a crowbar on the floor, and the place looked as though a hurricane had hit it. I didn't even have a chance to rummage through anything before these idiots showed up and arrested me."

"Who was it that called you in the first place?"

"How the hell should I know?" Dolores's eyes welled up with tears again. "It doesn't matter anyway, now that my baby's dead. Christ, I need a drink."

She'd been set up, pure and simple. "Do you have a lawyer?"

The tissues I'd given her lay in shreds, a storm of tiny blue raindrops at her feet. "Hillard's getting me one."

Somehow, I didn't find that very consoling. No one in

their right mind could suspect this fragile old woman of having spent hours neatly slicing up Valerie Vaughn. She couldn't even massacre a tissue efficiently.

"I'm sure Captain Kroll will have you out of here and home in no time at all. Has he stopped by to see you yet?"

Dolores stared transfixed in wide-eyed fright, like an animal caught in a set of bright headlights. "I'm afraid I don't know who you're talking about." She began to cry once more, hiccuping on her sobs.

If their motive had been to scare her into silence, it had worked. "Dolores, did you ever own a diamond necklace at one time?" Looking at me blankly, she continued to hiccup. "With a large pear-shaped diamond pendant?"

Dots of red appeared in the middle of her cheeks. "Are you telling me Hillard bought that slut a diamond necklace when he wouldn't buy one for his own wife? I'll kill him when I get out of here!"

I had my answer. Whatever else Dolores knew, she wasn't about to reveal any more right now. Between Fifi's death and her incarceration, she had been sufficiently muzzled for the moment. But I had also learned that Kroll frightened even the likes of Dolores, who stood up to both Vinnie and Gunter on a regular basis. Assuring her that she'd probably be home by the end of the day, I promised to check in with her as soon as I could.

I walked out of the building into the thick, blistering air of midafternoon. Passing images shimmered in sultry heat waves in the street where a swanky black BMW sedan sat waiting, its engine purring quietly. Opening the door to slip in behind the wheel was the tall, slim figure of Gunter Schuess. With little to lose at this point, I ambled over as the car door closed and knocked on the glass.

Gunter's head turned slowly in my direction. He stared out through green-tinted sunglasses that lay streamlined against his face. Showing no sign of recognition, he looked away, his hand curling around the gearshift. I rapped harder this time and motioned for him to roll down the window. Taking his sunglasses off, he gazed at me as the glass magically lowered and a blast of cold air rushed out. I rested my elbows on the window jamb, enjoying the coolness as the hot air of the street flowed into his car.

"Hello, Gunter. Out campaigning for Hillard with our local police?"

He smiled slightly. "Agent Porter, I didn't recognize you at first. You do turn up in the strangest places."

"When I heard the news broadcast that Mrs. Williams had been arrested, I rushed right over."

Gunter's fingers tightened visibly around the steering wheel as his eyes widened in alarm.

"Relax, Gunter. It was just a bad joke. There wasn't any broadcast."

He allowed the sliver of a smile to return to his lips.

"An interesting sense of humor you have, Agent Porter. But, as I'm sure you must realize, this is all an unfortunate mistake. It is being taken care of even as we speak. So you see, I'm afraid you've wasted your time. Mrs. Williams has requested there be no visitors. Besides, I thought your jurisdiction was wildlife. Aren't you a bit out of your element?"

"I'm still investigating the death of that alligator we found in Vaughn's apartment. Anything that happens there affects my work. Speaking of work, I have a tip for you on a company with foreign interests that just might be willing to invest some of its business in New Orleans."

Gunter's mouth twitched in amusement as he reached over and turned up the air-conditioning a notch. "Really, Agent Porter. You surprise me. Who would ever guess you have such a wide range of interests? So tell me. What company might this be?"

"It's called Global Corporation. Ever hear of it?" I watched for a reaction, but Gunter didn't flinch.

"No. I haven't."

His eyes never left my face as the car window magically began to close, remaining open only a crack. Then, almost imperceptibly, they flickered to the right for the briefest moment. I turned to see what had caught his attention.

Connie Kroll was hurrying out of the precinct and heading toward the car. Bounding down the steps, Kroll suddenly caught sight of me and stopped dead. Pretending to search his pockets, he quickly turned and veered off in another direction. I followed the figure as it scurried across the street.

"Isn't that the captain over there?"

Gunter's eyes remained straight ahead as Kroll ducked into a nearby coffee shop. "I wouldn't know."

He shut the remaining inch of window, cutting off any further conversation. Shifting into gear, the BMW rolled out into traffic and disappeared into the afternoon crush of vehicles filling the downtown street.

Exhausted from the heat, I went home and lay down on my bed to take a short rest before picking up Terri. The wooden blades of the overhead fan clacked out a soft lullaby, and the air blew gently across my face. A whiff of salt water hung on the breeze as though the sea were outside my window, instead of the scent of mimosa and magnolias from the garden below. I knew I was dreaming as the sound of the fan turned into the putt-putt engine of a small boat guiding me through the swamp. Twilight hung heavy, and bands of phosphorescent insects flickered like Japanese lanterns flying through dead cypress trees. My hand brushed against cool, velvety green lichen and wisps of Spanish moss caressed my face. A bullfrog balancing on a lily pad added its deep bass to a choir of cicadas that had burst into song. Twilight faded into night. A lone white egret slowly flew off, its long legs trailing behind like slivers of silver ribbon. I found myself carried down a finger of still, black water as all sound began to fade. Only the beat of my heart grew louder, turning into the roar of thunder that shook sleeping birds from their nests in the trees. Long fingers of lightning cracked open the sky like a broken egg, and tiny birds rained down on my head. A final peal cleared the storm away. No longer in the boat, I found myself standing on a small spit of land. I waited, alone and entombed in the dark. A small beam of light drew near, like a firefly that had lost its way. Shimmering in a kaleidoscope of color, Valerie Vaughn was revealed in all her sliced glory, her hundreds of gashes a bright carnival of lights. Gliding toward me, her eyes locked onto mine, and each light turned into a brilliant diamond. She reached out, but was suddenly drawn down into a quicksand of swamp. Soon, only her hair lay splayed on the surface, around it a bloody halo of water. I stood perfectly still, my heart reverberating among the cypress and moss, its sound echoed up by cicada and bullfrogs, fireflies flashing on and off to its beat. I closed my eyes, the rhythm of my heart roaring through my body as I felt Valerie Vaughn clamp her hand around my ankle with the strength of a heavy chain. Wrapping herself around me, her body lifted out of the water and she whispered in my ear, drawing me close, until I was pulled off that small spit of land. Cold swamp water covered my legs, my waist, swirling up over my chest and rushing into my lungs as I clawed to reach the surface. But Valerie held me down, draping herself on top of me so that I sank beneath a weight of diamonds, as a muffled laugh roared in my ear.

Bolting up in bed, I screamed as my heart beat fiercely against my chest, my breath burning in my lungs. The pungent aroma of the swamp lingered on the air, and a low clap of thunder pealed off in the distance. Purple clouds of twilight gathered outside the French doors of my bedroom as I rubbed my eyes, trying to brush away the remaining nightmare. But Valerie's face stayed seared in my mind as I continued to feel the weight of her hand.

Fourteen

I peered into the hospital room to see Terri sitting up in bed. His head, which had been shaved, was now carefully wrapped in a stylish turban of bandages. But the face below looked as if it had been reassembled by a team of auto-body mechanics after a weekend of hard partying. His nose was flattened and veered off to the right, while a collage of colors formed a work of modern art on every inch of available skin. His room was filled to bursting with bouquets of flowers in oversize vases which competed for space. Yellow and pink roses vied with the cloying scent of narcissus, orchids, and magnolia blossoms, to overcome the generic odor of antiseptic out in the hall.

Terri's roommate was an elderly man from Jefferson Parish who was appalled at having to share his room with a drag queen. Terri paid the old man little mind, plying his family with boxes of pralines along with complimentary tickets to his club act, which they promised to attend. A mane of ostrich feathers gently framed Terri's face, to which a layer of makeup had been artfully applied to hide the swelling as best it could. His body was swathed in a pink chiffon robe the color of cotton candy. Slippers topped with pompoms of fake pink fur peeked from beneath his bed like two well-trained French poodles, while an assortment of fashion magazines lay precariously stacked on a table. A pornographic array of get-well cards was tacked to the wall behind his bed, and a collection of vitamins and herbs cluttered his nightstand, forcing the phone onto the floor, where it rang madly. Busy pushing away the thermometer that Dr. Kushner was attempting to put in his mouth, Terri barely seemed to notice the ringing.

"I'm very discriminating about what I allow in my mouth, and this is not on the list." Spotting me at the door, Terri slid off the bed and into his slippers to throw his arms around my neck. "Thank God! I'd given up all hope of ever being rescued from this place."

Kushner didn't bother to ask how I felt. Instead she examined the bump on the back of my head, which seemed to have grown in the past few days.

"Congratulations, Porter. I think you're actually worse than when you were originally here. I'm glad to see you've been following my instructions so well. No more midnight romps with Sam for a while, or you're grounded for a month."

"Would you believe I had the best of intentions when I left?"

"No."

She was right. I had only myself to blame for the headaches which had plagued me for the last several days, something I didn't dare mention.

Terri pulled out a canvas bag from Gold's Gym, already jam-packed with his toiletries, and began to change into a pair of loose pants and a flowing shirt. "Who's Sam? I'm still back with your knight errant with the broken-down LeSabre. See what happens, Doc? A few days away and the girl's running wild."

Kushner wrote out a few prescriptions, handing them to me. "Two are for Terri and one is for you. It's an antibiotic. Do yourself a favor and have it filled, or you'll find yourself eating bad hospital food and watching old movies in a room just like this. I'm serious, Rachel. If you don't take care of that gash in your head, an infection is going to set in. It's up to you."

I nodded my head in agreement, anxious to be on my way before she changed her mind and made me stay.

"Just so you know, I'd keep on top of Sam if you ever want that autopsy done. He has a tendency to let things slide."

I thanked her and made a mental note to check in with Sam sometime in the next day or two.

Covering his turban with a panama hat, Terri was prepared to leave. Having bribed an orderly ahead of time, his roomful of flowers was loaded onto a gurney and squeezed into my car. I felt as if I were driving a bad excuse for a hearse.

"Thank God I'm finally out of there. I thought Bubba in the bed next to me was going to hire a hit man at any moment. I had to bribe his family with candy just to stay alive."

It was good to have Terri back. I'd already picked up some Chinese takeout, which I planned to microwave as soon as we got home.

"By the way, I did some homework for you when I was whiling away the hours between the sheets. Kushner's not the only one with friends in important places. We're making a stop in Bourbon Street before we settle in for the night. There's someone I want you to meet."

I did my best to persuade Terri otherwise, but he wouldn't be budged. "Just don't blame me if you have a relapse, Ter. I'll let Kushner know I had nothing to do with it. You're completely uncontrollable."

Terri placed a hand gently against my cheek. "Look who's talking. You look nearly as bad as I do, and from what I hear you were knocking back a fair amount of cognac the other night. This isn't a social romp I'm taking you on, Rach. This has to do with Valerie. I've been asking around, and I found someone who might be able to help."

The mention of Valerie's name brought back the heaviness that had been hanging over me ever since I'd woken up from my nightmare. I knew tonight would be one of those evenings to be filled with late-night TV, a couple of stiff drinks, a hot bath, and the latest spy novel. Anything but facing my own dreams again.

I drove down the length of Bourbon Street, giving Terri a full view of the damage that had been done. He was quick to notice that the buildings avoiding the full force of destruction—the strip clubs, massage parlors, porn theatres, and sex shows—were at least partially owned by straight men. Passing by the Boy Toy, Terri flinched as he saw the slogan of hate that had been spray painted across his poster.

I stopped in front of the Kit Kat Club, which was already back up and running as if a riot had never taken place. In a city where the homicide rate makes Miami look good, the Kit Kat had come up with a gimmick to draw in new business. A sign in the window announced a "Murder Pool." Open to customers only, the pool was taking bets on what day the city's five hundredth murder of the year would take place.

Terri led the way through the darkened front room. A show was already in progress as a stripper clad in a sequined G-string twirled around a pole, an overhead disco light flashing a procession of dreary colors onto her body. Bored with her own act, she mechanically went through the paces.

We worked our way backstage, where Terri knocked on a thin plywood door. Decorated with the tattered silhouette of a female with cat ears and a long curly tail, the word "STAR" was written underneath in tarnished gold letters. The woman who answered looked anorexic except for her chest, which was swollen out of all proportion. Terri introduced her as Kitty Kat, the star of the club. We followed her into a room that was a notch below a flophouse. Star billing hadn't done much for her sense of self-esteem. A blue Chinese happi coat was wrapped around her thin body, with enough grease stains to make it look like a used dinner napkin. Her legs were the width of a small bird's, bearing an array of bruises, while her arms could have passed as twigs. Blue veins stuck out against translucent white skin lined with a row of track marks, their tiny red punctures looking like a gallery of bloodshot eyes. Short blond hair sprouted from a base of dark roots, standing straight up on end from her head in punk fashion, while large brown eyes rimmed in heavy black liner drummed up images of haunted waifs on black velvet. Though she might have been pretty at one time, heavy pancake now coated her face in an attempt to hide a network of lines caused by more than just age and hard living. But makeup couldn't cover one angry red welt which stood out on her skin, running from the corner of her drooping left eye to her chin. As she nervously puffed on a cigarette, her eyes searched each corner of the room.

"You look like shit, Terri. Maybe we should work up an act together. I'm ready for some new material." Kitty's laugh came out as a cough, and she reached for a tissue to spit in. My eyes were locked onto her scar, which moved as if it had a life of its own. Zeroing in on my fascination, she pounced.

"You like the look—what's your name—Rachel? Got it free of charge. It's even helped my act. See, now I wear a full headmask when I get up to dance." She reached over to a makeup counter filled with tins of face powders, cream rouge, and Max Stein pancake. Grabbing a black leather hood with slits for the eyes and an opening for her mouth, she pulled it over her head. The effect was that of an executioner.

"Looks hot, huh? It's great. Everyone gets to see my body, but they never see my face. Makes the guys go wild. You gotta catch my act later and tell me what you think." Her robe fell open as she twisted around in search of a cigarette, revealing the intricate lacework of cuts on her abdomen. Her exposed breasts stood erect like two hard rocks. Kitty didn't bother to close her robe, but stroked her hand across her stomach as she put her feet up on the counter, amid the chaos of cans. "I put makeup on all my little beauty marks here, and nobody even notices. It was thoughtful that he didn't scar up my tits, though. I thanked him for that."

Kitty laughed and nudged Terri in his crotch with her foot. "Look at him. He's jealous. I've already told him a dozen times where he can go and get the exact same boobs I've got."

Terri took hold of her foot as he glanced at her choice of makeup, shaking his head in dismay. "Don't be such a bitch, Kitty. God knows your skin should be in even worse condition than it already is, with all the shit you put on it. Why don't you just tell Rachel what happened?"

Looking at Kitty, I knew I was just beginning to learn about the world Valerie had inhabited every day.

"So, you're trying to find out what happened to Val, huh? Don't waste your time. Nobody cares." Kitty reached for a bottle of Jack Daniel's and poured some out into three paper cups.

I took a sip as I studied the woman across from me. Kitty made me nervous. I thought of myself as street smart, until I bumped up against someone like her. It was only then that I realized just how little I knew of a whole segment of society that intrigued me as much as it frightened me.

"I care, or I wouldn't be wasting my time on it."

"You said it, hon. You're wasting your time. You have no idea what you're up against, do you? What's that they say? You can't fight city hall?"

I wondered if this was what Valerie had been like. Except Kitty was a survivor. Valerie had died from her scars.

"Is that who I'm up against? City hall?"

Kitty coughed a smoker's hacking laugh as she filled both our cups again. "No names, hon. I still gotta stay alive in this town." She brought the cup to her lips and, for the first time, I noticed the slight tremor that ran through her hand.

"Some guy comes in here one night about a year ago and catches my act. This is when I've still got a face I can show onstage. Well, I must have been grinding something the right way, because the next thing I know, I get a note delivered back in my dressing room, asking if we can get together and make it a night. A hundred bucks is tucked in with it, and I have a feeling there's more where that came from. So, sure. I mean, why not? Right?"

Kitty lit a fresh cigarette with the remains of her old one.

She stubbed the butt out, smashing it into the ashtray until it had been pulverized. Shivering, she closed her robe, tightening the sash around her.

"So, after the show we go back to my place. We do it, and he's no great shakes, but who cares. I mean, I'm not planning on finding Prince Charming at the Kit Kat Club. Anyway, he goes into the bathroom, and I decide to do a little search through his pockets. He's already told me he ain't done yet, and I figure he's gonna owe me some more by the time he's through. I want to see if he's good for it or if he's planning to stiff me. Save myself some time, ya know what I mean?" Her hand shook as she raised the paper cup to her lips. A trail of Jack Daniel's dribbled down her chin and onto the blue robe, adding to the assortment of stains.

"Well, I don't find any cash, but he's got some powder wrapped up in a packet that's just ready and waiting with my name on it. What the hell. I deserve a hit. I mean, the night is young, and I got this deadbeat in my bathroom taking a shower. I figure I'll just cut myself a couple of lines and figure out a way to get rid of the hot dog later. So, I'm just beginning to take a snort when the guy comes out, with the water running in the bathroom, like he's tricking me that he's in there washing up."

Kitty stared into space. The scar on her face twitched with a memory all its own. She motioned for me to pick up the bottle, and I poured some more Jack into both our cups.

"The guy looks at me not saying a word, not getting angry, and I figure everything's cool until he starts to smile. And then I know I'm in trouble. I mean, this guy doesn't smile like anybody I've ever seen. This prick makes my skin go cold. The next thing I know, he grabs me by the neck and tells me I need to learn some manners. That Americans are pigs with no manners. Well, the guy's got a fucking pair of handcuffs on him like he's a goddamn cop. He locks my hands together and chains me to one of the posts on the bed, pulling out what looks like a pocketknife. Except when he flicks it open, its a straight razor that I think he's gonna slice my neck with."

Kitty's cup fell to the floor, the Jack Daniels forming a pool at her foot as she flung her arms around her breasts, her body shaking like a rag doll out of control. Her tough facade was broken, tears streaming down her face.

"I almost bled to death. And when the bastard is done, he makes me apologize. I mean, he's got a hard-on. Watching me bleed to death is turning this asshole on."

Taking a few deep breaths, I stared into the golden liquid in my cup in the hope of finding some answers. But Jack Daniel's wasn't giving away any secrets tonight. I looked at the girl in front of me and wondered what kept her alive.

"Kitty, this guy wasn't American?"

She shook her head no, pulling at the skin under her eyes with the back of her hand. "I think the bastard was German. A white-haired freak with eyes that could turn you to ice." Spitting into a tissue, she dabbed at her skin in the mirror. "But I gotta hand it to him. My act is better than ever now. This mask thing really gets them going, you know. And I don't even have to worry about my makeup."

There had to be more to the story. The man she was describing could only be Gunter, and I wasn't ready to believe he'd just walk away, leaving one of his victims alive to spill the news of his handiwork all around town.

"What happened after that? Do you have someone who protects you?" She would have known better than to go to the police. With their busy schedule of dealing with drug busts, murders, and general crime on the street, one sliced-up hooker would have been considered nothing more than a nuisance to be brushed aside as extra paperwork.

Kitty coughed out a harsh laugh. "Yeah. I got a big protector. The guy who owns the club. He did nothing except buy me a new mattress. Told me to forget the whole thing—that he'd make sure the guy didn't bother me again. Said he'd keep me working at the club as long as I covered my face and didn't fuck up my tits."

"Who owns this place? I'd like to talk to him."

Kitty inhaled sharply on her cigarette as she removed the top of a cold-cream container, and slathered a handful onto her face. "Uh-uh. No way. This is as far as I go. I don't want no repeat visit from that freak. I seen what happened to Val, and I know when to keep my mouth shut. You got your story, and that was only to pay back a favor I owed Terri."

"Don't you want to get this guy off the street? He could come back for you anytime."

"That's exactly why I'm not saying another word. I hate what he did, but at least I'm alive. I'm gonna have to get ready for my show now, so you'd better leave." Kitty took off her robe and began to massage baby oil on her breasts.

Terri adjusted the panama hat on top of his turban. "Come on, Rachel. Let's go. Thanks for your time, Kitty. I'll let you know about that offer for an act."

"Fuck you, Terri. You'd drag my business down."

Terri got up and directed me out the door. It was then that I thought of the tape I'd seen that afternoon.

"Just one more question, Kitty. There were two men who used to solicit Valerie on a regular basis. I'm wondering if you might know either one of them."

"Who're the johns?"

"Connie Kroll and Hillard Williams."

Kitty stared at me for a moment before shutting the door in my face.

I showed the tape of Valerie Vaughn to Terri that night as I dished out two platefuls of Chinese food from his favorite takeout. Rocky got a separate bowl filled with his own order of chicken chow mein. By the time the tape was finished, Terri had lost his appetite.

"What are you, crazy? You're in over your head on this, Rach. Look at who you've got involved here. Forget the alligator. Forget Hillard Williams! Jesus, the entire N.O.P.D. is probably helping to cover this thing up. Kitty's right: drop it. It's not worth it. Besides, I don't need to have my building torched."

He was probably right, but I knew that didn't make any difference. I had no intention of letting this case go. Not now. Not at this point.

"Who owns the Kit Kat Club, Terri? If you don't tell me, I'll find out anyway, so do me a favor and save me some time."

Biting into an egg roll, he pulled out a shrimp and bent over to feed it to Rocky. His fingers dangled as the cat licked the grease from his hand. "From what you say, it's a guy you've already met."

My mind raced through the mental index cards of people I'd racked up on this case so far. None fit the part.

"Does Buddy Budwell strike a chord? Fat, sweats a lot, considers himself a pedigree Nazi? He owns the business. In fact, he owns a couple of clubs on the strip. From what I hear, that's how Val got her job at the Doll House."

I had a hard time imagining Buddy as the brains behind a chain of strip joints. In fact, it was hard for me to picture him anywhere outside of a swamp, surrounded by dead gators.

"Think about it, Rach. It's a great way to launder money, along with his other businesses. Hell, the guy's into everything. I hear he's even got a fish packing house in Morgan City, and part ownership in a restaurant out that way."

"Why would he need to launder money?"

"Jesus, Rach. He works in cash businesses. He probably juggles the money around from one place to the other. Word on the street is that the mob has its fingers in each one, as well."

Terri surprised me. I hadn't thought he paid attention to such things. "When did you start learning so much about Buddy Budwell?"

He grinned until the swelling in his face took on the proportions of a painted Buddha. "I had some free time to make a couple of calls the past few days. A lot of information floats around the strip if you know the right people to ask."

It was no easy task picturing Terri as a supersleuth, lying on the couch dressed in his favorite fuchsia pajamas covered with naked boys. I picked at my egg foo yung.

"If I could only tie Valerie in with Hillard rock solid somehow. Why couldn't he at least have paid her rent?"

Terri put his plate on the floor for Rocky to finish. "He probably did. But there's no way you're going to be able to prove that. Val always paid in cash."

I heard my fork clatter against my plate without having felt it fall from my fingers. "How do you know that?"

Terri stared at me through swollen lids. "Well, for one thing, I rented an apartment from her landlady, Flo Henken, when I first moved here. The old bitch wouldn't accept anything but cash. She said a check was no better than toilet paper, and she had plenty of that. Secondly, Val would never open a checking account. She couldn't have balanced a checkbook. Besides, she got paid in cash, and that's how she covered her bills." Terri took a close look at me as I put my plate on the floor next to his. "Why? What's the problem?"

"I questioned Santou about the same thing. He told me that Valerie always paid her rent on the first of the month by check to her landlord."

Terri reached over and picked at one of the containers of food. "This isn't the Kennedy conspiracy here, Rach. I think you're beginning to go a bit 'round the bend. Could be Henken sold the building a few years ago. Maybe she kicked off. Who knows?"

I didn't understand why Terri was defending him. "But Santou told me she paid by check."

Terri popped a shrimp in my mouth. "So what? What am I, God? Maybe she did open a checking account. Don't take my word for it. Check it out for yourself. But I think you're jumping to dangerous conclusions, Rach. You're looking for any excuse not to let yourself get involved with this guy. If you don't want to get laid, then don't. But you're taking it a little far."

I smiled at Terri, trying to let go of the edginess that had hold of me. "You're pretty good at this. While you were at it, you didn't happen to find out who organized the head bashing that took place during the march, did you?"

"I'm still working on that, but you'll be the first to know."

Terri removed the pink paper umbrella from the glass I handed him. He placed it next to the blue one already floating in a fresh bouquet of roses, sent to him only an hour ago from a prospective lover.

"Do me a favor and let this one go, Rach. You're making me worry, and I'm going to have to pay for enough plastic surgery as it is. I don't want to think of you ending up like Kitty. Or even worse, like Valerie there."

We had rewound the tape to Valerie's big entrance, and watched again as she turned to face the camera and winked. She seemed more alive now than she had just a few days ago as she looked at me once more, overcoming time, space, and death to reach out through the camera and grab onto my soul.

Fifteen

Sleep didn't come easily that night. I stayed awake watching a battery of old comedy reruns, until the first ray of light hit the sky about five that morning. It was only then that I felt safe enough to finally close my eyes. Waking up wasn't any easier. I slept soundly through the buzz of the alarm clock, only to be jarred into consciousness by the persistent ring of the phone. Picking it up, I heard Santou's voice.

"*Chère*, how about we get together for some dinner tonight? Say someplace on neutral ground, away from the precinct and prying eyes."

A circus of moths flapped around in my head, the communal beating of their wings making the process of focusing in on the conversation a difficult one. I yawned, the muggy air of an already steamy morning rushing into my lungs, filling me with the stale fumes of cars that trundled by on the cobblestone pavement outside my window. The damp sheet clung to my back as if it were grafted onto my skin. I mulled over what Terri had said last night, and decided maybe he was right. Maybe I was making excuses out of fear of getting involved with Santou. Maybe it was time I got over that and started taking chances with my life again.

"Business or pleasure?"

Santou gave a low, throaty laugh. "How about we make it a fifty-fifty deal, sugar? That way we don't miss out on anything. Tell you what—I'll even give you the choice of where to eat. Just don't break the bank."

I already knew where I wanted to go, and the choice would cover both bases nicely. I checked in with Terri and Rocky, feeding them both some leftover chow mein, and then headed out of town. I drove past sugarcane fields quivering in front of my eyes like a mirage in the morning heat, past cypress trees standing half-dead in the brown, briny waters of the bayou. I raced toward Morgan City and Terrebonne Parish, to play out a hunch involving land records and deeds in the area.

As usual, my presence was greeted with less than the normal Cajun friendliness by any of the local officials. The clerk for the city hall was a woman who seemed as old as the building itself. Soft and round, Mrs. Jeanette Tercle was of a suspicious nature under the most normal of circumstances. Having a Northerner ask to go through the parish land records was deemed an unnecessary affront.

"What you want for to be snooping through our records over here, you? This don't have nothing to do with no business of wildlife. These be parish records. We don't be going into your office, wanting to snoop through your business, no."

It took fifteen minutes of gentle persuasion, along with pulling out my badge and threatening to file a complaint, before I was allowed to follow the waddling form of Mrs. Tercle into the record room where the deeded history of Terrebonne Parish was kept. A minor tug of war ensued in order to pull each folder from wizened fingers that clamped tightly around bulging files, refusing to let go. Every sheet I paused over was carefully noted with eagle eyes. When Mrs. Tercle wanted to take a bathroom break, I was expected to tag along rather than be left alone to rampage wildly through yellowed and disorganized sheaves of papers. But my persistence finally paid off. After hours of sorting through dusty, useless records, I found what I'd come for. I informed Mrs. Tercle that she needn't pull any more of her folders.

"What you find, you? I need to know so as I can make it official information."

"Nothing, Mrs. Tercle. I'm sorry to have taken up so much of your time."

Mrs. Tercle harrumphed in triumph as she shut off the window fan and closed the door behind us, entombing the folders within their rusted file drawers once more.

"I don't know what you expected to find, you. But I don't be having time for this kind of thing. You tell your boss and don't be bothering me with such nonsense again."

I drove back over the Huey Long Bridge and breezed down Interstate 90, as the information I had discovered sank in. It wasn't the local Mafia that Buddy was playing with. He was back in tight with the big boys. A co-owner was listed on Buddy's fish-packing business in Morgan City: none other than Global Corporation, alias Frank Sabino, alias New York mob. What I wanted to know was if Global Corporation was just receiving a piece of the action, or whether they were full-time players entrenched in the day-to-day running of the place for reasons all their own.

Playing a hunch, I had also tracked down the title papers on Pasta Nostra restaurant, just east of Morgan City in the town of Gibson. While the business was owned by Buddy, the building and the land it was on were rented from Global Corporation, giving Sabino a finger in that proverbial pie. I had a funny feeling I'd find the exact same information once I looked up the rest of Buddy's business dealings in New Orleans.

With little sleep and no breakfast, I pulled in to grab lunch at the first greasy spoon I could find. Abear's Cafe smelled of deep-fried grease, along with its specialities of coon stew and gator fingers. Its decor was an odd assortment of tables, with sticky, plastic-seated rickety chairs that didn't match. But the beer was ice-cold and the gumbo was hot and spicy. To top it off, Hunky Delroix was sitting at the next table with his back to me, crouched over a giant bowl of alligator stew. I picked up my beer and sat down across from him without waiting for an invitation. Glancing up, he dropped his spoon onto the table with a loud thud.

"Jesus Christ, Porter. Can't you let a man even enjoy his food in peace?"

"Relax, Hunky. This is a social call."

Hunky pulled out a handkerchief as red as his face and mopped his brow before plunging his spoon back into the stew.

"There ain't no such thing with you, Porter. You're just like your boss. If you ain't out arresting folks, you just ain't happy. Well, I'm plumb out of information for you these days."

"You've got it all wrong, Hunky. I wanted to pass on a tip to you for a change."

Hunky eyed me suspiciously as he tore a chunk of bread off the loaf in front of him. Scooping up some stew with it, he shoved the piece into his mouth. He washed it down with a slug of beer, wiping his chin with the back of his hand.

"Oh, yeah? What kinda tip you got for me? Maybe you wanna let me know a good place I can go to shoot me some ducks."

"Only in season, Hunky. No, I wanted to let you know about a place where I heard they're looking for some part-time help these days."

Hunky pulled a heaping plate of catfish in front of him. "You trying to find me a job, huh? Must be feeling a little guilty about always stealing food from me. Where is this place?"

Watching Hunky wolf down his meal, the last thing I felt guilty about was taking any food out of the man's mouth.

"It's a fish-packing factory just west of Morgan City, called Fin and Claw. I hear they're in need of a few extra hands."

Hunky finished off his beer and burped, signaling the waitress for another. "You kidding me, Porter? Where the hell do you get your information from? You don't know shit. That place is locked up tighter than a virgin. Hell, you gotta know the right people to get a job there."

"What are you talking about, Hunky? I'll put in a good word for you if you want. Maybe that'll help you on your job application."

Hunky sprayed a mouthful of beer across the table as he let out a loud belly laugh, leaning back in his chair. "That's real good, Porter. You're gonna get me a job with the mob. Wait till Hickok hears that one."

"You mean the mob controls that place? I thought Buddy Budwell owned it."

Hunky's face fell as he realized the information he'd just let slide by. "Damn you, Porter. Just do me a favor and stay away from me, unless you're gonna take me in."

Slapping down a few dollars, he grabbed his bottle of beer and pushed his way out the door. He had told me what I wanted to know. Sabino had to have more than a fondness for Louisiana gumbo and crawfish, to be investing so much of his business down here. He wasn't making a fortune in packing fish, and he could have run his own restaurant far easier up North. There was a bigger draw that was keeping him busy in the bayou.

Cattails fluttered along the banks of the bayou. I slowed my car to gaze at the water lilies that hung heavy with purple blossoms ready to burst, scattering their petals into the brackish water that lay still and stagnant under a hot white sun. A cottonmouth slept by the side of the road, too lazy to move, the seething blacktop warming its belly. Taking my time driving back to New Orleans, I sidestepped Slidell along the way. I hadn't checked in with Charlie in the past few days, and I didn't want to. I was too afraid of what would happen if he found out I'd stolen a ten-foot alligator being held as evidence in a case that might never be solved. Besides, he wasn't going out of his way to keep me informed on any progress he and Trenton were making. I'd been crazy to think the Dynamic Duo might ever become the Three Musketeers. I was more out of the loop than ever.

* * *

I spent more time than usual agonizing over my outfit for dinner that evening. It was one of the hottest nights I'd experienced here so far, and the thought of sweating through the next few hours was an unappealing one. At least, that's what I told myself as I put on a blue gauze dress that hung off the shoulder. I went downstairs to check in on Terri before heading out for the evening. Twirling me around, he approved of my choice.

"Congratulations, Rach. You just might get lucky tonight."

Digging through his jewelry box, he took out an antique locket on a thin gold chain and attached it around my neck.

"Accessories, darling. Never forget that word." Terri put his arm around me, and I laid my cheek against his shoulder as he kissed the top of my head. "You look so good, I almost wish I were straight. And that's saying a lot. So buck up and at least try to look happy."

I found myself brushing away a tear from the corner of my eye, unsure of how it got there or why. "I wish you were straight, too, Terri. I really love you, you know."

Another tear sprang up as Terri hugged me close. "I love you, too, Rach. God played a bad trick on us both. I should have been born a woman and you should have been the man. That way, we would have made the perfect couple." Terri reached for a tissue and dabbed at my eyes. "Better yet, I'll stay what I am and you could just have been a gay man." I laughed as Terri touched up my makeup for me. "There. All better. Now kiss mommy good night and try to be bad."

"I'll check in with you later."

Terri pulled Rocky onto the couch beside him as he turned on the first movie of a Tennessee Williams marathon.

"Let's hope not. Try to loosen up a little bit, Rach. Having fun isn't half-bad."

Santou let out an appreciative whistle when he came to pick me up, making me wish I had gone with my gut instinct and chosen something less revealing to wear. I've never felt very comfortable where compliments were concerned, and tonight was no exception. Terri always laughed when I told him such things, saying it just confirmed the fact that he should have been the one to be born a woman. I liked being one; my problem was that I just didn't know how to enjoy it.

"Where to, *chère?* And please, let's make it a place without a dart board tonight."

I had no problem with that. I was looking to play a different game. "If it's all right with you, I'd like to go for a drive. There's a restaurant I've been wanting to try over in Gibson. It's a place called Pasta Nostra."

Santou ran his finger down the long slope of his nose. "Are you sure you wouldn't rather just stay in town? You're looking so good, I'll even spring for Antoine's."

"I thought you wanted to stay out of the limelight, Santou. Remember, away from prying eyes?"

A hint of doubt began to eat at me again. I turned to face Santou, taking a good look at the man. Hooded eyes watched me intently under a mass of shiny, dark curls that clung to his forehead like wilted flowers. I was ready to call dinner off when, breaking into a grin, he leaned over and quickly kissed me.

"Alright, *chère*. If that's what you want, let's go for a ride."

The sun hung low in the sky, a burning red ball setting the earth on fire, the air heavy with humidity like thick soup on a slow boil. I could feel Santou's skin next to mine, even though we weren't touching. The silence in the car was as loud as the honking of horns at rush hour on Canal Street, as we drove down country roads. A black mushroom cloud hung over a chemical plant near a field heavy with green sugarcane. Lying on the side of the road, an old hound dog never bothered to lift its head as we sped by, raising a dense layer of red dust that settled back down on top of him. An ancient couple sat on the porch of their unpainted shack measuring time from their rocking chairs, escaping the heat which had collected inside their house all day. Screaming children in yards played hide-and-seek, using old, junked cars and the grey wooden boards of a dilapidated outhouse as places to conceal themselves. My mind was a million miles away as each scene passed. Santou spoke, startling me out of a daydream of secret videotapes and hooded masks hiding painful scars.

"Dolores Williams is out on bail and back home." He didn't take his eyes off the road, though no other traffic was in sight. "I thought you'd like to know."

There were a lot of things I wanted know, none of which I felt I was any closer to finding out.

"What's going on with this case, Santou? Who are the good guys and who are the bad?"

He kept driving, slowing down only to let an old, arthritic dog limp its way across the road.

"Are you still a good guy, Santou? Or were you ever?"

Santou turned off onto a dirt ribbon that wove through a grove of willow trees draped in shawls of moss. He drove until the main road was out of sight, leaving only a plume of dust to mark our trail. The LeSabre heaved onto the grass under a spreading live oak, where he parked the car, turning off the ignition. I had never felt more vulnerable than at that moment, sitting there in my thin cotton dress.

"You think I'm crooked, Rachel? Is that what you're saying?"

That was exactly what I was becoming afraid of. More than anything, I wanted him to convince me that it wasn't true. Taking a deep breath, I knew I had to confront him with a few of the things that had begun to eat away at my trust.

"I found a set of rosary beads inside Valerie Vaughn's apartment the other day, Jake. They're an exact match to the beads you gave me."

Santou sighed as he reached into his pocket, and my heart began to pound. One of the things I had found so intriguing about the man was that I was never quite sure what he was capable of. At this moment, it terrified me. I found myself wishing I had pants and sneakers on in case I needed to run. But looking around, I wondered, *run where?* I should have stuck my .357 in my bag, and felt like a fool for having left it at home.

"Did you give her those beads, Jake?" He looked at me without a word, his eyes guarded beneath hooded lids that began to strike me as more menacing than sensual. "Just how well did you know her?"

For some naive reason, I had always assumed they'd never met. Now I knew better. His eyes bore into me as what I feared most began to crystalize in my mind. "Were you sleeping with Valerie Vaughn?"

Santou leaned in toward me, but I backed away. "I thought you knew me better than that, Rachel. I didn't tell you about knowing Valerie, because I didn't think it was all that important for you to know."

The sun flared through the windshield as it clung to the rim of the sky in its slow descent beneath the horizon.

"Valerie showed up at the precinct about two weeks before she died. She came to see me with some lame excuse about building-code violations at the club where she worked. I told her she had the wrong department. The police couldn't help her with that. I knew it wasn't why she was there, though. It was obvious she had something else on her mind. We began to chat. She hinted around the edges about some kind of trouble, but she was too afraid to talk. Valerie was a Cajun, and we're a religious type of folk. So I gave her the rosary beads in my pocket. I hoped that would give her the courage she needed." Santou ran a hand through his hair, the silver strands looking like pieces of tinsel against the brown skin of his fingers. "There wasn't anything else I could do for her, Rachel. The next time I saw her, Valerie Vaughn was dead."

I knew he was right. If Valerie wasn't willing to talk, not much could have been done to prevent her death. But there was more that bothered me.

"Buddy Budwell bought Valerie Vaughn's apartment building two years ago. Why didn't you tell me he was her landlord?"

Santou didn't say anything as he pulled out a Tums.

"I did some snooping around in the Hall of Records in both Terrebonne Parish and New Orleans today. Buddy's chock-full of property and businesses, and oddly enough, most of it is co-owned by Global Corporation. Why didn't you tell me any of that?''

Santou popped two of the Tums in his mouth. ''None of it seemed relevant to this case, Rachel.''

''Then what makes you so sure that Hillard wasn't paying Vaughn's rent? Because Buddy told you so?''

Santou's skin grew tight against the bone. ''There was no proof of anything. I didn't need you running around on a wild-goose chase, tipping our hand on something it wasn't the right time to reveal. So I just didn't bother to tell you.''

He was dodging me. Just as Hickok had done all along. ''When is the right time, Jake? When Dolores Williams is locked up for murder? You know she had nothing to do with Valerie Vaughn's death. Dolores was set up to be at the right place at the right time, with a crowbar lying at her feet. Or was that just coincidence? It strikes me that Dolores was made to learn what the inside of a jail looks like, so that she'd keep her mouth shut about whatever she might know. What do you think, Santou? Did the lesson work?''

Santou's jaw clenched, letting me know I was on the right track.

''I don't know what to think anymore, Jake. You're the detective on the case. Why is it I feel it's being squelched at every turn?''

''I've got no proof of anything, Rachel. Only lots of loose ends, just like you. You wondering about Kroll? Yeah, I think he's a big supporter of Hillard Williams, and would do anything he could to protect the man from scandal. They go back a long way together and share a number of things, one of which is a fondness for the ladies, especially ones who play fast, loose, and enjoy certain games.''

That was information I already had, and Santou might have known that as well. It didn't explain why he wasn't pursuing this case to the fullest extent possible. Even worse, he seemed to be purposely lying low and allowing Kroll to cover up a murder.

''What about Gunter Schuess? I've got a woman he cut up

for fun, who now looks like one of his calling cards. It seems he has a fondness for razors, and his handiwork has an uncanny resemblance to what I saw done on Valerie Vaughn.''

Santou got out of the car and walked over to a stream of water near a group of willow trees. ''Will your stripper testify to the fact that it was Gunter?''

I followed his long, lazy strides. ''What makes you think she's a stripper? I never said that.''

Santou didn't reply. Hunkering down, he splashed a handful of water on his face. I was hitting home runs, but felt like I was losing the game. Though I'd withheld information from Santou, now I was sure he'd kept even more evidence from me.

''No, she won't testify. It seems she has an addiction to staying alive. But that information doesn't help you at all, huh?''

A pair of dragonflies darted through the air, racing to take cover as the blossoms of water lilies folded up in a nocturnal cocoon. A cloud of gnats hovered above Santou's head like a halo as his fingers splayed the water.

''What is it, Santou? Bad girls get what they deserve? Because it seems like the death of one hooker doesn't hold much weight for you. In fact, it sounds as if Gunter might have left his mark on a few other lucky women in town. So, do you at least want to tell me why you're protecting the guy?''

He turned to confront me, water running down his face, onto his neck and inside his shirt, his brown skin gleaming through the thin fabric.

''I'm going to get him on something much bigger, Rachel. I can't waste it over a murder charge on a stripper.''

There it was again. Disposable women for a higher cause. ''What have you got?''

''I can't tell you that. But it's going to happen. Very soon.''

The temperature dropped precariously, and I felt myself shiver.

"Is Kroll in charge of this?"

Santou moved close, and the temperature zoomed dangerously back up to a steamy ninety degrees.

"He knows nothing about it at all, and it has to stay that way. You've got to promise me that, Rachel. Otherwise, this whole case will be blown, and I've worked too hard and too long to let that happen."

I could feel the heat radiating off his body as he drew closer still. "This means a lot to me. Things have happened in my life, *chère;* things for which I need to make amends. This case is the one that will do it. If I can pull this off, we'll bag Hillard, Schuess, and maybe even Kroll. You've just got to trust me for now."

His fingers caressed my face and then moved to my neck, where they lingered for a moment, before sliding down to where the gold locket lay nestled between my breasts. Holding on to the necklace, his hand came to rest over my heart. My pulse raced with an exhilarating mix of fear and sheer sexual longing.

"I need a week, *chère*. Can you try to trust me for that long?"

I wanted to believe him as much as I believed that tomorrow would be another hot, steamy Louisiana day.

"Why should I? Why should I believe anything you say?"

His hand sizzled through my dress, burning into my bare skin as he leaned in close. "Darlin', if I'm lyin', I'm dyin'."

I sighed. "One week, Santou. That's all."

Laying the locket gently back down, his fingers played along my skin as he kissed me lightly.

"Let's go find that restaurant."

Pasta Nostra sat on the edge of the swamp, hidden away from view in a copse of ancient oak trees. Soft amber candles flickered in each of its windows. Inside, we were led up a flight of stairs by the maitre d'. An exotic mix of Cajun and black, his skin was the color of cafè au lait. Along with high cheekbones, full lips, and a slim nose, he had jet-black hair lying straight against his head, its ends pomaded into a small and perfect ducktail.

Seated on the second floor, we could see the swamp spread out beneath us, a tumorous growth encompassing everything in its path. A full moon's light shimmered on still, black water, dancing in and out of clouds in a seductive game of hide-and-seek. It disappeared completely for a moment and the swamp was left with a foreboding air, as if it might strangle the restaurant and its occupants with its decaying vegetation. But the moon revealed itself once more, and the marsh glimmered like a secret fairyland at our feet. Lying near my hand in a tinted ashtray was the same matchbook I had found at Valerie Vaughn's, and then again among the jumble of papers at Buddy Budwell's.

"Any particular reason you chose this place, darlin', or did you just miss being away from the swamp?"

"I thought you did your homework on Global Corporation, Santou."

"Obviously you did it for us. This is Sabino's?"

"Along with everything else Buddy Budwell owns."

Santou smiled and took a drink of his scotch. "One of which was Valerie Vaughn."

Valerie Vaughn. Her face was conjured up before me, turning in slow motion again and again with a conspiratorial wink.

"Have you ever been to New York, Santou?"

Chewing on a piece of ice from his glass, he shook his head no. "Why? Are you thinking that maybe I'm tied in with Sabino?" His eyes narrowed in on me and then he grinned, taking pleasure in the game of reeling me in.

"I just wondered if you'd ever been to Times Square. I suppose in some ways it's New York's equivalent of Bourbon Street. I've developed a fascination for Bourbon and the people who work there."

"Like Terri?"

"Yes." Terri, a transvestite performer and my best friend in the world.

"And Valerie Vaughn?"

Especially Valerie Vaughn. I wanted to know what made a girl from the bayou go bad, and what saved a city girl like me from falling into the same trap.

"Be careful, *chère*. Bourbon Street and its characters should scare the hell out of you. It's seductive from the outside, but that's one shit world, and the people are pure trouble. Believe me, even your friend Terri is eventually going to hit rock bottom."

A glass of white wine was placed in front of me.

"And what about you, Santou? You have no vices?"

His eyes pierced through me from under heavy lids. Hickok liked to say that Cajuns had more than their share of secrets. Santou was full of secrets. Secrets about Kroll and Williams and Valerie Vaughn. When he spoke again, his voice was so soft and low, that I found myself leaning forward to catch his words.

"I'll tell you a vice I had, Rachel, because I want you to know how dangerous getting involved in that world is. I used to be with the DEA, working undercover on the strip." Santou swirled his glass and stared into the liquid with all the desire and despair of a parched man confronted with a mirage.

"I loved that work—the life, the excitement, and the danger. It wasn't long before I also fell in love with the nose candy. Hell, it's part of the package. It comes with the lifestyle—free and easy for the taking. You just had to know the right places."

He looked at me so intently that I felt like a prize butterfly about to be pinned to a mount. "I made mistakes, got caught, and was kicked out of the agency. They said I couldn't be trusted." A telltale muscle twitched under his eye. "I'd sniffed my life right down the drain."

This was a revelation I hadn't expected. The admission made him seem all the more human, and more seductive than ever. My voice barely came out in a whisper. "What did you do?"

Santou finished his scotch and motioned to the waiter to bring another. ''I felt sorry for myself, until I realized that it wasn't doing me any good. So I went and got cleaned up. Then I got lucky. I was offered a second chance, and joined N.O.P.D.'' He ran a finger along the inside of one palm, as if searching for an answer to his future. ''The strip is a fascinating place, *chère*. But sooner or later, it will suck you under; and the price you pay is to lose your soul.''

Santou's melancholy was almost a visible throb as he continued to stare at his palm. The spell was finally broken when he looked at me and grinned a lopsided smile. ''But don't you worry. I've still got plenty of vices, sugar. They're even fun to share.''

I flushed as Santou's innuendo hit home. Without a doubt, the man knew how to get to me. My pulse began to race once more, and I took advantage of the moment to compose myself by going in search of the ladies' room.

I followed the curve of the wall down the stairs to the first floor landing, and past the swinging doors of the kitchen. A second set of steps appeared to lead down to a cellar. The ladies' room was just around the corner, in a hallway as dimly lit as the dining room above. Walking into the room, thoughts of Santou raced through my mind like an X-rated film. I once again felt his fingers trace the line of my face and slide along my skin, teasing with soft caresses. The more I tried to push such thoughts away, the more explicit the scenes became. I studied myself in the vanity mirror. The flimsy dress, my bare shoulders, the care I had taken with my hair, the receding bruises painstakingly covered over with makeup, were all unmistakable signs. I had a bad case of desire.

I walked out of the bathroom and was about to turn the corner, when footsteps echoed up from the basement below. The sound of voices drifted to where I had stopped. They were voices I had heard before. Peering around the corner, I was in time to see two heads bobbing up the stairs—one the size of a large melon, carpeted with thinning blond hair, the other draped in a bad toupee. Buddy Budwell and Clyde Bolles came into view together, just as they had been only a few days ago. I pulled back, unable to make out what was being said, but hearing enough to know they were headed in my direction. Sliding back inside the ladies' room, I kept my ear pressed to the door as they entered the bathroom on my right. Then I eased out and quickly turned the corner, heading for the unlit stairs.

I climbed down the dim steps, using the palms of my hands to guide myself along the rough wall of stone, until I reached the bottom. A heavy metal door closed off whatever lay beyond. Deciding to risk a look, I grabbed the handle, pushing as hard as I could, but the door refused to budge. At the same moment, I heard the two sets of footsteps again, coming around the corner from the men's room. I knew that my timing had failed.

I pressed myself tightly against the door, wishing myself invisible as the lump on the back of my head kicked into high gear, its pain a sharp, searing throb. Time seemed endless as I looked up to see two pairs of feet hovering at the top of the stairs.

I held my breath as I tried to melt into the metal. Closing my eyes, I didn't dare move. A moment later I heard the swinging of the kitchen doors, and looked up again to see both sets of feet move off in the opposite direction. I stayed pressed against the door for as long as I could stand it, before pulling off my shoes. Soundlessly scurrying up the stairs, I didn't stop until I had reached our table.

Santou was working his way through his second glass of Scotch as I sat down. "Do you always carry your shoes with you when you go to the bathroom, *chère?*"

Slipping them back on, I didn't bother to answer. I thought of the dark stairwell and of what possibly lay beyond. Ordering a second glass of wine, I made a conscious effort to relax during dinner, but I found myself jumping at every strange sound. I caught Santou watching me, but he made no further comment as we filled the time with small talk. Midway through the meal, I glanced out the window once again at the swamp below. Barely discernible through the shadows was the outline of a small boat pushing off from behind the restaurant, its destination somewhere deep inside the swamp. The boat appeared to hold three figures, and I felt fairly certain that two of them were Bolles and Budwell. It took the full moon gliding out from behind a cloud, like Salome ripping away the last of her veils, to reveal the third figure of the trio. Connie Kroll sat gazing up at the moon like a loup-garou, the Cajun version of a werewolf, come to life. I smiled as I felt my luck return once again.

Dry lightning danced in the sky, its long, thin fingers reaching down to tickle the ground, while off in the distance the low rumble of thunder sounded a drumroll. Thoughts of Pasta Nostra receded from my mind. I gave in to the wine and laid my head back against the seat of the car, reveling in the sounds and smells of the night as we headed back to New Orleans.

I sensed the warmth of Santou's hand before it brushed against mine. The rough skin of his fingers slowly explored my palm with the lightest tinge of suggestion. He ran his hand up along the bare skin of my leg, and a surge of heat coursed through me. By the time we arrived back at my place, the air, heavy with humidity, broke like a giant sponge that had been squeezed, and the rain began to fall in a steady sheet. There was no need to question what would happen next as he followed me inside.

I didn't bother to turn on the lights. Instead, I opened a bottle of wine as Santou grabbed two glasses, and we headed wordlessly into the bedroom. After opening the French doors to the balcony, we slowly undressed as we listened to the rain streaming onto the roof and down the eaves, covering the nude maidens in the fountain below. Santou made love to me as I had imagined he would, with all the slow intensity of a smoldering fire. Afterward, we lay on top of the sheets and drank cold wine, allowing the wood blades of the fan to cool our bodies before turning to each other again to explore even more slowly this time. I dozed off later, hearing his steady breathing beside me, and didn't mind that for once the only illumination in the room came from the lightning that ripped through the sky.

In the middle of the night, his hand brushed my hair away from my ear and I turned toward him, feeling his body hard and warm against mine. Whispering that he had to leave, he kissed my cheek and told me to go back to sleep. And I did. I floated on my dreams, and felt safe beneath the thin sheet that rustled against my skin from the breeze of the rain and the fan above.

Later on, I felt my hair once more gently lifted off my neck, and I smiled to myself in the secret knowledge that he had returned to make love to me again. As I lay on my side, the sheet slithered off my body and I remained still in the silent anticipation of his touch against my skin. In my semiconscious state, the realization that I hadn't given him a key rippled across my mind, but I wasn't worried about such things. Not with Santou. His hand played along my leg and up past my hip, to nestle in the hollow of my waist before moving on to cup my breast. It lingered there, exploring every inch before continuing on with its journey. I gave myself over to the delicious pleasure of his finger lightly gliding along the skin of my throat, as his warm breath brushed tenderly against my ear. His whisper soothed my body like a loving caress, and the gentle sound of the words could have been a baby's lullaby until their full impact registered like a bullet in my brain, exploding in a firestorm of fear.

"Wake up. I want to watch you die."

My heart pounded out of control as a sharp nick pierced the skin of my neck, burning as the pain raced through me. Confused as to what was happening, I rolled hard to the left and grabbed my pillow, holding it in front of me with all the conviction of an invincible shield. Struggling to sit up, I reached wildly with my left hand to grab onto the baseball bat that I kept by my bed. But before I could grasp it, a hand grabbed the top of my hair, jerking my head back hard. As my jaw snapped shut my teeth bit into my tongue, and a stinging slash ripped through my neck once again.

Pulling loose, I clutched the wooden handle of the bat and screamed, swinging as hard as I could. I felt the wood make contact, crashing into flesh and bone with a thud, and I struck again as the bite of a blade sliced into my flesh. Still screaming, I heard a pounding outside my door as Terri's voice shrieked above the din. Words hissed out as I continued to flail at the air with the bat.

"Take this as a warning."

But I couldn't be sure if that was exactly what was said, in my terror and confusion.

Then I heard the scuffle of steps on my balcony, as whoever had been in my room climbed over the rail. Terri's voice was immediately beside me, but I couldn't stop the cry which tore out of my throat, ringing in my ears to mix with the thunder that exploded in my brain. Until I realized that I hadn't made any sound at all. Terri held me as I wondered if I was losing my mind, if it had been just one more nightmare played to the hilt in the darkness of my room.

My fingers trembled as I reached past him and turned on the lamp. Light flooded my room, illuminating a pool of red that formed a ghoulish design of blood splattered with goose feathers. My pillow had been slashed into ribbons.

Pushing away from Terri, I made my way over to the mirror on shaky legs. Three long gashes encircled my throat like a jagged choker of blood red rubies. As the blood flowed freely down my neck onto my breasts, Valerie's reflection appeared in the mirror, tattooed in a lacework of slashes. And I remembered Kitty, the stripper I'd recently met, and her own angry scars. I had little doubt as to who my attacker had been, or that this was the prelude to a terror not yet over. The slashes sizzled on my neck, branding me as one more victim permanently marked with fear. It made me all the more aware that I was no stronger or braver or safer than either Valerie or Kitty had been. And I knew that my nightmares had now become my reality.

Sixteen

What was left of the night was spent with lights blazing bright to fight off the demons that had suddenly become all too real. My .357 explored every closet, every corner, in search of something to take aim at so that I would stop feeling so helpless and out of control. Terri helped to patch me up as best he could, staining most of a towel before the bleeding subsided. Refusing his pleas that I go to a hospital, I allowed him to cover the gashes on my neck with rolls of gauze. Pouring me a shot of straight bourbon, he poured another as I gulped down the first.

Then he rocked me as I sat in bed, the gun cradled in my lap like a sleepless child. Refusing either to call the police or to try and sleep, I watched one moth after another fly into the overhead light, where they departed as black ashes in a crisp sizzle of smoke, falling in a growing funeral pyre around me.

I resisted the temptation to phone Santou. At first I told myself it was because I was too shaken up to be coherent. But it was more than that. I was angry that he had left me alone in the dead of night. He'd walked out, as if that was all the evening had been worth. I tried to stop myself from thinking this might not have happened if he had been there. But it didn't work. Along with being afraid and angry, I was hurt. Finally, I caved in and picked up the phone to call Santou, only to realize that he'd never even told me where he lived. Instead, I called the precinct, letting the phone ring until I could no longer stand the unanswered buzz in my ear.

As I hung up, a new thought entered my mind that put my other emotions to rest. I began to wonder if this had all been a setup that Jake might have been part of. It was obvious he'd kept information from me, and tonight had continued to dodge my questions concerning Williams and Kroll. He'd even asked that I blindly trust him for one more week, and I had agreed. Now I began to question that decision.

Terri continued to hold me until I finally began to nod off, my body succumbing to the effects of bourbon and too much adrenaline. By 5:00 A.M., I no longer wanted to sleep at all, my nightmares rivaling my reality. I assured Terri that I would be all right, and he waited outside my door until he heard me turn the lock behind him.

Alone with my thoughts, I made a pot of coffee and dragged a chair out on the balcony, keeping guard until dawn crept onto the horizon and the Quarter came to life with the clatter and hum of its early-morning residents. The last visible signs of rain were already disappearing as the rising sun sucked up the wet wisps of steam like a red-hot vacuum. Taking a cold shower, I left the curtain open, afraid someone might sneak up on me. Scenes from *Psycho* played vividly on childhood nightmares that no longer seemed so childish. Standing under the stream of icy cold needles, I tried to focus my mind on what to do next. I was running out of places to turn in this labyrinth of events, in which I now stood dead center. Turning back to my New York roots, I decided to pay Vinnie Bertucci a visit.

By the time I finally got myself together and checked back in with Terri, most of the morning had already slid by. I was heading out the door as the phone began to ring. I didn't bother to stop, unable to think of anyone I really wanted to talk to right now—including Santou. The police wouldn't help me, any more than they had Valerie. Time was running out before the next attempt on my life became more than just a warning. Whatever I had stumbled onto, the pieces were all there. I just had to discover how to put them together.

I walked out to a day that was going on just as the day before had, and the day before that, driving home the message that it would make little difference in the grand scheme of things whether or not I was around to join in with the rest of civilization tomorrow.

The trolley seemed to clang louder as I drove to the Garden District. The grass was greener, and the black iron fences standing guard in front of each shuttered Victorian house took on the presence of sentinels erected to keep danger away. Walking quickly up to the lemon meringue house that today appeared larger, I rang the bell and was greeted by the massive form of Vinnie Bertucci. His pompadour stood higher and his chest was broader than I had remembered. He filled the doorway, dressed in a royal blue knit top and baby blue polyester pants, and I noticed for the first time that he was wearing black alligator loafers without socks. The diamond pinky ring on his finger beamed a flare of light into my eyes.

Vinnie stared at me as he rubbed one side of his jaw and then the other, checking himself for any unnoticed gashes on his own skin.

"Whatcha do, New Yawk? Cut yourself shaving this morning?"

Vinnie giggled, pleased with his joke as he stood aside to let me in.

"Ya got good timing. I got sausage and peppers simmering that'll make ya cry, it's so good. We'll eat and call it brunch."

I sat in the kitchen and wondered about the best way to broach the subject as Vinnie stirred his homemade sauce.

"I wanted to thank you for sneaking me that piece of meat the other day. I'm having it analyzed. We should know the results pretty soon."

"Yeah, yeah. No problem. I hated the mutt myself, but I'd never kill the thing, ya know what I mean?" Vinnie lifted the wooden spoon out of the pan and brought it delicately to his lips. "Perfecto! It's chow time."

I wondered if Dolores was home, but seeing her was more

than I wanted to deal with this morning. My hunch was that she'd probably gone on one long drinking spree after being sprung from jail. Vinnie filled me in without my having to ask.

"The old broad's upstairs sleeping it off. She spent all last night yammering away about her dead pooch and banging on the floor for more booze. For Christsakes, it was like being at a Sicilian wake. She's got me running up and down the damn steps all the time, like I got nothing better ta do around here. She can belt 'em faster than I can pour 'em. But youse ain't here ta talk about that stuff."

I watched as he threw handfuls of fresh pasta into the boiling water, wondering how he'd known I was here about anything other than Dolores Williams.

"So, ya gonna tell me whatcha here for, or did ya just stop by cause ya missed my home cooking?"

I decided to drop a few small bombs and see if Vinnie picked up the bait.

"I've been doing some research lately on business acquisitions in the New Orleans area, and I keep bumping into the name Global Corporation. Ever hear of them?"

Vinnie poured the pasta into a large ceramic dish decorated with bright red crawfish, their claws locked together in a jig. "So, whadda ya, changing ya line of work now, New Yawk? I thought youse was busy being like a dogcatcher or something."

I was silent for a moment as Vinnie tasted the sauce, adding a touch of fresh pepper. "I think Global Corporation might be involved in some illegal wildlife dealings. The president of the company was brought up on charges a few years ago for trading in illicit gator skins."

Vinnie popped a sweet sausage into his mouth, chewing on it slowly. "Illicit, huh? I guess that means they was being bad boys. Didn't play by your rules. See, ta me that sounds like they was just doing a little free enterprise, which is what this country of ours is all about. Ya follow me? Anyways, this Global thing sounds like kind of a common name ta me, but then I got no head for business. Though I am thinking of opening a decent place for Italian eats in this town. Whadda ya say? I'll give youse a job. Maybe we'll even name a dish after the mutt."

I wondered what Vinnie had done wrong back in New York to land him in the position of playing number one houseboy to Hillard Williams.

"You know what I found out about Global Corporation, Vinnie? The company is based in New York, but it has an interest in lots of businesses in Louisianna—from restaurants to fish-packing houses to hookers. They even deal in diamonds. Doesn't that strike you as odd?"

"Ya been sniffing around maybe too much, New Yawk. Better watch that your nose don't get bit off."

Grabbing the bowl of pasta, he kicked the kitchen door open with his foot and sat down at the table, where he dished a large portion of spaghetti onto my plate.

"I have reason to believe that Valerie Vaughn's death and Global Corporation might be tied in together somehow. She might have found out something she shouldn't have. It could be that she learned of some illegal deals going on. Maybe she even tried to blackmail someone in the company."

"Maybe ya need ta get out more. Make some friends, go out on a date, get yourself laid. Sounds ta me like youse are spending too much time by yourself in those swamps, coming up with wacko conspiracy stuff."

"You know, Vinnie, there was another girl on Bourbon who ended up tattooed just like Valerie Vaughn. Only she didn't die. And she remembers that the guy who cut her had a fondness for razors. Some freak with white hair and eyes like a couple of ice cubes. Sound like anyone familiar to you?"

Vinnie pulled the cork out of a bottle of Chianti and poured two glasses. "I don't know any guy with ice cubes for eyes. As for the hooker, those kind always meet with a bad end. What can ya expect?"

I took a sip of the wine, hoping it would help numb the

pain that had started to throb in my neck. I should have known I wouldn't be able to get much information out of Little Italy. Like all good soldiers, he wasn't about to drop his guard. Slamming the bottle of Chianti down on the table with a thud, Vinnie caught me by surprise so that I jumped. He stared at me for a moment, then leaned in, both elbows resting on the table like giant rib roasts.

"Listen, New Yawk, I like ya, which is why I'm telling ya not to go pushing your nose in where it don't belong, if ya know what I mean. This is New Orleans, and they don't play so nice. I'd hate ta see something bad happen ta ya, so ya get a warning, ya listen ta it. Play nice with the dead animals, and don't go poking around too much. Ya don't wanna get the wrong people pissed off."

I touched the gauze along my throat. "I've already had a warning, Vinnie. It's gone beyond that now."

Pulling out a book of matches, Vinnie lit the drip candle in a Chianti bottle that sat in the middle of the table. "Then if I was youse, I'd think about taking a quick trip outta town."

He threw the matchbook down in front of me, and the red letters of Pasta Nostra jumped out like a neon sign. It was time for me to let Hickok in on the situation already in motion. I just hoped he wouldn't be angry enough to sack me for it.

Having decided to make my confession to Hickok, I figured that now was as good a time as any to check in with Dr. Sam. I wanted the results on both Fifi and the gator, and if he hadn't already done the autopsies and test, I was determined to hang over his shoulder until he did. Once Hickok found out about my extracurricular activities, there was no question I'd be sent back out on swamp detail to rot among the cattails and the duck poachers for good.

I started driving back down St. Charles when I spotted a phone booth and pulled over on impulse. I got out and found myself dialing Santou.

"Yeah. Santou here."

My heart pounded wildly as I heard his voice, and for a moment, I couldn't quite catch my breath.

"Anybody there? Otherwise, I'm hanging up."

I knew I had to tell him what had happened last night after he'd left—if only to try and gauge his reaction.

"It's Rachel."

"How ya doing, *chère?* Sleep well I hope?"

My mind went blank, making it difficult for me to think of the right words to say.

"Something happened after you left last night, Jake."

He chuckled as though he'd been expecting just such a reaction. "Yeah. Same thing happened to me, darlin'. I decided I want a lot more nights like that."

My skin felt hot and the receiver was slippery in the palm of my hand, as a wave of anger and fear swept over me, along with the searing memory of what had taken place.

"Somebody broke into my apartment after you left. I was attacked." A split second of silence felt like an eternity before I heard his voice again.

"What happened, Rachel? Are you alright?"

I touched my throat, and fear overtook any anger I felt as my stomach contracted in a tight knot. "I got a bit cut up, but Terri came in and scared him off before anything worse could happen. It was Gunter, Jake."

"Did you see him?"

"I didn't have to. I know it was him." I was met with another pause before Jake spoke again.

"How do you know?"

I wanted to shriek in frustration. Instead, I took a deep breath before answering. "I just know. The marks look like slashes done with a razor. The same as I saw on Valerie Vaughn and the other stripper I told you about."

"But you didn't see him?"

"I'm telling you, it's Gunter! What else do you need to know before you finally do something about him?"

Santou's voice resonated in a placating tone over the line.

"You can't arrest a man based on assumption, Rachel. You know that. Have you been to the hospital yet?"

"No."

"Well, get yourself on over there and then go home. I'll take care of this. You just leave it to me."

I hung up without bothering to respond. I'd already seen how well Santou had protected Valerie. I didn't intend to be the next victim on anyone's list.

I didn't bother to call and make an appointment with Sam. Instead I just swung by his office. Dr. Sam stepped out of his examining room with an unkempt Yorkie tucked under each arm, his own wild bush of salt-and-pepper hair as badly in need of a trim as theirs were. Handing the dogs back to their owner, he locked the office door behind them.

"Hey, Rachel! I see you got the message I left this morning."

In my rush to discover why someone had developed a yen to cut my throat, I hadn't thought to check my answering machine. "Actually, I didn't. I stopped by to check on what you've found out so far."

Dr. Sam's round baby face crinkled up into a smile. "What I found can buy us two one-way tickets to South America, and a life of leisure spent drinking margaritas and working on our suntans, *señorita*."

His smile faded as he noticed the gauze I'd wrapped around my neck.

"You've got quite a gash there, Porter. Maybe we'd better swing by Charity and have that looked at."

I put a finger to the gauze and felt the sticky wetness that had begun to seep through, staining the layers of cotton I had covered it with. I knew the cuts required expert attention, but I didn't have the time or patience to deal with the bureaucracy of an emergency room right now. If I didn't start tying some loose ends together fast, the gashes on my neck would be the least of my worries.

"It's not a big deal, Sam. If you can spare some gauze, I'll stop the bleeding and bandage it up again myself."

"Not good enough, Rachel. If you're going to be pig-headed enough not to go to the hospital, you're going to have to contend with my skills. And I don't want to hear any grousing about it, either."

Dr. Sam removed the bandage from my neck, letting loose a low whistle.

"You want to tell me what happened?"

"Someone out there isn't my biggest fan. Last night he decided to show me just how he felt."

"Do you know who it was?"

"It was too dark to see, but I can make a few guesses. I might just take you up on that offer of sun and tequila. What did you find out about our two prize specimens?"

I followed Dr. Sam into a small bathroom, where he disinfected his hands as though he were scrubbing for major surgery.

"We're going to work on a reward system, Porter. You don't give me any trouble while I patch you up, and I'll tell you what I found. It's worth behaving yourself for a few minutes, I promise."

He led me into his examining room, where I hopped up on a portable table just recently washed down from its last visitor. Sam pulled out a syringe, along with a small vial, a long sewing needle, and some fine silk thread.

"Whoa! Hold on a minute. I was expecting something more in the line of salve and a Band-Aid, not to be a guinea pig for your needlework technique."

Dr. Sam smelled suspiciously of borax as he cupped my chin in his hand and examined the wounds, which stung more than ever.

"Cut the crap, Rachel. You don't want to go to a hospital, fine. But you can't walk around with gashes in your neck fast on their way to becoming badly infected. I don't know if you took a good look at these suckers, but some guy did an expert job of cutting through layers of tissue and skin. Unless you want to end up in the hospital for an extended stay, I've got to clean these wounds and sew them up before they begin to fester. Does that explain the situation enough for you?"

At a loss for a snappy comeback, I only hoped the man had a steady hand and could sew a fine line. Every nerve in my body screamed as Dr. Sam applied disinfectant to the wounds.

"I forgot to tell you this would be the worst part." Chuckling to himself, Sam plunged the hypodermic needle into a vial of clear liquid. I held up my hand as he approached.

"I really hate needles. Just tell me what you're going to do."

He took the time to knock out a few air bubbles that had collected inside the syringe.

"This is exactly why I treat animals instead of people. They're not nearly as much a pain in the neck, no pun intended." Dr. Sam stood in front of me with the syringe by his side.

"What I have here is a local anesthetic. All you'll feel is a slight pinch and ten minutes from now, the area will be completely numb. Then I'm simply going to put in a few stitches. There'll be some tugging, and you might feel a little strange, but believe me, it won't feel nearly as bad as it's going to if I don't sew these up."

Thirty stitches later, I studied Dr. Sam's handiwork in the bathroom mirror. While the job was neatly done, there could be no hiding the fact that I had been on the verge of having my throat slit. I pulled out a bandanna and wrapped it around my neck, hiding the stitches from sight.

"Hey, Porter! Enough with the vanity. Come in here and I'll show you something really interesting."

I followed Dr. Sam's voice next door, where Hook was laid out on a porcelain slab tilted down toward the sink. Covered up in a white smock and latex gloves, Sam had the look of a butcher.

"You're not going to believe what this gator ate for his last supper."

Sam directed me to the tail as he grabbed hold of the head, and we carefully flipped Hook over. Sticking his hand into a thin flap cut in the gator's belly, Sam's arm disappeared up to the elbow. When he slowly pulled it out again, his hand was clenched around an erect, tightly packed condom. Untying the knot at its end, Sam dipped his finger inside and then held the condom out toward me.

"Here. Try some."

I followed his example, wetting the tip of my index finger and sticking it inside. My fingertip came back coated with a fine layer of white powder.

"This is unbelievably good. Do you know how many dealers would kill to get their hands on this stuff?"

Popping his finger in his mouth, Sam rubbed the residue on his lower gum. "We're talking pure, undiluted cocaine here, Rachel. There are twenty of these suckers stuffed inside, one of which opened up while Hook was trying to digest the load. Your gator's diagnosis is easy. He OD'd on some very fine cocaine."

Everything began to make sense as the pieces fell into place. There was no way that Valerie could have had the resources or smarts to be a dealer herself. This was definitely a big-time operation. Global Corporation had to be the front for bringing cocaine in through the bayous and pipelining it straight up to New York, with the excess going to Europe. Buddy's businesses were used for laundering the money, while the diamonds were probably one more dumping ground for large bundles of excess cash. My guess was that Valerie must have siphoned off some dope to sell. Panicking when she was about to be caught, she'd probably fed it to Hook to try to hide the evidence. It hadn't done either one of them much good. As far as the diamond necklace was concerned, it was anybody's guess. It might have been given to her as a payoff to shut her up. Or maybe she had just dipped her fingers in and helped herself to the goodies.

"There's something else you should know, Rachel. Somebody got to the gator before we did. Hook had already been sliced open when we got him here."

My nice, neat package began to unravel once more at the seams.

"In fact, there could have been even more of these condoms inside. There's plenty of room in there yet."

The possibilities were endless. Plenty of people had had access to Hook up to this point. And faced with a million-dollar gator, the temptation would have been close to overwhelming. A few missing condoms could help boost the retirement fund, and who'd ever know? The stitches on my neck pulled at my skin like the teeth on a piranha. I rummaged through my bag to find the last Percocet, and swallowed it dry.

"Great. Just great."

Sam's face fell as if I'd just burst his bubble.

"Sorry, Sam. I appreciate all your work. It's just that I'm getting nowhere fast, and my time is running out where this case is concerned."

Sam pulled off his gloves. "Just let me know when you want to catch that plane to Rio. While I'm piling on the good news, I did a few tests on that chunk of meat you brought in. Fifi was knocked off by a monster dose of strychnine. In fact, I'm surprised their yard wasn't littered with dead critters by the time it was removed."

At this point, I wouldn't have been surprised to find out there was more than dead wildlife in the Williams's backyard. It was time to turn the mess over to Hickok, and watch how he chose to play out the deal. While I knew there was always the off chance that Charlie himself was involved in this up to his eyeballs, my gut feeling told me I had no other choice. Before heading out, I promised Sam that I'd have Hook removed the next day. Now that the euphoria of having discovered so much cocaine was wearing off, we were both frightened by the implications of keeping Hook around any longer than necessary.

Stalling for time to think, I decided to stop off at home before driving on to Slidell to face Hickok. Along with my decision to bow out of the case, I'd begun again to wonder if I was really in the right business after all. So far, I had proved myself to be nothing more than a rank amateur. My stomach growled, and I recognized the familiar sound. Depression and anxiety always made me ravenous.

I stopped off at the Central to pick up a shrimp po'boy, and then headed back home. What I found when I got there didn't make me feel any better. The place was a shambles, with all the charm of a Freddy Krueger film. My secondhand sofa had been slashed nearly as efficiently as Valerie Vaughn. Its foam-rubber stuffing was heaped on the floor in yellow clumps, looking like globules of chicken fat. Books were thrown from shelves and drawers pulled open, their contents strewn about. I found that I no longer needed an excuse to buy a matching set of dishes, with bits and pieces of my plates smashed all over the floor. The bedroom hadn't fared much better.

Through it all, my phone machine continued to blink steadily, its red light flashing on and off like a warning sign. Not knowing what else to do in the midst of so much destruction, I automatically pressed the play button. Hickok's voice boomed out as thick as gumbo with its Southern twang.

"Get your ass on over here, Bronx. You, me, and Trenton are goin' fishing tonight." The time stamped on the machine set the call at just after three o'clock.

I tried to call Hickok at work to fill him in on what had taken place, but it was after five and everyone was already gone, including, oddly enough, Charlie. It was only then that I remembered there should have been another message on my machine. The call that Sam had placed to me was missing. I frantically dialed his number, worried that I might already be too late. The first two rings bounced around in my head like a shrill scream in an empty theater. By the time Sam picked up, my throat was constricted with fear.

"Sam, get out of your office right now. I just came home to find everything in my place systematically decimated with a very sharp razor. It looks like a search-and-destroy mission over here."

Sam's voice rose an octave higher on the other end of the

phone. "What the hell do you think they were looking for, Rachel?"

For a former activist, he was slow on the uptake. "All that cocaine. Didn't you say a dealer would kill to get his hands on the stuff? Well it looks like you were right, and your message is missing off my machine. So just get the hell out of there now!"

"Fine. But I'm taking the stuff with me."

"What are you, crazy? Don't take the time. It's not worth it. Just leave!"

"Listen, Porter. I'm rolling the whole autopsy table into the back of my truck right now. Gotta go. I'll catch you later."

I was left holding a dead line. Sifting through my things, I wondered if it had been Gunter who'd returned in hopes of finding the cocaine. And then I remembered the one thing in my possession that someone could possibly want. Valerie Vaughn's videotape. That's when my stomach tightened into a knot. I had left it downstairs with Terri. If anything had happened to him I would have only myself to blame, and it would be more than I could bear.

I tore out of my apartment, taking the steps two at a time. Saying a silent prayer, I let myself in his front door. Everything was in place, just as I had left it that morning. The charcoal drawings and photos of long-dead movie stars stared at me as I made my way down the hall, their eyes accusing me of not being good enough to crack the case, not having made the grade, and not having been concerned enough about Terri's safety. My heart pounded so hard I could scarcely breathe as I peered into the living room.

Terri lay asleep on the couch, the television a crackling pattern of snow. I thanked God and pharmaceutical companies for the Valium he'd taken before I'd left. It had probably let him sleep through the ransacking of my floor above. I made my way back out past that gallery of eyes, which judged me as harshly as I did myself.

Closing the front door, I sat down on the stairs as my legs began to shake and my eyes welled up with tears. I had to find Hickok. He'd become my only cavalry. Without him, I was about to go down just like Custer, who'd been as stupid as I'd been up until now, with something equally intangible to prove.

Seventeen

A light mist had begun to fall, making the day darker than it should have been. Left to wonder where Hickok was headed and how I would ever hook up with him, I found myself driving deep into the heart of Cajun country. Billows of fog as thick as cotton candy rolled across the road, making it all but impossible to see the headlights of cars before they barreled past. My thoughts wandered back to Kitty and Valerie Vaughn as I questioned how close I was to becoming one more victim to be passed over, the case hushed up, just another statistic in New Orleans's growing homicide rate. I continued to drive on without thinking of where I was going, until I realized I was heading toward Trenton Treddell's.

The fog lifted as night cannibalized the last remnants of day. The moon rose, only a sliver less full than it had been the night before. I turned onto the dirt road that led to Treddell's house and immediately plunged my front tire into a deep rut, knocking out what little was left of my car's alignment. The blood-chilling cry of a nutria rose from a canal off to my right, and a second critter picked up the cry. Not a light was to be seen as I continued on, until finally, a small incandescent pinpoint radiated through the trees. Driving closer, I saw that it came from inside Treddell's house. Trenton's pickup was gone, but the pink Cadillac stood on the gravel drive, the moonlight reflecting off its polished surface.

Remembering my last run-in with Dolly, I prepared myself for the worst as I approached the front door.

"What the fuck do you want?"

Dolly stood framed against the light, her hair a flaming hibiscus that glowed as if on fire. She was squeezed into a one-piece black bodysuit, its low neckline showcasing the tops of her breasts, with their gathering of tiny wrinkles. Her eyes were bloodshot and her coral lipstick smudged, and the distinctive odor of Southern Comfort wafted toward me. Standing barefoot on the orange shag carpet, her polished toenails were as red as freshly drawn blood. Her hand itched to slam the door in my face. While I desperately needed information as to what was about to go down tonight, I held only the faintest glimmer of hope that Dolly would be of some help.

"Is Trenton at home? I have to speak to him."

Dolly glared at me, her eyes glazing over with tears as her bottom lip began to tremble. "Do you have any idea at all what your interfering has done?" A large tear rolled down along the side of her nose and into the coral cavern of her mouth. "For your information, you just might be responsible for getting my husband killed tonight. Or are you too dumb to even know what you're messing with?"

Taken even more by surprise at Dolly's tears than by her outburst of emotion, I found myself speechless as she slammed the door in my face. It was then that I knew Hickok's fishing expedition had to have something to do with the drug pipeline I had stumbled upon. While Hillard and Buddy might have been minor-league players with drugs during their former gator days, they were involved on a major scale now, with Global Corporation marketing the majority of the dope. There was nothing better than to have two homeboys who knew the ins and outs of every bayou and channel sneaking in dope, most likely from Colombia. It gave Sabino and his pals control over the Louisiana coastline, and that in itself was priceless.

I wheeled my car around and started to head back down the dark road. If Charlie and Trenton were out on a sting tonight, I had every intention of joining them, no matter what. The honking of a horn and the blare of a cracked headlight jerked me out of my thoughts as I swerved hard to avoid the oncoming pickup. Slamming on his brakes, Gonzales pulled up beside me. He squinted his eyes tight and thrust his head forward to see if it was really me. His hair hung in long, oily strands, resembling slimy earthworms, as he leaned his body halfway out the truck window.

"Miss Porta, you gotta come wit me now. Charlie, he cursing you out somet'ing good for not being here yet. He and Trentone, dey gone out into de swamp. But you come wit' Gonzales. I got us anot'er boat and we find dem."

Gonzales didn't wait for an answer. He maneuvered his broken-down truck around and took off, so that I was left scurrying to catch up with the trail of dust he left in his wake. Making a sharp turn onto the blacktop, he didn't go far before veering off onto another dirt road. That road forked onto an even smaller and more rutted path. My VW vibrated with an intensity that left me wondering if it could go much farther, when I caught sight of the swamp up ahead.

Making his way over to a small aluminum boat, Gonzales waited for me as I peered into the foreboding swamp that lay quiet as the dead. I hesitated for a moment before stepping into the bobbing silver can, then we pushed off into the murky water, where we were swallowed up by the darkness of night. Gonzales silently paddled under the skeletons of forlorn cypress trees that closed in around us. A nearby choir of green frogs sang a down-home version of country Muzak. Water hyacinths floated on top of the liquid swamp, their blossoms closed to protect them from the evil roaming through the night like a desperado in flight from the light of the moon.

"The devil lives in the swamp, Bronx. That's why the trees grow so crooked." Hickok loved to tell me that, feeling almost Cajun himself after having lived in the bayou so long.

The cypress trees were twisted, their trunks frozen in serpentine splendor as I searched for the devil now. The hum of cicadas swelled from a small chant to a roaring crescendo, as we glided past a log with bright eyes that locked onto mine. Taking a closer look, I saw a bony head with walnut-sized ridges leading to a larger series of bumpy protusions resembling a spine. A gator lay patiently in wait for his dinner. Hearing the swish of wings overhead, I lifted my face and was gently caressed by dry strands of moss, their lacy skirts hanging down from a row of cypress trees.

The night hung heavy as a beaded cloak as Gonzales paddled down one ribbon of water after another, its pathway an ancient memory. I thought I heard the grinding churn of a motor off in the distance, but the sound was soon swallowed up as each stroke of Gonzales's paddle took us deeper into the labyrinth. Turning toward the man who was a creature of the swamp himself, I dared to break the silence.

"Do you know where Trenton and Charlie are?"

Gonzales blended perfectly into the night, adorned in black tee shirt and jeans. Gaunt and gnarled like the trees, the trunk of his body remained motionless as he glided the boat on a shimmering mirror of ebony. Rays of moonlight played on the slick strands of his hair that hung listless as moss.

"Where dey are, is where dey is. Dey out here somewhere layin' in wait for de huntin' to begin."

"Are we going hunting, too?"

Gonzales grinned, his black teeth jagged as broken bottles.

"Yes, miss. Don't you worry none. We goin' huntin', too."

I drew my knees tight against my body. The swamp began to play games with me, blowing up my childhood fears. Holding my breath, I could almost hear the bogeyman sneak up from behind, his fingers running down the length of my back. Every tree was a ghost, the white moonlight its transparent shroud. Every ripple in the water was a hand reaching up to pull me into a black underworld. Gonzales began to mimic each sound we heard. I twisted around until I sat facing him in the boat, and leaned forward to whisper, afraid to intrude upon the silence.

"What is it about the swamp that you love so much, Gonzales?"

Looking around, his eyes sparkled like those of the gator who lay in wait for his prey.

"De swamp is like my mama's arms around me, an' I just a li'l bitty baby. Dis here is my home. It's where I always feel safe. I got everytin' I be needin' an I don't wanna be nowheres else."

A black stick came to life, wriggling close to the boat. Propelling itself away, one more creature disappeared, swallowed up by the swamp.

"If I couldn't be in de swamp, I just as soon be dead."

"You still do any outlawing, Gonzales?"

Gonzales grinned at me through broken teeth, grabbing the limb of a tree and placing the splintered end in his mouth. "Just a li'l bit, Miss Porta. A li'l bit a gator, a li'l bit a gro'bek. Not enough to hurt, mind you."

We continued on in silence. I listened to every twig break, every leaf rustle, until I could hear my own heart. A splash of water off to the left drew Gonzales's attention. Flicking on his flashlight, he shined its rays onto a cluster of snouts snapping at a meal that bobbed up and down like a giant cork in the water. Gonzales rowed closer to see what all the commotion was about, raising his oar and jabbing it in the reptiles' direction until the covey of gators broke up.

The smell was enough to tell me that what lay facedown like a hunk of floating garbage was a human body, as we moved in for a better view. A ring of blood glowed phosphorescent in the yellow beam of the light. Gonzales tucked his paddle under the balloon of clothing, straining his muscles against the deadweight, until the body slowly rolled over. The face was partially gone, along with an arm and a leg. But enough was left to be able to tell that the man bobbing like a half-eaten apple was Louisiana State Wildlife Agent Clyde Bolles, dressed in the same clothes I had seen him in last night at Pasta Nostra. Moving to the opposite end of the boat, I leaned over, intent on throwing up, until I saw reptilian eyes staring back at me through a bed of algae, patiently waiting for me to bend a little lower. I pulled back up like a shot with the gator following, determined to snag his retreating dinner. Grabbing my .357, Gonzales pushed me aside and took aim, shooting the gator straight through the eye. It fell back into the water with a thud, and Gonzales kicked its body away from the boat with the heel of his boot.

"Dat will keep dem ot'ers busy, Miss Porta. Dey don't be bot'ering us no more."

Gonzales handed me back my .357 and turned his attention to what remained of Clyde Bolles. Looping a piece of rope, he slipped it around the waterlogged body to tow Bolles behind us. We paddled on until a small slip of land covered with palmetto came into sight. Jumping out of the boat, Gonzales dragged the mutilated corpse onto the island, where he tied him upright to the trunk of a tupelo tree. Then we pushed back into the foreboding darkness, and I glanced around to see Bolles, a tattered and bedraggled rag doll, looking like one more bayou ghost.

Gonzales clucked to himself as his paddle fractured slivers of moonlight with each stroke.

"Dat was one bad man, miss. He kill more critters dan anyone else around. You pay him off, he leave you alone. Ot'erwise, he haul you in an' you can't feed your family none. De swamp take care of its own, don' you worry."

Petty corruption had always been an unspoken fact at State Fish and Game. And in the local system where one hand washed the other, all poachers worked hard to fix the law. Being from a city where payoffs are a highly respected art form, I shouldn't have been surprised. But I was. I pressed my hand against the butt of the .357 where it lay tucked inside my waistband, and was grateful to have Gonzales with me.

The swamp changed character as we turned down a narrow channel. The silence was heavier, the darkness impenetrable, and the chorus of frogs no longer sang. Hiding behind a bank of black clouds, the moon had vanished. Gonzales touched my shoulder, and I followed his finger to a cluster of fireflies through a labyrinth of dead cypress trees. As we glided closer, the fireflies became flickering lanterns, their reflections bobbing like miniature moons. Just ahead sat a wooden lodge on giant stilts, an enormous bug with its legs sunk deep into the muck of the swamp. The silhouettes of boats swayed in the water, looking like restless horses hitched up to the cabin's dilapidated pier. The loud din of voices drifted toward us, an underlying buzz of anger filling the air.

Gonzales maneuvered around back, secured our boat, and then pulled himself up onto the platform. Reaching down, his hands locked tightly around my upraised wrists and lifted me up onto the wooden planks, where I landed with a soft thud. Placing a finger to his lips, Gonzales motioned for me to follow as we crept over to a window, staying well below the line of sight. The glow of lamps spilled out in patchwork squares, forcing me against the weathered boards so that I had to crane my neck to see what was going on inside.

At one end of the room stood Buddy Budwell, his thin blond hair slicked flat to his scalp, with skin as bright red as a freshly boiled crawfish. The armpits of his dirty white shirt were stained with yellow half-moons of perspiration, and his belly jutted out like a ripe watermelon about to burst. The only difference in his appearance from the last time I'd seen him was the black armband he now wore, along with the rest of the men in the room. Snippets of conversation floated out the open window as a hayseed dressed in denim coveralls stood up to speak.

"We don't go begging to no Krauts to support us over here, so why the hell should we be giving them our hard-earned money? If they're having trouble, shit. That's their problem. I say it's time Schuess got his ass back to Germany and out of our wallets. I'm sick of this Brotherhood crap. It don't hold no water with me. It's time we took care of our own."

Aryan Brotherhood, neo-Nazis, white supremacists, or Klansmen—whatever totem the group was rallying under, it all added up to the same thing. Buddy leaned into the lectern like a preacher preparing to work up his flock.

"Y'all know that since Schuess has been here tapping into our funds, we've had to go behind some backs and stick our fingers into the cookie jar just to keep ourselves going. Well, that's all gonna end. Hillard's given me his word that once he's mayor, Schuess is out of the deal. Louisiana's just gonna be for Americans again. We're gonna make N'Awlins our own, send faggots and the rest of the scum packing to Miami, and take back what's rightfully ours."

I glanced around behind me, but Gonzales was no longer in sight. Reassuring as it was to see our boat still tied to the piling, I knew that without his help I'd be a goner. I would never make it through the swamp on my own. The voices rose into an angry clamor over Schuess's demand for more money, when a movement in the water caught my eye. Crawling to the edge of the platform, I spotted Gonzales's outline swimming from boat to boat, a hunting knife clenched between his teeth, to cut the ropes that held each skiff in place. One after another, a ragtag navy of pirogues and small motorboats floated quietly off on the water, as Gonzales gave each a shove away from the lodge. The crafts drifted slowly, transformed into a queue of bobbing ducks among the cypress trees. He caught my eye and waved as he swam on to the next piling to finish the job.

Relieved that I hadn't been deserted, I sneaked back toward the open window. The conversation had veered to Hillard's opponent, Sam Jeffers, and his appearance at an upcoming rally. I scanned each face in the room, drawn to the man who now held the floor. Tall and gaunt, his Adam's apple bounced in nervous anticipation as he began to speak.

"Y'all know what they're trying to do to Hillard, what with dragging his poor wife into jail on some low-down, trumped-up charge of killing a whore. Well, I hear it was Jeffers's lackeys and some of those gays that set her up. They even poisoned that poor woman's dog. So I think it's only right we get Jeffers in return."

Buddy surveyed the room as he bellowed out, "Y'all in agreement with that? Cause I got a game plan guaranteed to land that man's ass on the front page of the *Times-Picayune* with one hell of a headline."

A beer keg of a man in a hunting cap and camouflage vest slapped at a mosquito as he heaved himself up from his chair. Waddling out the front door of the lodge, he scratched at the seat of his pants and reached for his zipper, taking his time to rummage inside. I pressed my back against the outer wall and scanned the water, hoping he wouldn't catch sight of Gonzales. Pulling his penis out with a sigh of relief, the man urinated over the side of the deck, the stream hitting the water full force below as he raised his head from his chest to stare straight out at the night. The moon slid from behind its cloud cover so that the swamp glittered, a pool of silver coins with the small flotilla of boats floating in among the duckweed and carpets of plants. But the man didn't seem to take any notice until his hand fell away from his penis and a few remaining dribbles hit the tops of his shoes.

"Holy shit! We got trouble out here!"

I pulled back from the corner, searching frantically for Gonzales, expecting to hear the immediate pounding of feet on the deck. The low whistle of a night bird drew my attention to our boat where Gonzales sat crouched, his knife out and ready to cut loose from the piling.

Perching myself on the edge, I pushed off just as Budwell rounded the corner. My legs buckled as the soles of my boots hit the metal bottom of the boat, the sound echoing through the swamp like a shot. But I had little time to worry about the pain in my shins and knees as I caught Budwell's eye, his smile telling me everything I needed to know. We were as good as alligator bait if he and his men caught us alive. Gonzales's hand pushed down the top of my head, and my rubbery legs folded into the boat like a jack-in-the-box.

"Dose coon dogs are after us now, Miss Porta. Stay outta sight while I make us some fried chicken."

A high-pitched howl escaped his throat as he turned from man to wolf, baying at the moon above. I felt as if I'd been whacked on the head with a two-by-four, my senses reeling from fear—and the smell of gasoline. As my eyes watered and my lungs filled up with its fumes, Gonzales lit a match. With his mouth split wide open in a maniacal grin, he leaned down to ignite the slick pool floating on top of the water. Ribboning out in a stream, the gasoline wound around to the front of the lodge. Then Gonzales revved up the boat's engine until it roared above the confusion breaking loose around us.

As we pulled away, a chorus line of blue flames flared up into a blazing funeral pyre, and I saw the contorted figures of men, silhouetted against the searing night sky, diving into a steaming stream of moonlight. Budwell still stood on the dock, his body planted firmly as he took careful aim with a sawed-off shotgun through the curtain of flames. I shouted to Gonzales—too late, as his body jerked forward and his hand momentarily left the motor's rudder. A stream of blood flowed down his right arm, pinpointing the spot where he had been hit. He took hold of the rudder with his left hand, and we continued to tear through the night.

I stood little chance of hitting a target with my .357 as we ripped through mounds of water lilies, with the buzz of an engine churning close behind like an angry hornet out to exact revenge. Gunshots echoed, sounding like the raucous cry of a jay. Whoever was behind us knew the swamp nearly as well as Gonzales did.

Our boat wove down one narrow fingerway after another in an effort to shake our pursuer, as the water around us was peppered with birdshot. A spray of lead pellets ripped through the back of the craft with a metallic ring. Missing the engine by barely an inch, they lodged deep in Gonzales's thigh. He cried out, the skin on his face drawing tight against the bone, and tears seeping from his eyes. The boat slowed to a near crawl as Gonzales turned his attention to the wound that had begun to spurt blood. I took hold of the rudder, determined to outrun Budwell myself.

"You can't do any more, Gonzales. Let me take it from here. Just try and direct me as best as you can."

But Gonzales pushed my hand away, his eyes locked dead

ahead. "Don' you worry none, Miss Porta. Nobody gonna catch us in de swamp. You just hang on tight and don' let go. Gabriel gonna put wings on us now. We gonna fly like de angels."

I'd heard of swamp fever, and knew that extreme pain could produce its share of hallucinations. I was afraid this was one of them. Bringing the boat nearly to a halt, Gonzales swung it around and began racing back full throttle into the oncoming gunfire, with all the determination of a kamikaze pilot. His lips pulled back tight in a half-crazed smile, and the long strands of his stringy hair flew behind him like a flag rippling in the wind. The sound of engines and gunfire roared in my ears and Buddy Budwell came into view. Budwell sat openmouthed, holding on to the rudder of his boat, his shotgun at half-mast as he watched our suicidal run. A ball of flames burned a hole in the night where the lodge had once been. Bathed against the blood orange background, Budwell slowly raised the shotgun, steadying it against his shoulder as he took aim at our oncoming boat.

"Gonzales, don't do it!"

My scream was lost as Gonzales suddenly pulled the rudder sharply to one side, nearly capsizing us. We wheeled back around in the other direction once more, spraying a sheet of water onto Budwell. Gonzales threw back his head, letting loose an unearthly cackle as he floored the engine, and our boat flew across the top of the swamp. A sandbar loomed directly ahead, and he swerved to avoid the stump of an oncoming cypress tree.

"Hold on! Now we fly!"

I took a look behind, to see Budwell's boat gaining rapidly as he lined us up in his gun sight. Digging my feet into the bottom of the boat to prepare for the impending crash, I felt the nose of the craft rise, as if it had wings, as we flew over the sandbank. We remained suspended for an instant before landing on the opposite side of the swamp with a resounding jolt, water falling around us like rain. I turned to Gonzales and laughed in relief, as if we'd made it through a terrifying ride at an amusement park, until I saw Budwell's boat approaching the same sandbar at breakneck speed. The laughter died in my throat as I waited to see what would happen.

But Buddy didn't know the swamp well enough. He turned to scream at his pilot, but there was no time for them to pull back before the nose of their boat rammed deep into the bar. With an earsplitting crack, the two men were thrown clear to the ground.

Tingling with the pins and needles of pleasure that comes only after having pulled off the impossible, I felt almost immortal until I turned back to see the growing pool of blood around Gonzales. With the immediate danger out of the way, the adrenaline rush that had held him together left him just as swiftly.

I pulled my shirttail out of my jeans and, grabbing Gonzales's knife, ripped the fabric into strips, tying them tightly around his arm and thigh in a poor excuse for tourniquets. Sliding the knife back inside its sheath, I shoved it in my boot and took over the rudder. Gonzales guided me back as best he could, as I kept an eye out for upraised stumps and bayou spirits. Soon, the putt-putt chant of our boat became just one more voice blending into the chorus of the night.

Helping Gonzales into the pickup, I rummaged under the seat for his keys.

"We've got to get you to a doctor."

But Gonzales shook his head in refusal, biting down hard on his lip. "No doctor, *chère*. You take me back to Trentone's. Miss Dolly fix me up good."

I drove as carefully as I could over the rutted dirt roads, aware that every bounce was sheer agony for him. We made it as far as Treddell's front door before being stopped by the barrel of a shotgun pointing in our direction. Shifting the gun so that it was aimed only at me, Dolly's gaze wavered to Gonzales as I struggled to hold him up, my arm wrapped tightly around his waist. She opened her mouth to speak, then seemed to think better of it. Setting her shotgun against the wall, she helped me to get him inside. The smell of

Southern Comfort about her was stronger than ever, mixing in with a sharply pungent odor in the house. Moving Gonzales into the living room, we placed him on a discolored mattress that lay on a floor already stained with dried blood, confirming the stories I'd heard of how Trenton skinned gators at home.

Dolly gathered together bandages, hot water, a stiletto-thin knife, and an open bottle of Southern Comfort with all the assurance of a woman who had done emergency surgery before. Covering her black pantsuit with a well-used apron, Dolly could have passed for a butcher ready to begin her work.

"Are you sure we shouldn't take him to a doctor? He's already lost a lot of blood."

Dolly zeroed in on me with red-rimmed eyes. "Haven't you done enough for one night? You got a problem, go in the other room. I done this plenty of times before, and no one's died on me yet. Isn't that right, Gonzales?"

Gonzales nodded his head in agreement as she handed him the bottle of Southern Comfort, which he eagerly pressed to his lips.

Cutting away the jeans soaked with blood, Dolly sliced into skin, digging at the birdshot lodged in his thigh. Reasonably sure that I wouldn't be missed, I took Dolly up on her suggestion and fled down the hall. The kitchen was a jumble of pots and pans stacked in a delicate balance, one inside the other on top of her stove. On the table was a half-filled glass of Southern Comfort sitting in a puddle of water, the ice melted to a chip that lazily floated on top. Next to it, the remains of a frozen dinner had coagulated into a hardened generic lump. Continuing on down the hall, I saw holes that had been knocked in walls and doors torn from their hinges, adding weight to the legend of Trenton's notorious temper.

I glanced into one room where I could see dark, brooding paintings of the bayou. My interest piqued, I stepped inside and turned on the light. Paneled in cheap plywood, the room held a convertible sofa with a pair of dirty sneakers sticking out from beneath its frame. A baseball mitt was tossed in one corner and a poster of rocker Jim Morrison hung on the closet door. But what drew my attention was the photo gallery of family history, tacked to the plywood walls. In one snapshot, Trenton and a young boy stood beside a gator they had killed, while Dolly was posed with the boy in another, both holding fishing poles in their hands. A montage showed the same boy grown older, a rebellious teenager studiously bored, a cigarette dangling from his lips and a young Valerie Vaughn clinging to his arm. I realized this must have been their son Dale's room, and opened the closet door to peer at a rack of old cotton shirts and worn-out jeans. Going over to a bureau, I gave my curiosity free rein, poking through tee shirts and shorts that still retained their musky scent. I was about to stop when I spied a blue satin box, and knew what I'd stumbled onto before my fingers even opened the lid. A silent ballerina sprang to life, her pink plastic legs pirouetting round and round Valerie's golden bracelet with its three tiny charms. But something new lay next to it on the bed of satin. I picked up the locket I hadn't seen before, and flipped open the lid. A portrait of Fifi stared back up at me. Before I could fully comprehend all that it meant, Dolly's voice boomed down the hall.

"Hey, Porter! I need help in here!"

Holding on to the locket, I slid the box back into place, shutting the drawer behind it, and quickly began to head out of the room. But in my rush to leave, my feet tripped over the dirty sneakers sticking out from under the couch. They flew across the floor as I scrambled after them. I hurriedly tried to put them back in their place, but something beneath the couch blocked my way. Kneeling down to shove them back under, I caught sight of a tripod and video camera concealed beneath the frame. Dolly screamed out for me again, as I froze in place at the implications of what I had found. But the sound of approaching footsteps quickly brought me to my feet. Turning off the light, I walked out and smacked straight into Dolly. Blood was splattered on her apron, and the stiletto knife was still in her hand.

"What the hell were you doing in there, Porter?"

I shoved my hands in my pockets, hiding Dolores's locket from her view.

"I saw some paintings hanging up and wanted to take a closer look."

Dolly brushed past me, closing the door to the room. "This ain't no museum, and I didn't invite you to snoop through my house."

I followed her out to where Gonzales lay fully bandaged, with an empty bottle of bourbon by his side. Dolly wiped her hands and the knife on an old kitchen towel, mixing fresh blood in with brown gravy stains.

"Help me take him into another room."

Between the two of us, we carried Gonzales into a small bedroom, where a large wooden crucifix of Jesus gazed down compassionately on the mattress below. Gonzales lay awake, his flesh the color of chalk against the sheets, his eyes glazed from liquor and pain as they watched me closely. Turning toward Dolly, I began to guess who Valerie's conspirator in blackmail had been.

"I have to head back out to the swamp to get my car. If it's all right with Gonzales, I'll take his truck. Somebody can swing by tomorrow and pick it up."

Dolly stared at me a moment before pinning her hair back in place, the dark roots exposed at the base of her neck. "Leave the truck here. I'll take you myself."

Gonzales reached out a hand toward me. "*Chère*, you gonna go look for Trentone an' Charlie?"

I wondered the same thing myself. "I want to. I'm just not sure where to begin."

Taking hold of my hand, Gonzales turned my palm faceup, and traced two pathways along the lines in my skin.

"You see dese two lines, de way dey branch off? We took dis one. Now you try dis one. It lead you to Charlie an' Trentone. You trust Gonzales."

My heart sank as I tried to follow his directions along the wrinkles in my hand.

"I'll do my best, Gonzales."

"I know you will, *chère. Lache pas la patate.*"

My rudimentary knowledge of French roughly translated this into "Don't let go of the potato." It made no sense, and I didn't want to stop to ask what he meant. My mind was still reeling from the discovery I had made in the room at the end of the hall.

I settled into Dolly's pink Cadillac as she popped in a Waylon Jennings tape and cranked up the sound. Any suspicions about what I might have found in Dale's room were masked behind a stone-cold face as we took off down the dirt road. I wondered how much Trenton knew about his wife's extracurricular activities. And now, I had yet another suspect who might have set Dolores up. Dolly remained silent as the music blared loud, jarring the silence of night. Trying to start a dialogue with her was like playing a game of Russian roulette—short and foolish—but I decided to give it a try.

"Would you let Charlie and Trenton know that I headed home in case I miss them? I'll fill them in on what happened when I catch up with them in the morning."

Her eyes stayed dead ahead, but the muscles tightened around her mouth, the ebb and flow of moonlight creating heavy shadows on the planes of her face.

"You think I'm your personal messenger service, princess?"

I reached over and lowered the volume a few notches. "You don't like me very much, do you, Dolly?"

"You got that right. There's some bad shit going on in these bayous. Always has been. But Trenton and me were doing just fine the way we were. Trenton had his fun playing games with Charlie Hickok, and everybody knew the rules. We kept the lid on trouble. Till you came along—you've changed all that, princess."

Her headlights locked onto a nutria scampering in front of our path, and she swerved the wheel to try and hit it.

"You've opened a real can of worms, and you don't even know it. Should I be thanking you for that?"

I braced my hand against the dashboard as her car swerved back to the left. "Was that why your son died, Dolly? Because he played by the rules? Was that keeping the lid on trouble?"

Dolly was silent for a moment. "Dale was a bunch of damn heartache. But he was my boy, and I loved him. Nothing can ever change that, just like nothing can ever change the fact that he's dead."

She turned to stare at me, slamming on her brakes. "You got any kids?"

"No."

"Then you got no idea what the hell I'm talking about."

Jamming her foot back down on the accelerator, she sent the Cadillac jerking forward again. Dolly turned the volume all the way back up, so that Waylon roared as we hit the blacktop. I found myself screaming above the music in order to be heard.

"You know, I'm not the one who talked Trenton into getting involved in this. He seems to have his own reasons for wanting to nail Hillard Williams."

"Yeah. And you just want to find out who killed some fucking gator, isn't that right? Don't try to sucker me, princess. You'll use whoever you can. You're out to prove yourself the hotshot on the block. Well, let me tell you that if you think you're going to end the drug trade in the bayous, you're in for one hell of a surprise. You'll just be the latest in a long line of fish bait, which is alright with me. I already lost my son, and now Valerie. You just better hope you don't take my husband down with you."

Dolly made a hard right onto the dirt road that led down to my car. Her assessment of my character gnawed at me. It bothered me enough to make me feel I had to justify my actions.

"Listen, gators are still being poached by the truckload down here, and I have a sneaking suspicion that it's all tied in with the drug trade. Doesn't what's happening matter to you, Dolly? Your son is dead. So is Valerie. There have to be hundreds of others just like them back in this swamp. If

Hillard Williams is involved in this, so is the New York mob. They're getting rich off hooking these kids on crack and cocaine, and shipping the rest up to New York. It has to be stopped."

Dolly glanced at me and sneered. "And you're just the one to do it, right, princess?"

I reached over and shut off the tape. "And what have you been doing about it, Dolly?"

"I was handling it my own way, Porter. I was doing just fine taking care of Hillard Williams, till you started shoving your nose in where it doesn't belong. You Yankees are so damn dumb, thinking you can come down here and jump in with both feet. There are other ways to get things done, hotshot."

We were almost at the swamp, and I was running out of time to confirm my suspicions.

"How is that, Dolly? By blackmailing Williams and Kroll with some sex tapes? Valerie just might have you to thank for getting her killed. What were you doing, anyway, besides grabbing a few grimy dollars off the man who probably murdered your son?"

Pulling in close to my car, Dolly leaned across and opened the passenger door. Sitting back, she kept her face only inches from mine, the booze still strong on her breath. "That tape was sent to you as a warning, princess. Don't you know that nothing's ever gonna change around here? Valerie's death proved that to me. I was doing you a favor by showing you what you were up against. Hell, you've got the next mayor of New Orleans backed up by the chief of police. I was trying to help save your life and my husband's along with it, you stupid bitch."

I got out of the car as Dolly leaned still farther across the seat.

"Hey, princess. I got another tape to dig out for you. It's one you'll really like. It's got that detective friend of yours on it. See, he used to come around to visit Valerie, too. He started off asking a bunch of questions, but then he got to staying for dessert. Hell, it got to the point that's all he began coming for. In fact, I've got some of Valerie's best work on those tapes. Maybe it'll give you some pointers. She always had the most fun with him. Has he been good for you, too?''

Dolly didn't wait for an answer as she pulled the door closed. Shifting into reverse, her car churned up a mound of loose gravel, spitting out a trail of hazy dust as she tore down the road and disappeared around the first bend.

I walked over to the edge of the swamp, and, leaning in toward the cattails, threw up what little I'd eaten that day.

Eighteen

The revelation that Dolly had been the one to send me the videotape answered my question as to who Valerie's partner had been. But other questions were still piled up like dead bodies at a morgue. I slumped behind the steering wheel, my hands shaking from too much soda and candy and too little sleep. I tried hard not to think about Santou. I suspected every word she said was true. All I knew was that I was dead tired of thinking, and more than anything else, I just wanted to go home, go to sleep, and not ever dream again. I put my head down on the wheel, ready to burst into tears, when a hand reached out from behind the front seat and clamped itself hard on my shoulder.

"Where the goddamn hell you been, Bronx?"

I shrieked and jumped, then turned around to see Charlie Hickok. Having been scrunched down on my backseat, he was struggling to work his way into an upright position.

"I've been spending all night nearly getting myself killed looking for you, Charlie!" I barked at the man who I should have been happier to see than anyone else in the world.

Hickok let loose a chuckle as he played with the bill of his cap. "You mean that was your lil ol' bonfire I seen over in the distance? You've been busy tonight, Bronx. You can tell me all about it in the boat. Let's get the lead out."

Charlie's motorboat was tied up next to the one I'd stepped out of only a few hours earlier. I was no longer so anxious to head back out into the swamp, having had more than my share of adventure for one evening. Or, to use one of Charlie's phrases, I felt as if I'd been stonewashed and hung out to dry. I stalled to give myself some time.

"What are you doing here? I thought you were supposed to be out with Trenton."

Charlie untied the boat from its stump. "Hell, I been out there all night poking around. But things are just about to heat up now, so I thought I'd cut you some slack and deal you in on the action. Give you a taste of what real agents do."

Charlie stood up and waited for me to jump into the boat.

"That is, unless you don't wanna be an agent no more, Bronx. What is it? Make your mind up real quick, cause I don't have no time to waste on slackards."

I thought of New York and what my life had been. The auditions, the angst, one heartbreaking relationship after another. In a sense, it didn't seem as if anything had really changed all that much. But if I didn't follow through with this, it would be one more failure I'd have to live with. And then where would I go? Besides, I'd already become hooked on the adrenaline rushes, being in on the hunt, and the feeling that I was at least attempting to do something worthwhile.

I looked over at the man who'd fought both outlaws and the system every step of the way, dressed in his fatigues and duck-billed cap, handing out approval about as willingly as he would a hundred-dollar bill, and it struck me as the ultimate irony. Some people had their gurus, their shrinks, or their plastic surgeons. I had Charlie Hickok. Shaking myself out of the stupor that had overtaken me, I silently damned whatever forces had brought me to doubt myself and my work. I headed toward the boat.

"Get a move on it, Bronx. The night is young, and we got huntin' to do."

Charlie pulled out two Baby Ruths and threw me one as I took my place on the wooden seat in front of him. The motor on his boat burped in unison with the bullfrogs as we slipped away from land and headed into the swamp. This time I told Charlie everything I knew, filling him in on the tie-in I'd made between Pasta Nostra, Buddy's clubs on Bourbon, his fish-packing plant, and the connection with the all-encompassing Global Corporation.

Charlie sniffed at the air before turning down a narrow offshoot of water. "Global is right. Those boys are screwing up all over the damn place. That Sabino ain't nothin' but a straight-up hoodlum, who'd as soon snuff you out in a New York second as give you the time of day. Hillard's got himself back in it but good, this time."

There was something eerily familiar about this fingerway of the swamp, which made me wonder if I'd been down this route before. The faint sulfuric smell of fire still lingered in the air. Charlie took the last bite of his candy bar, and I handed him the unfinished half of mine. He crunched up the empty wrapper and the crinkling shot through me like machine-gun fire, causing every nerve in my body to stand on end.

"Little jumpy tonight ain't ya, Bronx? Must be Budwell gettin' to ya." Charlie chuckled softly. "That Buddy's always been an el kooko kooko with that Nazi stuff. But up till now it's all been fun and games. Still, I guess it had to go over the edge sometime. So, those good ol' boys have been holding their meetings back here, huh?"

"Those good ol' boys nearly killed Gonzales and me tonight."

"The key word here, Bronx, is almost. You're still alive, ain't ya? Calm down. You'll live longer."

I concentrated on listening to the sounds around me, to the chain-saw buzz of mosquitoes, the swirl of water from a gator's tail, the comforting hum of the engine. Anything to keep my mind off Santou.

Charlie tugged at his cap, as he always did when there was something he wanted to say. "Let me fill you in on a secret here, Bronx. If you're gonna think about what you're doing all the time, you'll never make it through the day. It'll blow your mind."

I studied Hickok's face in the darkness and wondered if I was looking at a preview of myself twenty years down the line. "Did it ever blow your mind, Charlie?"

"I've been run over in a boat and left for dead in the marsh a couple of times. I've had my personal life blown to high tarnation. Hell, I've even been shot at on special occasions. That's when you learn if you're really an agent. When you put your life on the line to do what you believe in. It happens to everyone, Bronx. Don't ever let 'em tell you different, or they're damn liars. It may be the first time when you think you've been caught in a sting, or it can sneak up on you later, like a bad case of heartburn. Either way, you make it through with your wits still about you, or ya don't. It's kinda like an initiation. So you might as well find out as soon as you can."

Gliding through the swamp with its carpet of duckweed and interwoven branches of cypress closing off the sky above, there seemed no more fitting place in which to be tested. So far I'd been in agent purgatory, my every move on trial, with Charlie as judge and jury. I was ready for it to end one way or the other.

The quality of the air changed as the bayou widened to form a small lake, and then narrowed once more to a thin sliver of murky water. Working its way out to Atchafalaya Bay and the Gulf of Mexico, the area was uncharted and unknown by all except local diehards, making it easy to disappear in this watery wilderness—or to hide whatever you might want kept secret.

"Something else, Bronx. I got tired of your constant yapping about that damn gator. So I slit the thing wide open about a week ago for a quick look-see, and you ain't gonna believe what I found. Seems someone got the bright idea of stuffing forty packets of cocaine down that sucker's throat. Each one wrapped in a piece of chicken, to make the going down easier. We're talking one hell of a last meal. That sonofabitch popped his lights with a major high on."

Charlie snickered as he waited for me to join in.

"Well, what the hell's the matter with you? I thought you'd be happy about the damn thing."

I was tempted to say "I told you so," but held myself back. I had to decide whether or not to tell Charlie just how easy it had been to swipe Hook out from under his nose. It was a foregone conclusion that sooner or later he was bound to find out. But it wouldn't be tonight. Not in the middle of this swamp, where I'd have no place to escape his wrath.

"Why didn't you tell me when you found out?"

Charlie snorted, scaring off a water moccasin that had wriggled over to the boat for a better view. "Why the hell should I? You ain't exactly my coworker on this case, Bronx. Just remember that. As far as you're concerned, it don't change the fact that we still got a dead gator on our hands, no matter how it was killed."

I didn't bother to argue his logic. "It had to be Valerie Vaughn."

"That's a guess, Bronx. What makes you say that?"

I wondered how much Charlie already knew, and how much of this would be news to him. "Because it all adds up. It was her gator. She was Hillard Williams's mistress. I think she was murdered not only for stealing his drugs, but because of what she knew. I've got a hard-core videotape of her entertaining both Williams and Connie Kroll together in her apartment. Valerie was getting to be too much of a threat for the powers that be."

"Does N.O.P.D., or should I say Santou, know about this tape?"

The one saving grace I had in this entire situation was that I had never trusted Santou completely. But it still didn't stop me from feeling like a fool. "I wasn't sure what would happen if I told him about it. For all I knew, it could have landed right back in Kroll's hands. I decided not to tell anyone for a while."

"Okay, Bronx. I'll give you some slack on that for the moment, only because it's pretty much common knowledge. That all you got after all this time?"

Winning approval from the man was like asking for the sun, the moon, the stars, and the next solar system.

"Williams must have tried to ditch her when he began his run for mayor. Valerie probably decided she deserved severance pay, and somehow got her hands on the cocaine. Between that and threatening Hillard with blackmail, it was enough to get her killed."

Charlie pulled at a reed, sticking the end in his mouth. "That it, or ya wanna go for the gold?"

If I was wrong and making an ass out of myself, I figured why bother to stop now.

"Gunter Schuess is the one who killed Valerie Vaughn. My guess is that when Hillard discovered part of their stash was missing, he demanded it back. Valerie probably denied having done it and creatively hid the evidence. When Gunter turned up at her place, he planned to murder her either way."

Charlie gazed off into the distance, as if he were looking for something. "So where does Global come in?"

I felt as if I were back in school, trying to pass a major test. "Global has to be the shell company that's used to cover the drug operation. It also launders all the drug money, along with Budwell's other businesses."

The air had begun to smell of salt. We were getting closer to open water.

"You ain't tied up all the loose ends yet, Bronx."

If what I had come up with so far was true, I figured I'd done a hell of a job. I ran the cast of characters through my mind, trying to figure out what I had missed.

"I'd say that Vinnie Bertucci was sent here by Sabino to keep an eye on both Hillard and Schuess. Sabino probably figured that either one of them was capable of getting greedy and digging into the communal pot."

"Not bad. But you haven't filled me in enough on Schuess."

"Besides the fact that he's a manipulative psychotic with a fondness for using razors on women, there doesn't seem to be much left to say."

Charlie ran the reed back and forth between his teeth, openly pleased at the fact he knew something that I didn't.

"Sheeet, Bronx! That lame-o story of his about being Hillard's liaison don't hold no water. That dog just don't hunt. In fact, his name ain't even close to being no Gunter Schuess. He's the Butch Cassidy of Germany. That loony toon has had the German police on his ass real bad since before he landed it here in Louisiana. It seems that sonofabitch was running some underground group of psycho skinhead Nazis. He escaped out of Germany after a shootout with the police."

It made perfect sense. What better place for Gunter to hide out than southern Louisiana, with its rednecks and outlaws?

Charlie grinned in an unspoken contest of one-upmanship.

"So, what did he have? A Nazi hotline that led directly to Hillard and Budwell?"

Charlie pulled out a Milky Way bar and bit off a plug, as if it were a wad of Red Man. "Something like that. All I can figure is that Gunter got himself cut in on the deal. Seems he plugged in Sabino and Hillard with a big-time drug outlet over in Europe. In return, Gunter receives a percentage of the trade. But from what you heard at the lodge, my guess is that he got greedy and has started demanding too much—and the natives are getting restless with it."

The engine of Charlie's boat sputtered a low, throaty growl as it made its through a bed of water hyacinths, reminding me of Fifi. "The only weak link besides Valerie in all of this, was probably Dolores, with her constant threat to spill all she knew. I figure Fifi was poisoned as a warning, and when that didn't shut Dolores up, she was thrown in jail for a night."

Charlie tugged at his hat to cover a slight nod of approval. "Not bad for a rookie, Bronx. Not bad. But don't be expectin' any medals yet."

A Mars bar sailed my way. Part of Charlie's private stash, it was the closest I'd come to receiving a gold star.

Charlie slowed the boat until it bobbed gently in the water. The wind picked up and the bearded branches overhead creaked like a bed of squeaky springs. An owl hooted off in the distance, and I shivered as the same call was repeated from behind.

"That's our cue, Bronx."

The putt-putt motor chugged along as we headed out toward the open water. Charlie carefully guided the boat into a bed of waist-high reeds, where we found Trenton Treddell. Hunkered down in his own airboat, he had a perfect view straight out into the Gulf, his craft camouflaged by dense foliage.

The air no longer held the breathless quality it had in the closeness of the swamp, but now carried a pungent sting that came in off the bay. Whitecaps stirred, rubbing up against the oyster grass in the marsh, as the sea nibbled yet another chunk of coastline away. Stretching out in an endless band, marshes buffered the Louisiana coast for as far as the eye could see, their canals intertwining among watery grasslands to provide both poachers and drug runners with the perfect escape.

Trenton handed me a pair of binoculars and silently pointed off in the distance. All I could make out at first was the dark expanse of open sea and sky, until I finally latched onto an odd shape bobbing in the foreground. After a minute my eyes adjusted to the light, and the shape took on the form of a small cabin cruiser. The distant hum of an airplane resonated in the still night air, and a yellow light began to flash along the water, blinking three times in steady succession. Stopping for a moment, the pattern began again, repeating over and over.

And then I saw it. A Piper Super Cub flew into view. Passing above the boat, it reversed direction in a wide turn as graceful as a heron in flight and then came in for a landing, its floats touching down on the water.

"I bet that's ol' Buddy himself in that boat there, picking up another load of good Colombian gold. Hot damn, Trenton! I have a feeling we're gonna hit the jackpot tonight. Somebody's ass is getting ready to burn."

The body of the plane shone in the moonlight as it anchored next to the boat. And then the transfer began. One box after another was off-loaded and hoisted onto the waiting cruiser. I watched through the binoculars as two figures on board carried the haul down below. Buddy probably had someone else waiting back in these marshes, in a smaller boat where the drugs would be transferred yet again, to be taken to their hiding place deep in the swamp.

Their business completed, the plane started up again and skimmed along the Gulf like a giant water spider. Slowly lifting off, it flew out over the water and circled back inland, heading for the wilds of Cajun country.

Charlie threw the flashlight to me as he turned to join Trenton in his boat. "Okay, Bronx. This is where we part ways. Me and Trenton are gonna stick on Buddy's tail as tight as a pair of leeches. Your end of the deal is to head back in and track down that plane. Santou's expecting your call, and he'll meet you with a search warrant. While you're at it, find out who the thing's registered to."

I stared at Hickok as what I heard began to sink in. "What do you mean, he'll have one ready? All three of you knew about this pipeline the entire time, while I was left out of the deal?"

Trenton's boat rocked madly as Charlie clutched onto its side to board. "Yeah, we been working on it for a while now. If it's what we've been suspecting, we're gonna make news big-time."

I was sorely tempted to give Charlie a swift kick, sending him headfirst into the water, as he threw one leg over the side of Trenton's craft. After almost getting myself killed tonight in my attempt to find him, I was once more being relegated to the role of errand girl to perform yet another menial task. Santou and Hickok must have been pooling whatever information I'd given to each of them all along, without my knowing. I'd been shut out of the old boy network, proving, yet again, that sexism was alive and well in the backwaters of Louisiana.

"Let me make sure I've got this entirely straight, Charlie. You and Santou have been working together on this thing from the start without ever telling me? What's going on here? I feel like the patsy who's been left out in the cold."

Having successfully completed the transfer into Trenton's boat, Charlie pulled his cap down tighter on his head.

"Listen here, Bronx. You're still a rookie agent, and until you've proved yourself otherwise, this is the way things are gonna work. You got a problem with that, take it up with me later. But right now get your ass back on land. We got work to do and no time to waste."

I thought of all the investigative footwork I'd done on the case so far, from ransacking Valerie Vaughn's apartment, to shaking up Gunter Schuess enough to be made the recipient of a late-night call. If none of this had yet managed to push me beyond rookie, I couldn't think of what else would. I decided to request a transfer first thing in the morning. Louisiana, Santou, and Charlie Hickok be damned.

"No problem, Charlie. You just want to tell me how I'm supposed to go about hauling myself back to where my car is parked? We're in the middle of a damn swamp. I think that with all the work I've done, I at least deserve directions back to town."

For the first since my arrival, Trenton finally spoke.

"You'll be fine, Agent Porter. Just keep to your left. Keep veering left, and you'll make it back to land."

He hadn't once looked me in the eye. Now I knew why. I headed out, not bothering to look back.

I brooded a lot about loyalty and all of its implications as I navigated my way back through the tangle of swamp. While it was true I had kept my own secrets while investigating the case, there was also no doubt in my mind that sexism was rampantly at play. Hickok's deep-fried logic didn't surprise me a bit, but I had been completely betrayed in every way as far as Santou was concerned. Pushing aside all my good judgment, I had given him access not only to my hard-earned information, but even worse, to myself. It seemed more than enough reason to get out of Louisiana as soon as I could.

Hickok's cornball wisdom came back to taunt me like a whisper lilting through the tupelo trees. "Every time you're about take a step, right before you put that sucker down, have the horse sense to make sure and check exactly where it is your foot's going."

Up until now I'd been stepping wherever I pleased, repeating the same mistakes again and again, especially where my dealings with men were concerned. After all this time, I still had yet to learn the trick of letting my head rule my heart. But I felt as if my heart would be closed off forever, now. Though I'd been hurt in the past, I'd never been played for such a fool before.

The flashlight's beam slashed through the jumble of swamp, illuminating a clearing up ahead. I had made it back to where the night had begun. It was already past midnight, and the idea of going home and letting Santou and Hickok fend for themselves was more than appealing. I docked the boat and jumped out, tying the rope to a stump, while I considered my options. I'd had more than enough of playing gofer where Santou and Hickok were concerned.

Caught up in my anger, I barely perceived the smooth blade sliding like silk along the side of my neck from behind, its honed edge nipping into my skin. Thinking it to be nothing more than the sting of a mosquito, I swatted my fingers up against the razor-sharp blade, the edge slicing into my hand.

"Out enjoying the moonlight, Miss Porter?"

The familiar accent and mirthless laugh sent shock waves racing through me. Gunter's hand ran up and down my body, his fingers skittering across my skin in obscene familiarity. Wrapping one arm around my waist, his hand pushed its way down into the front of my pants, latching onto the handle of my .357.

"Let me relieve you of this. Such an unpleasant thing for a woman to have to carry."

His fingers played suggestively against my skin as he pulled the gun slowly out, the back of his hand brushing up along my breasts. Cutting the bandanna from my neck, the razor pressed tightly against me, its edge positioned just behind my ear by the carotid artery. My pulse pounded hard against the blade, rising and falling to the tempo of my fear. I knew that one well-placed slash would mean certain death.

Gunter's fingers were cold and dry against my skin as he removed the blade and turned me around so that we stood face-to-face. His translucent blue eyes froze my soul. Glancing down along his side, I could see the razor with its long silver handle, like those still used in barbershops. He followed my gaze, taking pleasure in the effect his weapon produced.

"Agent Porter, I'm sorry to say you're not looking your best tonight. But then, I suppose one doesn't have to worry about one's attire in the swamp. Not when you've been out playing hide-and-seek with the locals."

He caressed my skin ever so lightly with the razor's edge, a low moan bubbling to his lips as the blade came to rest on my stitches. He played with the threads, running the tip of his index finger softly along them, up and down my neck in rapt fascination. I flinched from the sting of pain, scarcely able to breathe from fear of what might happen next.

"What have we here? It looks as though you suffered a nasty accident. How painful it must have been for you. Was it painful, Miss Porter?"

Gunter held me tightly in place like a long-lost lover, one hand gripping the small of my back as if to support me in a dance.

"I want to remember you as you were the other night. You were really very lovely. Do you remember that? I slipped off the sheet so that I could gaze at you, and you were pleased by my touch. I would very much like for you to take your clothes off for me now. Slowly, please."

My breath tore out of my throat in shaky rasps as I fumbled at the buttons on my blouse.

"If you know where I was tonight, Gunter, you must also know what I heard."

My fingers trembled. Gunter smiled as he watched, savoring my fear.

"What you heard, my dear, was a bunch of bumbling rednecks playing at being toy soldiers. I hope it was amusing for you. I know it usually is for me."

"Then I'm sure you're also aware of Buddy and Hillard's plans for you. It seems you're to be frozen out of the picture. Buddy has managed to rile up everyone with tales of how you've been demanding more than your fair share. But you must already know all that."

The first button on my blouse was nearly undone.

"Don't stop now, Rachel." Gunter brushed his lips against my ear, his voice a low whisper. "You don't mind if I call you Rachel, do you? I feel as though we already know one another so well. Now, please tell me more. Here, let me help you with that troublesome first button."

The razor hurtled on a downward arc, cleanly lopping off the button, its sharp edge barely missing my fingers. Just as deftly, the blade was once again at my neck, pressing tightly into the vein behind my ear.

"You may proceed with your story now, Rachel. And please, continue with your blouse. Unless you would like some more help."

I worked hard to keep my mind focused and to put aside my growing fear. "I'm sure it's no secret to you that Buddy isn't happy about your involvement. But it seems as if no one else wants anything more to do with supporting your group back in Germany, either."

"This is all you found out? How very disappointing. I'd hoped for better from you."

He smiled, and his teeth gleamed in the moonlight, iridescent pearls biting down on his lip as he focused his gaze on my throat. Without any warning, the blade sliced through my stitches, and I began to sway. But Gunter held on to me in a charade of a lover's embrace. I knew that my only chance for survival was to keep my wits and continue to talk, if only to stop myself from losing consciousness. If I lost consciousness, I knew I would die. I managed to undo the second button.

"No, there's more. Buddy's been skimming a good amount of cocaine for himself, without either you or Hillard knowing about it. Everyone at the meeting tonight believed that the money is being funneled back to them. But you know it's not going any further than Buddy's pocket. He also annouced that Hillard has made him a promise. Once Hillard's elected mayor, you're out of the game and on the first plane back to Germany. It seems that Global has suddenly become very nationalistic where business is concerned. They're tired of sharing the wealth, and you're the easiest one to cut out."

Blood trickled down my neck as Schuess pressed the blade deeper into my skin. His fist dug into the small of my back.

"Williams would never be foolish enough to do such a thing. He knows I could ruin everything for him."

"Maybe that's why he wants to get rid of you, Gunter. Or maybe he isn't worried about you at all. Sabino has plenty of resources for taking care of any trouble that pops up. You don't really expect you'll be going back to Germany sitting first-class on a plane, do you?"

I scarcely dared move. My skin burned as if it were on fire, as a mosquito landed on my neck and began to feed at the open cuts. Schuess's breath was hot against me as he leaned in to whisper in my ear.

"You're lying to me, Rachel. I don't like to be lied to."

I desperately wished for the sound of a boat or a car in the distance, but heard nothing. "I couldn't possibly know enough to make this up. Why don't you ask Buddy if you don't believe me? You don't seem to frighten him much anymore. I'm sure he'll be glad to tell you the truth." My pulse rang in my ears. I waited for Schuess to answer. It was the only bait I could offer.

"Alright, Rachel. We will play your game. But if you're

lying to me, Valerie's death will seem mild compared to what I have in store for you. Get in the car."

I made a move toward my VW, but Schuess gripped my shoulder and shoved me in the opposite direction.

"Not your car, Rachel. I wouldn't trust my life in that thing. Mine, if you please."

He guided me to where his black BMW was parked down the road, and opened the driver's door.

"Slide in very slowly. We don't want to have any accidents. I would also appreciate if you would try your best to drive smoothly, my dear. Blood is so difficult to get out of good leather seats."

I felt every bump in the road not once, but twice. First from the ride of the car itself, and then again from the pressure of Gunter's razor against my neck as it jerked in opposition. I kept the car to a crawl until we hit the blacktop. The road was completely deserted. The same oak trees stood along the bayou, and bullet-riddled road posts marked the way, but all signs of human life seemed to have mysteriously vanished.

We drove in silence for a while until I was told to turn down a narrow strip of road. Passing through a thick copse of oak trees, I saw Pasta Nostra directly ahead. Sitting on the edge of the swamp, it was sketched in ghostly elegance, dimly lit by the waning moonlight. At this hour, there were no lights burning in its windows. Gunter directed me around to the back, where a truck with the Fin and Claw logo sat parked facing out toward the swamp. He held tightly on to my arm as I slowly got out of the car, the razor slick on my neck from my sweat of fear.

I stumbled over uneven stone steps that led down to the restaurant's basement, until we stood in front of a large metal door. Gunter pounded on it twice, stopped, then pounded again. Receiving no answer, he pulled a key from his pocket. As the door creaked open, the sound echoed down the metal stairs into the cavernous cellar below. An amber light flickered up, as though a harvest moon were being held hostage. Reverberating from somewhere below was the dull thud of a metal top being pounded into place.

The stairway swayed before my eyes as if it were floating, and I realized it was my body that had begun to whirl. Whether it was the pressure of the blade against my throat, or the overwhelming heat combined with the sickeningly sweet smell of my own blood, my senses began to spin. I lurched forward as my limbs careened out of control, and caught hold of the railing only to realize that Gunter had shoved me toward the stairs. Watching me now, he was coldly indifferent as to whether I plunged headlong or made it down one step at a time on my own.

My legs were weak as I descended into the room I had tried so hard to gain entry to a mere twenty-four hours ago. I thought of last night and Santou. Of how he had asked me to trust him, and how I had done so. And then what happened later that evening. Every intimate detail flowed back, catching me unawares, until I was once more swept up in a torrent of anger that helped me regain my focus.

Reaching the bottom step, I found Buddy Budwell shoving a pile of freshly salted gator hides into a fifty-five-gallon industrial drum. Charlie had done a hell of a job of trailing him. If this was what he considered sticking to the guy as tight as a leech, no wonder the poachers were winning.

The basement was more of a warehouse than a wine cellar. Empty metal containers were scattered about the concrete floor, their tops stacked like a heap of giant pie tins. Other barrels, fully packed, were pushed to one side, waiting to be loaded onto the truck above. Upon seeing me, Buddy's expression quickly changed from smug satisfaction to extreme agitation, his skin flushing deep red as he turned toward Gunter.

"What the hell did you bring her here for? You lost your marbles this time?"

Gunter brought the blade up under my chin as he pulled my head back. "Relax, my friend. I thought Miss Porter might be missing New York about now. Since we have a delivery going up there tonight, it seemed the appropriate time for her to pay a visit. I'm sure we can fit her in somewhere."

Gunter laced his fingers through the top of my hair and pulled my head back farther until it rested on his chest. Buddy stared at the blood running down my neck before glancing back at Gunter, who watched him as if mesmerized. Licking his bottom lip, Buddy shook his head and turned back around, continuing on with his work.

"Fuck it, Gunter. I don't wanna get mixed up with no federal agent's murder. You wanna do it, at least dump her in the swamp where the gators can get at her."

I swallowed hard past the lump that had lodged in my throat. The razor pushed tighter against me as I spoke. "You're a good one to give advice, Buddy. You did a hell of a professional job on Clyde. Hickok and Santou found him about an hour ago, with enough of his face intact to make an ID. Have you made any other mistakes yet tonight?"

I choked but didn't dare cough, afraid that it would plunge the razor into my skin. Buddy pulled out a thick packet of cocaine from an aluminum case at his feet and wrapped it in one of the gator skins before stuffing it into the bottom of a barrel.

"I don't know what you're gabbing about, Porter. I ain't seen that peckerwood in days. If he got himself in some kinda trouble, it ain't got nothing to do with me. Besides, you shouldn't be worrying about anyone but yourself at the moment."

Gunter tightened his grip on my hair, the razor never leaving my throat. "You're absolutely right, Buddy. Miss Porter needn't worry about anyone else. But I do. I worry about you."

Buddy wiped the salt from his hands onto his jeans, where streaks of white already ran down his legs and along the broad seat of his pants.

"Ain't no need for you to be worrying yourself about me, Gunter. I got everything under control." Buddy turned back around and bent over another mound of gator skins.

"But I worry about all sorts of thing. Right now I worry about all the time you have wasted packing these barrels, when I'm going to have to ask you to unpack them again."

Buddy froze in midair, a ten-foot gator skin hanging stiffly in his hands. Looking first at me, his gaze slowly moved over to meet Gunter's. The pulse in his neck visibly quickened.

"And just what the hell would you want to go and do something stupid like that for?"

"Because, my dim friend, I would like to make sure that all the goods are accounted for. I'm afraid Miss Porter has been unkind enough to accuse you of stealing. I want to prove to her just how wrong she is."

Buddy blinked as drops of sweat rolled down his face, plopping from his chin onto his belly. Turning slowly around, he continued to wrap another package of cocaine inside the skin in his hands. "You gonna listen to that stupid bitch? She'd say anything right now to try and save herself. Hell, you're smarter than that, Gunter."

The blade moved lightly along my neck, and I knew I had little time left. My words tumbled out in a mad race against the razor's edge.

"It's true, Buddy. You had everyone riled up tonight, agreeing that Gunter's been receiving too much of the profits. I heard you laughing about how you've been conning him, skimming drugs off the top all along. I'm just curious about where the money's been going."

Buddy continued to fold the skins, refusing to look in our direction. "You're full of shit, Porter. You didn't hear nothin' like that."

"He's been playing you for a fool, Gunter. How do you suppose Valerie got hold of forty packs of cocaine? She and Buddy were working this deal from the start. That was just the tip of the iceberg of what they'd been stealing from you."

Gunter loosened his grip on my hair, his voice soft and low. "Do it, Buddy. Unpack it all. I have a sudden desire to count it for myself."

Buddy continued to move on automatic pilot, packing the gator skins and cocaine without bothering to look at Gunter as he spoke.

"Don't be an ass. It's all there. I ain't unpacking the damn stuff just 'cause that bitch says so."

The razor shifted away from my throat. "But she doesn't say so, Buddy. I do. You see, I'm beginning to think Miss Porter might be correct, and that would make me very unhappy. Stealing is one thing I won't abide. It makes for such bad business."

"You got problems, Kraut, you deal with Hillard. He's the only man I take my instructions from. So get off my back. I got work to do if we're gonna get this truck outta here tonight."

Buddy continued to pile the skins and cocaine into drums as Gunter moved away from me in a quicksilver glide. Moving behind Buddy, he jerked his head back and, in one violent motion, slid the razor across the width of his throat. Buddy stared in disbelief as he tried to speak, his blood gurgling out in tiny bubbles that floated on the air before bursting in a liquid drizzle. Bring his foot up onto Buddy's back, Gunter pushed him to the floor in a heap.

"We mustn't bleed on the skins now, must we?"

Gunter bent over and wiped his razor on Buddy's shirt before turning back to me with a chilling smile.

"Now, let's see what can be done to make accommodations more comfortable for you on your trip."

As I skittered away, Gunter slowly followed with a smile, taking pleasure in my fear and in knowing escape was futile. I broke for the stairs, but he easily blocked my way. Lunging to the side, I nearly tripped over Buddy's crumpled body as I grabbed a metal top from one of the drums and threw it as hard as I could in Gunter's direction, aiming for his head. But the throw went wild, and he merely stepped aside. My breath tore through me, searing my lungs as I desperately searched for anything else I could fight with. My pulse was racing and my body began to shake as Gunter moved in for the kill with an air of icy determination. With a desperate sob I darted behind two of the metal drums and frantically tried to push them over, but, filled with hundreds of skins, they were too heavy to budge. The effort cost me my balance, and I fell down hard on one knee.

A jolt of pain shot up my leg, as something hard inside my boot pressed against my ankle. I remembered the sheath, and hope flared within me.

Gunter smiled as he approached, holding the razor close to his face. Its blade glistened in the warm amber light as if it were a beacon in the night, beckoning me home.

"Oh, yes. I like that position. It gives you a moment to beg."

I kept my eyes locked on his as my hand slowly crept down to reach inside my boot. My fingers wrapped around the bone handle of the hunting knife, and my heart pounded inside my chest. I prayed that my skill at darts would pay off now, when I needed it most.

I felt light-headed, and my vision began to waver as Gunter slowly moved in for the kill. I had to focus my vision. If my aim was off, I wouldn't be given a second chance. Slipping the knife out of its sheath, I kept my eyes trained on his throat—and flung the dagger as straight and hard as I could.

Gunter's hands flew to his neck as the knife lodged in his throat, and his razor clattered to the concrete floor. Holding my breath, I waited for him to fall. Instead, he held his ground.

And then he did the impossible. Pulling the knife from his flesh with both hands, like a loup-garou come to life, he approached me once again.

My heart stopped and I froze in horror, unable to take my eyes off him. Then I heard the scrape of metal across the floor, as he inadvertently kicked the razor toward me. Grabbing its silver handle, I desperately slashed the blade upward with a sob. The razor ripped through his stomach, slicing it open as his hand shot down and clenched my wrist. He still held Gonzales's hunting knife in his free hand, and I closed my eyes, waiting for the blow.

But instead of the slash of the blade, a gunshot erupted down the stairs. I cried out as Gunter's head jerked up. A split second later another shot shattered the air, tearing through his back and out his chest above me like a crimson-streaked scream. He crumpled onto one of the metal drums, his hand still clamped around my wrist.

Wiping away blood and tears, I pried myself loose from his steel-trap grip, and pulled myself out of the way. The silver razor was still clenched in my fist, and my body shook out of control.

A hand wrapped itself around mine, the fingers trying to pry the razor out of my grip.

"Let it go, Rachel. It's over."

Santou knelt beside me. Laying down his .45, he ran his fingers gently along my face until they came to rest just above my neck.

Taking a deep, sobbing breath, I looked up and saw Charlie Hickok framed against the moonlight at the top of the stairs, a twelve-gauge shotgun in his hand.

"Congratulations, Bronx. You just made full-fledged agent."

I removed Santou's hand and dropped the razor to the floor. Pulling myself up, I staggered out into the bayou night, where my knees gave way beneath me. I knelt in the grass, wet with evening dew, and began to cry—harsh, wracking sobs of relief, that I had survived the ordeal, and that Gunter Schuess had been blown away, and would never harm another woman again.

Epilogue

The aroma of jambalaya filled the room, as Rocky nestled into a ball of fur on my chest and purred loudly. A hand appeared over my shoulder, and I took hold of the offered piña colada. Coming around to sit beside me on his leather couch, Terri lifted my legs and placed my bare feet on his lap. I brought the glass to my lips and took a sip. My hand brushed against the thick bandage Dr. Kushner had wrapped around my throat to protect my new stitches.

"Congratulations, Rach. How shall we spend that new raise you'll be getting?"

Hickok had bumped me up two levels on the pay scale, befitting the newly acquired status he'd bestowed upon me.

"Well, I could use a couple of new pillows. My old ones have gone to shreds."

Terri squeezed my foot as Rocky jumped down and headed into the kitchen in search of a handout.

"I think you deserve more than that. Let's treat ourselves to a makeover. Maybe a few nips and tucks."

Though the bust had been made, the case was far from over. Now came the frustrating part—dealing with the morass of the court system. With both Schuess and Budwell dead, we'd discovered there was little evidence to tie either Kroll or Williams into the plot. The drug link in the bayou was gone—but only for the moment. There was talk of an investigation into Kroll's activities, but, as with most interrogations, it would be a long, drawn-out affair. More than likely, most of the evidence would be destroyed before it was ever brought to light. As for Hillard, rumors were circulating through New Orleans about his connection to the trade, but without proof, the effect had been only a minor drop in his polls. However, he did have one less supporter: Hillard showed up alone at the last rally, a few days ago, Dolores having left town to visit an "ailing relative."

"It makes me crazy to think of Hillard Williams slithering around like the Teflon King. Even worse, he'll probably end up as our new mayor." Terri wrapped a finger around a blond curl on his new wig. "The bastard's going to get away scot-free."

"I wouldn't worry about that, Ter. I have a funny feeling Hillard will get what he deserves."

I'd been out to Treddell's yesterday, and watched as he fed a large gator that he'd grown particularly fond of. When I asked if he planned to skin it, Trenton had given me a funny look.

"No, I have a much better plan for this ol' boy. He's got a special job to do. Then, as his reward, I'm gonna let him go free."

I hadn't asked any further. I didn't need to. Trenton would mete out his own form of bayou justice. Besides, there was still that tape, showing how Hillard and Kroll spent their leisure time. A copy of it was already sitting at the local TV station, waiting to hit the evening news.

"What about the bayou mama who was tied in with Valerie?" Terri asked. "You know, her partner in crime? I suppose Williams stays free, while she gets hauled off to jail."

I watched Terri wipe a lipstick stain off the rim of his glass. His bruises had begun to disappear, and though his nose would have to be fixed, he still looked more glamorous than I ever would.

"I never told anyone about that, Ter. You're the only one who knows."

Terri opened his blue eyes wide in surprise. ''I thought you couldn't stand the woman.''

I shrugged. ''I changed my mind.''

Though Trenton hadn't known about her activities, Dolly had been handing out some bayou justice of her own. Not only had Hillard literally been paying for his crime, but an invisible ax had been held over his head, threatening to cut off his career at any time.

''Hey! Get outta my jambalaya! Damn cat.'' A voice roared out of the kitchen as Rocky came flying over the sofa to land in my lap.

Terri looked at me and winked. ''What do you plan to do about the main course in there?''

I could see Santou cooking up a storm in Terri's kitchen. He seemed to sense the attention. Turning around, he grinned and walked out, holding a spoon in his hand. Leaning over, he brought the spoon to my mouth.

''Taste this, *chère*. Good?''

I nodded. ''It's great.''

Santou kissed the top of my head and motioned to Terri. ''Set the table and we'll eat.''

Curling my legs under me, I waited until Jake had disappeared back into the kitchen. ''I don't know what I'm going to do. Maybe too much has happened. Especially that business with Valerie.''

Terri moved closer and put his arm around me. ''Now, listen to Mama. People get bruised. It happens with age, Rach, and there's nothing you can do about it. So he's got his battle scars. God knows, you have yours. You think he's more damaged goods than white knight? Well, sweetie, we're all damaged people in our own way. But take a good look. He's here, and he cares.

''Now you've got a choice. You can stay alone, holed up in your safe little tower. Or you can take a chance. It's worth it, Rach. Think about it.''

Terri began to set the table, and I put Rocky down and headed over to take my place.